BELIEVING CEDRIC

For Sarah's mom Louise,

To your pivotal moments?
And keep an eye on that drunk?

Mark Edward

believing Cedric

a novel by Mark Lavorato

BRINDLE
& GLASS

Brindle & Glass Publishing Ltd.
www.brindleandglass.com

LIBRARY AND ARCHIVES CANADA CATALOGUING IN PUBLICATION
Lavorato, Mark, 1975–
Believing Cedric / Mark Lavorato.

Issued also in electronic formats.
ISBN 978-1-897142-56-1

I. Title.

PS8623.A866B45 2011   C813'.6   C2011-904188-X

Editor: Lynn Coady
Proofreader: Heather Sangster, Strong Finish
Front cover design: Ruth Linka
Interior design: Pete Kohut
Front cover: mammamaart, istockphoto.com

Brindle & Glass is pleased to acknowledge the financial support for its publishing
program from the Government of Canada through the Canada Book Fund, Canada
Council for the Arts, and the Province of British Columbia through the British
Columbia Arts Council and the Book Publishing Tax Credit.

MIX
Paper from
responsible sources
FSC® C016245

The interior pages of this book have been printed on 100% post-consumer
recycled paper, processed chlorine free, and printed with vegetable-based inks.

1 2 3 4 5 15 14 13 12 11

PRINTED IN CANADA

For my sister, Gina

Reaching up to the frosted copper handle
and opening the door to air
so warm it stings the cheeks

Supper steaming at the window
with the sweet breath of fried onions
Mittens drying on the furnace duct
beside a lunchbox lined with breadcrumbs

Being lifted impossibly high
above the portrait frames and lamps
the sandpaper scraping
of my father's stubble
clenching my body tight
with laughter

I imagine there are questions
and answers about school
but these have all faded
unlike the tactile
The plump fingers of my
mother's hand on my head
The wet of the dog's delicate lips
as he pulled the gristle
from my fingers
under the table

This is what I would have told you
if you'd asked
what I remember first

But you never did

Melissa was seated neatly on her sofa, reading, her cat asleep on the cushion beside her, just out of reach, when a sleek car drove into view and turned with certainty into her driveway. She looked up from her book, sure that this car, which she'd never seen before, would reverse out and drive away in the opposite direction, something that happened quite often on the road where she lived, an almost dead-end lane in the small town of Haliburton, Ontario. But whoever it was had turned off his vehicle and was getting out, though with much less conviction than he'd had while pulling in. It was her father, Cedric, now slouching in her driveway, slamming the door while squinting through the front window, a hand held over his brow to function as a visor.

Melissa's lips hinged open. The last time she'd seen him was four years ago. He had gained weight since then, and had taken, she noted, to wearing a tacky gold watch. She closed her book, hesitated.

Outside in the boreal distance, a chainsaw puttered out. A crow complained in the quiet left behind. In the sky behind Cedric, a myriad of individual clouds—the kind that are only seen here in autumn, small and shaped like blotchy snails with grey-bottomed bodies and white-furrowed shells—glided through the sky, all of them moving in the same direction, from one nameless place to another.

Cedric made his way to the landing, where he gave two feeble knocks on her door. He waited for her to answer, glanced over his shoulder, looked at the clouds.

That morning—the morning it happened—Agnes O'Donnell was sitting in the window of her resource room, as she did every day before class, staring down into the schoolyard, thinking. This was her ritual. And though it differed very little from the rituals of other teachers at the school, it was something her colleagues consistently commented on. She would come in forty minutes early, pour herself a cup of tea, select one of the old *Lethbridge Herald* newspapers lying on the staff-room table, tuck it under her arm, and retreat into the tiny room attached to the front of her class. There she would sip from her cup and stare at the wide field, never reading, or even opening, the paper she'd brought along with her.

It was a Tuesday, and a thin layer of snow covered everything but the places the children had trampled on Monday, snaking footprints exposing the brown grass and lumps of earth beneath. Beyond these erratic patterns, there wasn't much distinction between where the school grounds ended and the closest farmer's field began, except for the rows of yellow stubble scarcely sticking out of the white, raking lines into the horizon where they eventually swirled with the clouds. As usual, Agnes surveyed as far as she could.

She began this routine soon after her husband died, after the initial wave of sympathy cards had subsided and were thrown away. Most of them she had barely read, folding them in half with a careless crease and dropping them into the garbage, knowing that her husband was the type of man who was neither loved, nor respected, nor likely to be missed by anyone at all. He had been a proud man: proud of his job, proud of the authority he held at the bank, and proud of the immaculate order of his tool shed, which he seldom used. They had met at a dance in the basement of a community hall only a month after she'd signed on at the school.

She was drawn to his posture, how he held his neck with an almost comical erectness, craning to look down at the room around him, and she'd made a point to stand nearby, scratching at her nape, her hair draped over her hand. They danced twice, and on the second waltz, with the base of his wrist pressing into the small of her back, it crossed her mind that this would be the man she would marry. And, as it turned out, he had a promising future, along with being the only bachelor to have ever taken an open interest in her.

When they'd made love he was swift and fervid, and she spent most of her energy, pinned below his rigid weight, attempting to calm him, to placate his mounting frenzy that bordered, in her mind, on dangerous, his expression fierce, eyes widening. He would finish by squeezing her shoulders tight with a sudden rush that seemed to drain him completely, flopping onto the sheets beside her afterwards, catching his breath in the dark. He was a man that never whispered, and slept deeply.

She had imagined her life unfolding in the same conventional way as other teachers she knew, first Normal School and her certificate, then marriage, children, perhaps a stint as a housewife, and retirement. But two years after the wedding she still hadn't fallen pregnant and had begun to be a little concerned. It wasn't serious enough to warrant seeing a doctor; no; besides, she wouldn't want her husband finding out she'd gone to see anyone, as they'd managed to carefully avoid the subject of pregnancy altogether, only having talked about it once, in the first week of their marriage. She was cleaning the plates off the table at the time, reaching in front of him to arrange the fork and knife so they wouldn't slip off. "I'd like to have a couple boys," he'd said. "One day." He picked up a carafe and poured some water into his glass, drank it down, and clunked the container back onto the table without looking up. She put the plates in the sink and started to fill the washbasin, saying nothing. That suited her just fine.

Two years later she was finding it hard to fall asleep after he had rolled off of her, feeling the sweat of his sides cool and become clammy against her forearms, wondering if she was doing something wrong, or not doing something right, missing out on some important step. She wished she had a woman in her life close enough that she could ask these things. Her sister, who was single anyway, and happened to be a horrible correspondent—capable of answering even the longest of letters with an aloof postcard— had moved to Saskatoon, and her mother was gone, and had been since she was eight.

Agnes told herself she would wait another year before going to the doctor, which amounted to 1932 in its entirety. The months seemed to dawdle out in front of her, to slow down, and even, on certain Sunday evenings, to stop. The local news inched along on its sluggish orbit. There were strikes and the threat of communism; the Ku Klux Klan set a cross on fire in a neighbouring town, while in another, rabbit roping was introduced to their rodeo, and still there were no cells amassing in her belly. She buckled before the year was through and made an appointment, arriving at the clinic an hour early. When the test results came back a few weeks later, she went to a different physician, who came to the very same conclusion. He was sorry. He really was. But there was nothing anyone could do.

She told her husband at breakfast, the radio crackling in the background with a local show that neither of them really liked but still tuned into every morning. She spoke suddenly. "I can't." He was chewing his toast at the time and his jaw slowed to do the processing, trying to piece together what she might be talking about. Then, as suddenly as she'd said it, he understood. She went to the kitchen window to stare out of it while he readied himself to leave for the day. She heard him use his copper shoehorn, hang it back on the hook where it belonged, straighten his tie in the mirror, and walk out the door. She stood there for a long while, the announcer listing the city's events and advertisements from the Philco in the corner. There was a sale on car batteries.

The following months found her spending the odd night on the chesterfield in the living room, the lamps turned out, watching the slats of light from the street standards tint the carpet, gradually brightening, then fading again as the dawn blanched the sky. And through these nights Agnes began to feel, physically, that her body had changed in some way, that it was missing something, something she would have described as being the size of a stack of nickels, and as heavy, in the space above her stomach, just before the bones of her rib cage began. And what had filled that space was a kind of hunger, which, she had found, it helped to sleep with her hand over, to have the warmth of her fingers on the skin just above. She would eventually grow used to it, and used to the way that it sometimes clinched tighter, becoming a sudden knot below her sternum that would have her standing still until it passed—in line at the grocery store, erasing the chalkboard at the end of the day, arranging flowerpots in the backyard—a hand pressed tight below her breasts, waiting.

Through the years her husband dutifully sidestepped the topic of children, even avoiding the mention of her students, but Agnes felt that it was always there, between them, a kind of onus that weighed on her side of the scale and lightened his. And adoption seemed to be out of the question for both of them, for him because the idea of raising a stranger's offspring (that no one else seemed to want) was somehow perverse, while for Agnes it was an unspoken fear that held her back, the fear of not being able to devotedly bond with a child that hadn't come from her own body, the fear that she would feel the same way toward him or her that she felt toward her students, which is to say very little. So then, a childless marriage was just something they would have to learn to live with, or through, around. Accordingly, their home became a place of hushed civility. They adopted habits that circumvented each other, moving to different parts of the house whenever the other person entered the room. And Agnes increasingly felt that they did this not because they wanted to avoid conversation, but because they simply had nothing left to say. They had reduced their lives to the efficiency of gestures and motions, to the common understanding of wants and needs.

Until one sunny spring day in 1953, when she came home from school to find him in the bathroom, sitting on the toilet lid, staring at the towels in front of him, waiting for her to ask what was wrong. His answer was multiple myeloma, a bone marrow cancer whose prognosis was "bleak at best." By the following week he had stopped work at the bank and was receiving treatment, which, as far as Agnes was concerned, did nothing but speed up the process of his death. He deteriorated rapidly and within a few months was bedridden, and she had to take a leave from work to look after him.

She rearranged the house so that everything, in one way or another, served to make him more comfortable, to minimize the stress of his pain. He reacted to this care and attention to detail with a kind of distant animosity, which affected her very little.

She had to be counselled on matters of nursing, to administer some of his medication and keep both his body and bedpan clean, which made her think of her mother—or what little she could remember of her—who'd been a nurse. And the more Agnes got into the routine and rituals of caring for her dying husband, the more she was inclined to recall everything she'd learned about the events leading up to her mother's "going." (That was the word her father had used to describe it. Gone. Your mother is gone.)

It had all begun with an argument, just before the mild winter of 1918. Agnes was eight years old at the time, her sister ten, and they were leaning out over the banister in their nightgowns, watching their parents in the front room below. Their father, always a nattily dressed businessman, had just come in the door with some news that had upset their mother to a degree they'd never witnessed before. She was agitated, a few fingers against her lips, pacing around the room in her "waist," a simple and elegant dress that was in vogue at the time, which swept out from the hem at her ankles with every turn she made. While she moved, her head remained fixed on her husband, who was standing near the closet.

"You must understand," he'd said, "I've made an investment here." He hung up his hat, lifted a hanger for his blazer. "If the theatre doesn't show the play, I . . . we—our family—loses money. A lot of it. And at a time, as you know, that we can't afford to. The Victory Loan drive's coming; we'd agreed to buy as many bonds as we can . . ." He shook the hanger to settle the shoulders of his jacket onto the wood, hung it in the closet. "And the boys down at City Hall have already given it the go-ahead. I'm afraid it's running. I'm sorry."

Their mother stopped pacing, considering something. "Well then . . . I would like very much for you not to go."

"Please," he said. "Be reasonable. I have to." He ran his fingers along the chain of his pocket watch, which drooped gold against the black of his vest.

When Agnes's father returned from the theatre that evening, on October 11, after having congregated with hundreds of people despite the order issued that morning by the Medical Health Officer, banning all forms of public gathering—schools, churches, galleries, markets, stadiums—he took off his creaseless clothes and kissed his wife an apology on the forehead. She was probably feigning sleep.

The next day saw a cataclysmic rise of Spanish influenza cases admitted into the temporary hospitals and a myriad of houses placed under quarantine. It was so dire that the city was calling for clinical volunteers to help with the epidemic, and though her mother hadn't worked as a nurse since the girls were born, she told her daughters that she would have to leave the house for a spell, "to help some people out." She readied the household for her absence, cramming the medicine cabinet: oil of eucalyptus, antiseptic throat gargles, nasal douche, formaldehyde atomizers, liver pills, iron pills, gin pills, and "miracle" vegetable compounds. She made the girls promise to stay inside, and to never let any of their friends through the door. She kissed them goodbye, strapped a piece of cheesecloth over her mouth and nose, and left the house with a small suitcase.

Two days later, with the breaking news that an armistice of some kind was to be signed, the city erupted into what would turn out to be a premature celebration of the end of the First World War. More than half the population left their houses and quarantines, flooding the streets to parade with every noise-producing mechanism that could be found on hand. When the next three days saw a helpless increase in the number of cases, it was announced that the entire city would be placed under quarantine, trains forbidden to open their doors while passing through, and police controlling all points of entry, permitting only dairy and mail beyond their barricades. Before it could take effect, Agnes's father drove her and her sister to the train station and told them they were going to Taber, where their aunt would be taking care of them for a while, until the flu had passed out of the city. It was safer there, he'd said. If need be, they'd be able to leave that town, to go to another one, a safer one. If need be.

The girls returned two months later but to a very different father, a man who was withered and sunken-eyed, who had sat depleted in his armchair as soon as they got through the door, his hat dangling from his fingertips. He told them the news with little delicacy. "Your mother's gone. She was . . . around it all day. Said she even napped downstairs, with the corpses. Said it was the only place to rest and . . ." His hat accidentally dropped from his hand and he leaned tiredly forward to pick it up. "And she's gone."

Agnes doesn't remember mourning her mother's death as much as she remembers moments of her childhood when she distinctly felt her absence. She found there were experiences that she didn't want to share with her schoolmates, or father, sister, just with her mother, which meant that, sometimes, there were events in her life that went untold. She had also never thought about the particulars of her mother dying, about what their home might have looked like in those months that she'd been away. But while caring for her husband, that all changed. She considered the understanding that her mother must have had, after watching so many vigorous people die from the same sickness she'd contracted. As well as thinking of her father, wondering if he'd nursed her while she was slipping away; if, like Agnes, he had put all of his dedication and energy into caring for her, given himself wholly to her state of decline, to a decay that worsened, always worsened, regardless of anything he did, or of anything that was in his power to do.

There was a day during her husband's disease when, in only a few hours, their marriage changed. Agnes had brought him some lunch and had sat down beside him to help him eat when she realized that the frustration over his illness had reached a kind of critical point. He was scowling at the end of the bed, at his feet bulging under the covers like two dormant volcanoes, long, deliberate breaths hissing through his nostrils. When he turned to look at her, it was with an indignant expression, as if she had snuck up on him, as if she had been spying on some private moment where she wasn't welcome. Impulsively, he reached over and pushed the tray of lunch onto the floor. Both the plate and glass shattered, shards sticking out of the food, a finger of milk jutting under the dresser.

Her reaction surprised them both. She stood up, slowly, with the marked sensation that she was becoming lighter, somehow released. Then she spoke in a low, commanding voice, not unlike the one she used to discipline her pupils. "Well then. That's what I made for you. If you don't like it, you know where the kitchen is." She looked out the window. "Now. I'm going for a walk."

She left the food on the floor, exactly as it was, put a shawl on, and stepped outside. When she reached the end of their lane she stood on the corner, hesitating. While she stared down the long block she imagined herself continuing on, imagined wandering through the grid of streets, beside the rows of flimsy poplars and planked fences, in the thick air of freshly cut grass, walking until her feet were tired. But she found she could not. Instead, she returned to the house and started cleaning, bleaching the sinks and cupboards, scrubbing the stove, putting the chairs on the table to mop the kitchen linoleum, the bathroom mirror, the bathtub, noisily cleaning everything she could think of, except the mess on the floor in his room.

Eventually, late in the evening, she heard him mumble her name. Agnes pushed the door open and leaned casually against the frame, the slat of light she was standing in crawling up the side of his bed. With his hands gathered into a knot on the blankets in front of him, he fumbled through an apology. "I . . . I . . . You . . ." He sighed. "Okay," he said, nodding. "Okay."

From that evening on, almost consistent with the deterioration of his body, he became increasingly gentle and, for the first time in their married life, somewhat affectionate. At times he would abruptly grip on to her hand in his gruff way and then spend a quarter of an hour staring out the window, blinking, unable to let go of it, both of them settling in the silence, in the warm light that bled through the edges of the orange curtains, listening to the hum of the cars passing by, to the unseen sparrows chirping from the neighbour's hedge.

At his funeral, sitting on a frigid pew at the church, staring into his coffin, she realized something that disturbed her: that she was going to miss, not the person she married, but the frail being who was lying on the rumpled satin, the man he'd become when he was most decrepit. Looking at him then, she was forced to admit to herself that the best months of her marriage were the months when her husband was suffering the most. What kind of person, she wondered, did that make her?

When she returned to work, some of her colleagues at the school made a point of inviting her for their weekly Saturday afternoon of bridge, but she'd hated every minute of it. They'd sat outside, around a table on the patio that was much too large, a dish of Nuts and Bolts and a bowl of Jell-O salad jiggling in the middle of it. They adjusted and readjusted themselves on the lawn chairs, the straps of webbing cutting into their thighs, all the while talking about the same conventional things Agnes had always imagined herself talking about but had somehow never gotten around to. The buying of appliances on "the instalment plan," the automated washers, barbecues, vacuum cleaners, motorized lawnmowers. Then on to neighbourhood rumours and hearsay: "You know what *I* heard?" one of them leaning in and folding over her bridge hand as if it were the incriminating evidence itself.

She became taciturn, looking around at the other women. She felt old, boring, especially watching two of the newer teachers who could have been teenagers for all Agnes could discern. They were girlish, stylish, confident, using words they must have learned from their newly purchased televisions or those radio shows that she now switched off. Gee whiz. Neato. Swell. "This salad is just *ideal*, Erla." They raised their hands every now and then to pat their hair into place, beehives and bouffant flips, providing glances down the short sleeves of their blouses, confirming that they took to shaving their armpits, wore bullet bras. Agnes noticed that even the older women looked more fresh and vernal than she remembered them being, every one of them disciples of *Chatelaine* Magazine no doubt, embracing its tips and secrets with devotion, with faith. Lipstick, bubble bath, blow dryers, Clairol, Noxzema, all of it, ensuring they resembled Marilyn Monroe as close as was womanly possible.

The following week, she turned down their invitation, as she did every week afterwards, until they stopped asking. No, she had decided, the only place she felt at ease anymore was in her house and when she was alone. And she was fine with that. She would resolve herself to a life of domestic solitude, to rituals that avoided people, to mornings spent sitting on windowsills before class, thinking.

And really, it was surprising the wonders that one could find while alone. Only last week Agnes had had an experience that could only be described as extraordinary. She'd been on her way back from some grocery shopping, and had decided, for the first time, to take a shortcut that skirted a marsh on the border of her neighbourhood. Along the way, she'd noticed some cattails jutting out of the marsh's edge, most of them having gone to seed, their brown velvet splitting along a seam that seemed to bleed out with a type of downy cotton. She decided she wanted to touch one of them, or maybe even pick it, but as soon as she put down her grocery bags and walked into the reeds she found herself stepping onto a ground that was veiled and unnaturally soft, which had her rethinking the idea. She stopped, looked around. A few remnants of fall colours were standing out against the browns and greys of early winter, a yellow leaf caught in the sepia culms, a brush-dab of maroon, a fist of rust. There were also birds, she realized, twittering and chirring in the rushes in front of her, hidden. On a whim, she clapped, just once, never for a moment imagining that it would have the effect that it did.

The entire marsh seemed to erupt, and the sky darkened with hundreds, maybe thousands, of small black birds. They formed a bleary cloud that spread and thinned itself one moment, then condensed and folded in on itself the next; but it was always whorled and synchronous, always acting as one. There was a point when the flock passed low over her head, and she was sure she felt the wind of their countless wings, and flinched beneath its tremolo, ducking low into the sedges. Then the flock collected and spiralled above the marsh that was farthest away from her and, rather abruptly, sunk into the reeds again, leaving the autumn air empty but for their sounds, now remote and muted.

When she stepped out of the rushes several minutes later, stooping to collect her grocery bags, she was struck with a strange sensation, a thought. It occurred to her that there might be someone else, maybe even somewhere out there in Canada, who'd experienced exactly what she just had, who had stood in some rushes mesmerized and half-frightened by a swirling flock of blackbirds. And for some reason—she couldn't even begin to say why—it was important that this person existed, that they were out there. She continued on, thinking of who they might be, imagining a younger woman, an older man, crouched in another marsh, another time.

She hoped to spend many a morning thinking about this experience, sitting on her windowsill before class. It would be so much better than the petty way she sometimes found herself counting down the years (and even the months and weeks) before she could retire. And even better than spending this time, as she had been lately, infuriated and thinking of Lyle.

Lyle was a fated pupil of hers, whom, she knew, no one would ever be able to reach. He came from one of "*those* families" living in the river bottom, where houses, which were unwisely strewn along the floodplain of the Oldman River, were the very cheapest to come by. She'd once had the misfortune of meeting his parents at the supermarket, which provided a glimpse as to how he most likely spent his evenings, breaking the bottles his father threw into the backyard—a child testing the weight of a stone in his hand while scouring the ground for others, distractedly circling the patchwork of lawn with its spots of yellow grass where the dogs squatted to urinate, the bottles lined up like pickets, poking above the neighbour's side of the fence. She imagined this as a fairly accurate depiction because Lyle seemed to deal with people in the same way he dealt with the objects of his playground vandalism, as a constant experiment to inflict the greatest amount of damage with the least amount of effort. He'd found the most effective ways to terrorize his classmates almost systematically and had even stumbled upon a way to browbeat Agnes.

He had discovered it innocently enough, asking her one lunch hour, likely out of simple curiosity, if she had any children. She made the mistake of reacting, of being affected, beginning with stammering the fact that it was none of his business and ending with walking away from him abruptly.

In the weeks that followed, Lyle was cautious with what he said, slowly testing the waters, choosing the timing of his questions to coincide with as many witnesses as possible. Agnes O'Donnell recognized it as simple manipulation, as a classic power struggle similar to others she'd dealt with in the past, only this time it felt like she was losing the skirmish. With each calculated question he asked, she could feel her authority slipping, her respect, her judgment.

"Mrs. O'Donnell? You said I could keep my jar of worms for fishing in my desk, right?"

"No, Lyle."

"Yes, you did. Jeremy was there. Didn't she, Jeremy?"

"It doesn't . . . I'm saying no now. It doesn't matter what I said yesterday."

"Oh. It doesn't? Never?"

And for the first time in her scholastic career, she wasn't sure if she could deal with the problem in a calm or composed way. It incensed her, and she wanted nothing more than to put him back in his place, to shut him up before any of the other teachers or administration started whispering about it—even if it was already a little late for that. Recently, she'd taken to stalling in her resource room until well after the bell had rung, the teachers of the adjoining classes hearing the bedlam of her students escalate to the point where they were probably on the verge of walking into the room and restoring order themselves.

Agnes heard two sets of small feet shuffle into the classroom and sit down at their desks. She reached over and picked up the morning paper, holding it in front of her face in case either of the children decided to lean out of their seats and peek around the corner. Inadvertently, she found herself focusing on one of the headlines. It was about Sputnik, a satellite that had been launched by the Soviet Union in October, and the expected response of the United States to outshine it with a far superior craft. Somehow, this information did nothing but add to the instability she already felt that day, and this, before the class had even begun. She was barely clinging to the authority she'd once held in her third grade classroom, and meanwhile, somewhere above the veil of blue sky over the school, astronauts were peering out of their windows and watching the Earth shrink like a playground ball that had been kicked impossibly hard into the air. She flopped the newspaper onto her lap and turned to look down at the schoolyard again, where students were arriving in ever-increasing numbers, fanning out across the snow like ants whose colony has been disturbed, funnelling through the small opening of the front door and into the network of corridors, filling what was serene and wooden and quiet with their collective bustling. She breathed a tired sigh.

As the children made their way into the classroom and hung up their coats, she leaned farther away from the gap where she could see the main room, hoping to avoid acknowledging any of them prematurely—which was the gesture that finally signalled how far she had let herself slip. This couldn't go on. She had to do something, had to take a stand. She was an experienced teacher who had somehow allowed herself to be strong-armed by a child, who had succumbed to the same juvenile tactics she had spent years effectively suppressing. Yes, she thought, reluctantly standing from the windowsill, yes, she had no choice but to end this Lyle business, and today, definitively, in a way that was severe enough that it would never come up again.

She tossed the newspaper onto the table and walked out of the resource room, standing beside her desk and giving a slow nod to the students. "Good morning, class."

The children droned in unison, "Good morning, Mrs. O'Donnell."

"Let us stand and say the Lord's Prayer."

The class rose and stood facing the cross, hands clasped in front of their chests, and proceeded to mutter the syllables in a perfect monotone. She joined them as she always did, hitting a slightly higher note in an attempt to give the words weight and meaning, but doubted it worked. While she recited the prayer, she eyed a few of her students: Julie, already staring out the window, something she would continue doing for most of the day, mouth ajar, her gaze remote and unfocused; Carol, rocking back and forth on her feet, whom, once sitting, would not stop fidgeting for a consecutive thirty seconds throughout the morning; and then there was Lyle, watching his feet as if he were already bored, no doubt wishing he could be out in the playground where he was lord of all he surveyed. He was wearing two poppy pins today, probably in response to the lesson she'd given the day before. She had told them that the pins were made in "Vetcraft" workshops in Montreal and Toronto, by ex-servicemen who'd fought in the wars, then went on to explain the poppy's symbolism, that the red was for the blood shed in battle, the green for the hope of a better future, and the bent pin for the broken bones and suffering endured. It seemed the kind of thing that Lyle wouldn't be able to undermine, but he'd somehow found a way. He'd asked why the poppies were made of plastic and not of flowers—did the plastic mean anything? He wanted to know. She'd answered, quite simply, that it was owing to there being no real poppies in Alberta. They didn't grow here. At which point every student paused to look down at his or her pin doubtfully, at this emblem that had no connection to their immediate world, or even to their landscape entire. It had suddenly become something disassociated, outlandish. She could have sworn she saw Lyle fighting back a smirk.

When the children finished the Lord's Prayer they hurriedly crossed themselves and broke into the singing of God Save the King, which they finished off-time and off-key, sat down, and waited for her to begin. She asked them to take out one of their workbooks, and there was a collective creak as they all hinged open their desks and took them out, closing the lids with many a raucous bang and ruffling their pages to where they had left off. The unit was about professions, about the correct naming of vocations and common careers.

The lesson began and continued unremarkably, until twenty-three minutes later, when her eyes happened to fall upon Cedric Johnson. There was something about him that struck her as odd in that moment. He had always been an inconspicuous student, unexceptional, one of those children who made up a rather plain colour in the mosaic, who made it easier for others to stand out. He was, now that she thought of it, the kind of child a teacher could spend an entire year with and, within a month after he left, forget that he'd ever existed, forever requiring the prompting of a photo to put a face to the name. Yet right now, this normally indifferent boy looked decidedly awake, his eyes shifting around with a kind of distraction, if not wonder, from one corner of the room to the next, focusing on the most commonplace objects as if they had just miraculously appeared out of thin air. He was particularly focused on the snowflakes Scotch-taped to the windows, the shapes of paper the students had folded, snipped, unfolded, and held up to the light before sticking there. Well, she thought to herself, something must be going on at home—fighting parents, nightmares, a dead relative—something out of the ordinary. She looked away, back down at her book.

A few seconds later, Lyle raised his hand to ask a question about careers, his other hand reaching across to brace the one in the air, as if it were unbearably heavy. Mrs. O'Donnell tilted her head to the side impatiently, half-wondering who had ever come up with the phrase "There is no such thing as a stupid question," because whoever it was had clearly never spent time in a third grade classroom, where the days were saturated with them.

She did little to mask her irritation. "What, Lyle?"

"Um . . . Mrs. O'Donnell? Um . . . did *you* always wanna be a teacher?"

She had almost answered him before recognizing what his question really was. He was prodding into her private past, into her life. It was an attempt to rattle her. Yes. This was it, this was the moment she had promised herself, twenty-four minutes earlier, that she would not, could not, shrink from.

She noticed her arms trembling. Then she looked down into her hand and saw that there was a piece of chalk in it, and, as if it were some kind of bloated insect larva that had wriggled between her fingers without her knowing, she gave it a quick, disgusted look and hurled it at the ground. It broke into several pieces, the fragments scattering under the students' desks, bouncing between their feet and under the heating registers. The children all seemed to press their backs against their seats in perfectly choreographed unison, eyes opening wide.

"I have had"—she pointed her finger at Lyle's face like a pistol—"*enough* of you!"

Then she let herself go. She began with yelling the age-old disciplinary spiel about how Lyle had a problem with authority, and that he had better learn to toe the line or else. But somewhere along the way she lost herself. She started ranting about how far he was going to get in life. "If—*if*, do you hear me?—you can learn to listen, and respect others, and quell your aggressiveness, you *might* get to the end of grade nine. After which, I have no doubt, whatsoever, that you will go on to be a gas attendant, or have some such menial job. You, Lyle, will be bringing the change to the windows of your former classmates until you are old and grey."

When she finished, she seemed to come back to herself, seemed to realize that she was standing in front of a roomful of children. She straightened up, smoothed the sides of her dress down, hearing, in the sudden silence, the clack of shoes in the hallway, walking slowly past her door. She could imagine the gossip: "The old woman's finally coming undone," they would be saying later in the staff room, murmuring in a volume just loud enough for everyone to hear. "I mean, we all know she's been losing her grip for a while now . . . ever since Frank died really. Poor thing. She can't even bring herself to come to our bridge games."

But Mrs. O'Donnell didn't care. What was important was that it was over. It was clear that Lyle wasn't going to be causing problems any time soon. He was slumped over in his seat, trying hard to hold back tears. True, she wasn't proud of her outburst, nor of the cruel bite of some of the things she'd said, but it had been necessary. That much she knew. And now it was over, and time to move on, time to release the class from the tension she had created and return to the lesson. She cleared her throat and was getting ready to turn around when a noise came from Cedric, a noise that didn't fully register at first.

"Jesus *Christ*," he whispered as if to himself.

She felt her neck pivoting slowly in his direction, her expression wildly dumbfounded.

Cedric was shaking his head, looking at the rim of his desk. But when he realized that the teacher had heard him, he looked up at her, levelly, calmly, and spoke in a matter-of-fact tone. "That was a touch excessive, don't you think?"

The other students shifted, not knowing whether to look at Cedric or Mrs. O'Donnell. Some of them looked back and forth at the two of them in rapid succession, as if watching a ping-pong match, trying to get the look on both of their faces at the same time.

"*What*," she spat, "did you just say to me?"

He grinned, raised an eyebrow. "I—uh . . . was just pointing out that you might've been a little out of hand there. That's all."

Mrs. O'Donnell's eyebrows were moving in strange ways on her forehead. Her mouth was agape, but it seemed very unlikely that any sound was going to come out of it. She turned to make eye contact with a few of the other children, as if checking to see that they were hearing what she was hearing. It seemed so. They were almost giddy with excitement, watching to see what would happen next, enthralled.

"I mean," Cedric's voice broke into the quiet again, everyone turning back toward him mechanically, including Mrs. O'Donnell.

He waved a flippant hand in the air as he relaxed in his seat, "That's my take on it, at least."

Mrs. O'Donnell swallowed. She noticed that her breathing had become quick and that there was a musty taste in her throat, the taste, in fact, that precedes the acrid tang of bile. Then she heard her voice, speaking as if it were far away, dampened and muffled like something was covering her ears. "Cedric, I want you to go out into the hall. Right now. Do you hear me?"

He shrugged his shoulders. "Sure." He stepped out of his desk and walked through the classroom, slowly, with a confident gait— not cocky, not a strut, but like someone who knew how to walk away from a confrontation with the air that he had won.

She followed closely behind him, almost drunkenly, the heels of her shoes catching on the floor in ways they never had before. When she closed the door behind her, she led Cedric into a book room across the hall. There was a single chair in it that the teachers sometimes used to stand on, to reach the books on the higher shelves. She pointed at it, feeling like everything she was saying and doing was automated, empty. "I want you to sit there until I come back. Understand?" She watched him carefully as he stepped past her, and without even meaning to, she added another banal disciplinary remark: "And I want you to think about what you said to me."

Cedric got comfortable on the seat; and once he had made sufficient bodily adjustments, he turned to her, smirking.

"And just what are you grinning at? Do you think this is funny? Is that it?" She hadn't meant to challenge him either. In fact, the only thing she wanted to do was leave him be, contain him in a place where he couldn't be heard, and walk away. But now, after having explicitly confronted him, those same eyes were fixed on her again, teasingly clever, knowing. His smirk grew into a half-hearted smile, as if, yes, there really was something that was funny, a private joke that belonged to him and him alone. Then he looked away, beginning to inventory the rest of the room with the same hungry attention that she'd noticed in him a few minutes prior.

She didn't dare say another word. Instead, she closed the door and made her way to the ladies' room, where she leaned against the tiled wall and watched her reflection gawk back at her in the mirror. What exactly did this all mean? Was she going crazy, finally losing her grip, like everyone thought she was? Because, being honest with herself, as it stood, the only thing she could be absolutely certain of was that the child who was holed up in the room a few doors away from her was not a child at all. She shook her head. No, she knew children, understood them. She could recognize when a child was simply reciting adult words, repeating things he'd heard his parents say, trying out snippets that he'd picked out from restaurant conversations and bus-stop arguments, but this was different. There was a cognizance with the language, a natural ease with it that could only come from profound maturity, from worldliness. And this, this was the only thing she could be sure of.

So what was she supposed to do now? There was no one to help her, no one to ask advice from. It wasn't as if she could just stroll up to the principal's office and let him know that there was a man in the skin of a boy locked in the book room downstairs. It would be a matter of minutes before she was injected with sedatives and wheeled away to some institution for the rest of her life. No. She had to deal with this alone. And quickly.

She noticed that her reflection didn't look healthy, her complexion pallid, sickly. She stepped forward to the sink and turned on the taps, splashing her face with lukewarm water. When she was finished, she put a hand on the cold porcelain of the basin and leaned closer to the mirror. Her other hand wormed between the third and fourth buttons of her blouse and found the skin above the empty space there, pressing down on it, her fingers cold as a stack of nickels.

The thought crossed her mind to just leave, to walk out the

front doors and never return; let someone else clean up the mess. But she also knew that, if she did, she would be admitting to herself that she was insane, or at least incredibly unstable. Besides, if she just walked out now, wouldn't they try to take away some of her retirement fund? And if so, how many friends did she have on the school board who would stand up for her, speak in her defence? Few. Maybe none.

No, what she needed to do was to look at this problem with rational eyes, as something real, as something that actually happened to people. Then she could deal with it.

She considered how he'd addressed her, the way he'd held her gaze as if he were on the same ground, the same standing, and it came to her that the best thing to do was to confront him in that light, as an equal. She would have to walk into the book room and have a rational, grounded conversation with him, a conversation that was going to be every bit as squeamish and gawky as standing her ground with another adult; one of those cumbersome situations that everyone has been in at some point, a colleague who has overstepped his or her boundaries, a supervisor who has made a mistake. This was going to be about diplomacy, about reasoning, about seeing where the other person was coming from and, possibly, even admitting wrongs and apologizing. This is what it had come to. It was the only reasonable way out that she could think of.

She felt edgy as she walked out of the bathroom and down the hall, where she paused for a slow minute before putting a hand on the door of the book room. She opened it quickly and stepped forward, standing tall, holding her chin as high as her husband would have. However, she could tell instantly, just by looking down at him, that this wasn't the same person she had left in the room.

Cedric was standing in the middle of the floor, gawping up at her, his face long, eyes glossy, his shoulders seeming to hang from his neck. His hair was somewhat dishevelled, like he'd been holding his head for some time, squeezing tufts of it in his fists.

"Mrs. O'Donnell?" His voice was pitched high, meek, submissive. "Um," he looked around at a few of the shelves, "why am I in the book room? I don't . . . I . . ." he paused, as if wondering whether or not he should admit this next part, "I don't remember coming in here." Then he broke off, looking at the floor, and within seconds had started to cry, quietly, shamefully, like he'd wet his pants.

She let him whimper for a while, watching him skeptically, churning over the absurd thought that this could possibly be a grown-up in a child's body just pretending to be a child. But she heard the pathetic ring of paranoia and delusion in this reasoning. No. Intuitively, she understood that this was just a boy in front of her, a boy who was confused and afraid.

Agnes crouched down and held on to his shoulders. "It's all right. Everything's going to be all right now. Okay?" But Cedric couldn't look her in the eyes as she reassured him. He was discomfited, embarrassed.

She flattened one of the raised clumps of his hair. "Come on," she said, standing up. "Let's get you back into class."

For the next hour, Mrs. O'Donnell's movements were stiff and awkward, her instructions to the students imprecise and confusing. She found herself constantly checking to see that Cedric was still in his seat, still watching the class with his usual appeasing eyes, still writing in his usual complacent way. And, to her relief, he always was.

The day passed without further incident. As did the next. And then the next. Until, eventually, Agnes began to have a hard time believing that anything strange had ever happened at all.

No one knew exactly
how far to run
Starting, stopping
like deer spooked
with that curiosity that
has them lingering dangerously
between the line of knowing
and knowing it's too late
We'd watched him light the fuse
and drop it into the pail
with an unceremonious plop
breaking the meniscus
then scattered, wavering
gathering, tightened

How soundlessly
the pillar of water
geysered into the sky
and held there, weightless
towering colossal

Until the spout fanned
and began to drop away
falling into an explosive rain
that smacked at the pavement
with swollen globs
soaking some of the other boys' shirts
Cotton clinging to their backs
as slick-tight as bravery

Mine
was dry

Being on the road, traversing the country again on the way back home, put Melissa in an odd mood. Particularly here, in the landscape of her father's upbringing, which she had never before spent time in. She was leaning against a car, waiting for her roadtrip companion to come out of the gas station, when she noticed the train standing still on a set of tracks across the highway and decided to cross the asphalt to take a better look. She walked up to the car that was most heavily graffitied, an enormous rusted barrel with the fadings of the words "Government of Canada" on its side, in two languages, streaked with corrosion, mechanical grease, and bird droppings. It made her think about how far this one car had travelled, how many times it had made its way across the country. Then she thought about that greater context, picturing the nation's trains whistling over desolate tracks, then of its planes, like stubby pieces of chalk pressed sideways and pulling across the length of blueboard skies, and the night roads that stitched the cities together through a patchwork of cricket rumours and bat-fluttering expanses; binding us, dividing us.

But these thoughts were soon interspersed by wonderings about school and debt, where she was going in life and why, about travel and where she would find the money to do it, thoughts about her chances of becoming just another woman living a mostly painless fifty-two-week-a-year emptiness, interrupted, at best, twice, by all-inclusive resort packages. Thoughts that the chances were pretty good.

It's interesting how countries, considered Melissa, have a way of having their way with us. Though, she countered, so does the world really, our biology, our nature, time, the cosmos. They all have their way with us. In the end, those inspirational posters and movies and New Age propaganda professing how one individual can make an enormous difference are wrong. In the end, there is room for our smallness, our insignificance. Infinite room.

October 23, 1962

It was five o'clock in the afternoon, and Peter Kushnir was in his backyard striving for numbness, taking generous swigs from what was now his third glass of whisky. But it wasn't working. Instead, with each coating of warmth that drained down his gullet, he felt his despair mount. Within hours, he was sure of it, a nuclear holocaust would sweep the globe as bare as a slate, and he couldn't do anything—*no one* could do anything—to stop it.

He was, however, doing a pretty good job of getting himself drunk. He had never had much tolerance for alcohol, only really partaking at Christmas and New Year's get-togethers, retirement parties, and when he was handed a cup with an ounce of sour champagne at the railway yards, to be raised into the sooty air at the welcoming of another newborn. Other than that, he avoided it, convinced that drink was one of those things that made people turn on you, made seedy colleagues into friends and friends into enemies. Today, of course, none of that really mattered anymore.

Peter emptied his glass and poured a fourth, the spout of the bottle wobbling above the edge of his tumbler. As the liquid neared the rim, he heard the distant sound of voices and laughter, which belonged to a group of boys who gradually came into view. The boys were walking along the crest of the coulee that his yard opened onto, and he recognized them as kids who lived in the neighbourhood on the other side of the draw.

As they came closer, three of them broke into a jog and steered themselves down a long hill, their feet slapping at the dirt to keep up with their bodies. The last boy looked to be limping a bit, like he'd just twisted an ankle in a gopher hole or foolishly jumped from a branch that was too high, and so continued walking toward Peter's house, where the trail that dipped down and crossed the draw wasn't as steep or long. He recognized him as the Johnson kid, who lived close by and whose father worked down at the flour mill. Hearing the others call up to him, he learned that his given name was Cedric.

He watched the boy as he limped along, oblivious to what was happening in the world, oblivious to the very volatility of his own existence. There he was, concerned about his sore ankle, about catching up with his friends, or maybe just about finding something sufficiently rotund to topple down the hill. Lost in play, on the eve of the Third World War. Much in the way, come to think of it, that Peter had been (for a short period at least) during the First World War. That was, until he had learned better. Which happened on the day that he and his brother, Michael, had gotten into some serious trouble, and for the strangest reason imaginable.

It had been right in the middle of the Great War, when, he recalls, the weight of the daily news visibly slumped onto the shoulders of everyone in town. He was only eight but old enough to recall the unnerving quiet, the way people walked through the stores and sat in restaurants as if they were secret places, their conversations hushed and serious. The day it occured, Peter had been walking back from school with his brother, nearing the point on the road where the two rows of houses on either side stopped and gave way to a farmer's field—the field that their father rented, on the corner of which was a modest house that their family called home. Peter and his brother had found an old bicycle tire to push along the pavement and had gotten lost in play, constantly adding new and varied obstacles to manoeuvre the tire through, upping the ante. And because the game was being invented on the spot, they needed to shout out the rules to each other while they wheeled it along. The two brothers were speaking Ukrainian, as they often did when playing alone, and a woman stood watching them from her front yard as they weaved back and forth through the street, her expression as unmoved as a garden ornament's.

At some point, Peter became aware of a man yelling from far away, in a voice that was shrill and foreign, but thought nothing of it. Meanwhile, Michael challenged him to bounce the tire over a rock in the middle of the road but to keep the tire rolling in a straight line. It didn't, and they swerved to chase it in a long, sweeping circle, giggling.

The extraneous voice grew louder, more insistent. "You must come home! You must come!"

Then Peter dared his brother to roll it right along the gutter without letting it fall inside, and Michael told him that he doubted it was even possible, for anyone, even a grown-up.

"Zamóvkny!" they heard their father yell. Shut up. And they spun around to see him marching along the street from the field. Neither of them moved. The tire faltered beside them, spinning onto its rim, gyrating faster and faster until it had settled on the road and was suddenly still. "Zamóvkny," their father muttered again. Then he was speaking English, something they had never heard him do before. "You must come home." He gave the woman a quick nod. "Home," he pointed over his shoulder and turned on his heels to walk back in the direction he'd come. They followed, none of them speaking until they'd crossed the broad field and were inside the house. When their father closed the door, he turned around and slapped Peter, whose hand shot up to his face and started rubbing the cheek that was hit. Then his father walked to the table, sat down, and told them the child's version of what was happening in town.

Which was that on the bare soil north of the slough, the city had taken the framework of a sturdy chicken coop and turned it into a concentration camp, which was to be used for interning "enemy aliens," meaning anyone who had emigrated from Germany, Turkey, Austria-Hungary, or Eastern Europe. That included the Ukraine, from which Peter's parents had immigrated ten years earlier. Already some of his Ukrainian friends from the mines had been taken, and he'd heard of a carpenter a few blocks away who was arrested and carted off for having a German-sounding name. German-*sounding*, that's all the evidence that was needed. And did they realize that their name, Kushnir, could sound German too? Did they know that there were labour camps all over the province that were filled with Ukrainians, just like them? People *just* like them, he had said, poking an emphatic finger into his own chest.

At that point, their mother came out of the kitchen, wiped her hands on a towel that was draped over her shoulder, and sat down on the other side of the table, moving the chair without making a sound.

And what could they do about it, move? Of course not, because that would implicate them, it would be an admission of who they were, and someone—probably the Meyers, from whom they rented the land—would report them to the Home Guard, and they would be picked up within days.

No, the best thing to do was be quiet, to look like everyone else, to stay out of trouble, and under no circumstances holler out to your brother in Ukrainian when everyone in the neighbourhood could hear you. Was that understood, was it? He wanted to know.

Peter's memories of the months and years that followed were flashes of jittery apprehension. He had the feeling that things would fall into a natural pattern of school and chores and talk of the war, and the minute, in fact the very second, that he felt like his life was becoming safe, words would rise up out of the play-ground or the street, or from people milling in their backyards, talking over the splashes of watering cans, a few syllables jutting from the sentences like bayonets. Words like "Huns," or "Central Powers," or "the six escapees that tunnelled out of the henhouse." Or sometimes they were whole sentences: "And why *wouldn't* they have tampered with the threshing rigs? I mean, they've been called what they're called for a reason. They probably see it as an obligation of some kind. It's like in Hillcrest, I guess they had five hundred of them working in the shafts, until the other miners just had enough, you know? It's a question of safety." Peter would walk away from his eavesdropping with hands sunk deep in his pockets, watching the ground, the sidewalk, his shoes, and looking up at no one. Because it was his family they were talking about—his parents, his brother, himself—they were enemies, aliens and enemies. And someone was bound to find out at some point.

Sometimes he heard noises at night and would slip out of bed, careful not to wake Michael, and press his nose against the window to see if it was the Home Guard coming to take them away, having already imagined what they would look like when they did, a squad of men marching across the night fields, rifles swinging above their shoulders with each step, the muzzles catching flickers of frozen light.

And out of all these vivid images that stayed with him, there were none of the day that the war ended because for Peter, that feeling that his security was tentative, was faltering, never really abated.

He grew up in the 1920s, a decade candent with destructive fires in the area. He spent it farming with his father and brother, watching from a saddle or the seat of a tractor as columns of wavering smoke rose from the city as something else ignited: factories, houses, granaries, whole blocks, and at times enormous swaths of farmland. There were areas of town that were ablaze so predictably that the firemen would joke for months about the "winter annual" coming up. Then it did, and people were trapped on the higher floors, calling through the smoke until their shouts turned to coughs, and their coughs into that uneasy silence that follows a tactless punchline.

In the summer months he spent a great deal of time looking over his shoulder for anvils of hail clouds that listed toward the farm like collapsing buildings, purple flashes illuminating their cerebral folds from the inside out. Once, he watched as a pasture just north of their property was pounded to mulch by fists of ice that were the size of onions and layered just as delicately.

Today, there were only a few, thin high clouds hovering over the mountains in the distance. Peter, adjusting the glass of whisky on his lap, looked away from Cedric for a moment, up at those thin clouds, then down at the bottom of the draw where the group of neighbourhood boys were inspecting something they'd found. Like most twelve- and thirteen-year-old boys, thought Peter, these ones also seemed to spend most of their time and energy trying to kill themselves, in the winter finding the steepest slopes to toboggan down, crashing into rosebushes or rusted car frames at the bottom, and in the summer scavenging anything that would roll downhill and pushing it over the edge, cheering as its speed escalated in sluggish leaps, gouging deeper divots into the clay with every bounce. He'd once seen them line up an entire row of tires along the lip of his draw, and it was only when they'd pushed them over at the same time and yelled, "Initiation!" that he realized there was a boy at the bottom, cowering close to the ground in a tiny hollow that somehow managed to save his life, vicious blows of careening rubber hammering the grass and cacti around him. They were the kind of boys that made him happy that his wife had given him daughters instead of sons.

On the night that Peter met his wife, he and a friend had gone to a public dance in town. It was six days after the summer solstice, a glow loitering on the horizon, and there he found himself, nineteen and leaning on his elbow, managing to make a young woman laugh so hard she was covering her face with embarrassment, a woman who struck him as being sparrowlike in every way, petite and sharp and amber, with two rims of freckles masking her eyes. It was the first time in his life that he felt infallible, and the sensation lasted all of four glorious minutes. Then the chairs began to reverberate until they were floating along the floor, the electricity flickering in frenetic strobes, and something heavy and glass toppling from a shelf and shattering as the band stopped playing, an accordion hurriedly dropped into its case. As far as earthquakes went it was a piddling one but was enough to lose her in the chaos of evacuation, everyone scampering outside and into open ground, watching the sky as if the tremors were coming from above. He walked home that night without knowing her name, kicking at pebbles that were in his way on the sidewalk.

The second time he saw her she was standing at an intersection, waiting for a streetcar to pass, and he'd followed for three full blocks before working up the nerve to stop her, having reached out to touch her shoulder twice before actually doing so. They married in 1926 and, as the farm wasn't big enough to support two families, they rented a house in town. As luck would have it, her father was a divisional trainmaster for the Canadian Pacific, who managed to get Peter a job as a fireman, shovelling coal into the furnaces of the locomotives on their runs to and from the Crowsnest Pass.

When their first daughter was born, Peter started looking to buy a home, hoping to find something that was affordable but that also overlooked the coulees, wanting the guarantee that he wouldn't be boxed in by other houses as the city grew. His farm life had instilled in him a need for open spaces, the walls and fences in the city seeming to grow higher and closer every month that he lived there, a clutter of new constructions that invaded his periphery, crowded him in. His father told him about a woman who had some land and a tiny house, which had just been cleaved in half by a tree snapping with the weight of a freakishly early snowstorm. He went to the property and saw the gaping holes in the roof, the walls buckling around the diameter of the tree. But more importantly, behind these ruins, was a yawning skyline that opened up onto a yellow carpet of prairie that unrolled all the way out to the Rockies. "Perfect," he'd said, looking into the coulee draw just beside the house, which snaked an auburn path of hawthorn and snowberry down to the river. "Perfect."

He bought the house and the three acres it was on for only eight months' wages, quickly putting an addition on it and fixing the roof with the help of his brother on the weekends and after work. His father, who had probably had the idea in mind when he'd recommended the place, asked Peter if he would take his horses, whenever their working years were over with, and put them out to pasture on his land, instead of having to shoot them. He arrived with the lumber and some friends from church, and they built a modest barn in the better part of a day.

After they'd moved in, their daughter was just learning to walk, and the three of them would shuffle out to the barn to feed the horses in the evenings. At the end of one of the hottest summer days that Peter could remember, they were standing just in front of the barn doors after he'd spread some oats into the trough, listening to the horses grind their feed, watching the bulky workings of their jaws, when a woman started screaming across the coulee behind them.

Her scream was hoarse, panicked, and when they turned to look at her, all they could make out was that she was pointing at the cement on her driveway. Her back was against one of the outside walls of her house, and her other hand was blindly searching along it, as if for some kind of magical door to escape through. Within seconds, a neighbour sprinted toward her, sized up the situation, and swiftly returned with a garden hose, water jetting a thin arc through the air and splashing the spot she was pointing at. The man seemed to be washing whatever it was down the gutter toward the coulee, and when he looked up and noticed that Peter and his wife were watching, he hollered out a one-word explanation, managing to sound a little embarrassed, "Rattlesnake."

They relaxed, turned back to the horses, both of them dropping a hand down to touch their daughter, who was between them. Only she wasn't there. In the few seconds of their distraction, she had made her way into the barn and was now walking in the space under the horses' bellies, between the restive stilts of their legs as they transferred weight from one limb to another.

"No," Peter whispered, "please, no." Then he started moving toward her, gently easing into his steps while his wife tried coaxing the child out to safety.

"Teresa, sweetie! Come over here." She held out her arms wide, and then opened them even wider, wiggling her fingers with overstrung enthusiasm. "Come and see Mommy. Come on. Come here."

But Teresa didn't move. She was watching the strange way her father was creeping closer, working the soother around in her mouth. At one point she pivoted to the side and fumbled, holding out a hand to steady herself on one of the horse's fetlocks, as if it were the leg of a table. It happened to be too far and she managed to regain her balance on her own.

And all that Peter could think about as he stepped closer— watching the enormous disks of the horses' buttocks as they trembled to shake off flies, listening to the thump of their hooves as they distractedly shifted and jittered—was that, yes, he understood, he *knew* that his world was frail and prone to collapse, but what more could he do to be prepared for it? How could things like this happen to people like him, people who mistrusted every situation, who never let their guard down, not even for a second? Because he hadn't, he was just busy assessing another danger, which happened to be in a different direction. What exactly did it take to make a life safe?

And then he was there, at the horses, managing to reach far under their stomachs without touching them and clenching on to his daughter's shirt. He pulled her out as smoothly as he could, and up into his arms, the horses flinching and clomping the ground as he straightened up beside them.

On the way back to the house, he talked about having another baby, a boy, a brother who would be able to look after his sister. But a year later, following the crash of Black Tuesday in 1929, they had Marianne instead. Then, after a long debate over the prospect of another mouth to feed, they tried yet again, and in 1931, had Susan.

During the 1930s when work was hard to come by—and whatever work there was, labour conditions were degenerating—Peter kept his job at the railway and prudently held his tongue about it. Because between the incessant talk of unemployment relief camps, unions, and strikes, there was an animosity in the air, a desperation that sometimes swelled to the point of bursting: news of daring robberies, of communist polemics, of riots and violence. Peter kept quiet through it all. He went to work in the dark of morning, accepted his pay cuts with a phlegmatic nod, and avoided clusters of men on his way home.

In 1935, the same week that a mine blast in a neighbouring town killed more than a dozen people, he was demoted to track maintenance and spent the coldest days of the winter swapping the worn-out rails in the bends that wove toward the mountains. Once, while having to do some work between two parallel tracks— a place he'd heard other workers refer to as the "devil's strip"—he was caught by surprise and cornered there, being deafened by a train that was passing on one side of him and not hearing a second that was coming from behind on the other. The colliding gust of air jarred him to his knees, a thunderous roll reverberating in his chest cavity, the shriek of metal screaming above it. He covered his ears, cringing at the loudest sounds, and looked forward until the optical illusion that he was spinning became so overwhelming that he had to bury his face in the shivering rocks. It wasn't until both trains had passed, and the ground had stopped rumbling, that he got to his feet and looked around, the prairie landscape widening with his focus. He had never felt so small in his life.

Then, just as the drought and dust of the decade seemed to be settling into a tolerable future, the Second World War rose out of it. Only this time it was another list of people who had taken on the role of "the sudden enemy." Instead of the anti-Chinese, anti-Mennonite, and anti-Eastern European tendencies of the First World War, the politicians were flaring up with comments and actions that were in turn anti-Semitic, anti-German, and anti-Hutterite. The worst of it being against the Japanese, who, if they weren't interned, had to eke out an existence under a rain of bigotry and insults that pelted them from the moment they left their houses to the moment they'd locked themselves in again. Peter felt sorry for them, but not as much for their hardships as for their naivety, the fact that they'd let themselves believe—because they were integrated, because they were Canadians in Canada—that that would be enough. He could see it in their faces, the disgusted surprise, the shock at how easily a community could turn on itself. Their assumption that everyone would be seen as equal in the gloom of hard times, was a mistake he knew, they wouldn't make twice.

In 1940, as it became increasingly clear that the war would be a long one, the government revoked its "no conscription" policy. He was thirty-four years old, which wasn't the most sought-after age for a soldier, but it was young enough. He began the habit of walking into the house after work and, before even taking off his shoes, sitting heavily on the bench beside the door to sift through the mail, scanning the return addresses for anything that looked official or military. He did this religiously for five years, chewing the inside of his lip as he placed the scanned mail on the wood beside him. A draft letter never came.

Within only four years of the war ending, he had given away all three of his daughters, two of them to men working in the growing sugar industry and one to a returning air force pilot who had never gone overseas or been under enemy fire but had somehow managed to crash two farm planes in the months before their wedding, his arm in a cast as he walked down the aisle. One of his daughters became a school teacher, something Peter had always thought of as a noble pursuit, as well as his being comforted by the fact that nothing unsafe, nothing destructive, ever happened in classrooms.

When his father turned seventy-five in 1956, Peter and his wife had the entire family over for a meal and a drink to celebrate. Peter nursed a single rum and Coke throughout the evening, until, with the ice having melted and the taste gone flat, he went into the kitchen and poured it down the sink, spattering water around with his hand to rinse the brown film from the enamel.

Near the end of the night, after most of the grandchildren and great-grandchildren had gone home, his father pulled out a carton of eggs—a treat for the horses that he never failed to bring—and gestured to Peter that he was going outside. The two of them stepped out and walked through the dark, the frost on the grass crunching under their feet, until they were leaning on the barbed-wire fence near the barn. The horses, recognizing their previous owner's smell and shape, had soon gathered in front of them, nickering in low murmurs, their heads high, ears pointed and quavering.

His father hinged the carton open, and there was just enough light to see the two bulging rows inside. "So," he began, "the Russians went back into Hungary. Like I thought they would." He said this naturally, as if continuing a long conversation they'd been having, speaking in Ukrainian, as he always did when addressing his immediate family, or animals. "Crushed their revolution. Now they're back to where they were." He cleared his throat again. "Always the same."

Peter didn't reply. As a rule, his father spoke very little, and even less about politics or the country he'd fled fifty years earlier. Which meant that, when he did, Peter usually stopped whatever he was doing—hammer in hand, shovel in dirt, standing in the cold—and listened.

"Like in the Ukraine, same thing. People trying to make changes, getting killed. And it's just simple things they want. To farm and go to church, read. But you know what? You can't change a Russian's mind. And as long as they're there . . ." He shrugged.

Peter watched his father take an egg out of the carton and hold it out to the closest horse, who wrapped its velvety mouth around it, lifted its head into the night sky, rolled the egg down the length of its tongue, and quietly crushed it at the back of its throat.

"I've heard stories about what Stalin did to us in the thirties.

Had soldiers guarding the harvests and stock. Then he sent all the food away. They say there were so many starved bodies you couldn't count them."

He took another egg from the carton, wrapped his fingers around it, and reached out farther, to a different horse. He waited for its nostrils to brush against his hand, then slowly opened it.

"I heard that, when the Nazis invaded, people were cheering. Thought they were finally free. But after the Germans did the same, the Russians came back anyway."

He rubbed his knuckles along the same horse's forehead, working them into its broad swirl of hair, the horse pushing lightly against his hand. He didn't speak for a while. Then, "There are still stories about the concentration camps they made for us here in Canada. You know they kept them open for two years after the war ended, kept us working, men in bunks, behind barbed-wire, shooting at those who tried to escape. Afterwards, Ukrainian newspapers here were outlawed. But we slowly blended in. We have learned to be quiet."

The shyest of the horses, which had been just off to the side of the others, began digging at the ground, swinging its head like a pendulum. His father noticed and walked over to it, getting as close as he could, trying to give it an egg before the others could crowd in. "We have worked hard to be out of Russia's reach," he said gently, leaning farther over the fence, talking toward the horse's face. "We have worked very hard."

When the others had reached him and were gathering closer, one of them nudged his arm and the egg fell from his hand, landing in a clump of bunchgrass, still intact. The timid horse had heard it, and sidled closer, surreptitiously manoeuvring through the others, and when it found the egg in the grass, it threw its head back high to swallow it, stamping the ground once.

His father straightened up, speaking through a smile, "Perfect."

Now, six years later, Peter holds that conversation in his mind like a piece of incontrovertible evidence. He'd been following the lead-up to the Cuban Missile Crisis for weeks without even knowing he was. The US had been debating whether or not to invade Cuba for months, while the papers printed clips of a Russian naval buildup in the Atlantic that didn't make any sense. Then, the day before, Kennedy finally set the public straight, announcing that the world was indeed in crisis and that he had just given the Russians an ultimatum: Cuba was quarantined, lines on ocean charts were drawn, and the consequence of crossing them was firmly implied. The Russians, however, hadn't shown any sign of stopping.

Then today, after coming home from his shift, he'd picked up The *Lethbridge Herald* from the doorstep, flipped through it, and within minutes had walked to the cupboard of dusted bottles and pulled the whisky from the shelf. The front page read, UNITED STATES AND RUSSIA MAY CLASH BY NIGHTFALL, with a subheading stating that both US and Soviet forces had been ordered into a "state of combat readiness and diligence." But what had struck him the hardest was a political cartoon inside. It had pictured the two leaders of the superpowers at a poker table, the tense faces of the political world watching from the barely illuminated sidelines, the smoke of Castro's cigar threading through the lamplight. Kennedy was sliding a teetering heap of poker chips into the centre of the table, Khrushchev eyeing him coldly above his cards. The president's mouth was open to say the one word in quotation marks below. "Call."

True, he didn't know Russians in the same way his father had, but he was sure he understood them better than most people, and certainly enough to know that the world was about to see a nuclear exchange of some kind. Because the situation had already snowballed too far, too fast, and now, at the very least, one or two buttons would have to be pushed, and this, out of the simple need to maintain posture. Something, *somewhere*, had to be annihilated. As his father said, you cannot change a Russian's mind, and within days, whether the world realized it or not, those missile-laden ships carving through the sea toward Cuba had come to signify the

very embodiment of Russia's political conviction, of its tenacity, of its bold and stubborn determination. Could anyone really picture such boats being snubbed, being wrist-slapped, and pointed back home like a child kicked out of a game for disregarding the rules? Not likely. No, Peter thought, sliding the newspaper onto the kitchen counter, this would come to blows. In the end, his father, thinking that they were out of Russia's reach, had been wrong.

As it happened, Peter's wife spent her Tuesday afternoons at a friend's house, and the fact that she wasn't there to spend time with, on this day of all days, seemed almost poetic. Because, as Peter was now substantiating, that was how you had to do it, you had to live like nothing was ever going to happen to you—you or anyone else you cared about. You had to buy your groceries, keep to schedules, and check your wrist for the time, all while you plodded along across this no-man's-land of a world, with catastrophes flaring up in every direction around you. That's what you had to do—that and nothing else. Peter was done with trying to calculate the statistical likelihood of getting hit between the frontlines. It was high. Higher than ever. And no amount of guessing or preparation could do a single thing about it.

Which, naturally enough, led him into his backyard, to sit with a bottle of whisky and watch the sky like it was Dominion Day and the fireworks had just popped from the ground and fizzled into the night sky, wavering sparks tracing them to the spot where they would detonate. There was even a part of him that was half-curious as to what it would look like, wondering if he would see the wave of destruction fanning out over the land like he'd seen on some of the safety commentaries before movies—which made you feel anything but safe—houses pulverized in microseconds, frames of instant tinder skeletons that wouldn't even have the time to topple to the ground.

Peter returned his drunken gaze to Cedric, who was now nearing his house. And as Peter was watching him, something bizarre happened: the boy stopped in his tracks and, blinking hard, held his hands out in front of him, turning them over, inspecting them. When he was finished, he let them drop to his sides and started taking in the rest of his surroundings, pivoting in a full circle, absorbing the details of the skyline, the knee-high grass, the coulee where his companions were climbing up the other side. Then, as if remembering something, he turned directly to Peter and started walking toward him. He was walking, Peter noted, in a very different manner now, with confidence and direction, ostensibly forgetting his sore ankle altogether.

Impulsively, Peter raised his glass at this strange Johnson boy, feeling a little dizzy, a little unsteady in his chair. "Hey, kid," he mumbled, waiting to hear what would come out of his mouth next, "here'z . . . to th'end o'the worl' tonight." He pushed the glass out to clink with an imaginary counterpart and took a sip.

The boy didn't flinch at what he'd said or at his inebriation. He had walked straight toward Peter and stopped just in front of him, placing his foot—his bad foot, as far as Peter reckoned—onto the raised deck where Peter's chair was perched. "See," Cedric said, "the thing is, you're wrong about that. The world's not gonna end tonight, or tomorrow, or any time soon for that matter. Trust me." A practised smirk, a sweep of his blond hair.

Peter shifted in his seat. "Oh yeah, kid? Wlll . . . I'm sher yer parens tellya everythin's fine'n'dandy, but I'm afraid th'truth is—"

"No," Cedric interrupted. "That's not what they tell me. Not at all. In fact, if I was to go down that street *right* there," he pointed, "and ask my parents about what you just said, about the world coming to an end tonight, they wouldn't be able to reassure me in the least. Instead, they'd exchange this kind of serious look and avoid the question, which, if you think about it, is the kind of thing that would make a boy lose sleep for weeks, months even, waiting around for the world to blow up. I mean, *Christ*." Cedric shook his head. "What a thing to say to a kid."

Now Peter was squirming in his chair, feeling more than uneasy and, to his unpleasant surprise, somewhat nauseous.

"Look," he slurred, "whut I'm talk'n'bout is politics, kid, 'bout com-plucated . . . adult things, 'kay? 'Bout Russian boats and Kenndy and . . ." Trailing off, feeling weary, annoyed even, Peter looked over Cedric's shoulder at the barn not far behind him, then at one of the horses he'd put out to pasture for his father. It *was* strange how calm the horses appeared, standing placid and regal.

Cedric cleared his throat.

Peter shook his head. "Anyweh, like isaid, these'r complu-cated . . . gron-up things, kid. Ya wuldn't unerstan."

"Oh believe me," Cedric said, smiling, "I know all about those adult things." He straightened up. "Just like I know this crisis'll blow over. Like I know that, after it does, the Cold War will just build and build, long past Kennedy's assassination, and will only dwindle away just before the Soviet Union collapses." The boy, looking quite happy with himself, gave Peter an exaggerated wink. "That's what I know."

"Wha'ju . . . ? *Whah?*" Peter squinted.

Cedric removed his foot from the raised deck. He placed his hands in his pockets. "And I know much more than that," he said, looking for a moment into the dry grass at his feet. "Much more. I mean, don't get me wrong, it isn't roses for everybody. Bad things happen. To the world. To me." He swallowed. Then, shifting his weight, Cedric pulled a sudden finger from his pocket and pointed into Peter's face. "But it doesn't play out the way you think. So keep the doomsday trumpeting to yourself. You hear?"

Cedric turned and started down the hill. He dipped into the draw and climbed up the other side, stepping out of the coulee and onto the road. He was still looking around at the houses and yards as if he'd never seen them before. Then, abruptly, he lost this acute focus and was looking just in front of his feet again, walking like he had been earlier, less self-assured, smaller, limp-ing to join his friends.

Peter found himself staring down into his glass, hazily con-templating what had just happened. But, as it was, he was having a hard enough time focusing on the glass itself, the colour of the whisky blurring into a shapeless froth in his lap, let alone digesting word for word something that hadn't made any sense at all. There was, however, a single allusion that the boy had made that kept rising in his mind; something about J.F.K. getting—stabbed, did he say, shot? Either way, Peter thought, it was laughable. Imagine, someone killing Kennedy. He was sniggering now. "Crizzy kid."

There was, however, something troubling about the incident, something he felt quite compelled to push away. Resting his head against the back of his chair, he resumed the woozy task of watching the sky, waiting. In the pasture in front of him, one of the horses lifted its head and turned toward the clouds that hovered over the mountains, as if watching too. Its tail swished, an ear cupping to the side. Tuning into something unseen, unknown. Or tuning out.

Peter admired how the clouds above the mountains had fixed themselves onto the glass sky with such serene stillness. A stillness, in fact, thought Peter, sinking farther into his chair, that was perfect. Perfect.

When the first of us got his licence
we stood on the driveway
passing it around like a chalice
our voices still crackling with pubescence

That night we drove beyond the city limits
into the dark where moths struck the windshield
and flashes of green eyes stopped frozen
in the ditch to watch us pass

Inside the dashboard glow pressed at the glass
with the images of our faces sated with freedom
and distorted only as much as the radio swells were
electrified with our wildness and youth and abandon

Outside the fields were strewn with hay bales
like course-haired creatures hunched over
and sleeping, oblivious to the wide-open night
and the infinite promise it held

Somewhere above the car I imagined
a meteorite slicing open a slash of sky
and sealing it up instantly
with the dwindling haze of its tail

All while we raced along at a floating speed
with our headlights opening the gravel road
the white noise of rubber on stones billowing
red dust into the tail lights to close it

Melissa was thinking a lot about poetry. About how it was the oldest art form in existence, and how, despite that, she didn't really—really—know what it was, couldn't define it. And she very much wanted to, wanted an answer of some kind. So she asked the one person she was sure would know. She hadn't expected his response.

"I think," he'd said, "we all, poets or not, have the feeling of what poetry is. We know when something poignant, something song-worthy, passes through our lives, makes one of our days more of a story worth telling than just another empty orbit of the clock. We know what poetry is when we hear it, when we see it, touch it. That much is almost simple. But what poetry is to me, personally, is the larger complex that it produces, that we are imbedded inside.

"If you think of your own life," he continued, "you might be able to string its narration together using the exotic beads of those few, most singular moments that you've experienced, the big turning points, the poems, until you could look at those glass colours all butted up together, side by side. But what you don't see looking at it—or even stop to consider—is that every human being that your path collides with at those poignant moments also has a string of beads, which is now intersecting with yours, and so is woven into it. And I think that this network of blindness to the poetry of other lives, this reluctance to penetrate such an expansive yet simple code—to admit the verse that is beneath everything, behind everyone, impelling its way through every existence, silently, cloaked and teeming—that we could exist without acknowledging this interplay around us, is, to me, exactly that: poetry. Poetry is being deaf to the extravagant choir that is behind you, below you, above you. But singing anyway. It is the collective and soundless cacophony of our solitary melodies, which is humming, even now, ringing in our ears with its almost perfect silence."

Melissa considered his take, often. So often that she'd been thinking about it just a few minutes before her father dropped by, unannounced, after a four-year hiatus from her life. Just before she'd closed her book and stood to answer the door, hesitating at the door handle.

June 11, 1965

The policeman twisted around in his seat to speak to the two girls in the back. "Now you're sure," he paused, looking at each of them individually, "*real sure* that this is your uncle's house?"

"Oh yeah. I couldn't tell before cuz we drive a different way, but now . . ." Hilda Crowfeathers leaned toward the window, giving the house another thoughtful appraisal, "Yeah, that's it. I'm sure."

The officer looked them over skeptically, a voice crackling numbers out of the dispatch radio behind him, "That's five-two-five at station, confirm." He lifted his hat and scratched the line of moisture-matted hair beneath the brim. Then he gave them one last serious glance, got out, walked seriously to the front door, and rapped on it three times with a serious fist.

While his back was turned Hilda let out a stifled giggle and, as always when she smiled, used the tips of her fingers to cover her teeth, which happened to be immaculate—well aligned, large, so white they darkened the russet of her skin.

But her cousin sitting beside her, Brandy, wasn't joining in the amusement. The truth was that, to her, things had stopped being funny ever since they were ushered into the backseat of the police car and the door—with its blank panel that was missing a window lever, ashtray, lock, and handle—was slammed shut. She wondered where this was going to end, when she would be able to return to her normal life. To the red-lined coulees she called home.

Brandy Weaseltail had grown up on the reserve, just off of the Old Agency Road, which snakes north between the river and the delicate ochre lines of the Belly Buttes. For most of her life, she had believed that every hill in the world was striated with red streaks like the ones that layered the land behind her house, and even now, at sixteen, seeing the lacklustre clay running down the ravines in other places just made her that much happier that her home was tucked between the shoulder blades of those colourful buttes.

Her family's house had one room, three windows, and, like most residences on the Blood Indian Reserve, no running water. And because her father usually had jobs for her two older brothers—like cutting wood, hauling building supplies for his carpentry work, and hunting—the job of getting water automatically fell to her. Every morning, and sometimes late in the evening, she would walk with two plastic buckets out to the closest spring, which was a little more than a mile away, and would linger there for a long while, visiting everyone else her age in the area who was doing the same. When she left, she would lift the two buckets, one of them being slightly larger than the other, and walk lopsided back to her house, a scale tipped to one side.

She had gone to school for as long as one could on the reserve, which was until grade six. But it hadn't been an easy time. It was a place with bizarre rules and rituals, where, to start with, they were exposed to English for the first time, and forced to speak it, with every Blackfoot word that was uttered getting them a ruthless mouthwashing, faces held over sinks, having to lick their soapy palate for hours until the tallow and lye was finally gone from their lips. Brandy considered English an ugly language, the tone flat, the words strung together without so much as a hint of lolling melody. And if the priest and nuns weren't speaking English, they were speaking an even stranger tongue, one that had either the letter "M" or "S" droning or whistling at the end of every syllable, a language that not a single one of the students understood or even, for that matter, knew the name of.

Her parents were Catholic, so she had at least some familiarity with the rites and ceremonies at the school, but what she could never get used to was the severity with which they were practised. There were prayers every morning, before lunch, after lunch, at the beginning of classes, of recesses, and after school; they had to constantly rehearse hymns and songs for the masses that observed a list of saints and holy days that Brandy doubted even the priest could keep track of. And they were strict, the nuns seemingly bent on catching you whispering during class or lingering outside after they'd rung the bell. If you were caught, they would stand over you, waiting until you shrank under the weight of their stare, their giant black garments flapping in the wind and framing the unnatural white of their faces. There were times that she suspected there wasn't a single thing you *could* do without getting disciplined for it, and that discipline was increasingly harsh and peculiar. Atonement usually meant some kind of embarrassment, having to act out your punishment in front of the class or the entire school, standing in the corridor facing the wall while the other students scuttled through the hallway behind you. Once, having giggled during prayers, Brandy was sent out to stand in the hall for three full hours, studying the flakes of paint as they peeled away from the walls, even helping to liberate some of the blisters of gesso and letting them fall to the floor where they lay like fish scales gleaming in the flat light. She was there for so long that one of the Sisters—a different woman, a nun who had a quiet kindness to her and even seemed to like Brandy, handing her a pear whenever Brandy showed up without a lunch—touched her on the shoulder and told her she could go back into class, that she had been there long enough. When she opened the door to let Brandy in, the two nuns exchanged a severe look that wasn't broken until the door, swivelling on its well-oiled hinges, closed soundlessly between them.

As soundless, in fact, as the house that the police officer was still standing in front of, now growing impatient. Brandy and Hilda watched him as he bent low, leering into the front windows of the bungalow, looking for movement—a cat, dog, anything. It was apparent he had come across few signs of life. He turned to look once more at the girls in the backseat of his cruiser. Something in Brandy's chest fluttered. She doubted very much he would see the humour in this when he found out. She remembered the only other time that she'd seen the police take someone away. They weren't, if she recalls, known for their levity.

It had been in her final year of schooling, when she was eleven, and there was an incident where the RCMP had to be called in. It began when Theron, one of the boys from the south end of the reserve, stole some coins from the priest's jacket while it was hanging in the cloakroom. Unable to make him confess, the priest found the boy playing marbles in the schoolyard one afternoon and calmly asked him to stand and turn around; then he swung wide with a fist and cracked him on the side of the head. When the child fell to the ground the priest continued beating him until one of the nuns ran out to pull him off. The next day Theron's mother came to school in a pickup truck, walked straight into the priest's office, shoved him to the ground, and started kicking. For the second day running, the same nun found herself scurrying to a scene of violence to try to stop it but in the process was punched as well, given a bleeding nose that streamed for several minutes, splashes of red staining the white of her habit. By the time the RCMP arrived, Theron's mother had calmed down, even seemed placid as she was escorted out of the school and taken to the police station in Fort Macleod. The priest stayed where he was.

Other than that, the only other connection she had to the police was the fear that they might come and take her away to a special school. After her years of learning on the reserve were over, Brandy had spent the next while helping out at home with her family, like most of the other students. It was law, however, for Indian children to continue on with their studies at residential schools, which were located far off the reserves, often in other provinces that Brandy had never even heard the name of. But at that same time, there was speak of unspeakable things that were surfacing, things that had happened, and were still happening, behind those holy walls. When Brandy's mother received the letter that allotted Brandy into the same residential school she'd gone to herself, she outright refused that Brandy be carted off. And she'd refused more adamantly than Brandy thought she ever had reason to. Which was somewhat strange. Regardless of how inflexible her mother was on this point, Brandy still secretly feared that the police would show up one day and whisk her away. Thankfully, they never did. Only now, she wondered if it was just because she hadn't given them a reason to.

The policeman placed his hands on his belt, which holstered an array of threatening objects in black-leather pouches. Hilda, who seemed bent on making their predicament worse, suddenly gestured to the policeman that the *real* door was in the back. He replied to this gesture with the most unimpressed, world-weary expression he could muster and went around into the backyard. Hilda giggled again. Brandy did not.

Because this really wasn't funny anymore, or fun. She wanted out, out of this car with its faint stains running along the stitches of the upholstery, the material panging with the remnants of urine-soaked pants and bloodied shirts pressing against the fabric, of alcohol-sweat and the hunched-over thoughts of brutal retribution that lingered inside it. She wanted it all to stop, wanted to go back to where people knew her, accepted her, where no one jabbed at her with their hard-judging glances. She wanted the ochre streaks of the Belly Buttes, delineating the soil like contour lines on a map of the way home.

As she was thinking this, a group of boys about their age came out of one of the houses and started walking down the street toward them. They were staring at the police car, mumbling, laughing. Hilda turned to face them, her knees on the seat, and waved them closer. They stopped beside the car, looking around for the policeman that the cruiser belonged to, and, failing to find him, loitered uncomfortable on the sidewalk like they were lost in their own neighbourhood. They were all smirking, mumbling out one-liners that neither of the girls could hear.

"Hey," Hilda yelled into the glass, her breath spray-painting a misty halo in front of her mouth. "Could you guys open the door?

I have to talk to my grandma. Can you hear me? My grandma. She's in that house there."

After a moment, the coast still clear, the entire group of them felt confident enough to bend low and peer through the windows, as if they were looking at animals in a zoo. They were pretending that it was impossible to hear what Hilda was saying, one of them feigning to clean out his ears, another cupping his fingers into a dish on the side of his head, all while they continued to murmur their snide jokes, letting out hissing bursts of laughter every now and again. Brandy wished Hilda would just be quiet, would stop making everything worse than it had to be.

She looked beyond the boys, at the bungalow looming behind them, and found herself also wishing that her grandmother was actually inside. Both Brandy and Hilda had spent every summer of their lives at their grandmother's house. The fact was that both of their mothers drank quite a bit, and their grandmother, who lived alone, liked to get them out of the house whenever she could, along with genuinely needing the help, keeping the girls busy with jobs like getting her water, driving her around on errands and visits, and cooking—fried baloney and bannock, Kraft Dinner and fry bread.

Recently, her grandmother had been going out of her way to keep Brandy out of trouble. In her own manner, that is. For starters, she'd taken to gathering medicinal plants from different parts of the reserve, instead of the short walk around her home that had always sufficed before. Her grandmother insisted that Brandy drive her to these new places, and she soon got the feeling that finding plants had little to do with the excursions, as sometimes they wouldn't even come across any calamus root for her toothaches, or yarrow for her stomach, sagewort for her arthritis. Instead they would find a cairn where, her grandmother would tell her tangentially, it was said that archaeologists had found arrowheads five thousand years old; or they would stumble upon a teepee ring with a story to it, a family, perhaps, who didn't want to live with the tribe after the reserve broke up, or a camp from the great battle of 1870, when the Blackfoot defeated the Cree; or sometimes it would just be an old landmark that was newly explained, like The Little Hill, with its soil as red as the buttes in Brandy's backyard, where in only thirty years, almost three-quarters of the reserve's population died of small pox, measles, and scarlet fever. When they left the hill, her grandmother had called it by a different name, pointing back at it with her wrinkled hand, her fingers unable to straighten, "Ab-ki-e-nab Es-koo." The Graveyard.

Her grandmother had also set her up with a job, something hard to come by on the reserve. One of her neighbours had been commissioned to make handicrafts and beadwork for the tourists that were passing through the area on the national-park circuit, on their way to Waterton, and she offered Brandy a small wage to lend a hand. The commission was a private one, from a white and tidy man who ran a bright and tidy souvenir shop in Cardston. Twice a week Brandy walked the two and a half miles to the woman's house and would sit at a white table with long dishes of vibrant beads splayed in front of her like the rays of a prism. While she worked, the woman, who was about the same age as her mother, talked incessantly, rolling through her array of opinions, often looking up and waiting for Brandy to acknowledge that she agreed in some way or was at least listening.

"I'll tell you something: life on the reserve," the woman said one day, speaking in Blackfoot but mixing English words into her sentences without much rhyme or reason, "it's changing. And people who can't keep up with it, they'll be left behind. That's just how it is."

Brandy stopped to watch her as she slipped the beads down the string, threaded the needle through a piece of leather, and pulled it tight.

"You know, the other day, an old woman—I won't tell you who—saw the work I'm doing here, and do you know what she told me? She said it was wrong. The colours, the patterns, they're not right. That's what she said, 'Not right.' But I'll tell you something: I'm making money. My own money, not just what I get from the treaty payments; like other people—like her."

She rolled her eyes. "Can you see what I'm talking about? Now that woman—I won't tell you who—she just doesn't get it; no one cares what the colours mean anymore. Not the tourists, not my generation, not yours. And why don't we care? Tell me, why? Because we know: life on the reserve is changing."

She worked quietly for a long while before pausing to look into the middle distance, nodding to herself. "That's just how it is."

Brandy walked home that day through a strong Chinook wind, the silt that her footsteps disturbed along the gravel being swept off to the side. She thought about what the woman had said, about everything changing around her. But the truth was that she didn't feel like it was. She looked up at the Chinook arch over the Rockies, bridging one side of the skyline to the other with a ribbon of cloud that was as grey and rounded as bone. No, as far as she could tell, everything was the same: the same road, the same buttes, same river, houses, and all of them enveloped in the same wind, like they always had been. A gust of it whipped her hair into her eyes and she flinched, pulled it out, and tucked it behind her ears, where it didn't stay.

Brandy loved the wind. She loved it because it was like a living thing, like a temperamental creature that had a thousand moods, a thousand voices. She loved how it yowled through the power lines with angry groans that made up the deepest sounds of winter, how it whistled through the cracks around the doors and windows, the pressure filling the room like a rigid lung, the reflections of shapes in the windows bulging, thinning, bulging again. She loved how it could flap cowboy hats off men and untie women's scarves as they walked across parking lots, how it whirled empty grocery bags in the eddying corners of buildings for days, then randomly plucked them into the air and lifted them higher, netting them in the branches of winter trees where they rattled wildly, flailing with a popping resonance that filled your ears, even after the car door was slammed shut and you sat in the vehicle, which jostled on its springs with each gust, and cleaned out the sand and grit that had collected in the corners of your eyes. She loved how that same wind, sometimes only inside of an hour, could become quiet and giving, could turn into a whisper in the grass that moved as fluidly and hushed as a garter snake. But mostly she loved it because everyone else she knew—even Hilda—hated it, endlessly complained about it, scrambling from one form of cover to the next. It made it hers somehow.

"Come on. Open it. Please?" Hilda continued to plead with the group of boys. "I have to talk to my grandma . . . like right now. Come on, guys. Open the door. Just for a second."

But the boys were also growing nervous, knowing, as the girls did, that the policeman would be returning within minutes, seconds even. So they eventually stepped away from the glass, and, glancing guiltily up and down the street for a moment, they walked away in a single huddled group.

Except for one of them—the one who had been gaping around at the neighbourhood while the others were teasing them. He had started to walk away with everyone else, but stopped for some reason, and was now hovering beside the car with a searching look on his face, like he was using this moment, of all moments, to decipher some annoying riddle that had been bothering him for days.

One of the other boys noticed he wasn't following and turned to walk backwards for a few steps. "Come on, Ced," he called out, his tone disappointed, even bored. "Let's get outta here."

"Hey, Ced," Hilda shouted through the glass. "On your way, open the door, will ya? Come on."

The boy, who was blond, the collars of his short-sleeved shirt ironed crisp, took a step toward the cruiser, hesitating at the door handle. It wasn't quite clear if he was gazing in at the girls or at his own reflection in the car's side window. Either way, he looked satisfied.

"You know, I think you want to open it. Hey?" Hilda giggled, turning to look at Brandy for a moment. "I think he wants to."

This was how it always was with her cousin Hilda. She could often get people to do things they shouldn't. Especially Brandy. But this was mostly because she never meant anyone any harm. She just had a knack for finding enthralling things to do (climb that tree, hide there, scare him, "borrow" that). And as she'd been Brandy's closest friend for as long as she could remember, there was also an unspoken obligation to follow along. And most of the time, it was fine. Things rarely went this far. The mischief they usually got into was spontaneous and felt like it was over in seconds. Like the last Sundance they were at.

Brandy and Hilda would invariably get dropped off for a few days at Sundance, and sometimes for the entire length of it, having to help out like the other young people there, looking after children, gathering things for the elders, the boys digging postholes for the lodge. During the ceremonies, they would sit off to the side, feeling a little embarrassed, wearing blue jeans and T-shirts, watching the older people dancing around in headdresses and moccasins. It was a strange sensation because there was a part of her that wanted to stand up and join in, ask questions, be taught, and a part that didn't, that felt silly and withdrawn. And these two feelings seemed to rise up in her with equal strength, until the only thing she could do was just sit there, still and awkward.

But then, in the middle of a long dance, the drumbeat rising insistently above the singers, two motorhomes had turned off the road and were driving toward them, looking for a place to park. At first Brandy and Hilda thought they were drunk because a few of the men walked briskly out to tell them they couldn't stay, which is what you did with people who wanted to drink at Sundance, you ushered them away, coaxed them into a car and took them back home. But it turned out that these people were white, with their faces gawking out of the windows as their vehicles turned around. Later she'd heard rumours that they were anthropologists from a university in Edmonton who had driven eight hours in hopes of taking pictures and filming the event, to document whatever they could, before it was gone.

As the motorhomes crawled away, back over the dirt road toward the highway, Hilda had pointed at the ladders that were fixed to their backs. "Let's get on," she'd said, already jumping to her feet. And they were off, both of them laughing, sneakers kicking up dust. Hilda leapt onto the closest ladder, and as soon as she was secure, she reached an arm back to help Brandy up. They bumped along the road for only a minute before the motorhome slowed to turn onto the highway, where they jumped off before it sped up too fast to do so. Once on the ground, the wide-eyed driver spotted them in his mirror, pulsed his brakes. They waved, smiling, Hilda covering her teeth with the tips of her fingers.

A few days later, in Standoff, Brandy and Hilda had talked to one of the young men who had turned the motorhomes away. His name was Mike, a wiry young man, a bit older than they were, though he kept his hair in two braids like a grandfather. He was among the few people who had continued on with his schooling off of the reserve, and he'd even graduated. After working in Calgary for a year he returned and opened a confectionary in the back of one of the community buildings in Standoff. The location left something to be desired, his only window tiny, tinfoiled, and looking onto an alleyway where two deserted cars were busy rusting, gradually sinking into the soil. But in spite of the locale he had a decent clientele base and was constantly disappearing into the dim of his shop to rummage through the cardboard boxes on the floor, bringing the items out to people waiting in the sun, digging in his pockets for their change. Hilda and Brandy saw him as one of those people who could say things others could not.

"Hey," he greeted, seeing the two of them walking through the alleyway, "girls come for s'more liquorice?"

Between the collective pockets of both girls they scraped together thirty-five cents and asked Mike for as much candy as that would buy. After seeing that it was really all they had, he gave them an extra Twizzler each, on the house.

After Hilda recounted their daring tale with the motorhomes, she asked Mike about the people driving them. Who were they exactly? Mike only answered with a grin at first, leaning against the granular cinder-block wall outside, arms across his chest. While he thought about how to explain it, he watched the ramshackle cars as if they were important to the process. "I think, in the end, I understand it—or a bit anyway—from when I was out there, in the cities and stuff. Sometimes, when you're workin', or in bars and stores, you hear people say things 'bout Indians, like you're not one of 'em, standing there—like you can't hear." He smiled to himself, shook his head. "And I'd say, mostly, they think we're all drunks and dumb and crazy."

The girls laughed and he crouched down to pick up a pebble from the pavement. "And yeah, sure, we are all that. But we're also more. And that's somethin' most of 'em don't get. Which is why them people in the motorhomes came, cuz they think we're all gonna die away in a few years. Either really die, or become white, like them."

He watched the tiny stone rolling around in his palm. "But that's just not gonna happen." Then he closed his fingers around it, bouncing it up and down in the dark of his hand. "Nope. We're a strong people." Brandy and Hilda ventured a snicker, but he didn't seem to mind, his expression unchanged and serious, until, tossing the pebble at a clump of grass between the two cars, he turned to look at their faces, smiling with them now. "And we're not goin' anywhere."

It was a sentiment Brandy didn't feel particularly confident about at the moment. Even if, that morning, she and Hilda had woken up safe and stable in their grounded, regular lives, at their grandmother's house on the reserve. Just before noon, their grandmother had asked them to walk to a neighbours' place to check on things, as the neighbours had gone to the States for a few weeks.

The girls reasoned that, seeing as it was only another mile farther on, they would pay another neighbour a visit as well, while they were out. Which meant they wouldn't be expected back until later in the evening.

After the hour it took to walk to the first neighbour, they dutifully sauntered around the perimeter of the house without seeing any broken windows or other signs of damage, and so were crossing the yard to leave, on their way to the next house. They passed between a few old cars that were parked near a shed, the grass growing high around them, their dashboards sun-faded and cracking like dried mud. Hilda noticed that there were keys dangling from the ignition in one of them, and they jumped inside to see if the radio worked. It didn't, but when Hilda turned the ignition farther than she'd meant to, the car suddenly coughed into life, idling roughly but with assurance, getting smoother with every second. They looked at each other, faces lighting up. Instant co-conspirators.

They crept down the lonely road away from the house, talking about what they should do. "We could drive to Cardston," Hilda offered, "get some candy or somethin'." They searched their pockets for money and, to their surprise, each of them had a five-dollar bill and some change.

"I don't know, if we're gonna risk goin' all the way to Cardston, might as well go to Standoff . . . or Fort Macleod even!" Brandy was getting excited.

They stopped at a T-intersection to one of the main gravel roads in the area, Hilda giving the gas gauge a long assessment before a new look spread across her face. "No. We're goin' all the way to Lethbridge," and she turned onto the road and gradually sped up, the ashen-brown dust filling the rear-view mirrors until it was useless to look back.

Up until now, Brandy had liked driving in cars. After having to walk everywhere, your eyes got so used to the slow lag of the grass under your feet, the landscape changing in such measured degrees, that when you started accelerating in a car it felt impossibly fast, like you were a rocket rumbling just above the blurry ground. She rolled her window down and leaned into the flapping air, and there, again, was a different kind of wind, a different voice, one that was heavy in your ears and somehow both musty and dry at the same time. The shadow of the car sped along in the ditch beside them, jumping up toward her with every approach they passed and plunging down on the other side of it, trembling over the grass that was mottled with pieces of paper and coloured plastic.

The adventure of the road combined with the mischief of "borrowing" a car was delicious, and she could see that Hilda felt the same. Her face kept breaking into a smile, and as one of her hands lifted to cover her mouth, the other would be tapping at the steering wheel with some internal rhythm that was fast and elated.

Once, as they were nearing a bridge on the highway and the edge of the prairie fell away, opening onto the folds of a river valley below, she shouted above the engine and the pulsing gusts of air from the windows, delivering the same joke her brother had told over and over again: "You know what we called this land, before the white man came?" She gestured out in front of her, a hand sweeping the windshield.

Brandy smiled, holding her breath, knowing what was coming and getting ready to laugh, the car tipping down the slope and their stomachs lightening with the drop.

"*Ours.*"

They burst at the same time, convulsing with laughter until well beyond the bridge and up the other side of the coulee.

As they drove under the first traffic lights, they talked about what they were going to do in town. It was then that Hilda raised the notion of alcohol, and to Brandy, who had last been drunk at an epic Christmas party where she'd had to stumble outside and vomit in the snow, thought the experience was finally far enough in the past to consider it again. The plan then was to go downtown and find someone to bootleg for them, drink while wandering the streets, looking into shop windows, and make their way to the movie theatre, where they would see if they still had enough money for a ticket.

They left the car in a store parking lot and soon found an outlet of the Alberta Liquor Control Board (a name, Brandy had heard, created at a time when anyone of Indian blood reported drunk was fined, imprisoned, or both, and their informer given half of the funds collected). Hilda, looking confident, stopped a man at the door before he went in. He'd been grinning to himself, his weekend having just begun, and was wearing blue overalls that were speckled with paint and blotches of mortar. He stood in front of them, listening, and looked them over carefully before taking their money and nodding at the short list of things they wanted. But just as he walked through the door with hesitation, he came out with conviction, handing them back their five-dollar bills and saying, "Actually, I . . . this isn't really something I wanna encourage." He looked around, then waved a hand toward an old and withered Indian man hunched over on a cement parking block across the street. "Get him to do it for you. Sure he wouldn't mind."

As he walked away a woman passed by and gave them a piercing look, a look that was pitying and resentful, a look that brought Brandy back to the first time she caught a bus in Lethbridge. She had been with her brothers, and after they'd dropped their coins into the glass tube and were monkey-barring down the aisle, the bus canting and shifting gears, she could feel everyone's gaze stabbing them. And when the other passengers looked away, it was only to watch them out of the corners of their eyes instead. Brandy had sat down by herself and was trying hard to ignore it. Then she saw the woman sitting across from her remove her purse from the seat and sling it around her shoulder, on the side farthest from Brandy.

Hilda looked disappointed, offended. "Encourage? Who does he . . . ?" She looked across the street at the only other non-white human being they'd seen since entering the city limits, who was slumping to the side now, as if he were about to fall over. "Come on," she said, taking Brandy by the arm. "Better'en nothin'."

But it was the worst idea they could have come up with. The old man could barely walk, and by the time they had helped him across the street and prodded him through the door, watching him disappear down one of the aisles, he'd become the heaviest burden they could have asked for, the critical flaw in their plan, their day. He collapsed just out of sight, grabbing for something to steady himself before hitting the ground and clutching on to the most expensive bottle of Scotch on the shelf, which broke on the floor beside him. They saw the woman at the till make a phone call but didn't realize she was talking to the police until a cruiser rolled up beside them a few minutes later. The girls made a break for it and ran four blocks before jumping into their car. Hilda eased out of the parking lot like a model driver, but by the second set of lights they heard the short bleat of a siren signalling them to pull over. She did, and turned off the car, the sound of the engine being replaced with the traffic humming by, neither of them saying a word.

The officer radioed in their licence plate before sticking his head through the driver's side window, forearms resting on the chapped ledge of rubber-lipped seals. He just had a few questions for them, that was all; like their names, where they lived, and whether or not they knew anything about two minors attempting to buy alcohol, who seemed to fit their description perfectly. No? Hmm. Well, could he see their papers then. A quick look exchanged between the girls. Silence. Papers, please, he repeated. They shuffled madly through the glovebox, the pouches in the door panel, under the seats, their pockets. Nothing. Let me get this straight, he conferred, you have no licence, no registration, and no insurance? More silence. Cars purring past. Could you both step out of the car, please.

Which would have been more than enough trouble for one

day. But then, for some reason, Hilda had the great idea to improvise a new story. She'd said that this was really their uncle's car, and that he had given them permission to take it. Honest, you can ask him. Which would be easy enough, seeing as he lived close by—on the north side—and she proceeded to lead him through a labyrinth of streets before deciding on an anonymous house where anyone's uncle could have lived, including the policeman's.

Now, before he returned from a fruitless search for a family member in the back of this random house, Hilda was soliciting the help of a cruel neighbourhood boy to make their predicament even worse. Or at least more humiliating. Cedric was still staring at them, his face pushed up against the window, Hilda's face close on the other side, the safety glass compressed between them. She was eagerly pointing down at where she imagined the handle to be. "Come on, open it," she urged.

The blue of Cedric's eyes suddenly flared with an idea, and he stepped back from the cruiser to address the boys farther down the street. "Hey, Dave!" he yelled.

They all stopped and turned, one of them answering impatiently, "What?"

"You were in my grade three class, right, with Mrs. O'Donnell?"

"Yeah?"

"Okay, remember when she lost it on that kid—like *really* lost it. You remember that?"

The other boy looked up into a tree as if consulting it. "Uh, yeah, I think so. Why?"

"Do you remember me saying something to her—about what she'd said—and then getting kicked out of class for it?"

The other boy gave him an incredulous look. "No. You mean— *you*, saying something to *her*? No."

Cedric took an enormous amount of air into his lungs, letting it out with the slow sinking of his posture. He was thinking again, working out some private complication that seemed to have nothing to do with any of them.

Hilda knocked on the glass as if to wake him. The policeman's radio crackled, a woman's voice doling out numbers in a monotone. Brandy watched Cedric as he wavered, sure that he was about to make the girls the brunt of a joke, again. But she was wrong.

Cedric straightened, again stepped up to the door, let his hand rest on the latch for one thoughtful moment, smiled, and opened it.

Brandy and Hilda exchanged a quickened look while shouts from the group of boys filled the street.

"What are you, an idiot?"

"Close it!"

"What are you doing!"

But Cedric had made a decision, and was standing straight, holding the door wide like a chauffeur, even gesturing like one, rolling his wrist elegantly toward the sidewalk.

Hilda grabbed onto Brandy's arm and the two of them fumbled out of the car and started running, quickly ducking between two houses, crouching down amid a mess of salvaged lumber, bald tires, and rusting bicycle frames. Brandy positioned herself so that she could just, just see the police cruiser. They had made it without a second to spare because the policeman soon appeared from behind the house, suspecting nothing, his hat off, scratching at his hair again.

He looked up to see Cedric, with his hand still on the open door of the sedan, and threw his cap back on, tugging it tight. "Hey!" he called out, then repeated himself, his surprise amplified threefold, "*Hey!*"

He darted out onto the sidewalk, looking around for the girls and finding nothing but a cluster of boys milling about, analyzing the asphalt.

He chose the wrong direction to start off in pursuit. As he passed Cedric, he pointed a rigid finger into his face. "You're in serious trouble, kid. You don't move an inch—hear?"

As the man jumped to his toes, breaking into a jog, he glanced over his shoulder to make sure Cedric had understood the gravity of his words. But, by the looks of it, that was unlikely. The boy was beaming, slowly lifting his arm out toward the officer, raising his middle finger. The policeman slowed to a standstill, his mouth open.

"Nope," said Cedric, "I think you'll find I'm in no trouble at all."

The officer nodded gravely, "You just stay right there. You hear me? Right there." Then he turned and ran in chase of the girls. Completely flustered, he soon disappeared between two houses on the other side of the street, probably having heard someone working in their backyard.

The girls didn't wait to see what happened next. They erupted from their place of hiding and began running toward the alley, still between the two houses. Brandy felt like she was floating, like she was wind. Hilda was laughing out loud. Though, with her arms out, hands running along the wall and fence, steadying her as she clambered through the salvage heap, she couldn't cover her teeth the way she normally did. Instead they were bare, sun-emblazoned, and wildly free.

It was nothing like the movies
no hard-won courtship or balcony ballads
no moaning promises
lips muffled against flesh

Instead it was the dusted symmetry
of four desk rows
ruler-straight and name-tagged
so we were close enough to whisper

Over the years she would tug me
to walls, to lockers, and point out
the graffiti etchings of our names
inside oblong hearts
as grey as pencil lead

We lost our virginity before prom
in my father's Rambler
the fumbling of hands
groping over bodies
as if feeling for a light switch

Until somehow
the kinship became habit
comfortable
like a gift sweater that fits well
and has a nice-enough colour

though you wouldn't
have chosen it
yourself

Melissa switched on the tape deck, turning it up a bit, rolled her window down farther, and went back to watching the fields as they moved past, fields strewn with hay bales now, like course-haired creatures, she fancied, hunched over and sleeping, oblivious to that exceptionally wide-open sky and the elephantine clouds that padded along the prairie with their shadows.

They'd driven past most of the exits to Lethbridge and were cutting between the coulees, crossing a broad river valley where Melissa watched an extensive railroad bridge as it ran parallel to the highway, towering pylons as black as the coal it was built to transport. It struck her as one of those industrial eyesores that had since become quite funky, in that chic-urban-steampunk kind of way. She was about to comment on it but didn't. They drove up the other side of the coulee where the highway opened onto a yawning skyline and a road-gridded carpet of prairie that unrolled all the way out to the Rockies. They found a cheap-enough campground just as the peaks started to rise and shoulder into the wide panorama that their eyes had become used to. It was near the site of a devastating landslide that had buried part of a town in 1903, the sprawling boulderfield so barren it could have happened yesterday. They clambered to the top of one of the larger rocks and ate submarine sandwiches for dinner, talking disjointedly about all the houses that had never been excavated in the wake of the disaster, the homes that were buried beneath them.

April 18, 1969

The college band had found a disco ball in someone's garage and had proudly hung it from the ceiling with a thick and unlikely rope (the kind one might see hanging from the rafters in a barn). The disco ball was the only light on the dance floor now, a projected net of blue dots circling the massive space of the gymnasium, gliding over the wood strips on the floor and the painted sidelines, between the churning bodies where it climbed the fabric of dresses and descended the broad shoulders of suit jackets.

Denise Colwell leaned back against the wall, her hands behind her, a palm flat on the white painted brick. She had been scanning the faces for several minutes now, looking for Cedric Johnson. Earlier that day she'd overheard his friends talking in the hall, and knew that he was supposed to be there; that and the fact that he wouldn't have his mousy girlfriend in tow. His friends, incidentally, had almost used those very words while they loitered in front of their lockers shell-shocked and vacant, having written the last of their final exams, their conversations shifting from "forgetting" to study, to completely blanking out when the test papers slapped down in front of them, to the end-of-semester dance that evening—who would be there and who wouldn't. It was then that one of them mentioned how Cedric's girlfriend, Julie, was away in Red Deer, and that "of course" he would still be coming to the dance. This was, after all, Cedric they were talking about.

She'd already decided exactly what she was going to do when she saw him tonight. She was going to walk right up to his back, tap him on the shoulder, and say something that, only a week ago, she would never have imagined herself saying. Because it was now or never, and because the swirling pattern of light was making the dark of this college sports hall something feral and primitive, something turbulent; but mostly because of the way Cedric had looked at her every time they passed in the hall, or leaned over a table in the fluorescent quiet of the library, talking in a low, suggestive voice about absolutely nothing.

During the past week, Denise had been thinking a lot about her life, and had come to the realization that the only thing that was really exceptional about it was how ceaselessly ordinary it had been, how the years had managed to stream by without so much as a single drama, or grief, adventure, yearning. Nothing. She just *was*. That was the only way she could think to put it. She was. Of course she had had her bruised knees and birthday cakes, favourite toys, been on sports teams, and had learned shorthand and how to type one hundred and twenty words a minute. And yes, yes she'd had her romances too, which even seemed to be relatively sweeping at the time, though they soon fizzled out into an oblivion so insipid it was almost difficult to remember their names.

Her latest was a fling with a fellow college student named Robert. He had told her, on their first date, that she, and she alone, could call him Bobby. She smiled politely at the gesture but couldn't bring herself to do it, awkwardly reverting to the standby pronoun usage, "Oh . . . *you!*" On their second date, he'd walked her to her door and leaned in to kiss her after standing on the doorstep for three gauche seconds, which started out fine, until his tongue began jabbing into her mouth like a child's thumb squishing ants. Then, as if that weren't enough, he pressed himself up against her, his penis bulging stiff in his pants. She stopped kissing him and fumbled in her purse for her keys, but he still hadn't gotten the hint. Instead, he proceeded to grind away at her, as if he were an overzealous German shepherd and hers was the closest leg he could get to after the urge had struck. She pushed him away, coldly thanked him for the movie, and never talked to him again. And it had occurred to her, at some point throughout the week, that that pathetic bungling on her doorstep happened to be the most interesting thing that had ever happened to her.

She'd never been an introspective person, had never lain awake wondering at the ceiling above, until the party last Saturday night, where everything changed. Since then, she'd spent *most* of her time thinking, digging into her formative years, trying to find things that stood out, things that would make her life a little more than a simple going-through-the-motions. She hadn't come across much, but she had revisited one distinctive afternoon quite a few times, mulling it over, sure that there was something in it worth considering.

It had been a blue-sky day, early summer, and she was eleven years old, in the backyard and playing with her Barbie, a craze-toy that had been released the year before, in 1959. She remembers that she was sitting alone at a table near her mother's flower garden, a table she appreciated for the fact that it was perfectly aligned with a birdbath in the yard, which rose out of a pool of chrysanthemums like a whale spout. She remembers considering the birdbath as being mythical or sanctified in some way. And looking back at it now she's sure that, if she hadn't been playing in the way a girl should, with her doll, sitting at a table being discreet and innocuous and complacent, she probably would have had her hands in its water, knee-high in the bee-drunken flower heads, maybe playing with the floating curls of down that birds sometimes left behind on the water, blowing on them like miniature sailboats; she could have been an epic wind to an epic ship on an epic voyage. But she was playing like she should have been instead.

She remembers why she held the birdbath in such a fabled light but isn't sure if what happened with the grackle took place that same afternoon, the same blue-sky day that her brother leapt from the garage roof. She doesn't think so.

The event with the grackle probably happened earlier, and it was a simple one, but striking, extraordinary. She'd been crouching down near it, at the edge of the flowerbed (maybe stealing a petal, maybe spitting onto the dirt, inspecting the gummy flesh of a worm that had surfaced, maybe even touching it while no one was looking—who could say?) when a dark form flapped into view and splashed into the water only three arm-lengths away from her. The bird, a common grackle, began to wash itself immediately, oblivious to her presence, shaking long drops into, then out of, its iridescent plumage, raising its head after every dip to survey the yard with its piercing yellow eyes, which never managed to pierce her, to see her as a threat, as a potential predator cloaked in a pink dress. She watched it, mesmerized, as still as a statue on the edge of a fountain. In the sunlight, glistening, the bird was almost candescent, a metallic sheen, like oil streaks filming over a dark puddle, every colour in a nighttime rainbow. When it flew off, abrupt and without warning, a drop from its feathers had landed on her arm, and she'd held it up close to her face, as if to look for colour, for some kind of tint in its clarity. But it was only water.

Yet it wasn't. It wasn't *only* water. Now it was something more. It was a drop of water that had fallen from a flying grackle. Just because something was commonplace, she thought, didn't mean it had come from a place that was common. Wasn't it possible that the soot from a volcano was more than just soot, that the coating of frost that smudged a plum was more than just frost? Or that a piece of corrugated cardboard, from her brother's makeshift flying machine that he'd jumped off the roof with, was more than just cardboard?

That day, while she was playing with her Barbie on the table (as a girl should), her brother had been busily constructing it in the back alley with three of his friends. Using a two-by-four, the box from a newly purchased freezer procured from somewhere in the alleyway, and two rolls of black electrical tape, he'd fashioned an impressive wing, complete with two slots cut out for his hands to grip on to the two-by-four frame inside, for steering purposes. It took all four of them to manhandle it, first onto the high fence, then onto the roof of the garage itself. Before lifting the contraption onto his shoulders, her brother looked up to the sky professionally, searching for wind and pivoting in a full circle, akin to a weathervane. The air was still. A seagull—six hundred miles from the nearest sea but only a mile from the local dump— glided through the blue and screeched as if in response to so many eyes following it through the sky. Her brother, giving the conditions a serious sniffle, lifted the wing onto his back.

Denise remembers that in the days leading up to this, her brother had become fixated with the idea of air resistance, jumping off trash bins with a small piece of plywood in hand, off a ladder with a garbage bag, lugging their aluminum toboggan to a playground to hurl it from the top of the jungle gym. He had an easily engaged, though some would say obsessive, personality. A toy in a catalogue would suddenly catch his eye, jump out at him from one of the glossy pages, and inspire him to rip it out, Scotch-taping it to his bedroom door, and saving allowances, mowing lawns, shovelling walks, and collecting bottles from corner-store garbage cans until he'd saved enough money to buy it. Likewise, he seemed confident in his methods and preparation here, teetering on the apex of the roof with the long cardboard wing on his back, focusing on the edge that fell away. When he was ready, he sounded a barbaric yawp over the rooftop and broke into a sprint down the slope to the overhanging eaves. There was no hesitation.

Denise was standing on the lawn below, with the others, and had innocently envisioned him gliding around the neighbourhood for a while before landing, and, as such, had looked at his trajectory, the line he would be swooping in directly after takeoff. But right across from the garage was her father's greenhouse, a recent addition to the shed, which had grown into something much larger than the shed itself, a framework of opaque plastic that was misted with transpiration, the odd droplet of water trickling down its sides like a shower stall. Her brother would crash into it.

She stepped forward as if to yell a warning, as if to implore him to abort mission before it was too late. But nothing came out. And realistically, nothing would have stopped him anyway. He'd made up his mind. About what, Denise couldn't be sure. She suspected, thinking about it now as an adult, that it wasn't even about flying. It was about something else entirely. Maybe a test of conviction— where even the failure to take flight would carry with it, somehow, the taste of success; the flavour of something won, something magic, a precious metal, the acridity of brass in the blood that was about to run from his mouth.

He leapt. The cardboard folded up like an inverted umbrella, and he plummeted to the grass, legs collapsing on impact, his body crumpling forward and, with his hands still clinging to the two-by-four in the wing, onto his face. Pushing the flying machine off him, and already crying, he peered up at his shocked audience, his teeth coated red. The three boys who'd helped him, swapped a stunned look, turned, and fled the scene. Denise wasn't much better in terms of assistance, only managing to stare down into his face, unable to move, playing with her hands, biting her lip.

Eventually their father came running, and her brother was soon whisked off to the hospital, gagged with a tea towel to stop the bleeding. He'd broken his fibula, chipped a tooth, bit his tongue open, and would spend two months in a heavy cast, hobbling around on crutches, recounting the story to any and everyone that asked, without the faintest tenor of regret.

While he was away at the hospital, Denise had knelt on the grass, avoiding the dark stains, and had torn a piece of cardboard from the corner of the failed flying machine. She doesn't remember ever seeing the piece again, which means she'd probably thrown it away, or hid it somewhere so particular that she'd forgotten where it was. What she does remember clearly is that, the following morning, she got in trouble for leaving her Barbie outside on the table all night. "The poor thing was left out in the dark," her mother had scolded, "not put away, unattended to, uncared for. How would you've liked that?" Denise went outside to collect her doll, who'd been lying on her back in her fur-frilled gown, white gloves up to her elbows, her earrings lobed, lipstick crimson, staring up at the night sky with her flawlessly eye-shadowed and mascaraed eyes, wide open. While the stars blinked back.

As strange as it was, Denise had actually gone to the party that had changed everything in the way she saw her life by accident. Cedric had asked whether or not she was going to "the shindig on the weekend," using the crucial misleading word: *weekend*. Then, during her bookkeeping class forty minutes later, an acquaintance invited her to a get-together on Saturday night, owing to someone's parents being away. And how many different parties could there possibly be in one junior college? So she'd accepted the invitation, done her hair and makeup for an hour, and arrived to hear people talking about the wild bash that had happened the night before, on Friday, and caught Cedric's name wafting in and out of the tales of inebriation. Great, she'd thought to herself, just great.

She looked around the room for somebody to talk to, somebody she liked, but hardly recognized anyone. It was a different crowd than she was used to, the kind of people who were going to school to become park wardens and Fish and Wildlife officers, where the hot topic, besides the bigger party that she'd missed the night before, was fishing. But out of common courtesy, she resolved to mingle for an hour or so, then slip out the back. She said a few hellos and accepted a snub-necked bottle of Lethbridge Pilsner from a guy she'd once been introduced to, though had since forgotten his name. He asked her if she had come with Patricia, one of her classmates, who was apparently with her sister downstairs (at the word "downstairs," he had widened his eyes with drama, but Denise didn't feel like taking the bait and asking what he'd meant by it). "Not really," she'd answered, already looking for the stairwell, thankful that there was at least someone in the house she knew. She lit a cigarette, left the conversation, and, beer in hand, started down the unlit steps.

The stairwell descended to several small landings, the second of which was the porch for the back door. Just outside, Denise saw three men through the doorglass, standing in a circle, passing around a hand-rolled cigarette, each of them squinting as they took their turn to suck in an enormous lungful of abnormally blue smoke. They were dressed like they hadn't showered in days, weeks maybe, their hair unkempt and greasy, clothes more colourful than they should have been. And as she turned on the landing to continue down the steps, she caught a sniff of their skunky smoke, and it all came together. They were hippies! And that was marijuana they were smoking, here, behind the very house she was in!

Like everyone else, she knew all about the *existence* of the counterculture, had seen the Vietnam protest marches on television, the banner-waving tie-dyed processions, the braless women with their beaded headbands, and the men with their patchy beards and circlet sunglasses. But those types certainly weren't seen around Lethbridge. The police had made it clear that such antisocial behaviour wouldn't be tolerated in the city, making all sorts of inquiries and arrests at the mere rumour of drugs and printing an anti-narcotic series of articles in the newspaper. In fact, only a month before, four raggedy-looking people were seen standing in front of the local theatre, and a paddy wagon promptly appeared to take them into custody, for questioning under suspicion of drug possession. It turned out that they were actors taking a cigarette break at a dress rehearsal days before the premiere of *Oliver*; Fagin's grubby apprentices from a Victorian society gone wrong, a perfect match to the modern version, who were slipping down the same criminal slope.

Not knowing what else to do, Denise pretended she hadn't seen a thing and continued downstairs. But as soon as she stepped into full view of the basement, she wanted nothing more than to turn around and run. The suite was split into two large rooms, the first with a pool table as the focal point, five or six respectable-looking college students scattered around it, none of them women, and most of them using their cues as a crutch while they paused to leisurely look her over, and the second was candlelit and blaring with music, every piece of furniture draped with real true-to-life bona fide hippies.

There were only two people she recognized, a young man named Arthur, who was holding a beer and watching her, leaning with his hand on the green felt of the table (to the understandable irritation of the players), and her classmate Patricia, who was in the other room with the hippies, having what seemed to be a heated argument with one of the women.

Denise gave them all a sheepish grin. "Hi."

Arthur perked up. "Hell, it's Denaise! How y'all doin', sweetie pah?" Arthur was one of those people who liked to do accents and impersonations, the Texas cowboy theme one of his trademarks. Two of the pool players rolled their eyes at his back.

"I'm good, fine," she said, taking a long sip from her beer and looking around the room. She could see that the basement suite belonged to a hunter, who was trying his hand at amateur taxidermy, stuffed birds flying out of the walls, an antelope head mounted on a velvet plaque and craning its neck to look in her direction. Right beside her, frozen into a stance that had it snarling into her face, was a mink or weasel perched on a piece of driftwood, eyes shining black, nose threateningly wrinkled, its teeth bared and even linked with a silicone stream of saliva. It occurred to her that the animal itself was thinner and more fragile looking than her wrist.

Arthur strutted over from the table as if he'd been riding a horse for five too many decades. "Ah know whucher thinkun," he drawled, "that that there weasel there ain't so beg. But I'll tell yuh somethin', them creatures is right vicious thangs." He swigged his beer, wiped his mouth, nodded. "Trust meh, it was him . . . er may."

She smiled and pointed into the other room. "Sorry, I'm just gonna go'n say hello to Patricia for a sec." She squeezed between Arthur and the weasel and excused herself through the other men as well. Then she stepped into the clatter of music and the thick haze of incense that threaded the air of the second room.

To Denise, if anything was immediately clear, it was that the hippies had full control of the music. There was certainly no Tammy Wynette standing by her man in this crowd, no sir, it was more the likes of Janis Joplin bellowing out to a microphone whose metal stand she was probably thrusting her pelvis at, and Jimi Hendrix, squelching through an electric guitar like he was wringing the life out of a six-year-old plugged into an amplifier. Denise had no idea how people could listen to such noise. The only thing she could be sure of was that this sound, this new "genre" of music, wouldn't last. It couldn't. It just happened to suit these counterculture types because it balked at the contemporary ideas of what music should be.

It occurred to her that the coarse and aggressive sounds that were blasting from the speakers couldn't have been more incongruous with the way the hippies were acting. Their eyelids were half-closed, eyes bloodshot, glassy, and staring into the centre of the room. Except for the two women arguing, no one was saying a word, or nothing intelligible anyway; one of the men was nattering on about something in the music, pointing his finger at the stereo whenever it—whatever "it" happened to be—pounded out of the speakers. "There! Right there! Just *listen* to that shit!" Though, aside from him, no one really seemed to be. They were ogling at nothing, focused on nothing, grinning at nothing. They were, thought Denise, people who had abandoned themselves. They were lost.

Seeing as Denise was standing directly behind Patricia, and the two women were so involved in their dialogue, neither of them noticed her. And though all Denise wanted was to say a quick hello and leave, she wasn't about to cut into an argument to do so, and soon found herself squatting down to a shelf, running her finger across the spines of a record collection, tilting her head to the side as if reading the titles but really only eavesdropping on the squabble. She had been wondering what someone like Patricia, who seemed to have her feet on the ground, would be doing in the farthest corner of a basement, arguing with a hippie. But it soon became clear.

"No way, Patty. A chance like this won't come along again. There's enough room in their van, and Fawn knows this cat in the city that we can stay with for a while. I'd regret it forever, not going."

"Regret? You're throwing your life away here, Joan! Can't you see that? I mean, just forget about Mom and Dad and everything else you hate about this town for a second, okay? Think of how you're gonna get by. You don't have any money, any *skill*. What are you gonna do, marry one of *them*?" Patricia waved a hand at one of the chesterfields where four of these "cats" were sinking into the creases of the cushions like jellyfish into quicksand. "Find yourself a nice drug-dealer husband who'll do what for you—what? Pimp you out in some slum, spread you around to his friends so you both can have a roof over your heads? Is that the plan? I mean, wake up."

Her sister laughed, trailing off into a cold trill. "Would you *dig* this! *You* telling *me* to wake up? That I'm throwing *my* life away? Just look at you, for Chrissake. Going to school for Mommy, prancing in and out of those stupid classes. Secretarial Studies. More like How to Please Men 101. Every one of you wearing the same skirts, same length, same shoes, bobs, same little cat's eye glasses. For what? To get behind some reception desk where some rich boy can cherry-pick you, pluck you out of the office and into his little house for you to spit out a few kids, iron the smears of lipstick out of his shirts for forty years? You think you'll be touching a typewriter in two years? I mean, Jesus, Patty, that's some high horse you're sitting on. You could write the book on selling yourself short."

Patricia buried her face in her hands and let out an annoyed groan. Meanwhile, Jimi Hendrix sang on about being down on the ceiling, looking up at the bed, and, as if on cue, one of the hippie girls looked up at the light fixture and shook her head to clear the hair out of her eyes.

Denise had made herself into a progressively smaller ball of limbs crouching on the floor, hoping not to be noticed. She felt a kind of burgeoning instability in her stomach, like someone had reached into her belly and knocked over the first of a coiling network of dominoes that she hadn't known resided there. She wanted out of this basement, wanted to walk away and forget that her life choices had ever been challenged, that her unspoken incentives to go to college had been spoken, by a stranger. Luckily it was by some waste-of-a-life drug addict.

She noticed an ashtray on the shelf in front of her and laid her cigarette against its rim, getting ready to leave, still hoping to slip out of the room unnoticed. But just then the three men who had been smoking outside walked into the room and stepped past her to slump onto the arms of the sofas and anywhere else they could fit. One of them greeted her with an offhand, "Hey, what's happenin'?" but instead of replying, she'd bent closer to the record titles as if having found an album she'd been looking for. Which is when the debate behind her ignited again.

"And all these drugs?" Patricia began. "You really think that smoking them—or injecting them, or whatever you do—isn't gonna catch up to you? You're gonna kill yourself. Eventually. Can't you see that? Can't you at least wake up to that much of it? For me?"

"Okay," her sister began in a calm enough tone, rattling the bracelets on her arms, uncrossing her bellbottomed legs, "if it's really just the pot and love and freedom that get to you, let's just— for like a second—pretend that they have nothing to do with it, okay? And let's take a good look at that nice square world you want me to 'wake up' to. Don't worry, you don't have to go far, just take a look around in your little junior college canteen, with its new microwave oven zapping food with some kind of *rays*, and read a few titles of the books people are holding: *Naked Ape. Diary of Che Guevara. Electric Kool-Aid Acid Test.* Or if it's magazines, read the headlines: peace marches, rallies for the Poor People's Campaign, Red Guards disbanded in China, Vietnam casualties, amputee vets, draft dodgers smuggled over the border, a black model on the cover of *Glamour*, only a year after Martin Luther King was assassinated . . ."

"Oh so that's why you do drugs. That's just great," Patricia interrupted, "to bury your head in sand cuz things are . . ."

"Shut up. Now students burned the Paris stock exchange, the Orangeburg Massacre, riot police mowing down thousands in London, Black Panthers, John and Yoko's album banned, Trudeau trying to legalize abortion, the pill, double helix, pirate radio, superpowers scrambling to put a man on the *moon*! *Christ,* Patricia. Don't tell *me* to wake up. The shit is hitting the fan all around you. In a couple months, your little square world won't even *be* there to wake up to.

"So you can spare me the lecture about . . ." she continued, but Denise wasn't listening anymore. She was surprised to find herself standing, looking down at her bottle of beer on the carpet, her cigarette in the ashtray with a strand of smoke rising from its tip. Jimi Hendrix was blurting out with a different tune now. "Hey, Joe," he was asking, "where you goin' with that gun in your hand?"

Then she found herself walking, quickly, pushing past the men playing pool, Arthur half blocking the door to the stairs, standing beside the weasel again. "Yer not headin' aowht so soon, are-yeh, sweetie pah?" He posed in front of her, chin out, eyebrows raised. But she shoved past him, up the stairs, out through the back door, and into the unlit yard where mounds of disturbed earth were lumping the garden, pickets demarcating rows of future tomatoes, the wooden stakes pointing inflexibly up at the clouds that striated the sky, starlight piercing their fringes from tens of thousands of light-years away, many of them suns that were, she'd recently read, already extinguished, transformed into something else entirely, their history lagging far behind their projection. She stumbled around on the grass, looking up at them, blinking wildly. The stars blinked back.

Then she was running, to her car, lurching on her raised heels under the illuminated orbs of two streetlights, into her seat, where she slammed the door and locked it shut. She fastened her seatbelt, put the keys in the ignition, took a long look at the dashboard of her 1964 Ford Comet, then slumped over the steering wheel and wept.

The following Tuesday, she went to the first of her final exams and saw Patricia there, looking unhappy, listlessly arranging her pencils on the table in front of her. Which must have meant that her sister Joan had really gone through with it, that she was in the States somewhere, right then, marching in front of government buildings, protesting wrongs, advocating rights. Denise wasn't sure anymore if she viewed this as reckless or courageous, wasn't sure if it was authentic integrity that Joan was acting out of or egotistical abandon, hedonism. Who could say? The only thing she could be certain of was that Joan believed in something, and she believed in it strongly. Whether it was piquing her own pleasure or placating humanity's pain, she'd chosen an epic voyage and had set out on it. On an epic ship. In an epic wind.

What did she, Denise, believe in? What poignant speech could she deliver to the furtively open ears of the world, crouching in corners to overhear?

As the exams were passed out, she placed her purse on the floor and, in doing so, looked around at everyone else's handbag, noticing that they really were, as Joan had pointed out, all the same size and style, even the colours varying within only a few shades of one another. She noted other similarities of the throng, wondering if there actually was an irrevocable change that was pervading the globe. What if, within a few years, no one would see an exam room like this one, ever again, where virtually every individual dressed and spoke and cut their hair in the same way? What if they were all going to look back at themselves, rows of their smiling faces staring out at their future children through yearbook mediums, and laugh.

It was a long week for Denise, and what little time there was between studying and writing her exams, she filled with pensive silences. Once, she had sat in her room with the lights off, curtains drawn, breathing evenly and soundlessly for so many hours that she lost track. And by the time she found herself standing there at the dance, her back against the wall of the gymnasium, she felt like she'd had some kind of epiphany. It was slight; no tectonic displacement in the foundation of her ideals—she wasn't about to become a flower child and abandon her secure life, no—but she was going to take charge of her direction more consciously, become less passive. She was going to let herself go every now and then, follow her instincts into a direction she wouldn't normally step. And she was going to start tonight, with Cedric Johnson, because if there was anyone that made her feel a little dangerous, a little impulsive, it was him.

The last time she and Cedric were at a party together, he had waited for his girlfriend to disappear into another room and had approached Denise, who was standing alone in a corner. Without saying a word, he held out a pack of cigarettes to offer her one, watched her long fingers slide it out, unfolded a book of matches, struck the phosphorous so the flame illuminated his face, unhurriedly leaned in to light it in her lips, and lingered there, intimately close, his breath on her neck, studying her mouth as she blew a stream of smoke into the room. There was something so carnal, so implicit in the act, Denise had to smile. Cedric didn't, the air sticking between them like sweaty skin.

She finally spotted him at the dance, walking through the dark along an imposing gymnasium wall, dwarfed by its height, and passing under the tactless decorations and hand-drawn posters, where the words END-OF-SCHOOL BASH had been coloured in with permanent markers, the letters unaligned and uneven. He stopped and leaned casually against the white-painted brick, his back to her, exactly as she'd envisioned he would.

She eased herself away from the clammy wall and started toward him, feeling tense, thrilled, uncomfortably warm. But when she tapped him on the shoulder, to her surprise, he didn't turn around like he should have. Instead, his body stiffened, and he looked up at the poster on the wall, the ceiling, the disco ball, the dance floor, as if he were taking in the scene for the very first time and was unaware that anyone had even touched him. So she tapped him on the shoulder again and was almost startled by how quickly he spun around to face her, his expression light and playful.

"Of course," he said above the music, clapping his hands once and holding them together as if he were praying, "Lest we forget: Denise."

She pulled her head back. "And what's that supposed to mean?"

Cedric let out an ambiguous chuckle. "It means . . . I guess it just means I'm glad to see you. Glad it's not all—I don't know— trauma of some kind or another."

"What?" This wasn't how she'd imagined it. He'd always been so down to earth, so predictable. And if he hadn't been looking her over in the same way he normally did, letting his eyes slide shame- lessly down the curves of her body, she could have mistaken him for someone else entirely, someone who only looked like Cedric Johnson, a double.

"Look," he said, "I know I'm not making sense. It's just . . . I mean, something's happening to me that I . . . can't even . . . *pretend* to understand." He ran a hand through his hair and gripped the top of his head, squeezing it tight.

Then, seeming to let go of whatever it was that was bothering him, his arm dropped to his side, relaxed. "But I *do* know a place out there in the hallway that—uh . . ." he nodded toward the steel doors of the gymnasium, "that you could show me." He held a hand out between them, waiting for her to take it.

She didn't move, stunned. How did he know that she'd poked her head into one of the recesses along the corridor, a classroom entrance, and had imagined leading him there, had intended on doing exactly that? Did that mean he had done the same?

"Go on. Take it," he urged. "Lead the way." He winked at her.

Glancing down at his palm, she saw a dot of light streak across it and realized that everything, however outlandish it was turning out to be, had become titillating, enticing. The walls of the gymnasium seemed to pull in toward them like a levee on the verge of bursting, a levee that inevitably would. It was decadent.

She took his hand and they walked into the harsh light of the hall, past a fountain where a girl was drinking, straightening to wipe water from her chin, where they slipped into the doorway that both of them had apparently noticed. In the hidden alcove, Denise leaned back, her hands behind her, on the doorknob, while Cedric brought his face up close to hers. He moved in closer until his mouth was at her ear and whispered, "You'll never guess what door in this hallway just happened to be left unlocked."

Not believing him, she gave the metal knob a twist, and both of them fell into the room, stumbling awkwardly into the cool and chalky air. They shut the door behind them, laughing, and instantly, in the sudden dark, everything had become even more alluring; they were alone, unseen, and anonymous, the band's guitars shut out and muffled, strumming the standard folk songs to a crowd that had no idea where the two of them were.

"How did you know?" she asked while her eyes adjusted to the glow seeping under the door.

He stepped closer, put a hand on her hip, his other on the side of her neck, his fingers moving along the downy edge of her hairline. Then he dipped his head under her chin and carefully touched the skin of her throat with his open mouth, hovering there, not kissing her.

His words registered as vibrations in her trachea more than sound. "I knew ... because of this strange thing I told you about . . . that's happening to me. It's part of it. Like I know that, after this," he let the wet of his bottom lip catch on her skin and dragged it along the warmth of her neck for a moment, "after this—this first time—cheating on my wife will just get easier."

It took a second for this to fully register, and she struggled to pull away from him, trying to read the expression on his face but seeing only blurry features there. "What do you . . . you're not married to her, are you? No."

"Not yet. No. But I will be in a few years."

She pushed him farther away. "Why would you say something like that, right now?"

"You're right," he whispered, stepping forward and trying to touch her again. "It has nothing to do with right now." At first, she pushed his hands away, but he persisted, getting closer, until his face was right in front of hers. "Absolutely nothing."

Then he kissed her, softly, firmly, with a kind of learned concentration. He was calm, assured, and moving down her neck again, the moisture of his mouth tracing a cool line along her skin like a vapour trail in the night sky above the college. He unzipped the back of her dress with a sleight of hand she hardly noticed and eased her onto the carpet.

Denise's thoughts were moving farther away, her arms on the floor above her head, arching her back, feeling the wineglass smoothness of one of his fingernails as he ran it across her lips, his other hand busy taking off his own clothes. And just before her mind was emptied of the last of its conscious streams, before she plunged into the warm water of focus, it occurred to her that Cedric had said things that were much more than peculiar, and that he might be doing this purposely, in an attempt to make himself more mysterious.

She didn't really believe him. In fact, the only thing she believed was that there was a new world wobbling on a new axis, and that she was on her way to becoming a woman that might be able to thread her way through it with a kind of quiet daring. She believed that, from now on, she would be able to lead the things that she wanted into unseen corners and taste them. She wasn't a conventional girl anymore. Now she was something else, something more. And that was all she believed. Not in Cedric, not in his strange words and countenance. Not really.

She tilted her head back, his hands slipping over her bare thighs like water, and smiled into the dark. Feeling like every colour in a nighttime rainbow.

We crossed the country towing a bantam trailer
Crammed with boxes we couldn't trust the movers with

Sleeping at motels in nameless towns, our only food
Cellophaned or deep-fried in truck-stop diners

We watched the landscape change by degrees of longitude
Adjusting the hands of our watches while our daughter's

Fingers pointed out the red of granaries, the stretch of aspens,
And finally the blushing granite the highway cleaved between

It was on a long stretch in Ontario that I nodded off
Both of them asleep in the dim of the sedan, mouths open

And breathing against the windows while the patient
Hum of the engine lulled my head into a slow dip

Jerking awake with a panic so raw I had to stop, pulled
Into a picnic area with signs a national-park green

And surprised that neither of them woke when I turned off
The car, I stepped out into a night that smelled of waves and

Walked to the edge of the trees where an expanse of black
Water opened up so wide it swallowed silence

Grumbling swells rolling up slopes of rock, hesitating,
Then slipping back into the surf to boil in the dark

While in my mind the car-crash *what if* churned
Over and over on itself like a precarious shoreline

Melissa went down into the Don Valley Brick Works with the stack of pages and a lighter, setting them on a rock amid a tangle of small trees and long grass. She lit the wad of papers and straightened up, already satisfied, watching the line of char creep and boil, the corners curling like gangrenous tongues, velvety and cresting to lick the roof of a mouth that wasn't there, and so continued to furl and lift, until they were floating, the ashes rising, whirling into the air, only to settle farther off, into the bushes and grass, the fireflies of their sparks still glowing. Melissa stepped back, suddenly panicked, realizing the potential disaster. She ran over to one of the larger embers and stamped it into the reeds, looking over her shoulder as another feathery-grey parachute landed onto a shrub. She darted over there next, shoes crunching through thorny branches, then began moving out in a wide circle, patting and stomping, already humiliated, thinking in headlines, mortified that the cinders would spread, that the singeings of her scribbled lines might catch fire, the embers of her words growing into a swath of something wide and consuming and precarious, until she was laughing, madly laughing at the idea of it, knowing that this, her ridiculous scene, was sure to become a poem she would need to write someday. Words smouldering to take on a life of their own.

"Kóstas! Yórgos! Grigora, uh!" said Helena, coming into the kitchen and picking up Kóstas's sweater off the floor, neatly draping it over the chair beside him. Kóstas took little notice. "You know, I tell you both there's people coming into the house this morning and what do you do? What do you do?" She was speaking to her sons in Greek, which, normally, was more readily understood than her clumsy English, but today she had the distinct feeling that whatever came out of her mouth, neither of them were in the mood for listening. "You take an hour to eat your breakfast. One hour. Now I have to clear up in here. Right now. So get out. And hurry up." She tapped her closest boy, Yórgos—who, at seventeen, really should've known better—lightly on the back of the head.

Yórgos also took little notice. He was bent over the table, absorbed in the narrative on the back of a Sugar Puffs cereal box while abstractedly scooping spoonfuls of the product into his mouth. "It was Kóstas," he said, answering his mother in English, still fixated on the box. "He was the malaka that wanted toast and a million jams."

"Oh," Kóstas retorted. He was the younger, at fifteen, but more than capable of holding his own. "Eh, malaka, who's the one who spilt the juice, huh?"

"Hey, hey, hey! Skasei, uh!" Helena held her hands out. "I don't care! I don't care. Just get out of the kitchen. Or better yet, get out of the house. Go play outside or something."

"It's too cold out." Kóstas put his arm out on the table and rested his head against it as if needing a respite from the mere thought of going outside. And Helena knew he had a point; there'd been a trace of snow on the ground almost every morning over the past week, with the nights dipping well below zero.

She started clearing off the table. "Well, go watch some cartoons then. Or . . . I don't know! Just do *something* outside of this kitchen!"

"Ma," Kóstas began quietly, as if confiding something grave and unfortunate. "We're too old for cartoons."

Helena flashed him a look that had both boys reluctantly getting to their feet and disappearing into the living room. She heard the crinkle of a magazine and one of them settling onto the chesterfield while the other turned on the television and stood in front of it, flipping through the channels, the dial clicking until it finally stopped at a station that was playing Saturday morning cartoons anyway. She heard another magazine now, rustling above the squeak of the springs in the armchair. Helena considered the volume, especially for cartoons that neither of them were watching, as being a bit loud but didn't say anything.

She was half-listening for a piece of news to be inserted between the programs, as the news seemed to be interrupting everything in Toronto these days, and it was mostly about the gay people in the city. The police had done something only a month before that had finally made sense, arresting almost three hundred of those homosexual types in their prancing bath houses. But since then, the city was up in arms about it for some reason, angry protests in the streets at night, a gay rights activist announcing plans to run as a candidate in the provincial elections as a demonstration, a pastor on a hunger strike demanding an investigation into police policies, and, only yesterday, a Gay Freedom Rally, where all kinds of important personages (whom Helena had never heard of, mind you), authors, lawyers, and politicians, were speaking out in favour of the gays. Helena really had no idea what the big deal was; she just hoped her sons didn't see or hear it and get any ideas. Imagine it: Gay rights! If you weren't normal, you didn't get normal rights, thought Helena. That was obvious, wasn't it?

She finished clearing off the table, wiped it down—careful to find the spot where Yórgos had spilt some orange juice—did the few dishes, and even gave the floor a quick sweep. She liked to make an effort whenever she invited future tenants into her house, liked to have the place looking impeccable, because if eleven years as a landlady had taught her anything, it was that tenants were generally the kind of people who were always watching, always looking for an opportunity to overstep the boundaries she set. If you wanted to protect yourself and your property, thought Helena, you had to start at the outset.

Not that she was expecting any problems with the young couple that were about to drop by and sign their lease. The Johnsons had let on that they wanted an apartment to rent just for the time being, while they looked around for a house to buy in the suburbs. They had a two-year-old daughter and the straight-laced air of people who did things by the book, who followed the rules, respected guidelines, due dates. In fact, so much so that when they first came by to see the apartment, and Helena learned that they were new to Toronto, she'd thrown out a few of her own "tenant terms and conditions," just to see how they would react. She'd watched their responses cautiously, ready to amend the fact that these were just—if they didn't mind anyway—some of her *personal* requests. But every time she tossed a proviso into the air they simply exchanged a look of mild surprise, shrugged, and agreed. Which was good because when it came time for them to leave, the figures would work out a little better on her side of things, something that, Helena believed, had happened very seldom in her life.

The buzzer, which her son Yórgos was fond of saying sounded exactly like a strike on *The Price Is Right*, let loose with an abnormally long ring. Helena took one last look at the lease papers on the table, a pen resting diagonally across them, and hurried to the door, opening it to a gust of cold air that flecked her welcome mat with a spatter of wet snowflakes. Cedric and his wife were standing shoulder to shoulder in heavy coats, smiling with plastic congeniality, their daughter in her mother's arms, straddling her waist and wearing an overly puffy snowsuit, gazing at Helena the way two-year-old children do.

Helena bent out of the doorway and scowled up at the grey sky. "Stoopid weather."

Cedric chuckled in accord and held out his hand, shaking Helena's too firmly, as opposed to his wife, Julie, who offered her limp fingers to squeeze, which felt to Helena like the tiny wings of a dead bird.

She let go quickly, smiled. "Come in, come in, it's a freezing out hhere."

She led them into the kitchen and pulled out the chair in front of the papers for Cedric to sit in. "I hhave to tell you something. You know, in my country—you know I come from Greece—and, I tell you, in Greece, in March, it is already sooooo hot." She closed her eyes and arced her hand through the air in the shape of a sweltering summer sky.

"But." She shrugged. "Now I am hhere. Where, in March, it snows. And you know, sometimes, in April, it snows too? You believe it? I khan't believe it." She laughed to herself. "Is it so cold in . . . ? Uh . . . where you come from again? You tell me Alberta, no? It's big city Alberta?" Helena pulled out the chair even farther and gestured for Cedric to have a seat. "Sit, sit." She stepped closer to Julie and pinched the child's cheeks, leaning in close. "How are you, Kouklitsa, good?" Then up at Julie. "You guys want some coffee or sometheen?"

"No, thank you," said Julie, putting her daughter, who had begun to squirm, down onto the ground. "We just had breakfast. But thanks anyway, really." The little girl clung on to her mother's leg like a sloth to a tree and looked up at the three adults, wide-eyed, mouth open, the cleft below her nostrils glistening.

The adults stared back, smiling, which was a natural enough thing to do, until, Helena thought, the moment had gone on for too long and she broke the child's gaze to look over at Cedric. To her surprise, he didn't look so well, suddenly pale, gawping down at his daughter like she'd just appeared out of nowhere, miraculously.

"Melissa," he whispered, as if he were alone in the room with her, "baby." He squatted down to the child's level while both Julie and Helena stood by, confusedly watching him.

He brushed his knuckles across his daughter's cheek, then touched the tip of her nose with his pointer finger. She blinked hard, once, but otherwise continued to scrutinize him as warily as the two women.

Cedric shook his head. "You see? See what you were like before? Hmm? Before you . . . went and . . ." He stopped to chew the inside of his lip. A cartoon explosion bellowed from the television in the other room, followed by a clatter of animated pots and pans caroming off of one another. Birds twittered in the quiet aftermath, flying, presumably, in a halo formation around a character's head.

"You know," Helena finally broke in uneasily, "hhi think you guys have a good idea to rent apartment for a year. Like this you can take your time and look around, find a nice house for good price, you know? No hurry like this."

When she met Cedric's eyes, who was still squatting on the ground in front of her, she let out an unnerving simper. "What is it?" Looking up at Julie now. Another simper. "Your hhusband okay?"

Julie, a hand on Melissa's head, looked Cedric over. She seemed to agree that there was something about her husband that was most definitely not okay. He turned his manic attention back to his daughter.

Helena let out a shallow sigh. She suddenly had a bad feeling about this. You see, she thought to herself, you see? She was wrong. These will be bad tenants. Strange man with strange ways. They'll be trouble. Which meant that, somehow, in some way, the Johnsons were going to cost her money. Money that neither she, nor her family, had.

Which (Helena slouching now), anyone had to agree, seemed to be her lot in life. Why was it exactly that she *always* had to be weathering the storm of bad luck or faulty circumstances; and here, of all places, in this frozen country that God had forgotten. But what Helena considered most tragic about this was the fact that it hadn't always been this way. There had been a time, a brief time, when the universe hadn't conspired against her, hadn't revelled in her wanton hardship. And it was a time that she reminisced upon likely more than was healthy. A time that she missed with every Greek bone of her body.

Specifically what she missed was gathering eggs from the chicken coop as a girl, cupping her hand into a tangled nest of fingers and carrying them into the kitchen, gently placing them into a chipped blue bowl on the table; or running home from school to cook lunch for her family, who ran a small farm outside of Kalamata, butchering the worst-laying hen with a method she'd devised herself, which had made her father beam with pride; or the honey melon that he would bring in for breakfast in the summer, stabbing perfect cubes of it and doling them out on the end of a knife, Helena pinching the cold flesh from the end of the blade and placing it in her mouth with a shiver of sweetness; or setting out before sunrise with a wicker basket to pick mushrooms, taking a break when the cicadas started up, looking out through the pines to the landscape beyond, where sheep dotted the scrubland like ant eggs under an overturned rock.

It was all so ideal (or so she remembers), until she was sixteen and one of her cousins moved to Athens to work in a textile factory. Helena's father thought it might be a good idea for her to do the same, make some easy (and much needed) money for the family. So she left her parents' farm and entered the industrial sprawl of the metropolis only to find that she could barely earn her own keep. About to admit defeat, about to return to her family as a failure, her cousin read her a fortuitous ad in the paper that she'd cut out, which was looking for textile workers overseas. The tiny rectangular clip of text said that interviews would take place the following week in Athens. A dazzling bulb of promise lit up in both their minds. Canada.

Helena was one of the youngest women standing in line that day, the queue twisting around corners and filling several hallways of an office building. When it was finally her turn, she wiped the wet of her hands against the sides of her dress and gave a quick glance back at her cousin, who mouthed. "Kali tyhi." Good luck. She walked into the room to find just one man sitting behind a desk, an enormous bulk of a figure who was so large she couldn't even see, let alone guess at, what kind of chair he was sitting on. She stepped forward, trying not to stare, and placed her application on the desk in front of him. "I . . ." she hadn't meant to speak, "I'm probably too young."

He ran a heavy finger down her application form to find her age, then looked up at her, staring at her breasts. "I'd say you're old enough." His accent in Greek was a strange one, and Helena, having never heard anything but local dialects, took it for the inflection of someone who was well educated, opulent. Still watching her, he picked up a rubber stamp, worked it into an inkpad on the desk, and thumped her application so hard that the unseen chair beneath him complained with a crackle. "Hired. We'll send a package in the mail with the details and flight times." He began writing something on her form and spoke at the papers, "Send the next girl in on your way out."

Her cousin was hired as well, and the two of them left the building running, out into the street, looking for a phone booth to squeeze into and give their parents the tidings. Helena talked to her father, her tone secretive, as if she were divulging a complicated plot. Her plan was to go to Canada, work for five short years, and come back rich, free—free to do whatever she wanted. As reluctant as he was with the idea, he assented because, really, she was right: once she was rich, she'd be free to do whatever she wanted.

The flight from Athens to Toronto was a memorable one. There were seventy-five young women on the same plane, sponsored by the same Canadian company, en route to a city where, it was rumoured, there were skyscrapers as impressive as the ones on postcards from New York City. When they landed in Toronto, they were ushered, still giggling with excitement, into a yellow school bus that had been rented to bring them from the airport to their living quarters, which, like Helena's tiny apartment in Athens, were at the edge of a large industrial tract. Only instead of apartments, these were dormitories, two sets of bunk beds in each room, with a single toilet, bath, and kitchenette assigned to every floor. A man with a clipboard gave them a brusque tour, allocated rooms, and went through the rules, the women looking around at one another while they listened, waiting for someone to complain. The man spoke Greek with the same accent as the one who'd hired them, and when he was finished listing the many rules, he also clarified some of the finer print that they may or may not have been aware of, like the fact that not only were they to live in these quarters that were nothing more than glorified berths, but they also had to pay a substantial rent for the privilege to do so, a rent that managed to carefully tread the line between just affordable and cheaper than any other option available to them in the city. It was then that a few of the bolder women spoke up, asking to see someone in charge. He countered with a terse remark and inferred a threat that was severe enough to silence both present and future griping. Did they happen to be aware, he wondered out loud, that the company could, at any time, strip a worker of her visa and immigration papers, hence taking what the Canadian government viewed as a produc- tive worker who was contributing to its economy and turning her into an illegal noncitizen who was leaching from it—the very kind of criminal, mind you, the authorities in this country actively pur- sued? Which was something they should consider before opening their little ungrateful mouths again. After all, this *was* better than jail, wasn't it? Because if it wasn't, then, hey, they were always free to go and battle for immigration themselves. In fact, they were free to do whatever they wanted. So look, see, there was the door, he dared them, go ahead, a slack wrist motioning a flick at the reality on the other side of it, see how long you last out there. The women looked first at one another, then down at the floor.

She worked in sweatshop conditions for almost two years at the textile mill, living with other young women like herself who could afford nothing outside their dormitories but fanciful wishes of finding Greek men to save them. Which was unlikely. It was harder for Greek men to get their papers than it was for women (or so it was said in the dormitories), owing to the country's focus on bolstering its population and the fact that women were the surer bet, being more liable to stay in the country once they started producing offspring. Helena wouldn't get nearly as upset as some of the other women, who saw themselves as simple pawns who had been pencilled into a government stratagem, as an italicized letter in a demographic equation, the margin of its error.

But Helena wasn't giving up. She saved what she could, shopped on her only afternoon off, and managed to live on a single chicken throughout the week, a hen, she realized, that had been raised without seeing the sun, mechanically slaughtered, plucked, incised and gutted, Styrofoam-tray inserted, plastic wrapped, freezer-truck distributed, price-tagged with a sticky label, and shelved, all for her convenience. And if she could get her shopping done in time, she would make her way to Greek Town, on Danforth, which is where, at age eighteen, she found her ticket out of the textile mill, with no apparent ramifications to her immigration status. In retrospect, she was really only trading in one form of slavery for another. But, as Helena was beginning to learn, that was undeniably her lot in life.

She'd gone inside a restaurant to ask if they might need some help in the kitchen or with the cleaning and had made an impression on the woman who was running it. She walked out with a new dress to wear as a uniform, and a room to let above the bar. Within a week she'd moved in and was working both the lunch and dinner shifts, and found, for the first time ever, that she could make enough money to pay all of her living expenses and still have a few tips left over at the end of the week. She kept these in cash (assuming that the banks would dole out her figures to Revenue

Canada and swindle her money away in the form of taxes) and stashed them in her room, keeping track down to the penny.

Then, on one of those muggy summer days that Helena despised in Toronto—where the heat clung heavy to her body in a way it never had in Kalamata, weighing her down, making her movements sluggish and arduous as if she were wearing three-too-many wool sweaters—Yannis Andreadekis came into the restaurant, his shirt stained with lines of sweat along his spine and sternum, splotches of dark spreading from his armpits. He gracelessly asked for her phone number within minutes and, not getting it, came in every other day, demanding refill after refill of coffee and asking questions about Helena's private life while she topped off his cup. It was how he hung on to the few details that she'd inadvertently given him, how he repeated them the next time he came in, always asking for more in a way that seemed genuine enough, that made her finally accept one of his invitations out for dinner.

Throughout the evening, she learned a lot about Yannis Andreadekis, and the more she learned, the less he sounded like a find. To start with, he was the only Greek she'd ever met who had landed in Canada illegally, having gotten work on a ship in Greece, then, wanting to avoid military duty, leapt overboard just outside the port of Montreal, almost killing himself in the process, nearly drowning in the grimy water, was hypothermic for hours, and survived only for the kindness of the proprietor in a dépanneur who'd fed him fatty bacon and tea while he ran on the spot over a heating duct. He had been working under the table and dodging the immigration authorities ever since, he told Helena, winking, without the slightest bit of shame.

He began asking her out more often, which had Helena asking a few discrete questions to the regulars at the restaurant about how, theoretically, an illegal immigrant might eventually become legal. And she could never be sure if it was *because* of those questions that Yannis was suddenly plucked from work by Immigration Canada one day. He was brought to a prison to await trial and a seemingly inevitable deportation. Helena, feeling guilty, contacted everyone she knew, assertively cashing in favours, and hesitantly promising new ones. Until, through the restaurant owner's daughter-in-law (who had a close friend whose father worked in immigration), she found her in. She then contacted everyone who had ever known Yannis and, through the neighbourhood lawyer (who always brought his family for Sunday dinner at the restaurant), compiled documents that vouched for him, illustrating that he had several people willing to sponsor him in the event of his release, and, most importantly, someone with landed-immigrant status waiting to marry him.

When Helena signed the final papers, it occurred to her that, as far as marriage proposals went, this couldn't have been further from her adolescent daydream of a sharply dressed gentleman sitting at her father's table, listing his innumerable assets and proclaiming his unwavering love for her, not a whisper of a dowry, with the entire family rushing in afterwards, already celebrating. Instead it was she, the woman, offering her hand, and only as a means of getting a coarse labourer she had somewhat fallen for out of prison. It looked like, even when it came to getting a husband, she was destined for difficulty and hardship. With a sigh, she dotted the one "I" in her name and slid the papers over to the lawyer, watching them disappear into his briefcase, the lid being swiftly shut and sealed with two professional clicks. Yannis was released within a month, and, in accordance with certain clauses and stipulations, they were married almost immediately, a slapdash ceremony at the nearby Orthodox Church, with her cousin standing at her side in a dress she'd borrowed from a friend. The day after the wedding, she moved the little furniture she'd acquired over the years into a small apartment Yannis had found for them off of Arundel and placed a planter of red geraniums on the doorstep.

In 1964, after waitressing well into her eighth month of pregnancy (making sure the owners knew what this did to her back), she gave birth to her first son, Yórgos (though, as to avoid giving other children the chance to pick on him, his Greek name was pronounced only in the house; "George" in the playground). Two years after Yórgos was born, to the month, she had Kóstas (a name chosen for its ease of use both in the house and playground), and with the money Yannis was making, which, after becoming the co-owner of a growing and reputable painting company, was always on the rise, they managed to get a mortgage for a two-storey apartment building on Langford. The complex looked great from the outside, had four suites, and after choosing to live in the one with the small garden in the back, they rented out the other three, providing them with a bit more than their monthly payments to the bank, hence making it a legitimate second income. And seeing as Helena was at home and would be able to keep track of the comings and goings of the tenants better than Yannis, he asked if she would act as the landlady; take care of things so he wouldn't have to worry about the apartments "as well as everything else." It was remarkable to Helena how, sometimes, others weren't capable of seeing her suffering for what it was.

Working as a landlady suited her. She was good with money, and good with people too, always smiling, asking about their lives, making them feel as at home and relaxed as she could. Understanding how these few simple gestures and niceties could make the business side of things go that much smoother. It lowered people's guard, had them throwing out fewer questions and demands. Because Helena detested demands, detested when people cocked one of their thighs out to the side, hand on their hip, and spoke like they'd just been coronated the sovereign of a newfound state. The problem was (and throughout the 1970s she became increasingly convinced of this) that people in Toronto were watching too many courtroom series, eating pizza slices off TV trays while admiring graceful lawyers strutting the floors in front of jury boxes, giving inspirational speeches and instilling viewers with a false sense of empowerment, as well as all the words that went along with it; words like "legal privilege," and "within my rights."

Thankfully, in the last year or so, Toronto had entered a unique era, a period in the city's history where these words had come to mean less and less. It was due to another word that was being thrown around at the time (and with much doom and gloom attached to it): "recession." But for reasons Helena didn't understand, some provinces were being hit much harder with the term "recession" than others, like Ontario. Which had people flocking to Toronto. The vacancy rate was close to nil, and to address the housing shortage there was an abundance of new apartment complexes being built and renovations being done to existing ones to create extra suites, hammer falls counting down the seconds of summer. Which in turn had Yannis's painting company making a bundle and a queue of prospective renters at Helena's door, ready to put a security deposit down months ahead of the end-of-lease dates she gave them. Whatever this worrying phenomenon "recession" was, it hadn't come to the Andreadekis household.

For once, Helena thought, finally, the world wasn't working against her. Though, as she was sure it would revert back to its old ways very shortly, she thought it best to benefit from it while she could. Understanding that there was a limit to what people would pay for an apartment in their area north of Dundas, she was interested in finding out (as anyone would be really) where that limit capped itself off. Which had her carefully, and with quiet persuasion, encouraging tenants to move out of their suites as soon as possible, at which point she could change the contract and increase the rent to whatever she deemed fit.

Because, really, when it came time for them to leave, there was always something that needed repair; and even if there wasn't, what about the general wear and tear on things that she'd have to pay for down the road? Helena wasn't responsible for that wearing and tearing, so why should she have to waste her money refurbishing things that hadn't been cared for as well as they should've been? She was a businesswoman, and she was just adopting some justifiable common business sense.

And it wasn't as if it was making her rich—by any stretch of the imagination. If she were rich, she wouldn't have to watch her money like this in the first place; in fact, if she were rich, she would *lower* the rent, practically give the apartments away to people. And, let's see, what else: she'd have a garden, a nice one, something bigger than the meagre backyard plot they had now, big enough that she could invite people over for the Feast of Dormition in August, with a firepit where Yannis could set up a spit and knock down the cinders, stirring the coals until they were the perfect temperature to roast a lamb. And if not a garden, then maybe a holiday, back in Greece. They could visit her parents, spend Easter there, in the way that Easter should be spent: go to the vigil in church on Pascha Saturday, watch the lighting of the Holy Fire at midnight. That's what she would do. And while she was there, she'd be sure to go to the beach near Kalamata where the shore slopes into the Mediterranean, and she'd swim in that sea that she remembers so well, in the water she can picture even now, water that was always calm and blue and clean. That's exactly what she'd do if she ever made enough money. She'd spend it. Because she would be free to. Free to do whatever she wanted.

Cedric, still squatting on the kitchen floor in front of his daughter, looked up at Helena, and, as if suddenly recognizing her, was beaming. He shook his head, something cold, something sardonic in his expression. "You don't say. Why it's Helena Andriakolopolisalis." Cedric stood up tall, until he was looking down into Helena's face. "I'm sorry. Am I pronouncing that correctly?"

"Whhell." Helena took a step back, exchanging another look with Julie, trying to smile. "Is Andreadekis is how we say."

"Cedric," Julie mumbled, "is everything all right?"

"Yes, Julie," he said with an odd formality. "Fine. Things are just fine. We're here, if I remember correctly, to sign a lease." He looked around the kitchen and pointed at the stapled papers on the table. "Yes, that lease there. You see," he said, addressing both women while tapping the side of his head. "A memory like an elephant." Cedric stepped over to the table and slid the papers into his hand, scooping them up as if they weighed several pounds. "Oh, Helena, you'd never believe the things I recall. In fact, I wonder . . . knowing what I know now, if I could just . . . ask you a few questions about the details in this contract."

Helena attempted a smile, scratched the back of her neck. "Yhess. Off-course." She took two further steps back, leaning against the kitchen counter now, crossing her arms over her chest. She watched Cedric as he flipped the pages of the contract over. His wife and child watched as well, everyone in the room feeling the volatility in his gestures, everyone afraid to speak, as if the cartoon noises from the other room were fragile and sacred.

As the seconds passed, Helena felt herself becoming less afraid and more annoyed. You see, she found herself thinking again, do you see what the world had dealt her? No breaks for Helena. Never. She looked at her feet, wondering how long she was going to have to wait in this awkward silence while Cedric perused the clauses in the lease.

Cedric lowered the paper from his face. "You know, Mrs. Andriakolopolis . . ."

"Is Andreadekis." Helena shifted her feet.

"Exactly. Well, you know, I can't seem to find anything in here about your needing both 'key money' to secure our placement *and* three full months of 'last-month's-rent deposit.' Strange it wouldn't be here because I think that's what you told us we had to pay. Now, you wouldn't . . . dream of taking advantage of us, would you?" Cedric let out a humourless chuckle. "I mean, that would make you a kind of . . . conniving, corrupt—well, for lack of a better word— bitch, wouldn't it?"

Helena gave him a toxic grin, then looked at Julie, who in turn looked down at her daughter, feeling the sudden need to pick Melissa up. "I wonder, honey," Julie mumbled toward the back of Cedric's head, bouncing her daughter as if the child desperately needed placating, "if we shouldn't come back a little later."

"You know, Julie . . . I'm afraid 'a little later' is not quite something I can do. Besides," he smiled at Helena, cordially dipping his head before returning his attention to the lease, "I'm thoroughly enjoying myself here. So then, where were we?" He flicked the papers, turned the page.

Seeing the frightened look on Julie's face, Helena shot a quick glance toward the living room, where the Saturday morning cartoons were still safely blaring. She found herself wishing her husband were there. Why did he never drop by anymore in the middle of the day, with his transparent detective work, his jealousy, looking for clues of the illicit lovers that Helena had never had? Not that she was afraid for her safety (she doubted this odious man would lash out with his wife and daughter right at his side), but she could feel that his resentment was seething. Everyone could, including the little girl, who now looked like she was about to cry, gawking at her father, tuning in to his hostility.

"Now this is interesting," Cedric said, having found (or not found) another clause in the lease. He laughed, shook his head, and took a step toward Helena. Julie reached out with her only free hand, Melissa in the other arm, and held on to his elbow, as if to restrain him. He responded to this by wrenching his arm free.

Helena straightened.

Melissa started to cry. Everyone turned to her.

"Oh just great," Cedric said, tossing the lease back onto the table. "Do you see what you've done, you stupid cow? Do you see that?" He gestured at Melissa, now wailing in Julie's arms. Julie, an appalled look on her face, headed for the door, opening it wide and stepping out into the blowing snow, leaving it ajar behind her.

"Just fuckin' great."

Helena looked Cedric over disgustedly, finally slipping off the end of her tether. "Ande gamisoy, uh! Esy eksogamo tekno! You! You go out of my house! Now, you *katharma*! Out!" She pointed. "Go!"

Kóstas and Yórgos quickly appeared in the living room doorway but stopped there, not moving, watching the scene unfold. A clip of classical music played from the cartoon behind them.

Cedric headed to the door, looking more in pursuit of his wife and daughter than someone obeying the order to vacate. He spoke to Helena over his shoulder, "Anyway, don't forget to hit us up for the paint job. And a new bathtub too while you're at it. You'll make a bundle on us, don't you worry." He stepped outside and gently closed the door.

"Julie," Helena heard him call. "Wait. Just a second. Hey, I said *wait*!"

Helena had followed closely behind him, and she locked the deadbolt as soon as she was within reach, then stood on her toes to peer through the peephole. She saw no sign of Julie and the little girl out in the street. Just Cedric, standing alone on the sidewalk, rubbing his forehead and looking around the neighbourhood like he was lost. Eventually, he hunched his shoulders, pulled the collar of his coat up over his neck, and walked out of sight.

"Ma?" asked Yórgos to his mother's back. "Who was that guy? I mean, what . . . was that all about?"

Helena returned to the kitchen table and picked up the lease papers. She noticed her hands were shaking. She filed the forms neatly into the drawer where they belonged and remained standing there in front of it, the drawer still open. "Notheen," she answered. "That was about notheen. Just some stoopid katharma, thinks he knows everytheen."

The television in the other room filled the silence that followed with the beginning of a commercial break, a man's voice like an auctioneer's, rapidly endorsing the "All-New-Hot-Wheels-Ultra-Hots, in stores everywhere."

She closed the drawer and turned to her sons. "Honest," she was speaking in Greek again. "Just some guy who's going crazy. That's all. Nothing more."

She walked to the sink, turned on the tap. "Nothing more."

the one free afternoon i'd had in
ages and thought i'd spend it
answering her tireless pestering
taking her by the hand into
the backyard to look for
something to do
dog days
toronto
syrupy heat
gooeing the tar between the
cracks like charcoal bubblegum
so I lugged the pool we bought
for her out of the shed
the one I wouldn't have
dreamt of having as a child
and she stood there
in her bathing suit
six and already shy
covering her sex
while i filled the
plastic with every
floating toy in production
water rippling at her ankles
glistening in a barbie-doll pink
and all she could do
was watch me
the hose drooping
from my hands
in a pout as
low as
hers

Melissa stood in front of the spray-painted train, thinking, thinking about the immensity of where and how we fit into it all, what we're forced to dwarf ourselves in measurement against—it's almost natural that such an overwhelmingness manifests itself physically, inspires something tangible, like graffiti, something left behind for the wayfarer to read, see, witness. Even if it's simply to say. "I was here. We were here. Once." Wasn't that why people scratched their initials and names into newly paved slabs of cement, brandishing sticks to etch out letters and dates, children squatting down to push their palms flat into the congealing mud, why travellers, merchants, and crusaders of antiquity inscribed other cultures' holy buildings and landmarks? They were all saying the same thing really. They were saying, quietly, soberly: "We weren't important. We weren't someone whom you would normally remember, someone who altered a heroic past or a courageous future. And why didn't we? Well, it turned out to be much, much bigger than us, so big that we couldn't. But we could change this wall, this train, this rock, this bathroom stall. Maybe even with something aesthetic or poetic, something thought-provoking, challenging, something that we drew or wrote in protest, disgust, dissent—or maybe, maybe it was just something. But something that was ours. Exactly ours. Put down in precisely the size and colour we intended it to be. It's not much, of course, but it was born solely from our choice to leave it behind. This, here, is our paltry stain that we've chosen over sterility, our tiny peripheral shout over silence."

September 14, 1985

Steven was walking toward the bright lights of a gas station at Pearldale and Finch, his hands in the pocket of his hoodie, one of them fingering the blade of a knife. He knew that a switchblade would have been more formidable, dramatic, and so probably more effective, but an old folding penknife—with its pin so caked with grime that he'd struggled to open it—was all he could find rummaging through the drawers of the house he'd woken up in. Which meant it would have to do. He saw an expensive-looking car pull up to one of the pumps, a chubby man get out of it, unlock his gas-tank cover, and hinge it open. He was blond, dressed in pricey casualwear, and looking around a little uneasily, probably feeling more than a touch out of place, as if his low-fuel light had just flickered while on his way out of town, up the 400, heading to cottage country, ready to spend a day and a half at his own personal plot of furbished boreal shoreline, with its dock and covered boat, with its weathervane mounted onto the apex of his boathouse, for aesthetical purposes only. The man looked critically at the grease on the pump and hose, put the nozzle into the hole, and twisted around to watch the digits of the pump flitter into higher values.

Steven Greig had a mother somewhere, a mother that had given birth to three children, from three different fathers. The oldest of her children, a girl, had been promptly whisked out of the delivery room and adopted at birth. Steven imagined her sometimes, sure she was living a well-adjusted life somewhere else in Canada, somewhere green and kind. After her, Steven's mother had a boy, who was also taken out of earshot before he'd cried for the first time, and was probably then rewarded the same fate, jumping through the sprinklers in some architecturally controlled neighbourhood in Ontario or British Columbia, a neighbourhood that was, again he imagined, green and kind. But on the afternoon that Steven came into the world, things were different. His grandmother happened to be in the same hospital, on the same day.

She'd accidentally learned, by means of an overly helpful assistant at the registry, that her very own daughter was in the hospital as well, and in the natal wing no less. Not having seen her in more than five years, she thought the coincidence providential, in the same way it was providential that she was in the process of turning over a new leaf—swore to it, honest to goodness, once and for all—and had been straight and sober for almost three days consecutive, following the bleak news about her liver, and a few lumps that were awaiting removal and testing. After wheeling her IV pole through several fluorescent and disinfected corridors, she learned that she was a grandmother for the very first time (having never heard a word of the grandson and granddaughter who'd preceded Steven). She demanded to see him, this newborn, her blood. The disinclined hospital staff checked records, papers, legalities, murmured to one another behind high counters, and finally assented. She picked him up, rocked him, stuck her pinkie into his mouth, cooed. She had a great idea.

A month after she'd taken him home, her concerned neighbours had called the police so many times to complain about the child's incessant, brutal, and—the most pressing reason for the phone calls—noisy neglect that Steven could legally be taken out of her custody. However, as he was officially under the care of a blood relative, Child Services was obliged to contact other genealogical connections in hopes of finding another, better suited, family member who might be interested in taking him in. His aunt, who had eight children of her own, and was living in the largest low-income housing project in North America, Regent Park, in inner-city Toronto, reluctantly agreed, in the diminishing hope of receiving more—and maybe even, for once, adequate—child support cheques.

Steven's first memory was one of contentment and self-worth. He and his cousin were walking to a corner store (he used this term "cousin" because of its blanketed convenience; though he'd never actually sat down and calculated his relation to the people he lived with, whether they were step-cousins, first, second, third, half-cousins, or no relation whatsoever, he referred to them all, simply, as "cousins"), and as they were walking, this particular cousin, Kipp, was shrewdly and subtly pointing out policemen along the way. He was teaching Steven to look for the cars with OPP written on the side, or the unmarked sedans that parked like slinking (though always well-buffed and Armor-Alled) ghosts in the backdrop, the only vehicles that had two men sitting casually inside them, as if having nothing better to do with their days and nights than chat in the comfort of a Buick, nonchalantly raising a pair of binoculars to their eyes every once in a while. His cousin also pointed out the neighbourhood snitches, who had been black-mailed into collaborating with those very men in the sedans. He made sure that Steven could identify them all. "Hey, Stevie, see these guys over there, on your right? No, no, your other right, bud—yeah, that's it, good man. See those guys there? Snitches. Fuckin' snitches. The whole group've 'em. Gottem? Good. Good man." At seven years old, Steven appreciated very much being called a man. He was important. Already.

Sometimes they would go out after dark and stop just before the door of a tiny store that had closed for the night, his cousin crouching down on his haunches, talking softly into Steven's face. "Okay, little buddy, here's what's gonna happen: I'm gonna go inside and get us some treats, okay? So if you see anyone coming, any cops or snitches, or anyone else who looks pissed off, I want you to knock on the glass, like this." He wormed a knuckle between the bars on the door, tapped three times. "Okay?"

Steven would comply gravely, understanding.

"Good." His cousin would stand and take a few steps towards the back of the building but would often stop, hesitate, then bend down again to ask what kind of treat, exactly, he wanted from inside.

Steven was the ninth child in the house; five boys, three girls, two rooms. He understood that he was living with his aunt and uncle instead of his parents, but didn't know why, and already knew better not to ask. His aunt and uncle weren't happy people at the best of times, but questions of any sort, about school, clothes, milk, eggs, seemed to reliably set them off into a frustrated rant that often spiralled into rage; the mayhem of nine children weaving skittishly between them, trying to get out of the house, or, if it was winter, trying to get away into the farthest corner; someone getting slapped in the head as he or she passed, another shoved onto the ground, bouncing against the drum-clang of the stove. There were only two people in the house that could talk back and deal with the consequences: Kipp, who, at sixteen, had already found several ways to make his own money, and Natalie, whose glamorous air came from her well-earning job as a stripper and the near super-idol status she'd attained at having been a Sunshine Girl on the third page of *The Toronto Sun* (the picture of which Steven had her sign). Everyone else had to make themselves as small as they could when it came down to it, or run.

The first time Steven saw someone shot, he was ten years old. He had a friend who lived across the way, at Sackville and Gerrard, whose house he would sleep over at, sometimes for days at a time, no questions asked. His friend's mother was bedridden with pulmonary emphysema, which amounted to the house being reigned by her teenaged sons; the walls lined with calligraphy, illustrations, and graffiti by anyone who could wield a felt pen and was struck with the inclination, dishes festering in a sink that was perpetually backed up with an orange and oily scum, and adolescents sitting on a sofa they'd dragged into the kitchen, passing around a box of artificially sweetened and coloured cereal through a mist of narcotic smoke, threads and clouds of hashish, pot, and sometimes something else that was mildly sweet or mildly sour. He and his friend were standing outside when it happened. A young man with a bulky jacket was pacing in front of the house, as if waiting, as if wanting to talk with someone inside, but was uncomfortable with entering. One of the boys from in the house stepped into the doorway for no apparent reason, saw the young man with the bulky jacket, and stiffened, terrified, hands out on the doorframe on either side of him. Steven was watching his reaction, so didn't see the gun, just heard the staccato *bam*, and watched his body fold onto the porch, limp and lifeless. He remembers hearing the other boy sprinting away, and the sugary smell of burnt gunpowder.

Steven came to learn that this was how violence worked. It wasn't logical or predictable, it wasn't a buildup of reasonable causes that led to an unreasonable effect, an argument that escalated, a series of increasingly potent threats exchanged; it was just suddenly there, abrupt and conclusive. And it was something that couldn't be questioned. Its aftermath could, yes, but not the certainty of the act itself. The act was final, absolute, definitive. And it was something you had to be ready for, everywhere, always.

The second time, he was twelve. It was near the Boardwalk, where the dealers strutted invincibly along the pavement until they spotted a ghost car on one of the periphery streets, when they shuffled timidly out of sight. This time, he and another friend, a girl named Kirsti, to whom he would lose his virginity before either of them were pubescent, were loitering in the wading pool, built only four years earlier but already largely dilapidated. There were tiles missing, grout chipped and peeling, hammer dents in the moulding, a half-submerged shopping cart poking above the surface like a miniature shipwreck, the fountain of water spewing out at crooked angles. (Steven understood, and at a very early age, that his neighbourhood was not green, not kind.) *Bam.* A body crumpling to the ground at the edge of the pool, a dark puddle fanning out from beneath it. No warning, no pre-empt, just screams to follow it through, round it off. Kirsti grabbed his arm and together they fled deeper into the housing complex, the wet of their footprints chasing them.

Steven was dealing drugs long before he was aware that drugs were even dealt. His cousin Kipp had him running around on "errands" all over Regent Park, bringing wads of something to someone's living room and running back with a wad of something else. In return Kipp would give him some money for candy, chips, and pop whenever he wanted it, reminding him, offhandedly, handing him a ten-dollar bill, "not to take shit from anybody."

And Steven was getting the hang of that too, was less and less afraid to tell people off when he had to, to push people back. He'd even taken to testing the limits with his aunt and uncle when they fomented into one of their screaming fits. He was thirteen. It was 1979. And life was good. The Montreal Canadiens had won the Stanley Cup, there was a new television show called *You Can't Do That on Television*, and the movie *The Warriors* was playing in theatres with authentic and exciting brawls spilling out of the cinemas afterwards. Steven even had friends, or at least people he could hang out with—break bottles with, steal from 7-Elevens with, and stand in alleyways with afterwards, smoking purloined cigarettes in a contemplative apathy. He'd found, in his own awkward way, a niche, a place to belong.

Then, on a cloudy day in March 1980—when the remnant piles of ice leftover from the snow removal of the winter had turned pebbled and muddy, water fingering out from beneath them and streaking the cement between the apartments with glistening pinstripes—everything changed. He had just finished running an errand for Kipp and had rounded a corner where he came face to face with a police officer, uniformed, polite. "Hey," he greeted, hands on the black implements of his belt, "I was wondering if you could help me out here, bud. I've got a couple questions for some kids, about your age, but they're not at their house. Maybe you can tell me where to find them. Their names are, uh . . ." he produced a small spiral-bound notepad, flipped the page, and stepped closer, to show his list. At that point, a strange impulse came over Steven, and he couldn't explain why, it was just there, and happening, automatically. He noted the proximity of the policeman's foot to his, lifted his leg, and stomped his heal onto the polished black toe of the man's boot, spat in his face, turned, and ran.

When he was caught and put into the officer's cruiser, it was the first time in his life that he'd ever felt constrained, confined, and couldn't explain his reaction to this either. He flailed, screamed, bit, clawed, pulled hair, spit until his mouth was dry, lay down across the backseat and tried kicking the windows out, and when none of this worked, he managed to get his pants below his waist and piss everywhere he could fling his urine with furious pelvic rotations. He was further restrained, driven away, pulled into a tall and official-looking building, and heavily sedated. When he woke, bound to a bed, he could only think of his cousins, how they were going to laugh at this story, how Kipp would tell his friends about it while rolling a joint over the coffee table, how Natalie would probably ruffle his hair, call him a brat, chuckle. He'd be a kind of hero in their eyes, he imagined, standing up to the police like that. He was brave.

Eventually a woman came to talk to him, gently, calmly, like you would talk to an animal before opening its cage to transfer it to another. She wanted to know about his family life, wanted to hear about his house, his aunt, uncle, his "cousins." Steven was struck with another clever idea. He began to speak in a whisper, like there was something in his throat, something painful and swollen, and when she brought her face closer to listen, he spat in it, screamed at her to release him, struggled in his bonds, writhed on the polyester sheets. She called out over her shoulder and three large men appeared bearing one small needle and another day was gone. Or was it a week. A month?

When he'd finally agreed to cooperate, to sit and talk like a regular human being, the theatrics having become less a novelty, less worth their future storytelling, Steven found himself sitting across from a more stern-faced woman. She placed the news onto the table like stolen coins, her gestures half-guilty, half-smug. It seemed, she'd said, this "incident" had been coming for a while now. She'd met with his aunt and uncle several times, had been to see his home, interviewed his family. She'd learned that, apparently, he'd always been a bit of a problem child. Always a little wild, a little devious. He had, she warned, the potential makings of a criminal or, at the very least, of someone slightly unstable, depressed, with the traces of an anxiety disorder. Which had sparked some research into his parentage. Did he know, she asked rhetorically, that his "maternal associations" had a history of mental illness? Perhaps not. Well. She was afraid that, yes, that was the case. And these things could be hereditary, she wanted him to know.

Steven started shifting in his chair, shrugged. "Look, lady, I don't give a shit. When can I go home? I'm fuckin' bored here."

The woman scratched the back of her hand. "I'm not sure you understand. Your aunt and uncle . . ." she turned her hand over, looked into her palm for a moment, then back up at him, "they don't want you back. That's not going to be your home anymore. We're going to find you another one instead. With a foster family at first, but I'm sure you'll be adopted in no time."

Steven felt something growing inside his stomach, rising into his chest, and this time he knew what it was. Once, on a hot August day, he and one of his cousins had gone down to the Harbourfront, where the Gardiner Expressway thrummed at their backs, and had walked through sites of demolition and construction, the old factories with massive machinery rusting behind splintered windows, shards dangling in the frames like loose teeth. They watched as a thunderstorm edged across the lake, toward the city. It was so hazy that Steven could barely make out the contours of its cauliflower clouds, but he could feel the air turning viscous and weighted, becoming slower, electric. Until the growling of the storm had swollen above the burr of the freeway, the flickers of lightning piercing through the sooty veil like tracers of siren strobes. He and his cousin stood below, shrunken. It was mammoth, fierce, inexorable. And now it was welling up inside of him, lifting him as if he were caught in one of its updrafts, floating above his chair. His arms bolted down abruptly, finding ground. He flung the table aside, lunged to grab on to one of the woman's hands in the air—which had been raised in surprise, in fright—and sunk his teeth into her fingers until he had the taste of pennies in his mouth.

The juvenile ward of the psychiatric hospital was not a nice place. It consisted of three wings. One for the criminally deranged, people who had violent and aggressive tendencies toward others: pedophiles, child murderers, adolescent rapists, and chronic assaulters, all of them heavily medicated, strings of drool from the corners of their mouths indicative of how well they were being kept in check; another ward for those who did damage to themselves: anorexics, bulimics, substance abusers, the manically depressed, suicide attemptees, and self-harmers; and another ward that was reserved for borderline cases like himself, who were in danger (and seemingly the "imminent" kind) of slipping into the preceding two categories.

Because his was the least secured of the wings, Steven soon saw the potential of making a break for it and within a week had made the first of his two escape attempts. Looking back, however, he could admit it was a stupid move, ill thought out, ill timed, ill executed. Had he not spent the afternoon in therapy, the impulse probably wouldn't have risen up in him so strongly, and he could have bided his time a little more wisely.

The problem with therapy was that people bought into it not because it was helpful or they believed in the process, but because if you cooperated during the sessions, you were rewarded with "off-ward privileges": like going outside onto the grounds, a patch of cement enclosed with an impossibly tall chain-linked fence, where you could mingle with older people who'd been institution-alized most of their lives; or to the rec room , where the recreation included puzzles with pieces missing or their cardboard swollen with dried saliva, boards with checkers from five different sets,

Connect Four apparatuses mended with Scotch tape). For these honours, people let their emotions fly, sincerely pouring them out to the good-natured therapist and to everyone else who was forced to be there and listen.

"Me?" someone began that day, pointing at his sternum. "Well, this morning, I just . . . I wanted . . . I mean, I had this urge to, like, feel my bones somewhere, you know? Like with a knife. Like, cut to the bone and push on it, against it, you know? Like a steak. That feeling. You know what I mean?"

The therapist, slowly, earnestly nodded his head, narrowing his eyes, trying, seemingly *straining*, to understand. "Okay. Okay," he said conclusively. "Thanks for sharing, Jamie." At length he looked up at everyone else. "Okay. Okay, who's next?"

When the group of them were being escorted from therapy (a citrus-scaled room with brown flooring, yellow walls, and orange plastic chairs arranged in a circle) to school (a citrus-scaled room with chairs arranged in a square), they passed a door that looked to have access to the outside world and, without thinking, Steven broke away. He slammed through it and was sprinting down a lane that had manicured trees and grass that was greener than any he'd seen in his life. He was tackled before even reaching midway along it.

This stunt didn't just get him demoted from the P3 wing to the P2, he was also introduced to some of the rooms that were designed for the "implementation of disciplinary measures." First, as he'd come back inside screaming obscenities at any and all of the staff, it was The Quiet Room, a cushioned chamber with thickly insulated walls and a door that appeared to have fingernails imbedded in the foam near its edges. There were no windows—not to the outside, not to the hallway—only a closed-circuit video camera mounted in one of the corners, a black iris steadily fixed on him. (When he first noticed it, he'd given it the finger.) He walked around in circles for several hours, maybe the better part of a day, finding the tender floor the most disturbing aspect of the room, the ground sponging under his sneakers like an orange quilt of moss. He thought of his family while he treaded around, which, of course, had never really been his family. He wondered why he hadn't seen this all coming, seen the fact that he'd become not only another mouth to feed, but another delinquent to bail out of trouble, another stress in his aunt and uncle's already stressful lives. He wasn't even their child; they hadn't brought him into the world, into their house, hadn't asked for him; they'd taken him in as a kind of regrettable favour, and that was all. Yeah. He understood where they were coming from. Sure. But that only made him hate them more.

No. He was on his own now. For good. Just him. And that was fine. That suited him just fine. (Throughout his day in The Quiet Room, the most defiant thing he could think to do was, ironically, be quiet, and so didn't make a sound padding around in front of the camera, didn't even whisper.)

Then, after lunging at the first person that came to speak with him, he was introduced to The Bubble Door Room. There, the priority was in keeping the hospital staff safe, with a Plexiglas bubble on the door that they could put their heads inside, in order to see if he was huddled in either of the blind corners, readying himself to lash out again, but mostly to check that he was still sufficiently sedated. The sedative of choice was chlorpromazine (affectionately referred to as CPZ), and the instant it was injected, his vision became blurred, the sounds in the room muffled. But worst of all was what it did to his mouth, his tongue becoming gluey, a thirst coating his throat, scratching at it—a thirst impossible to sate. Always asking for water, dreaming of the rim of a paper cup, what it would feel like against his lips, the cool liquid slipping down the walls of his esophagus, wetting the membranes. But water would never come. Just the thought of it, the asking of it, the word spoken out to an empty room, muted echoes pasted onto the baby-blue walls: "Canuhave somewadder please?" Tongue doughy, flour-frosted. "Please? Coulduhget a lill' water overhere? I'm real thirsty. Please? Just a cuppowadder?" Head tilted to the side, blinking slow blinks, eyelashes raking through the recirculated air. An epoch of stillness, of nothing.

Then someone would open the door, and be moving too fast through the room, suddenly standing in front of him with a paper cup of water, and a smaller paper cup of pills, a weaker dose of CPZ—provided he was good. He would look at the water, swallow the dust deeper into his throat, look at the pills. Reach a heavy hand out to the water, have the cup of pills placed into his fingers instead. A hesitation. "Are we going to have a problem here, Steven?" a voice would say too quickly. Another hesitation, blinking at the line of water in the paper cup, out of his reach, tasting it, smelling it. "Fine. Have it your way." The faceless body turning around too fast, walking away too fast, calling out to someone as they disappeared through the door. Then the door filling with another body, someone carrying a syringe.

"No . . . Please . . . I . . ." His shoulders wrestled square, vein found, a new surge of limpness, new rush of thirst. He would coil into a ball and turn to the door where a face with glasses would be filling the bubble, looking at him, expressionless, now writing on a clipboard, now pushing the glasses farther up the face's nose. In an alien and faraway consciousness, Steven understood that he was in very big trouble, understood that mental asylums were places where, the saner you were, the crazier they would make you. He knew he had to get out. At whatever cost, in whatever way. But he would have to be smarter this time. He would have to plan it through, think of everything. And he would have to play their game until it all fell into place, was in perfect alignment.

Which is what he did, amounting to his second time being less an attempt and more an actual escape. It began by asking for extra jobs around the ward, to keep him busy, he'd said, out of trouble, and he started helping the kitchen staff clear plates after meals. He would scrape off the plates—instant potatoes and powdered gravy, a rectangle of meat tissue, and the only thing coloured a kind of indistinguishable vegetable matter—organize them into bus pans, and slide them into a dumbwaiter where they were lowered to an anonymous dishwasher in a kitchen where, he imagined, the security was minimal. This miniature lift was operated by means of a cable on a pulley, and he could picture himself crawling inside, gripping on to the steel line, and shimmying down it. The rest was in the timing. He waited two weeks, waited for October 31, 1980. Halloween.

He lingered around the dining hall until the dinner dishes were most likely done below, fire-poled down the cable in the dumbwaiter, skulked through the dark kitchen, left through a service door out the back, across the hospital grounds, and onto a sidewalk to join zombies, draculas, ghosts, and kids with bloodied hockey masks passing one another with little ceremony. He spotted a Zellers and, realizing that it was a Friday night and they were open late, went inside. He found a shirt, pants, and sweater that fit, then went into the bedding department, grabbed a pillowcase, shoved them all inside, and walked out the front doors, even getting a few Rockets thrown into his pillowcase from a woman who stepped out from behind her till to toss them in, wishing him a Happy Halloween.

He went to a few other houses while mulling over his next move, ringing doorbells, saying nothing, fluffing open his pillowcase. There was no look of shock on people's faces, hands digging into bowls of candy, reaching out, hovering over his pillowcase, eyeing the grease streak from the cable that ran down the middle of his mint-green hospital scrubs. "So what are you supposed to be?"

"I'm an escaped mental patient."

"Oh. Right. Good one," tossing in a few lollypops.

Steven knew that, though he'd never really even been out of Regent Park, he'd have to leave Toronto altogether. And tonight. But before that could happen, he needed money; and it occurred to him that if he were to go into backyards and back alleys, listening at the doors for hollers of "Trick or Treat!" or for the doorbells themselves, he could be sure the people inside were distracted, and could check the latch, slip in, and do a quick scan for purses lying around. He headed in the general direction of the bus station and took every alleyway he could find. After trying only two doors, he imagined he had enough money for a bus ticket to another city. And any other city would do.

He changed into his freshly stolen clothes in the washroom of the bus station, shoved the remaining candy into his pockets, and walked up to one of the ticket windows. Unfortunately, there wasn't anyone else in the lineup before him, so he didn't have time to scan the list of places and prices to choose, at the very least, a place he recognized the name of. Improvising, he played the village idiot. "I want to buy," he spoke in a slow nasal voice, slurring clearly, "a ticket." Steven placed his money with overstrung care on the counter. The woman behind the glass fingered the bills, waiting for more details, and when they didn't come, she offered the most likely possibility, "Looks like . . . to Kitchener? Leaves in fifteen minutes?"

Steven looked relieved, "Exactly."

It was the shortest one hour and forty minutes of his life, the man beside him with a Walkman blaring his cassette of *Back in Black*, nodding his head to AC/DC, mouthing the words, "And youuu, shook me allll nighhht long," his half-whispers in the eerie Greyhound dim, strangers in rows sitting still, sitting alone, together. Then the new bus-station lights were passing overhead, the door hissing open, the coach emptying as people dispersed habitually into taxis, into rides parked to pick them up, lovers embracing on the platform, mothers taking their sons' arms, fathers their daughters' backpacks. Steven walked alone with his pockets of candy and found a bench in the station to sit heavily upon, looking down at his new corduroy pants, pinching them. He noticed a pain in his throat, and he found himself blinking back tears. He had to be hard. Had to be harder than the world was to him. That was the only way to pass through it. Wasn't it? He took a toffee out of his pocket, unwrapped it, squished it between his thumb and his forefinger. Then turned it to the side to do it again.

He stared into his lap until a crazy man passed in front of him. Steven watched him pluck an aluminum can of Canada Dry out of a garbage bin and slide it delicately into a black plastic bag.

"Hey, guy, can you show me a place to sleep?"

The man stared at him for a long while, then broke off to scratch violently at his nose. He turned and walked out of the station, never acknowledging that he'd even heard Steven speak. But from the other side of the glass, his body already enveloped in the dark, Steven could just make out the man looking back inside, gesturing for him to follow.

He never did say a word. They walked together, on his rounds presumably, checking garbage bins as they went, slipping cans and bottles into his plastic bag until he had to hoist it over his shoulder like Santa Claus. He smelled of urine, caked body odour, the dry rot of refuse. His seamed fingers were so dirty that Steven thought they looked gangrenous. He finally stopped outside an abandoned house, pointed.

"I can sleep in there? You sure?"

He nodded deeply, stopping with his chin against his chest, as if he were holding back a burp, then carried on.

Steven looked up and down the street, the last remnants of trick-or-treaters straggling along the walkways to and from the warm homes. The doors and windows in the front of the abandoned house were boarded up, but in the back, after threading through high weeds that were bolted and frost-limp, he found the back door ajar, pushed it open to the flickering light of a candle, casting quavering forms on the bare walls.

"Uh oh. You O-P-P?" a deep voice called out, two other people chuckling.

"Fuck no." Steven approached them, stepping into the candle-light. He could just make out a pile of ratty blankets against one of the walls and in a corner, a rust-stained mattress, threadbare, dark blotches in its centre.

"Pheeuuw. Lucky for us I guess." The young man looked him over. "New in town?"

"Yup. Comin' from Tronno."

"Oh yeah. Runnin' or hidin'?"

"Both."

Laughter.

"Well then, have a seat there on the floor, brother. I'm Larry, that's Sam," he picked up the candle to light a joint he'd produced, gesturing to the last of them, "Dingo." He drew in a lungful of smoke, passed it to Steven. "Welcome to the Hilton."

The group of people he found in the same plight were surprisingly diverse, some of them youth that had gone AWOL from orphanages and group homes around Kitchener, escapees from abusive parents, crazies, biker-gang misfits, older hobo types, or failed hippies whose peace and love and purpose had faded into a narcotic haze of bitter anti-conformism. There were even a few Natives, who'd fled their reserves in hopes of finding a better life but who'd found instead that no one in their right/white mind would hire an Indian. It was a community in constant turnover, people arriving one day, getting caught by the police the next, appearing again after days of being away, only to disappear once more. Their one common thread was poverty, survival their one common goal.

Steven lived on the food he could steal from convenience stores, and though it wasn't the first time he'd stolen things, it was the first time he saw it as an art to be perfected. To start with, he'd learned, you had to look like you owned the place, walk like you had nothing to hide, nothing to lose. It also helped to appear as if you were looking for something specific, hunting for it, craving it, and turn out to be disappointed that that particular establishment didn't carry it, maybe even mentioning this while passing the proprietor, pockets stuffed, jacket bulging. "You don't have any dill-pickle Doritos, eh? No?" A listless look down at the

Scratch'n'Win lottery case that made up the counter. "Well." A shrug. "Thanks anyway." And because this wouldn't really work at grocery stores, butchers, bakers, or markets, his sustenance was composed exclusively of junk food: unmicrowaved microwavable hotdogs, Twinkies, salty soothers, jawbreakers, Gummy Bears, Blue Sharks, Black Nibs, ketchup potato chips, and cans of root beer.

Having nothing better to do one day, he walked with an older boy to buy some hashish, then over to a few high schools where he sold it at lunch hour and recesses, making an easy twenty bucks. Steven watched how he cut it, listened to the prices, and was making his own money, even enough to scrape by on, in only a week. He realized that, were he to have shared in the profits that Kipp had been making (while he did all the running, mind you), he would've been rich.

As the winter set in, Steven followed the general migration into the basement of an abandoned apartment complex, where the boiler room was far enough below the frost line to be an even 14°C all winter, not warm, but not freezing either. Part of the deal of this unpaid co-habitation was for each person to supply as many candles as they could, which, besides the obvious light needed in a building with no electricity, helped to take even more of the edge off the chill. While walking between the schools where Steven made his money, he would pass by a few of the known make-out spots in the city, points with some kind of vista where teenagers brought bottles of wine and drank them with their backs against derelict walls, far from the disapproving eyes of their parents, running their clean fingernails—or so he imagined—through each other's freshly shampooed hair. He would pilfer the candle stubs they left behind, wax-fastened to logs and stones, amid a scattering of milky condoms, their wrappers, the plastic shards of busted lighters.

He imagined that the courting and coupling done in these places were the very antipathy of everything he knew. In his world, there was never a gradual and delicate breakdown of inhibitions, the slow stripping of cultural restraint before getting down to something carnal and animalistic. It was the other way around. Everything began in that state, and often stayed there. Since there was no water or functioning sewage, people—teenaged girls, boys, men, and women alike—urinated and defecated where they had to, preferring the squalor of gas station toilets but often finding it easier just to squat in the alleyways, piss in the open air of parks, steam rising from the saffron arcs and vertical jets during cold spells. Sex was open and candid, and often referenced before anything else. "I'm not a whore," a new girl said as she settled into some blankets in the corner, "so no one try anything or I'll fuckin' cutcha." Or: "Uh-uhh." Dingo's posture becoming aggressive, bordering on hostile. "This's the second day y'owe me money—so, like, pay up or give me a blow. Now," already unzipping his jeans, the other person resignedly beginning to crawl toward him. There was no dignity, nothing holding anyone back. But that didn't mean there weren't glimpses, albeit rare ones, into something else. Like that afternoon with Sam.

The two of them had gone out to get some food, and it started to rain. Hard. Steven doubted very much that people who had homes ever thought about how people who *didn't* coped in the rain. It was a real problem, with no raincoats or umbrellas, and nowhere to go. If it was warm out, you could sit under a bridge or overpass, pigeons made anxious by your presence. The other option was under stairs, doorways, or buying an order of fries and spending the day in the abrasive colours and child-hectic ambience of McDonald's. On this particular day, they'd sought shelter inside the closest building around, an office tower with a vestibule, where they could be dry and "inside" without actually entering the building. They lingered for a minute or two, still cold, bored, before deciding to wander around inside. They made it five metres into the lobby before being spotted by a security guard who approached and, when they ran, gave chase, deeper into the labyrinthine halls, both of them laughing, looking for a way out, the number of security guards increasing in their wake, until Steven ducked into a narrow hallway with a small bathroom at its end. They locked themselves in and listened to their searchers scramble past on the other side of the door. Minutes passed, and Sam, still cold, ran hot water onto her hands, vapour smoking the mirror.

It was her idea. She thought to make the most of the hot water, the privacy, the unlikelihood of being found, and take a sink bath. In her coarse way, she demanded he bury his head in the corner and never turn around. Ever. He promised, and was good to his word, listening to her undress, then splash water carefully onto herself, pushing the pink foam out of the soap dispenser, droplets running down the sink, plumping into a puddle on the floor behind him. He heard her use what sounded like the entire roll of disposable hand towels to dry off, then get dressed, tucking in her shirt, zipping up her pants.

"Your turn," she'd said, shouldering him out of the corner. But as he turned around, she was too close, and his erection brushed against her on his way to the sink. As opposed to Steven, Sam wasn't good to her word, and halfway through washing himself, naked and squatting over the faucet, she turned around, grinning at him seriously. She stepped forward, put her hands on his thighs.

The sex was fast, urgent, both of them fumbling onto the floor with their arms out, gripping onto whatever they could, the edge of the sink basin, the tiled walls, the base of the toilet. She kept her mouth open the entire time, Steven noted, and she tasted of pink dispenser soap.

That night, they went together into one of the smaller nooks of the boiler room, where she usually slept alone, both of them with a candle, two orbs of undulating shadow walking along walls of cracked cement, a hand in front of the wicks, steadying the flame. They put the candles where others had been before, a wavering flagellum of carbon flaring up through bits of chipped paint. They smoked a joint (as this was the only way for her to find sleep, he knew) and instead of having sex a second time, she asked him to lie down in front of her, and she spooned him, adjusted the blankets around their shoulders. Before she fell asleep, she whispered that she'd only ever slept like this with a dog before, a mutt she found in Toronto and panhandled with for a while (cuz, she added, people tended to give more if they thought the money was going to a canine). Steven couldn't think of what to say in response so kept quiet. Even though he really wanted to know more, more about her story, how she got there. He knew she'd lived in a group home for young women, a place designed to teach girls in foster care everything they needed to know about both the business end, and the frontlines, of prostitution. As it turned out, that night would have been the only occasion to ask her; the next day she disappeared, most likely picked up by the police. He never saw or heard anything about her again. Then, three days later, it happened to him.

Coming out onto a sidewalk from an alleyway, he felt a tap on his shoulder and was asked for his ID, for reasons he didn't hear, due to the pulse thumping in his eardrums. He would've run, but with another police officer flanking him (with the apt impression that he was about to bolt), there wasn't much point. He refrained from spitting in either of their faces and was brought back to the juvenile wing of the psychiatric hospital, where he met with a woman he'd never seen before who'd recently replaced the previous director. He told her, flatly, that he'd escaped because he wasn't crazy, that he didn't belong there, that he belonged in a normal home, with normal people. She explained to him that, if this were true, he would have to prove it, that his behaviour alone would dictate the length of his stay. She promised. And, likewise, Steven understood. He realized that, in the end, it wasn't only a matter of playing their game, it was a matter of winning it; that the one way to get out of an asylum and stay out of it was leaving it through the front doors, "healed."

He asked one of the staff in the rec room about it, what he

could do to expedite the process of his "recovery." The man suggested helping out with the recreational side of things, namely doing the jobs that he and his colleagues didn't like to do. So Steven took to raising and lowering the volleyball nets, setting out other equipment, watching the games from the sidelines before gathering everything up again and putting it back in its rightful place. He was also asked to go into the adult ward to host the bingo games, picking small white balls out of a giant transparent one, staring through it as he did so, the images distended and blurry (not unlike The Bubble Door), the wobbling shapes of people sitting nearby, their giant craniums funnelling into pinheads, then widening again, eyes bulging.

Then came the day that one of the staff, who was somewhat tolerant toward Steven's general harshness and smart remarks, asked if he wanted to do a few other jobs besides just his normal routine. "Sure." He shrugged. "Whatever. Better'en just standin' round." When he was mopping one of the halls, knowing that there were hospital janitors paid to do that very thing, knowing that he was being tested, and was passing, he could barely keep the smile off his face.

The following Monday, he had a meeting with one of the administrators, and another two weeks of dutiful chores, behaviour that bordered on polite, and a subsequent meeting with several other administrators had them talking about releasing him into a foster home. They even believed that they'd found one suitable for him: in a suburb north of Toronto, where the lawns were nice, where the people were nice. Green and kind. Did he think he could manage that? they asked. Of course he could, he'd said, looking out the window with nonchalance. Of course.

The foster family Steven had been assigned to was in Brimley, a residential area with regularly maintained streets and brightly painted fire hydrants. His new family had come outside to greet him as he arrived, standing on their driveway, wondering where his luggage was. The family consisted of a couple that ran a flower shop together, the man's biological son (who was quite young), another foster child like Steven (even younger), and himself, who, at fifteen, was tall, lanky, with a voice that was pubescent and breaking. To Steven, they seemed like one of those families on TV, well adjusted, clean, friendly, smiling at nothing. It put him on edge. For the first week, he walked around afraid to touch things, easily startled by their salad spinners and steamers, their food processors and sprinkler systems. Conversely, he seemed to offend them with his language and mannerisms, most noticeably at the supper table, while he wiped his constantly runny nose with the end of his sleeve, coughing out over the salad, standing to snatch things from the centre. Once, after they'd finished eating, and a full ten days had passed of Steven going to a nearby school without a word of the friends he was supposed to be making there, they asked him to stay behind after the younger boys had excused themselves.

"So . . . Steven," his foster mother began, "you haven't told us . . . about what you like to do in your free time. Do you—you know—have any hobbies or . . . anything like that?" Steven looked down at his plate, which matched the designs on his cup, his fork, even the colour scheme on his cloth serviette. "Because I know Brady likes putting those models together, ships and cars mostly. And John flies those little Styrofoam planes."

"And they both like sports," Brady's father inserted. "Play them, watch them, collect cards."

"Oh, and those wooden model dinosaurs! I don't even think you have to glue them, isn't that right, Walter? You don't have to glue them?"

"Nope. No glue." ·

His wife tried to laugh. "Anyway," she said, turning back toward him. "We just wondered what *you* like, Steven?" Both of them grinned warmly, waiting.

He blinked, eyelashes raking quickly through the freon-circulated air. What, he wondered, if he really *was* crazy? Or worse, what if he was too sane, what if he'd already lived too much, seen too much, understood people too well? What if he'd become the type of person who would never be able to pretend this greenness, this kindness? What then? Where would he go then?

It soon came to his attention that the monthly allowance his foster parents provided didn't amount to much. Even if he'd had the fervid hankering to click together these non-glue dinosaur skeletons (as a means of whittling away those pesky free hours he might find between his birth and his death), he barely had enough coinage for a bag of chips and some Gummies to keep him from stealing over his lunch hour. Fortunately, he knew a simple way to make a little extra cash on the side and had soon gravitated toward the only other dealer in the schoolyard. The principal notified his parents of this poor choice in company, and when they confronted him with it, he told them what he thought of *their* company, spitting invisible saliva onto the ivory-coloured carpet in their living room. Once the unhappy decline had begun, phone calls made, meetings had, it only took two months for another car to appear in the driveway, this time with a social worker from Child Services, who stood beside the car while Steven got in, wondering why he didn't have any luggage.

The mould was cast. For the next three years he would almost lose count as to how many foster care placements he had, how many municipalities (and hence social workers) he was put under the jurisdiction of, how many times he ran away and lived on the streets until he was picked up a few weeks later, how many schools where he was scribbled onto the end of the attendance rosters, then scratched out again. From emergency shelters to group homes, from foster parents with extended families and low incomes to middle-class nuclear units, all of it interrupted by "trial weekends" with potential adoption couples who would always find him "too" something. Too coarse, too vulgar, abrasive, deviant, or too angry, too quiet, too brooding. Until he was too old for adoption at all, while still, luckily, remaining too young for incarceration.

And for the system, the idea of juvenile detention was indeed a viable option, and one that was even recommended to him by a social worker who'd seen Steven through five of his "transitions" in a single year. It was following his fifth that he said it, sitting behind a desk eating an apple, chewing it quickly while looking Steven over, who sat with his arms across his chest, scowling at his feet. "Steve, I'm going to be frank with you here." He was clearly exasperated, swallowing large chunks of apple-matter down his gullet, throwing a hand in the air to help him explain. "I think we both know that you're . . . well, you're a bit of a fuckup, hmm? But the problem is that you're *such* a fuckup, you can't even fuck up right. I mean, you *could* do something really bad, couldn't you? Get yourself landed in kiddy jail, keep yourself away from functioning families and other people who are just trying to care for you, provide for you." He checked himself, sighed. "We just . . . we all want what's best. And you? You throw it away, every time. Every time, Steve."

He lowered his hand, looked out the window, pointed. He was speaking quietly now. "That's Alex in the parking lot. Nice guy. He'll drive you to your new home. It's a . . ." he leaned forward to read from a piece of paper, "a family running a bed and breakfast in a small town up north, cottage country." He waved a dismissive hand toward the door, pulled his chair closer to his desk. "Now go. I'll probably see you in a few weeks anyway."

Besides the stream of highway images while driving to and from these different placements, flashes of linking towns and sprawling municipalities, Steven had never really seen life outside of a city, didn't even understand how it could exist. The term "cottage country" made him uneasy, knowing that, were the need to arise, he might not have the option to run, deal, beg, or even find a warm squat to sleep in. There was probably nothing for miles around but inbreeders, bleak forest, and muskeg, moose standing docile and still, shredding twigs between their molars.

It was near Algonquin Provincial Park, or so he assumed, with all the brochures and tourist information piled high near the reception. The bed and breakfast was supposedly "family run," but it was really the couple's twenty-two-year-old son and the foster children that did the work, changed the sheets, made breakfast, and cleaned the rooms; duties that, surprisingly, he didn't really mind. There were six foster children in all, most of them girls, and as Steven was a burgeoning man of seventeen, the person he should have related to most was the couple's son; however, as he essentially held the position of "boss," Steven made a point of steering clear of him whenever possible. He spent most of the time that he wasn't working alone and, something else that surprised him, outside. Because the residence was on the distant outskirts of a drowsy town that took five minutes to walk the breadth of, there wasn't much point in going there, and his bedroom was nothing but a gloomy hovel, in a basement, with no television. So he spent his hours sitting in front of the lake that bordered the property, smoking slow cigarettes near a dock that pointed its planked wooden arm out into the water. A dock where herons sometimes landed on its tip and stood, pensive and regal, for so long that they became part of the landscape, their poise both curled and erect at the same moment, like lifted shavings from a planer still attached to the wood. A tall bird, a tall boy—staring out at the featheredge horizon where lake sheen met the clotted reflections of spruce trees—gradually forgetting each other.

Until the evening he went outside to find a person on the dock, one of the younger girls, clamped up into a ball, rocking back and forth, apparently crying. He looked over each of his shoulders, not knowing what to do, feeling stupid. While thinking he would have to find someone else to talk to her, he sauntered in her general direction until he was there, squatting down next to her, like his cousin Kipp had done with him. When he put an awkward hand on her back, she seemed to wake up, snap out of the trance she was in. She twisted around to look disgustedly at his fingers, flung them off, and ran away. He watched her disappear into the trees, mulling the incident over. Until it all fell into place.

The suspicion that there was sexual abuse taking place at the bed and breakfast worked in the way that suspicions do, clinging to clumsy phrases and glances, to the words that were being so carefully left unsaid. It was, of course, the family's one real son, who had limitless access to empty rooms, unseen corners, and moments in a day to take advantage of his foster sisters. The suspicion was finally verified with Steven's own ears while he was changing the sheets in one of the rooms and heard an unnatural scuffle in one of the adjoining suites. He pressed his head up against the wall, heard a rhythmic whimper that, the closer he listened to it, only became more subdued, more painful, more ugly. He stepped away from the peach-painted gyprock, staring at it. It occurred to him that, were he a hero, like the ones in the movies—Sean Connery, Harrison Ford, Roger Moore—he would have kicked open the door, pulled the man off, punched him out. Saved the day. But a hero he was not. He didn't even have the mettle to tell anyone about it.

And he hated to admit it, he really did, but he also didn't want his summer to end just yet, which is exactly what would happen when the police came round. As it stood, things were good for him there. It was a nice place, a place where he felt something inside of him shifting, changing form, maybe even mending. Yeah, sure, sure it was all fringed with a fifth and sordid defilement. But wasn't everything? And for once, finally, it had nothing to do with him. He was out of the loop. And was only making a conscious decision to refrain from stepping into it.

Steven skirted the times and places where the abuse took place, and it continued much as it had before he'd sussed it out. Sitting at his spot by the lake, black flies eventually gave way to mosquitoes, to horse flies, to acid flies. To nights with a cool edge, where stars punctured a crisp dark, and geese trumpeted by in invisible formations, sounding closer than they really were. Until, at last, when one of the teenagers being raped ran away, was picked up by the police, and told all, it came to an end.

The hammer dropped quickly. And as the evidence mounted, Child Services thought it best to—at least temporarily—close down the foster home. The police arrived as the transport, in order to interview the remaining foster children, ensuring they build a solid case before they all dispersed to other homes. When Steven saw the officers strolling toward the dock, he felt something storm-like rising in his chest again, jumped to his feet, and fled.

He ran first along the lakeshore, then into the forest, crashing through the undergrowth, over rose-hued outcroppings of Canadian Shield, hollows of bunchberry and horsetail, stands of aspen that shivered above him, until he realized he'd gotten himself a bit lost, the trees dead-ending where sentinel snags rose out of a wide marsh that spread out around him. At first he'd thought to walk through it, part the sedges, and end up on the other side, but as soon as he walked into the reeds he found himself stepping onto a ground that was veiled and unnaturally soft, which had him rethinking the idea. He turned back and found a bed of moss that was as soft as the padding on the floor in The Quiet Room, where a lump of exposed granite offered him a spot to catch his breath. He sat down, looked around.

There were some cattails jutting out of the marsh's edge, most of them having gone to seed, their brown velvet splitting along a seam that seemed to bleed out with a kind of downy cotton. He noticed the fall colours standing out against the browns and greys of the wetland, a yellow leaf caught in the sepia culms, a brush-dab of maroon, a fist of rust. There were also birds, he realized, twittering and chirring in the rushes in front of him, hidden. He wondered what they looked like. He wished they would fly, wished he could see them in the whorled cloud of their beating wings.

Then he heard the police in the distance, quashing through the sphagnum behind him, getting closer, following the path of his broken branches, the logs he'd folded over, grass he'd trampled. He knew he was only postponing the inevitable. But he also knew that he would remember this. This place. His time by the lake. The feeling that he was slowly, slowly, becoming connected to something. Something worth submersing himself inside, surrendering to. Something bigger than him. And what he liked most about this "something" was that it didn't require a name. The only thing it required was countryside, and silence.

Steven was eventually taken to another group home in Toronto, where he put on a nice face, said his pleases and thank-yous for two days, and, after dinner one night, found a small window to slip out of. He had five months before turning eighteen, at which time he would no longer be a "crown ward of the state," a pawn that could be displaced at any time, according to the whims of people who didn't know him or his history. Twenty weeks to lay low and avoid the police, with the understanding that he was becoming less a priority to them with every day that passed. And with that in mind, he had a plan.

He was going to save as much money as was possible for a petty criminal, and with it, he was going to go back out there, into the woods. Somewhere up north, or anywhere really, as long as it was by a lake. He'd find a spot and get himself set up there, look for a place to live, pay rent, and all the other things you had to pay for. (He wasn't sure how this worked either: electricity, heating, water—did you have to pay for water if you lived on a lake?) Then he'd find a job, cutting wood or something, building brackets to store canoes, cleaning fish—whatever. Because now he knew that there was actually work to do "out there," had seen it with his own eyes, whole communities of people with jobs, houses, and vehicles, people who lived entire lifetimes in these places. His plan was, simply, to become one of them. And he wasn't naive about it. He understood that, to get there, he'd have to fight more than they'd had to. But the way he saw it, if he could pull himself back from the vacuum of the psychiatric system, he could pull himself out of the inner city as well. Yeah. Of course he could.

He remembered the dealers on the Boardwalk in Regent Park,

how they carried around fisted wads of twenty-dollar bills, how his cousin Kipp kept a roll of red fifties down the front of his pants, with one or two halos of brown hundreds layered between them, like the rings in a tree that denoted an exceptional season. After all this time, those spools of money were still the largest he'd ever seen, had access to. And it was just the kind of money he needed to make now.

So Steven found himself walking in the general direction of his old home, passing haunts that had changed, and haunts that had not. It was 1984, the name of a famous book, he'd heard, about authoritarian figures watching you as unwaveringly as the camera in The Quiet Room, as the ghost cars that cruised the perimeter of the Boardwalk. And because this was his first night AWOL, when more than ever, the surveying eyes of Toronto would be on the lookout for him, he decided to take to the back alleys.

Steven loved alleyways, loved how they were made up of the parts of people's lives that were most hidden, most indicative, most real. The only cars that were parked in them either gleaming-new or corroding-old, tiny mouths of rust around wheel wells flaking open like cold sores; televisions with imploded cathode-ray tubes and screens a spiderweb grey, spun around the point of impact; broken umbrellas pressed flat on the ground, tattered and bat-winged into a sprawl like the fossil of a pterodactyl stretching out into mudstone; and brick walls frosted with the acrylic of vandalism, graffitists with their strange hierarchy and one-upmanship, spray paint cancelling certain designs while others were left expressly untouched, framed by signatures and symbols encroaching with tentative caution.

Steven crossed Parliament and into Regent Park and had soon found someone he recognized to bring him up-to-date. He learned that his aunt and uncle had moved away (probably for the best, as he'd intended on pounding at their door the first time he passed by, giving them an earful, maybe more). Of the two cousins he revered most in the household, Natalie—of past Sunshine Girl fame—had become a prostitute and rumoured heroin addict, while Kipp, quite the reverse, was cleaner than ever and had ambitiously moved up in the world. Leaving his small-time dealings and corner-store robberies behind, he'd gained himself the reputation as the savviest mover of handguns in underground Toronto. By Regent Park standards, he was rich.

Kipp was glad to see him, reaching up to ruffle his hair when he opened the door, pulling him inside. As they caught up and reminisced, they were both careful not to broach the topic of his aunt or uncle or the fact that Steven had been committed after they'd outwardly rejected him, beginning a long list of tribulations that also went unmentioned. References to the past were kept nostalgic and fleeting. Besides, the present was much more interesting. And as if reading Steven's mind, Kipp handed him a bottle of Moosehead, walked to the window to steal a look outside, and started talking about the entrepreneurial mood in the streets, how, these days, and in only the last few months, the opportunity to make big, *big* money had sprung up out of nowhere. Steven chuckled, pried the cap off his beer, and listened like a fox to a rodent under the snow.

It had come in from Los Angeles, and had swept across the continent as fast as cars could drive. It was a drug that hit hard, didn't last long, and every first-time buyer became an instant regular customer. It was essentially cocaine, but instead of needing a laboratory, dangerous reactions, and chemists to produce it, anyone with access to coca bushes, baking soda, and water could do the trick. The water inside caused it to sizzle and "crack" when you lit it, hence lending it the name that most people had adopted. And as long as you didn't screw up like his sister Maya, he'd warned, and start smoking it yourself, you could be a rich man in no time. Kipp weighed out the look on Steven's face, then picked up the phone. "I know a guy who just got a ton of the shit. Start you out." He dialled a number, ear to the receiver, stole another glance through the window. "Hey, Stevie," he said before the person on the other end had answered. "Need a place to stay till y'get settled?"

It was better money than he'd ever hoped for. Supply could barely keep up with demand, and people naturally trusted him, many of them remembering his face and name from the days he'd run errands for Kipp. He soon acquired the reputation of being a "smart kid," someone who steered clear of the hard stuff and had a commercial edge, someone who was either going to become a formidable presence in Regent or find a way out of it.

By the time his eighteenth birthday came around, he had a coil of bills so thick he'd stopped counting them, roughly dividing it into thirds, carrying two on his body and stashing one in his room at Kipp's place. However, as good as things were going for him, the scene had its drawbacks. Crack was everywhere, and everyone was smoking it, a constant burnt-candy smell wafting between the walls and blocks of the housing complex, puffs of sweet-plastic smoke rising from corners where kids were crouching in the dark, glass pipes hovering close to their lips, having just bought a "twenty" from him. Twenty bucks for a half-gram enveloped in Saran Wrap, ripped away and lit up every few minutes to maintain the effect, which would, at most, last a half-hour, only to find them strung out, open-mouthed, and frantically looking for more. Or ways to get more.

He sometimes traded it for sex but was famously choosy with whom he made this arrangement. One of the girls he slept with surprised him one bright winter afternoon with yet another draw-back. She'd just heard his family name for the first time. "Steven Greig, eh?" She looked him over impishly. "How much you wanna bet I know all about the first time you got laid," hands on a set of bony hips, "Steven Greig."

"Yeah?" he said with little interest really, reaching into his pocket and producing a "forty" for her, as agreed. She told him how she knew Kirsti Farley, how they'd become good friends after he "left" the neighbourhood. Kirsti had talked fondly of him, said they'd both been at the wading pool when someone got shot there, that they ran away and hid together, said she'd lost her virginity to him before either of them had hair below the beltline.

Steven nodded, asked how she was doing now, where she was, in Canada, the world.

She rubbed her cheek, "Well . . . last time I saw her she was talking shit. Smokin' lots and had, like, this great idea to like, *pretend* to hook. You know? Like, agree on a price with the guy, get the cash beforehand, as usual, but then, like, pull a knife or something, tell the guy to get out of his car, then drive a few miles away, and like, dump it and walk off. Said she did it once, and it worked like a charm, so . . ." she finished, seemed about to leave, find a warm corner to smoke in.

"And?" Steven asked, holding on to her arm.

"And nothing." A shrug. "Haven't seen her since." She pulled her arm out of Steven's grip and walked away, across an empty courtyard, over compressed snow and fairy rings of dog urine. He watched her knock on a door, exchange a few words with the fat man who opened it, and disappear inside.

It got him thinking, all these unhappy endings. Maybe it was time to go, take what he'd managed to save and run. Make do. Make it make do. Because, though he'd always known that the world in the inner city was in a state of constant and varying decay, it occurred to him for the first time that, possibly, he had no choice but to decay a little along with it. Maybe the easier money was to make, the more, somehow, it cost.

That night, he promised himself he'd leave in a week or two. Swore to it, honest to goodness, once and for all. But then came the evening he was walking back from the Boardwalk, turned a corner, heard a thump, felt nothing, no pain, no panic, just a slow and slothful writhing to wake up, lying face down on a frigid sidewalk with the biggest headache of his life. His pants were still undone, and he didn't have to feel for the hidden wads of cash on his body to know they were gone. Furious, he almost told Kipp about it. But in the end refrained, knowing that, if he did, *someone*, somewhere, would have been shot, probably killed. No, he had to keep looking ahead, far ahead. And he had to stay focused on that place—wherever it was—that place with a lake by its side. So, with a strained and less-than-stoical resolve, he used the last third of his savings to buy as much "cornbread" as he could get his hands on. Then got back to work.

Only now he was more cautious of where he walked and dealt, and less cautious of who he sold to, even dealing to one of the local prostitutes who everyone else who was working a corner refused, on account of her being pregnant. It seemed absurd that drug dealers should have ethical inhibitions, but they did. And it was for that very reason that Steven went out of his *way* to sell to her—it was a matter of principle.

Because if there was anything he detested, it was how, when one human being held something that another desperately wanted, they acquired an instant self-righteousness. He'd seen it living on the streets; the ridiculous things people did with the homeless, crazies, drunks, and addicts who were begging there, middle-class men and women delivering a sanctimonious speech while handing down an apple or a half-eaten sandwich, explaining in a sympathetic voice that they weren't giving money as they feared it would be spent in the wrong way. He sometimes daydreamt of the perfect reaction to this, picturing himself dangling one of those good people's paycheques in his hand, miming that he was just about to hand it over, saying, "Now, you poor misled thing, I *want* to give you this, but I'm pretty sure you'll spend it on wrongful things, on things that won't nurture you or fulfill you in any way, but will empty you instead—like an Audi, or needless renovations, or manicures for your lawn, your nails, your Chihuahua." His eyebrows raised piteously into a sloping capital "A." "Okay?" Then he'd place their cheque in his pocket, hand over some food stamps instead, pat them on the brow with condescending benevolence, and prance away with an air that was so self-satisfied it would look like he was floating.

In Steven's mind, he sold crack to a pregnant woman *because* it was ethical, because it was her choice to make and not his, or anyone else's for that matter. However, such progressive thinking *also* had its drawbacks. In mid-July 1985, her water broke, and knowing she would have to go to the hospital and through the double ordeal of childbirth and withdrawal completely on her own, under duress and in pain, she stumbled out onto the Boardwalk to find a little peace and euphoria to inhale just before the ambulance could take her away.

It was a mess. Seeing her, people who normally stayed away from the brazen and troubled youth came out of their houses and crowded around, the skin of their bare arms representing every shade in a caramel rainbow, Irish descendants, Sri Lankan immigrants, Bangladeshi, Chinese, Vietnamese, Philippine, Indian, Jamaican, Somali, Congolese, their languages washing into one another, making the same urgent observation that no one seemed to really understand but Steven. Sirens undulated, became swollen, grew closer from two directions. The prostitute screamed. The throng pulsed with the sound of her voice. Some men ran to help guide the ambulance to the scene while two women moved in closer, touching her belly, her back. She shoved their hands away, faltering onto the cement now, her mini-skirted legs straight out in front of her, filmed over with the glistening of amniotic fluid speckled with blood capillaries, like black lint on a pink sweater. She held her head, quivered, seemed about to scream again. Someone shawled a thin blanket over her shoulders, which she tried to shirk off but didn't succeed. The bleat of a siren close by, doors slamming shut, a white-uniformed man muscling through the bodies for a preliminary assessment of the situation, then back out for the stretcher, clearing people away.

What happened next happened fast. Steven mumbled a demand to someone standing beside him, took their pipe, un-Saran-Wrapped a rock from his pocket, then straddled her from behind, squatting, hands out in front of her face—and lit it. She knew what to do. The crowd did not. When the paramedics parted the mob, they paused to gawp at Steven in the same way that everyone else was. No one was able to speak. He stood up, pocketing the spent pipe, meeting their eyes. Were it another time in his life he would have happily spat onto the ground at their feet, but now, all he could think to do was turn around, pull the hood of his hoodie over his head, hands in the kangaroo pocket at his belly, and slink into the afternoon streets.

He saved manically for the two months following this, talked less, thought more. He thought of the people in the asylum, of the families in the baroque suburbs that he'd briefly been a part of, of the pushers and gunrunners around him, of the pregnant prostitute, of Kirsti, of Sam. And he wondered, maybe there was no such thing as "getting out." Maybe everyone was living in a kind of institution, just like the asylum was, where the fodder was feeding the stock feeding the fodder. Maybe everyone was festering in their own self-inflicted wounds.

Then the opportunity of a lifetime landed in his lap. It presented itself one commonplace morning after he'd groaned out of bed and was walking into his living room, adjusting his testicles deep in his jockey shorts. He stopped, standing there looking at a man with a handgun raised up at him, a revolver. He was checking it, winking an eye through the holes of the cylinders as if Steven were the sun, rotating it full circle, deliberately, steadily, like a sundial in time-lapse photography. When he was satisfied, he set it back in its housing with the dark of his hand.

"That's the kid you should talk to," said Kipp, delicately gesturing for Steven to take his hands out of his underwear.

"Y'don't say."

"Got *my* word. But ask around if y'like. He's sound." Kipp looked pleased that Steven's hands were now in his armpits, forearms across his chest. "Stevie, this's Brice. Brice needs to move some shit."

Brice then explained his predicament. He wasn't from around there, was just passing through in fact, had heard Kipp's name from a few different people, and needed to buy some guns. He also needed to unload a bulk of crack he'd fortuitously come into. And fast, before he started crossing borders. When he said the weight and price—no haggling tolerated—Steven could barely believe his ears, trying to shift coolly, still standing around in his underwear. Okay. Deal. Brice wrote an address on a ripped corner of a flyer and told him to be there at nine that night, sharp. He bought three handguns from Kipp and, before closing the door, addressed Steven once more, leaning on the doorknob in his stylish clothes, his shirt a faded pink, hair feathered, a sapphire-coloured stud in one of his earlobes: "See ya t'night then."

This was it. Steven could resell the shipment to the guy who normally supplied him and in this one transaction make enough money to leave the inner city for good. He counted his pennies and was short four hundred and eighty dollars. He borrowed five from Kipp and waited for the sun to rise through the smokestacks, leisurely arc over the wires, and ebb behind the apartment blocks.

It wasn't ideal that the address was in the Jane and Finch area, the traditional rival of Regent Park, but he doubted it mattered much. He was meeting someone who had nothing to do with the city, knew nothing about the squabbling of adversary neighbourhoods, the politics of local demographics. He took the bus, even paid, and arrived early, more excited than nervous, rubbing his hands together as if he were cold. And when he walked into the apartment and got a sense of the general atmosphere inside, any apprehension he might have had thinly slipped away like sweetplastic smoke. This wasn't a drug deal from the movies with shootout potential; it was real life, with real synthesized music from a ghetto blaster, real middle-aged men sitting comfortably around a table who were benign-enough looking to be real store owners and restaurant proprietors. They looked so respectable, in fact, that he doubted any of them even lived there. They were the kind of people who had houses, and in nice neighbourhoods. Green ones. Kind ones.

Business first, they exchanged merchandise for money, Brice counting it cautiously and Steven taking a good whiff of the drugs, which smelled and looked exactly like the stuff perpetually jammed under his fingernails from cutting it. Done deal, duffle bag in hand, standing a bit gawkily, they asked if he wanted to stay for a drink, somebody pouring a glass of amber fluid from one of the three bottles on the table, lighting a cigarette. The liquor looked expensive.

Steven glanced at the door, back at the table, down at the bag in his hand. He felt light, calm, like he was about to go on his first-ever holiday, already packed and ready. He hadn't had much to celebrate in his life, but he certainly had something now.

"Sure." He found himself shrugging and sat down beside the most taciturn of them all, the duffle on the floor beside him, leaning against his foot.

"Bourbon?"

"Sure." Steven had only ever heard of bourbon before, never seen it, tasted it, smelled it: a smell of perfumed honey, he noticed, now that he was swishing it around in his glass.

"Cheers."

"Cheers."

"Chin." *Clink-clink. Clink.*

And it even tasted good. Velvety and smooth, a welcomed warmth slipping down the walls of his esophagus, wetting the membranes. A second sip. Conversation rolling along easily. Cigarette offered. Thanks. Lighter sparks. A third sip. One of the men starts telling a long joke about a crocodile in a bar, which even turns out to be funny. Laughter. A fourth. The man to his right sidles closer. Steven eyeing him. A fifth. Slower now. The sixth more syrupy than the others, while a fuzziness rises from the miniscule hairs that cover his body, pushing through like dandelion heads above the grass and blossoming across his skin. He finds himself struggling to keep his eyes open and has the sensation that he's gyrating with a kind of elasticity, like his head is a bowling ball slotted onto the end of a car antenna, slowly tipping over, a tug-of-war against gravity, where gravity is sure to win. His hair eases onto the tabletop, ear to the cool Formica surface. Laughter swells in the muted background like sirens. There's a hand on his lap, sliding up his leg. He feels the bowling ball of his head becoming heavier. Pressing into the table now. Sinking into it. Someone else's hand is in his hair. On his scalp. Which is imbedding itself deeper into the Formica where it's— all. Suddenly. Black.

It was morning. September 14, 1985. Blinds drawn, light seeping in around the edges. He'd been slipping back into a dream he couldn't remember, into a sleep that was hungry and avid, that clawed the hours into its dark mouth one at a time, never quite satiated. When he finally managed to ply himself into consciousness, he was unable to stop blinking, a room he didn't recognize gradually coming into focus through an opaque film.

He was on a bed, on his stomach, wrists bound and tied to the headboard. He could feel that his T-shirt was still on but that his pants, socks, and underwear were not. Struggling to focus on the knot, the two separate images from each of his eyes slowly melding together, he wriggled himself closer, clumsy hands beginning to untie it. Having freed his wrists, he explored the back of his head, which was sore for some reason. He found tingling bald patches there, where, it seemed, his hair had been torn out. When he rolled over, the pain smarted for the first time in his sphincter and far up into his rectal cavity; blood was on the sheets, marbled with the brown of his fecal matter and suspicious pearly threads.

It hurt to walk, toilet paper clotted between his buttocks, coagulating into his underwear. He crept through the house until he was sure there was no one there, then started rifling through it noisily, through the fridge, cabinets, drawers, tipping over chairs, overturning sofas. No duffle bag, no money, not even some pocket change on a bedside table.

He stopped in the centre of a ransacked bedroom, standing on a tangle of sheets, catching his breath, needing to think. He thought about his next move, which was clearly to get out. Out of Regent Park, out of the crack scene, out of this vile, sickened city forever. And he was never coming back. Never. He didn't have it in him to ploddingly work off his debt to Kipp, to start saving from scratch—again—to have to explain to everyone what happened to his "big out."

What he needed was some quick money. Greyhound fare. That was all. And he even knew how he was going to get it. He found a knife in a drawer, and unable to think of anyone else who would carry around a coiled fist of cash, the idea of mugging a fellow dealer crossed his mind—as had been done unto him. But he happened to know, and from a very reliable source, that most of the dealers in the Jane and Finch area had handguns. No. No, what he needed to find was some stupid piece-of-shit yuppie and snatch his wallet from him. That much would be easy. And no risk involved. Just a clueless rich guy who wouldn't know poverty if it walked right up to his back and stabbed him.

He stepped outside, got his bearings, and started walking. Then walked faster. The brisk stride caused the rips along his rectum to sting and burn. And the more he felt the damage, the more he wondered if there was a foreign body left inside him, like a sliver—slivers? Maybe they'd done it to him with something wooden as well. A cooking spoon, the handle of a toilet plunger, the leg of a chair. He bit his lip, tightened his grip on the knife in his pocket, and saw a gas station ahead, an expensive car pulling into it. He angled straight toward it.

The chubby man that stepped out fit the bill perfectly. He was blond, dressed in pricey casualwear, busy checking his watch like his time was the most precious thing in the universe. He was looking around a little uneasily, probably feeling more than a touch out of place, as if his low-fuel light had just flickered while on his way out of town, up the 400, heading to his cottage and a piece of property he took for granted, no doubt, which had fallen into his lap in the way that it did for rich people.

Steven clenched his jaw. He didn't even care if something went wrong when the blade came out of his pocket. No. He didn't care about anything anymore. He had to be hard. (Hadn't he already learned that somewhere?) Harder than the world was to him.

As Steven approached, he felt himself becoming increasingly acrid, numb, a loose canon. He stopped just within reach of the blond man, at the same time as the trigger on the gas pump clicked shut, the man's tank finally topped up with premium unleaded. The man was still looking away, replacing the nozzle into the pump while Steven waited for him to turn around, waited for him to take notice, to clue in to what Steven was there to do.

Then something happened. The rich man paused, stood suddenly still, looking around as if he were gathering critical information of some kind, searching up at the signs, along the street, through the store window. Then he stiffened, petrified, like he knew what was going to happen next, knew that Steven was right behind him and about to take a grimy knife out of his pocket and threaten him with his life. There was something unsettling about this, troubling. But Steven took the knife out of his pocket anyway. Then he squeezed the handle until his fingers were white, and stepped forward. The microseconds ticked by, Steven was growing uneasy, nervous, involuntarily tightening his sphincter. He winced.

Then, all at once, the man spun wildly around and threw his hands into the air like he was in a bank robbery. "Ohhh . . . nn . . . uhhh," he muttered, paralyzed.

Steven wiped his nose with the hand that wasn't holding his knife, though it also panged with the scent of the oxidized blade, of copper pennies melting in his palm. "Give me your wallet."

The rich guy was frozen, unable to respond.

"I said give me your fuckin' wallet!"

The man whisked it out, held it between them. Steven lunged forward, snatched it, and ran.

On the bus, he picked Cedric's wallet apart, held his driver's licence up to look at the picture. His mind was blank. He thought nothing, felt nothing. Outside the window, flashes of linking towns and sprawling municipalities streaked by, the highway a black thread stitching cities together. Up ahead another city cinched closer. Another city. Steven dropped the emptied wallet onto the Greyhound floor, looked outside.

Another city.

There is a light that emanates from
the limestone bricks of big centres,

a disparate one, singular even, which
you can only catch at the rarest moments,

dusk, dawn, one of those non-rush-hour hours.
When the buildings covet and cradle their

grey stillness so tightly you'd think
it was sacred, and mistake it for being.

Quiet dangling from their walls like ivy, as if,
on the other side, there were a small-town home.

Not like the kind we were born in, or the den
we rebelled to leave, nor even the one we swore

we'd build ourselves, placing everything—just—
so—but instead the one we should have.

The kind of home that knows so well, forgives
so wantonly, that there isn't even blame there

that we didn't.

Melissa's cross-country travelling companion broke one of their rare no-music-or-radio silences just after Medicine Hat. "This just . . . this feels so Canadian. Don't you think?" she asked.

But what Melissa thought was that she was about to come across as a humbug again. Because to be honest, she'd always hated the question, had never seen the point of it really—all the literature and art collectives, the radio programs and television documentaries that explored the query of what it meant to be Canadian. In our scrambling need for an identity, thought Melissa, we'd opted for the worst way of acquiring one: namely by working backwards. We started with the naive idea that we could find a parameter for us all to fit inside, trace a silhouette with all the things we are and aren't, define a "we" by using the paltry measure of our few, few common denominators. Why should we care about the shape of the one paper-thin shell that might encapsulate us all? What kind of culture would be driven by such a manic search for its own confinement? If we spent half as much energy not in concentrating on what this fictitious capsule might look like, but instead on filling it, on cramming it with original art and thought and science and cuisine, on driving forward unimpeded by our own backward clichés and questions, those blurry lines would draw themselves. The truth was that Melissa didn't feel very Canadian, didn't feel moved when she saw her flag rippling in the wind. But she did feel that she liked the wind. And it's there, she knew, that the drawing should really begin. Right there. At the beginning.

"Good question. I don't . . . really know what I'm in the mood for. Think I had the ribs last time . . ." Neil was scanning the George Bigliardi's Dining Lounge menu, a blind hand reaching onto the table in front of him, finding his ice water, fingerprints smudging the condensation along the sides of his glass. "How about you?" he asked, looking up at Cedric.

Neil Murray was a man who had always understood that there were things that permeated quietly, things that leached into our veins from other places we've lived, other skies that we've walked beneath, silently coating our arterial walls like minerals rimming a water pipe, a thin dusting that patiently bloomed into something like frost, slowly thickening, making our future movements less sudden, less sure. Yes, some things permeated quietly. While others, like this lunch hour with Cedric Johnson, did not.

Neil wavered. Shifted in his seat, anxious. He sipped his water again. Put the glass back on the table. "Cedric? You okay?"

"Neil," Cedric declared, his pupils wide and glossy, holding his closed menu like a plaque he'd just been presented with much custom and import. He placed it gently onto the white of the tablecloth in front of him. "Neil, I am *so* glad to see you."

Neil picked up his water again, sipped from it. As a rule, Cedric wasn't an odd man, wasn't given to unpredictable episodes or capricious outbursts. And the fact that he'd just said he was *glad* to see Neil, of all things, was an undeniable red flag. Because Neil happened to know that, this noon hour more than ever, he was the last person in the world Cedric was glad to see.

"Oh. Well." Another sip. "I'm glad to see you too." He lied unconvincingly, looking around the room. One of the restaurant hosts was leading an older couple to a spot against the wall. Brass railings divided the chain of tables, the antique light fixtures refracting only a slight sheen off the dark-wood panelling, creating a cave-black dim that was difficult to adjust to when stepping in from the bright streetscape of fresh snow outside. Three other businessmen were settling into their chairs nearby. "So then," Neil ventured, looking over his business partner (*ex*-business partner now) with circumspection, "what are you gonna have? The ribs?"

Cedric rested his hands on his closed menu, slid forward in his chair. "Neil. Listen. You remember when I was mugged, by one of those greasy . . . hoodlum . . . *vagrants*? Remember that?"

Neil smacked his lips, eyeing the upper reaches of Cedric's potbelly, the blond of his hair tarnished with strands of grey, the upper corners of his forehead beginning their sparse, patient climb. His expression was utterly sincere. "Uh, yeah. Yeah I think it was right after we met, at a gas station around Jane and Finch, right? Must have been five, six years ago now?" Neil shook his head regrettably at his glass on the table, which, he noticed, at this rate, would need refilling soon—immediately, in fact. He picked it up and took a final noisy gulp, tossing it back like a tequila shooter.

"Exactly," Cedric agreed. "And you wanna know something crazy? I just, seconds ago, went through the same thing. The exact same shit."

Neil feigned shock. "My god, in the bathroom . . . or . . . ?" knowing that Cedric had been in front of him over the last "few seconds," along with the entire morning for that matter. They'd been making phone calls, moving the last of Neil's files into the back of his SUV, finalizing the mini-takeover. He glanced around for the waiter, not knowing what to do with his hands, wishing he had more water.

"And you know what's even crazier? Even though I knew everything about it, *knew* that he wouldn't stab me or . . . even hurt me, I was just as scared the second time around. Scared shitless. I mean, this is all," he held up his hands to indicate the dining lounge around him, "all so real. You know? Just as real as that greasy little . . ." he cut himself short as the waiter had appeared abruptly, interjecting.

"Sorry, gentlemen. Can I get you something from the bar to start off?"

"Look." Cedric made another gesture with his hand, shooing the man away, rolling his fingers out to another part of the room, seemingly a faraway corner. "Could you just . . . screw off for a bit? I've only got a couple seconds here."

Neil and the waiter both hung in the moment, stunned, not knowing what to do, watching him closely.

Cedric leaned farther into the table, the crease at the centre of his forehead etching a rift down his face, a blue eye pinned to each side, a kind of dividing line, Neil had once thought—half the man that he'd liked and half he despised. How similar the two looked.

Cedric continued in a lowered voice, undeterred by the waiter still standing by, still dumbfounded. "I'm having the strangest experience of my life, Neil. And I know this'll . . . this'll sound crazy. I know. But . . . I'm having these flashing *moments*, where I'm back, in my own skin, during these—I don't know—*instances* in my life that were . . . big, I guess. And I mean that I'm physically, actually, there, reliving them."

The waiter stepped back, smoothly slipping away into the din of the restaurant, watching Cedric over his shoulder as he walked to the bar.

"I see," Neil muttered, sitting back in his chair. "Moments . . . like . . . now?"

"Yes. Moments like now. Because this is pretty much the last time we speak, isn't it? We leave here, without saying a word of what we're both thinking through this entire lunch, and we walk away."

Neil's expression was a concerned one. "Hmm." He'd recently read about a rare form of epilepsy where, instead of going into a grand or petit mal seizure, the person experienced "a slipping" into another personality or reference of time. Though he wasn't sure where he'd read it, could have been a cursory glimpse over the tabloid rack while he was waiting in line somewhere. "So . . . let's just pretend for a second that . . . this isn't crazy, and that you're really sitting here . . . again. For the second time."

"I am, Neil."

"Right." Neil rubbed the back of his head. "So, when . . . I mean, how old are you?"

Cedric squinted, looked at the carpet. "I . . . don't know. What year is it?"

Neil noticed that the melting ice in his glass had produced a few more millimetres of water. He sucked what he could out of it, placed it back on the table, and lowered his voice, almost to a whisper, "The year is 1991."

Cedric looked back down at the carpet, more busily this time. "I . . . don't really know how old I was in '91; I'd have to figure it out. But, I mean, how does that matter? If I *could* tell you how old I was back then . . . offhand . . . how would that help?"

Neil sank back into his chair again, though this time very slowly, the dark wood of it pressing along his spine, his sides.

The candle lamp on the table fluttered for a moment, then, as if to compensate for its transitory quavering, continued to glow with an even brighter, steady flame.

"So then . . ." Neil began after his drawn-out silence, "tell me, now that you're here, reliving this, are you . . . gonna do anything different, say anything different . . . the second time around? I mean, do you think you're here to—I don't know   change things? Do something right . . . for once?"

"No," Cedric said, clearly smarting a bit from the jab. "No, it doesn't seem to work that way. I can't really *change* any-thing . . . except the moment I'm reliving. And no matter how radically I change it, it doesn't seem to have any effect on . . . on things that happen afterwards."

"Hmm. Right. Yeah. Guess that makes sense." And it did to Neil. He thought about himself in the past, as a boy, in South Africa.

And in looking back, he could only see himself as a fated individual, fated to move to Canada, marry, have a daughter, divorce,
get screwed over by his business partner. Now that he thought
of it, it was intriguing to consider that fate couldn't exist in our
present or future, but that it could in our past. Which was apparently the case for Cedric, in this experience he was having. While
he might be able to revisit a past moment, a past self, he would
have to be doing so as a self who had an unalterable future. The
past we can visit. But we can only do so *as* visitors; our itineraries
already printed, stamped, and unredeemable. Like a tourist in an
old photo—already destined. Already damned.

"So if you *can*, as you say, at least change these moments
you're reliving," Neil posited, "what're you gonna change about
this one?"

"Well . . . I guess . . . I guess to start with, I just . . . I'd want
you to know that I—you know—felt bad that . . . we . . . our little
agency . . . uhm . . ."

"That you fucked me over?"

"No. Neil. I *didn't* fuck you over. I mean . . . it was just . . . it
was a clear and simple business decision. And one that, believe
me, you would've made yourself. If the tables were turned."

"Really? You happen to know what I would've done? That's
great. You're a regular clairvoyant, in all kinds of ways, it sounds."

"Look, what I'm saying is . . . I'm saying . . . well. I guess I'm
trying to say I'm sorry. Okay? I'm sorry for the way it all turned
out, for you, between us. I mean . . . it was . . . it was unfortunate."

"Well, I'll agree with you there." Neil hadn't meant for his tone
to be quite as icy as it was. He *was* being apologized to. Though
at the same time, he was glad for the effect his cynicism was
producing.

"Yeah." Cedric sighed, looking down at the cover of his menu.
He ran a slow, thoughtful hand along its surface. "Yeah."

Cedric Johnson had come into Neil's life in 1985 while playing
on one of the local golf courses. They'd both heard of each other in

the insurance business, and when a common acquaintance introduced them, they took the opportunity to shake hands, exchange cards, network amiably. It turned out they had a lot in common. They were both the leading brokers in each of their small agencies, loved cars, hated sports, had blasé marriages, an only daughter, and lived to golf. They'd also both had nightmarish run-ins with corrupt landladies, excitedly swapping details to see if it had been the same one. They began meeting to tee off together somewhat often, going for a drink after the last hole, and when Neil started complaining about the fact that his agency had just lost one of its major multinational insurance companies to write for and that his clients were more than unhappy about it, Cedric pointed out that there was a position opening over at *his* agency, complete with an empty office and that same multinational company to sell for. Allowing Neil to keep his clients, keep them happy, and even have a modest increase in his monthly income. It was a nice thing to do.

However, a year later, there was a management shift at this new office where both of them worked, and the person that Cedric and Neil had to answer to, and deal with on a day-to-day basis, was, in Neil's words, "a manipulative power-happy prick." Cedric wholeheartedly agreed with this assessment, and as the atmosphere in their workplace disintegrated, he took to meticulously reading over the company's contracts of employment, looking for a way out. Which he found, a loophole that would allow them both to leave the agency and take with them the bulk of their clients as well. And, they theorized over beers and potato skins, with their two unencumbered portfolios—the two largest in the company—they would easily have the critical mass to set up their own agency, be their own bosses. They discussed it for months, met with lawyers, and, finally, made the bold move and put in their notices.

It worked flawlessly. Their new agency soon became a thriving and lucrative venture, with little overhead and heaps of profit. Each of them bought a new car, looked into cottage real estate, either did renovations on their existing house or bought a new one altogether. Bright kitchens, sterling pot sets hanging in a descending row, jars of olive oils crammed with aesthetic herbs, lined up on backlit shelves never to be touched, chic sofas and armchairs aligned to a new and towering entertainment system, complete with surround-sound speakers and state-of-the-art VHS.

The two families got together more often, even if their daughters didn't really get along, despite being about the same age. Neil's daughter was an outgoing and playful girl of eight, and Melissa, Cedric's daughter, was a nine-year-old who was brooding, reticent, and only wanted to be on her own to draw and paint pictures. And in Neil's household, there were no paints. They made a mess.

Until the time came, in 1989, that their client base had grown too large for them to deal with themselves, and they had to hire an additional broker. With the acquisition of another person into the company, they also needed to revisit their initial contract. Both of them would remain the co-owners but would have one and potentially more employees beneath them. Cedric, with his affinity for dealing with contracts, took care of it, and while doing so had his lawyer draft an extra item into it, known as a shotgun clause, which would allow either party to make a buyout offer to the other, at any time. However, if the offer wasn't fair, the other party could turn around and buy the company out from the offerer, for that same unfair sum of money. Meaning that if either of them were to come into financial hardship, the other could take complete advantage of his business partner's weakened position, swindling him out of his half of the company for very, very little cash. Neil noticed it, heard Cedric's plea to take it to a lawyer himself and have it looked over (costing Neil at least a thousand dollars in the process), thought about the unlikelihood of financial hardship coming his way, considered their friendship, the golf games, the endless banter of cars, the pitchers of beer, even the odd family holidays they'd taken together, and signed it.

He didn't think of it again until his marriage began to crumble, a fault line slipping between him and his wife, in the slow and steady way that fault lines do. He speculated that it had probably been there all along, unnoticed in the foundation of their relationship, steadily prying it apart.

Meanwhile Cedric had inherited a surprising figure from his passing parents, who'd been killed in a car wreck. Cedric was gloomy, but grateful, and the two men commemorated the bittersweet news with a bottle of single-malt Scotch, aged twenty-seven years.

"I'm sorry for your loss," said Neil, holding his heavy tumbler within reach of Cedric's. A slow clank. Settling back into his armchair, Neil noted how glassy his friend's eyes were. After taking a sip, raising his eyebrows, he added, "And I want you to know, if you ever need any help, at all, finishing this bottle, I'd be happy to oblige." It was the kind of remark Cedric would normally have chuckled at but this time only managed a cheerless smile.

A month later, Neil's wife filed for divorce.

Without surprise, and probably for the better, he was only given minimal custody of his daughter (every second weekend), he lost the house, the most expensive of his two cars, and had to pay what he learned was a steeper-than-usual alimony and child support. Neil was defeated, miserable, broke, and perhaps a touch guilty of neglecting his clients, and certainly of being seen less on the fairway than was good for business. Following Christmas, once the calendar had rolled around to 1991, with the US Congress authorizing Operation Desert Storm and a massacre in South Africa killing forty-five mourners at a funeral, Cedric chose to lay his offer down on the table. It was an absurd and petty sum, but a sum he knew perfectly well Neil would be forced to take.

Neil wasn't in the mood to beg or remonstrate. He'd almost become used to signing papers that were in the spirit of his losing streak. He did find another job easily enough, and when hired, asked for a full month before he would have to begin, feeling like he needed some time to reorganize his life, get his bearings back.

He found himself strolling through the underground mall system, looking for something he'd always wanted, though couldn't quite pin down what that was. He was in a peculiar mood, thinking too much, feeling like he was somehow on the verge, like he might do something out of the ordinary, at any moment. Something different, rash, impulsive.

He had sauntered into a novelty item store, lifted a few gadgets, ran his fingers across the illuminated bristles of a kitsch fibre-optics lamp. Then he noticed a prism. His mother had collected prisms when he was a boy in South Africa, and he remembered them being heavier as a child. He held it up to one of the ceiling lamps and grinned at the colours that came out the other side. It occurred to him that there was something there, something in this chunk of glass, in the light that was passing through it, in the movement of the rays as he tilted it in different angles. Something from another land, another sky, another time. Something that permeated quietly.

He bought the prism and put it on the kitchen counter of his new and echoingly empty condo. Whenever he passed it, it seemed to jog some other memory of his life—his life before it had all unravelled, that is. Some other hue in the landscape of his childhood, which, it felt, he'd almost forgotten.

He had been born in a coastal suburb of Cape Town, South Africa, in 1956, a time when apartheid was still quietly sinking its roots into the soil there. Though Neil recalls nothing about the politics, never having heard a word of the anti-gathering acts being passed or that segregation was being introduced into the cities, races being pushed out of them and into their respective townships and "Homelands."

What he does remember is driving around in his father's Hudson, sitting in the backseat with his face just above the rolled-down window, hair flapping, bare legs dangling over the edge of the upholstery, watching the world float by through the sea-salt air, the drifting of colourful shapes and murky forms. When his father drove to the harbour district to drop off the family's nanny at her own apartment, it was squatters and shanties that streaked past, smoke from a cooking fire, then, perhaps, in the space between a set of buildings, a woman's body fluid with dance, two notes of a singing voice filling the car's interior for an instant, then trailing off behind them, emptying it.

Neil's family had had three coloureds that worked in and around their house—a maid, a gardener, and a nanny. Of these, he and his sister (there were only two of them, two years apart) preferred the nanny, Ollie. She was a large woman, had false teeth that she would take out to show when parents weren't around, and a vibrant scarf that she wore over her head at all times: crimson, ginger, azure, jade. Ollie was, as far as the children were concerned, part of the family, a second mother, the one that comforted them when they scraped their knees at play, who washed their hands before meals, made them check under their finger-nails for dirt when they came in from their tree fort in the yard. She would even come along on holidays to take care of them, singing whenever she was alone with the children, alternating between humming and lyrics, both versions foreign and soothing to Neil's ear, both common and ethereal.

Neil's mother had—besides her family, of course—two great loves in life: Victorian literature and prisms. The latter was a hobby that came to her quite by accident, having toured through a well-lit house once where there were several prisms on display. There was something about them that captivated her immediately, the way this spectrum of tints and tones could exist, tightly bound, some-how encoded inside of a single ray of light, and she endeavoured to have a few around her own house. This "few" turned into many, and then to whole prism sets, prism apparatuses forming rings of glass triangles and hexagons where light was refracted and re-refracted through every one of them, creating impressive and vibrant patterns that changed throughout the day, even to—and this was Neil's personal favourite—a prism mobile, where a series of small Swarovski crystals dangled from glass rods like an invisible marionette, poised and waiting for a puppeteer. And when his father was having one of his cocktail parties, the heat and motion of bodies in the salon was enough to send this mobile turning on the axis of its nylon thread, casting colours in every direction like a disco ball, a projected net of spectral dots circling the open space of their living room, gliding over the yellowwood strips on the floor, between the churning bodies where it climbed the fabric of dresses and descended the broad shoulders of suit jackets.

But the real reason it was his favourite was that, sometimes, it moved for no reason at all. That is to say that there were mornings when there wouldn't be the slightest breath of wind, an immaculate calm. And still, the mobile found a way to stir, pivoting slightly, slyly, in miniscule degrees. Completely of its own volition.

If he noticed this when he was on his way outside to play, he would stop in his tracks to watch it for a minute, mesmerized. Because this was a mysterious thing, something he couldn't explain. And looking back at it, what Neil found interesting is that he never felt the *need* to explain it. Later on, as a Western adult, he would be surrounded by, and immersed in, a mentality that completely opposed this, where, if one were to encounter something they couldn't explain, it was understood that they should at least *try* to explain it, at least make an attempt, consult a resource, experiment. And for the most part, it was a mentality he subscribed to. Even if there was a part of him that still wondered whether or not it was the right thing to do, wondered if, perhaps, we were all, at every stage in our life, children first and learners—absorbers of knowledge, dissectors, and logical-conclusionists—second. Wondered if we all *understood* mystery long before we were ever taught to explain it away.

The first memory he has of this *need* for an explanation came with words. Scary words, which kept cropping up in his parents' discussions at the most unpredictable of times, discussions that were becoming tense and uneasy—loud when they shouldn't have been, quiet when they shouldn't have been. Words like: protest, bans, unrest, riot, treason, catalyst, Mandela, saboteur, militant, terrorist, Sharpeville, massacre, emigrate, stable, fellow, commonwealth, nation, Canada.

And then the news came.

"Hey." Neil's father was standing in the centre of the room after work, clapping his hands together. "Guess what, you kids? Daddy got another job today. And you know where it is? It's in a place where you can make *snowmen*! Can you imagine that! How fun will that be?"

Neil exchanged a look with his sister, who turned to look outside, at the planks running out of their tree fort. She spoke at the window, "Um—Daddy, are we gonna take Ollie with us? Like on holidays?"

Her mother chortled from the sidelines, using her pet name, "No, Meisie, Ollie has to stay here with *her* family. We're going to go to this new place with just *our* family. With just us. Okay?"

His sister was confused with multiple things that were layered into this statement, panic rising, tears flooding her eyes.

"So . . ." Neil broke in before his sister could burst, "in this new place, how far's the walk to the beach?"

It was their parents turn to exchange a quick look. "Well, I don't know, son," his father said, "I guess we'll just have to see, won't we?"

It was late October 1966 when their plane touched down on the Toronto runway. Neil remembers it well. It was overcast, drizzling, cold. And let alone was there no beach with sand, waves, or fisherfolk, nor any of this oft-alluded-to "snow" to build snowmen with, something, some disease probably, or maybe just the cold itself, had tragically killed every tree in the country. The elms and maples in their new neighbourhood stretched up into the grey air with nothing more than naked twigs, branches that were as devoid of leaves as the root systems buried under the soil in his native, and increasingly beloved, South Africa. Dead leaves rotted in the dark spaces under hedges, festered on yellow lawns, clotted the gutters beside the sidewalks.

Their parents tried to lift the children's palpably heavy spirits by embracing the few local customs with enthusiasm, and with Halloween just around the corner, their mother brought them to a gargantuan drugstore and told them they could each choose whatever they wanted from the aisle of masks and costumes. Dragging their feet across the linoleum tiles, their first time ever with shoes on in a store, they stood in front of the synthetic jack-o'-lanterns. Neil lifted his arm as if it were unbearably heavy and chose the mask of a sad scarecrow. His sister a sad clown. When the big night came, they were pulled moping from house to house, walking on the implausibly long streets amid zombies, Draculas, ghosts, passing one another with little ceremony. When it was over, he and his sister traded candy on their living room floor, sliding like-groups of crinkling wrappers across at each other with the detachment of shifting commodities on the stock exchange.

There were two things that lifted Neil out of this slump. Springtime, when tiny but innumerable green flames began unfurling from every dead branch in the nation (turns out they weren't dead after all); and, two years after that first spring, when he got his hands on a car magazine, lent to him by a friend at school. Initially, the magazine helped transport him to the free and glorious sensations of driving in his father's Hudson, which the family, "perversely" to Neil's mind, also left behind. But then he realized that the magazine gave him an instant connection to other boys in his grade, as well as something to talk about with his father, something that put them on common ground for the very first time. He came to discover that the interest in cars was a kind of club where, if you had a bit of knowledge, or even a preference, you were automatically admitted into its innermost circle, its opinionated fraternity. His parents noted this budding interest, and he soon had subscriptions to several monthly and bi-monthly automobile publications, which were then left lying around the house, pages spilled open, photos of metal with gracile curves, pinups in his room.

When, in 1969, his father decided to buy a new car, Neil went along with him through every stage of research, test driving, selection, and purchase. Neil felt he could judge a vehicle best by how things looked from the driver's seat, carefully examining the interior, the dials and gauges. He preferred dashes that were clean, uncluttered, seats that were non-leather, supportive, comfortable. When his father had finally signed the papers at a dealership, Neil was sure that the decision was made more or less on his recommendations. He was happy to have been of service.

While growing up in Toronto, in the well-to-do residential area of the Annex, he'd had to find ways of integrating into city life, and when he couldn't, he utilized the newfound and applauded skill of not complaining. But that didn't mean that South Africa wasn't in the back of his mind; it was, and at times even came to the forefront, entered his conversations, became something that was important to highlight. "Me? No actually, I wasn't born here. I'm from SoewthAvrikuh." He liked how even the mere word "Africa" carried with it a certain exoticness, an instant flare, consistently conjuring images of leaping gazelles and elephants trampling the savannah, all to the mental soundtrack of bongo drums and monkey calls. Yeah, he seemed to imply whenever the wild continent was mentioned, that was him, that was Neil; he was raised there, was a direct product of that striking place; he'd *lived* those images his friends were conjuring. Whatever they happened to be.

Once or twice he was confronted with strange and slanderous references to his homeland, which, because they didn't make any sense at all (and were probably based out of a more than understandable jealousy), he'd thoughtlessly dismissed. Until he was in a classroom at the age of fifteen and his social studies teacher handed out the first hard evidence, sliding it lightly onto his desk. It was a photocopied article from *Time Magazine*, about apartheid, which, undeniably, was a word that Neil had heard before. It was even a word that was inherently understood—in the way that his relationship to the coloureds who had helped raise him was understood, in the way that mystery was understood. Without questions.

Before the class was through, he'd found himself in a desperate argument with the teacher, then with other classmates, the whole time standing firm behind the claim that *Time Magazine* was a sham, that it was making uninformed accusations on the actual, true-to-life *reality* of apartheid. Neil knew better. He was born and raised there, wasn't he? He'd seen this phenomenon first-hand, and everything was fine with it, he was sure, he *knew*. He was SoewthAvrikun.

He knew, that is, in the same way he had been sure he knew Cedric. Naivety is always obvious, glaring, tacit; unless it's your own. That day, at the age of fifteen, Neil began his personal, complicated, and three-decade-long slide from a head-held-high pride about his native country to a head-hung-low shame. From a boy who shouted out his origin above the squeaking of swing sets to a receding-hairline insurance broker on the golf green, leaning over his putter, hunched, small, and mumbling the same country name under his breath before quickly changing the subject.

As the topic of the injustices in South Africa mounted in the mid-to-late 1980s, pop culture picking it up and running with it—blockbuster films, television series, tabloid news programs, songs, concerts, venues—fingers began pointing. And it seemed like shame, as always, was appointed to the only people who kept their fingers to themselves. This, Neil found, helped let Canadians off in a way, let them conveniently forget about the long list of things that they had to be ashamed of from their own past. True, they weren't loud with their accusations, weren't belligerent, but they did make it clear that they believed they were in the right, and that, presumably, they always had been. It was a quiet pride. But it happened to be just boisterous enough to drown out the creaking rust of their wrongs.

Yes, South Africa had given Neil shame. But that wasn't all it had given him. Because what he had come to understand, and in the last few months more than ever, is that there were other things, things that permeated quietly, things that seeped in from the different places we've lived, the different skies we've walked beneath. Things that, for Neil, had to do with songs that his nanny had sung to him in another language entirely but whose meaning he had nevertheless understood. Things that had to do with the way sunlight could somehow move, ever so slightly, beads of glass that were suspended on a string. And something about those beads of glass themselves, and the way they could split the sunlight that was moving them, separate it, and lay it out in all its vibrant, disregarded fragments. Neil had been given a way to hold on to mystery, which he had almost forgotten along the way. Thankfully, he was able to recall just enough, enough for it to filter into his thoughts on this noon hour, January 30, 1991, while sitting across from Cedric Johnson. Just enough to allow for this strange conversation to take place, allow Neil to consider these claims of his now ex-business partner as being a real possibility. A small and archaic piece of him that could afford this one suspended moment of believing Cedric.

Cedric cleared his throat, looked into his lap for a second, scratched his chin. "And you know," he said abruptly, "while I'm at it, there's another thing. You remember that one night, when we were all over at your place and were—into the cognac, was it?—and I made a complete ass of myself? God, we were liquored. And there was that . . . I mean, when me and your wife were in the kitchen for that long while, mixing drinks and . . . And you remember all this?"

"Yeah?"

"Well, I just wanted you to know that . . . nothing happened."

"I know."

A pause. "How do you know?"

"Because she told me."

"And you believed her?"

"Yeah."

"Oh."

Cedric looked into his lap again, and this time noticed something. He stretched his back out against the chair behind him, running his hands over his belly. "Guess I was a bit thinner back then too, eh?"

"Thinner?" asked Neil, trying to assess Cedric's paunch that was protruding under the table.

"Well, thinner . . . than I become, I mean."

"Oh. Right." Neil broke off to look around the dining lounge, which was really beginning to fill up. This was crazy really. The conversation, the things exchanged, the suspension of reality. "Well, must say, whatever *is* going on in that head of yours, it's good . . . I mean, good . . . that you . . . kind of came clean, I guess." He turned back to Cedric, who looked suddenly quite concerned.

Cedric snatched his glass of water from the table, the ice tinkling against the sides, his eyes darting around the room as he drank from it. Then he put the glass down a touch too hard on the table, trying to smile. "Sorry?" he said, unfolding his napkin to dab his mouth. "Wha'd'you . . . wha'd'you mean—come clean?" He looked away quickly, scanning the room, pausing at one of the waiters, who was glaring at him while pouring a glass of wine at another table.

Neil observed him for a long minute, noting the slight changes in his gestures, in the nuances of his body language, until he'd watched him long enough to know. He let out a half-snicker, shaking his head, opening his menu. "Nothing. Forget it. I didn't mean anything."

They were words Cedric looked relieved to hear.

"So." Neil ran his finger down the entrees, trying not to look up from the list. "What'r'you gonna have?"

They ate their meals, exchanged pleasantries and chitchat about nothing in particular, and when the waiter stiffly placed the bill on the table, Cedric slapped his Visa onto the billfold without reading the total, signed it a minute later, and they stood to leave.

They shook hands in front of the restaurant, standing on the long-running sidewalk of Church Street, Neil offering Cedric a knowing, loaded smile, which found Cedric again becoming unnerved and ruffled, citing the cold as the reason for his hasty retreat. "Well, I'm off before I freeze to death. Talk soon, old boy," he'd said, turning his back with a final wave.

Neil waved at him in turn. "Talk soon."

Neil's car was parked at the curb, and he hopped over the slush ruts, got in, and waited for the engine to warm, looking in the rear-view mirror. Cedric was gone now. And once the exhaust of Neil's suv had clouded his view, he shifted it into drive and pulled out, his all-terrain tires plowing easily through the slush. He looked down between his arms to check the gauges, the focal point of his clean and uncluttered dash. No warning lights. Everything was fine. He turned left onto Maitland, worked his buttocks deeper into the seat. They were non-leather seats, supportive, comfortable. He could hear the radio just beneath the purr of the engine (a 3.9-litre, fuel-injected, 8-cylinder); it was calmly discussing the Hudson Bay Company's decision to stop selling furs. He switched it off, turned onto Yonge. Checked his gauges again. Everything was fine.

Everything was fine.

The rocks under the water were as speckled eggs
and noticing that, I noticed the swallows
taking no notice of me,

skilfully catching insects over the springtime lake,
swooping and diving in abrupt curves
until they'd caught one.

Then, somehow, they'd signal to their mate
who would meet them halfway, between
their catch and the nest.

And just before the two birds collided they would
camber up, until their bodies had stalled,
hanging there in an aerial balance,

where, at that deadpoint of slipping for an instant
out of gravity's fingers, in the pause of their
hovering weightless, beak to beak,

the insect was handed off. Then, dropping to the
surface with a twirl, a flutter, both would
glide away in opposite directions.

Such exactitude, delicate choreography in rearing their
chicks, squeaky with thankless mouths wide,
gawky and huddling in wait.

Thinking that our dance to do the same had so little elegance,
I picked one of the speckled stones from the water
to take home, but put it back for its weight.

Melissa pulled a sweater and the road atlas out of the car, slammed the door in the humming quiet of the gas station's fluorescent lights, and ran her finger along the red line of the highway as if to measure how far they were from Thunder Bay. Just then a sizeable moth plopped onto the map next to her hand and became instantly still, probably sensing that there was something large and breathing hovering over it. The moth was pale green with a delicate maroon outline and a set of discerning eyes painted onto its wings. Two long lobes dropped from the mimicked face like tusks, the insect's body in the centre making up a kind of furry nose. It was the most striking moth Melissa had ever seen, and she found herself looking up at the lights, as if to find more of them there. Once, her friend Nathan (some might have referred to him as an old boyfriend), who was a great collector and retainer of factoids and useless trivia, had told her about the way moths had evolved to navigate by the strongest celestial light: the moon—if it wasn't new—or one of the brighter stars, Sirius, Arcturus, Alpha Centauri. Which is why, he'd said, when they pass by an artificial light, naturally assuming that it's going to stay in the same place in the sky, directly above them, for example, they have no choice but to circle it in order to keep it there, at that one fixed point in their vision. They're not, contrary to popular belief, attracted to light; they just can't seem to get past it, disoriented by their only means of orientation—like an arctic airplane heading continually west in a spiral around the magnetic pole. They're drawn into danger by a set of intuitions that they know only how to trust, into a blindness by the very way they see. And there was some aspect in that, considered Melissa, folding the map as the moth flew away to bounce off the lights again, that was really, and quite wonderfully, human.

July 19, 1996

Nathan and Richard could be heard several houses away, walking along the slow-arcing street of Leaside's Sutherland Drive. The noise they were producing had people in their yards wandering to the sidewalk to stare at the teens as they approached. This was, after all, one of Toronto's neighbourhoods that prided itself on its quietude, on its elegantly bricked homes, its streets that were maple-shaded, lower-speed-limited, hopping-black-squirrel-abundant. The boys had just finished a bout of beatboxing, Richard working the throaty bass and snare portion while Nathan provided the clicks, cowbells, and hi-hats to the piece. But it was an oeuvre they'd been playing with for a few blocks now, and one they seemed to have exhausted, both of them breaking off after a minimalist closing, then wiping a slow hand across their mouths. (Regardless of skill or discipline, beatboxing had the tendency to produce a not-exactly-negligible amount of salivary spray.)

"Too good," chuckled Nathan, jumping up at a broken and dangling branch, swiping at it. He missed. "Too good" was a phrase oft exchanged between the two, and was more or less considered their trademark. Though in their minds it was something they used sparingly, reserved for only the most authentically funky, genuinely quirky, or wildly original things.

And in the spirit of using it sparingly, Richard didn't agree or echo Nathan's assessment. Instead he started into a jazzy walking bassline, the deep pluck of a contrabass resounding from his esophagus. Nathan waited, nodding to get the rhythm, then clamped his lips into a Miles Davis clench, eased open the far corner of his mouth, and broke in with something that sounded like a melange between a trumpet and an alto sax. They continued on this riff for another two blocks, until they arrived at

Melissa's house, where the party became louder as they strutted up the walkway.

They stepped onto the landing and Richard rang the door-bell while Nathan plucked a small purple flower from one of the planters beside the doorway, inserting it into Richard's hair. Richard lowered his chin and blinked at him in a gesture of bash-ful femininity.

The door burst open. "Ricardo! Nater! *Entrez*, gentlemen, *entrez*. And dude. Like the flower." It was Travis, a twelfth-grader who went to Leaside High School with them, and he was here, strangely, at a party of grade-eleveners. He was a nice-enough guy, even if he was only capable of rehashing the apparent hilarity of *Saturday Night Live* skits. And seeing as it was July, and summer was the season of reruns, it left him open to the previous season's gags in its entirety. "Hey, juguys see that one with Jim Carrey and the like, Roxbury Guys, pickin' up those geezers, noddin' their heads in the car like . . . boom, boom, boom . . ."

Neither of them answered as someone else had responded, bobbing his head in time to Travis's. They all passed through the hall together, two bobbing their heads, two not, and stepped into the living room, where the air was awash with music and captions of conversation overlapping one another.

". . . and the guy's like, screw that, I'm outta here . . ."

". . . we started doing tequila shooters and . . ."

". . . no way. Buffy is *so* lame. I mean, look at . . ."

". . . hey've you signed my cast yet? Cuz I, like, got this . . ."

The CD in the stereo was Weezer's *Blue Album*. A good choice as far as Nathan was concerned. He produced a mickey of vodka from the back pocket of his baggy cords (which were bought at a second-hand store, of course, like the rest of his wardrobe, with the exception of underwear—who bought second-hand underwear?) and he took a shallow swig, grimaced. He would have offered the next sip to Richard, but someone had already handed him a beer and was busy commenting on his flower.

"Thanks. Can't take the credit for the actual *innovation*, though, as it was the brainchild of this man here." Richard pointed at Nathan, who moved in closer to elucidate.

"My dearest Richard, I'm so very happy that you used the word 'brainchild' there, for the purple-flower-in-the-hair-of-naturally-curly-to-borderline-poodle-haired-young-men such as yourself came to me as an epiphany, as a cerebral-*birth*, okay? And it is undoubtedly set to be *all* the rage this year, on catwalks in Paris, London, New York, I tell you, la totalité du monde de la mode. The look has sparked several other creations, notably the main accessory to the flower thing, also sure to take the runways by storm in the coming months, which is the slightly protruding solar plexus muscle group as seen here." Nathan was arching his back and running his mickeyless hand over a belly that was indeed protruding. "To the uninitiated fashion eye this could be mistaken as mere fat, likened to that of a common sea mammal, whereas it is in fact the overdeveloped six-pack. Dude, this is washboard muscle that has, as yet a mystery to science, become so overworked, so strained, that it's begun to retain water. Fat? No. What this is, gentlemen, is cutting-edge-stylish water retention. It is now, it is hip, it is the very concept of sveltness—only *enhanced*."

Travis, who was in earshot, laughed.

Richard was smiling and gave Nathan a slow nod. "Nice."

"Thank you, dear sir."

"Hey." Someone else had noticed the two of them and was sidestepping through the crowd to come closer. "Hey! Thought you guys were in Nova Scotia still. Wasn't that right? You both went down there? *How'd'goi'dere'by!*"

"Aye laddie, 'tis true, 'tis true. Just got back the other day," affirmed Richard, who had gone there with the expectation of returning with at least a *hint* of a Maritimes accent. He'd also been waiting throughout the two weeks to hear himself referred to as a "*yung by*" or simply "*by*," but the cliché never managed to surface. Not that he was disappointed. The experience was priceless, enthralling. He'd never said "too good" so much in his life.

Nathan had enticed him to come along by relating a few of the idiosyncrasies of the tiny community where his grandfather was based, on the banks of the LaHave River on the South Shore, near Bridgewater. And though Nathan had spent anywhere from two weeks to two months every summer of his life in the area, he was seeing its quaint peculiarities as if for the first time, through the eyes of his neophyte counterpart, Richard. The two young men saw themselves as amateur documentary filmmakers, only without the cameras, essentially setting out to interview people, encouraging storytelling from anyone who had something to say, and boldly inviting themselves along with Nathan's grandfather on routine errands and the sorting out of everyday problems.

Nathan and Richard now had the unofficial attention of a small corner of the room, which had Richard taking the opportunity to recap some of the highlights of their trip. "Okay. So, full disclosure here: I am of the opinion that the place rocks. You should see, his grandpa took us to this, like, 'sawdoctor'—literally—cuz his saw was busted, and the place was this garage-cum-junkyard thing with, like, all this metal carnage and these amateur welding projects all over the place, these freakish birds and animals with nut-bolt eyes and shovel-blade beaks, all spray-painted in these, like, bright Moto-Master colours. Wicked. And then inside there were these five guys in stained undershirts with these little thin moustaches, and, like, this AM radio with a blown speaker crackling out seventies rock. Oh! And one day we pulled over to the side of the road, to this dock that was also this kind of impromptu end-of-the-day fish market thingy, and we walk up to this guy, who had a car door slammed onto his head when he was a kid or something—and crushed his voice box—and Nathan's grandpa taps his foot against one of the guy's plastic pails with all these mussels inside 'em, and asks the guy what he's selling them for today, and—no joke—the guy replies in this voice higher than Minnie Mouse's—on like helium—and wheezes out: 'Money.'"

Nathan laughed with everyone else and listened to Richard excitedly ramble on. He was on a roll, and not to be stopped, even if Nathan was pretty sure he wasn't quite doing the place justice. His grandfather, to Nathan anyway, was an epically cool, over-the-top man, who was to be unequivocally revered. He was a man who had immense hands, so thickly callused they were cigarette-stained yellow on the pads, and when Nathan imagined his life, he had always visualized it through the work that had gradually misshapen those hands. On the handles of his oars, heaving back, then lifting the shafts out of the water and placing them in his tiny dory, careful not to bash the wooden blades, standing up to tug at a longline, trawling for cod, hand over hand, deftly flipping the fish from the hook and into the boat, his dorymate re-baiting the line as it slipped into the water again on the other side, the fish utterly lifeless from the bends, being pulled up from so deep, some of their bladders protruding from their mouths, cleaning them back at the schooner, heads and gurry flung overboard, slime and bright blood stringing between his fingertips; or in the off-season when he would jump a train, gripping on to a rusted metal bar between two colossal railcars, pivoting noisily with the twists of the track, jumping off in the Annapolis Valley, rolling through a weed-choked ditch, standing up to dust off his over-alls, cracked and stunted fingernails tweezing thorns out of his ring finger, then climbing the rungs of a ladder, reaching through scratching leaves and branchlets to a lime-green apple, freckled, blistered with raindrops, plucking it from the stem and into his wicker basket; then at the helm of an oil tanker in the Merchant Navy, thumb in a crook of the chrome wheel, spinning it to star-board to steer clear of surfacing U-boats, corvettes carving into sight to gun the submarines down; then disembarking after the war, his palm squeaking along the gangplank rail and into the pub of another country, a cigar between his cigar-thick fingers in Cuba, raising a glass of stout in England, ouzo in Greece, kir in France, sake in Japan.

Nathan listened as the exaggeration in Richard's stories shifted into the direction of hyperbole. Which was fine. Made them all the more entertaining really. It was just that he felt Richard was missing a key point: that Nathan's grandfather was clearly made of stuff that they were not. Harder, firmer, truer stuff. And as the gaggle around Richard and his storytelling grew in density, Nathan decided to slip away, decided it was time that he found Melissa. When it came to Melissa, Nathan thought he could do with a bit of the stuff his grandfather was made of.

Nathan walked into another room, where he found mostly girls of his grade, along with a handful of the punks and "radicals" of the school, people who called themselves anarchists, eschewing the nutritious dinners their upper-middle-class parents placed in front of them at 6:00 PM, kids who left the table to spend the rest of their evening holed up inside their pastel-painted bedrooms, listening to Sonic Youth and tack-holing the walls with posters of Engels, Marx, and propaganda from the Libertarian Communist Committee of the Spanish Civil War. One of them, Chris, walked over and tried to greet Nathan with a fancy handshake: a series of grips, different fingers interlocking at different angles, fists connecting, one on top of the other, then frontal, palms sliding, slapping, perhaps some snapping added in for flare. It was a handshake that Nathan completely botched.

"Gee, I seem to have completely botched that handshake. I am really, really rather sorry. I suck. I suck and I'm embarrassed, mortified, worthless. And how about you, Chris? How are you? Keeping well?"

"Quite. Yeah. Thanks."

Nathan noticed the conversation being a little more elevated than in the front room. Current affairs mostly: the Olympics opening that day, Dolly the sheep, human cloning around the corner, the nonstop stream of recent plane crashes ("Who would fly these days? I mean, seriously . . ."), along with a peppering of the same subject matter that was prevalent in other parts of the house, recent episodes of *The Simpsons*, the most annoying vjs on MuchMusic, and O.J. flagrantly getting away with murder.

"Hey, man," Chris said out of the blue. "You're from Ottawa, right? Might be goin' there in a couple weeks. There's this, uhm, well, it's a protest, I think, that a buddy and I were thinking of joining. But it might not get off the ground. Anyway. Cool place?"

"Uhm. Yeah I guess. For protests."

It was true. Having grown up in Ottawa, Nathan had seen his fair share of picketers and lobbyists, from both sides of abortion laws and gay marriage to acid rain and public service strikes. He'd even seen breast-baring women march from Parliament Hill to the Byward Market for the right to be topless in public. In Ottawa, protests were just another part of the cityscape. Did that make it an alluring and exciting city in Nathan's opinion? Not really.

Nathan Amundsen had grown up in the Glebe, a charming area cradled into a "J" of the Rideau Canal, tight streets with semi-detached houses, specialty shops, quiet restaurants, and cafés garnishing many of its street corners. As a boy, he'd found it an excellent place for playing Dungeons & Dragons, usually in friends' basements, afterwards walking to hang out near Dow's Lake, thoughts of casting spells and goblins still fresh in his mind, settling onto his knees on the grass there, fidgeting, clicking his teeth to an unheard rhythm, distracted out of the conversation by every man, woman, child, dog, frisbee, bee, and scavenging crow that happened to pass into his line of sight. He was by nature a nervous child, which was something he'd never really grown out of. In his adolescence this became an attribute that, when coupled with his general love of punks, freaks, activists, and any other personality perceived to be "on the societal fringe," meant that he spent a good portion of his leisure time feeling apprehensive. (Though he did discover that beatboxing helped him cope.) Thankfully, this uneasiness was a private one for the most part, something he managed to keep concealed from his compatriots. Even if there were times that it escalated into an outright panic attack.

Nathan's father was an aeronautics engineer, an occupation that, even his son had to confess, was fairly cool. But what was not cool was his being unexpectedly transferred to Toronto one day. Once they'd moved into their new house in Leaside, everything seemed bleak to Nathan. He had left behind the painfully slow and anxious progress he'd made to second base with a girl in his grade, his mother had refused him the farewell party "he'd always dreamt of" (several bus tickets for he and his friends to Woodstock '94 in New York State), the first half of the NHL season was locked out, and Kurt Cobain was dead. Things, he figured, really, could only get better. And fortunately they did.

He met Richard, namely because both of them had the same eclectic taste in second-hand clothing and spoke so quickly that few other people could follow. Though the true forming of their allegiance came when, on only his second week in Toronto, Richard offered to show him around the city; but just the corners, he'd promised, that were most worth checking out. They spent an entire Saturday walking the downtown core, people begging via signed cardboard while they piled construction rubble into precariously balanced cairns; graffiti alley, where spray-painted scrawls were considered less vandalism and more art; Kensington, flea markets, thrift shops, experimental rooftop gardens, organic co-ops, all amid smokestack spires that jutted brick-red and sudden out of common neighbourhood streets. Nathan was hooked. Appreciating this, Richard introduced him around to other people, and he'd soon fallen in with a quirky group, making the acquaintance of Melissa and her artsy-though-not-taking-themselves-too-seriously crowd, and things had all been uphill from there.

Melissa reached around and tapped him on the belly. "Hey. You made it," she said above the music. Nathan's eyes flitted down to her body, then quickly back up to her face. She was wearing one of her favourite T-shirts, the fabric thin, its worn-in shape treading the line between hiding and highlighting the curves that lay beneath. She was drinking a cooler, pinkish, bright, her breath more sugary than panging of alcohol.

"Whoah, I see you've chosen to delve into the hard stuff. Wild berry-berrilicious, is it?"

"It's the red dye number three I'm after." She took a swig.

"So, where's the folks?" asked Nathan.

"Don't know. Something about Niagara something or other. My dad's got some business thing tomorrow, but they went a day early. Lucky for us."

"Luuuckee," Nathan agreed, looking out at the room and falling into what felt like a gawky silence. It was often how things were with Melissa these days: starting out fine until they trailed off into something clumsy. But who knew, maybe that's how it was with everyone in the same boat, every non-couple-continuing-as-friends who'd lost their virginity together. Maybe that, in itself, was a recipe for clumsy.

Sexually speaking, Nathan was no Casanova. He'd begun his exploits modestly enough, back in Ottawa, with two promising flings whose sole intention was to get as far down that road as was adolescently possible. Necking in a semi-private spot he'd found behind the Champlain statue near the National Gallery, his hands squeezing away at the soft warmth under their sweaters, teeth clunking, only to find himself ambling stiffly back home again, underwear sticky.

It was a pattern of relative failure that followed him through his first year in Toronto as well. But then, out of the blue, and completely unforeseen on his part, the night with Melissa transpired. It had happened only three months earlier, that May. He'd just turned seventeen and it was springtime, nature broadcasting its brazen pornography from every green space in the city, courting calls, dances, songs, pheromones, nectar, everything alive pulsing with an undeniably voracious urge to mate. He was fidgety with it.

It had been a simple consequence of friends cancelling at the last second. Normally, Nathan and Richard were invited to hang out and provide the entertainment whenever two or more were gathered, which was the case that evening. But Richard had a surprise-to-him family get-together, and the two other girls who were supposed to show up had caught wind of a band that Melissa hated and they loved playing at a café with no cover charge. When Nathan walked through the door, he noted the quiet of the house, and innocently asked the whereabouts of Melissa's parents. It turned out that they would also be in absentia for most of the night, at one of those networking dinner parties her father, Cedric, was so fond of. It was then—while both of them leaned casually against the white kitchen cupboards, sunlight seeping in through the man-tled window between them, the pendulum of a clock ticking loudly, rhythmically, randily—that the atmosphere between them became laden. Nathan tapped the counter with a hectic beat, in time with the clock, lost for words.

So they opted for the safety of the television, Melissa channel surfing until she found MuchMusic, sliding the remote control onto the coffee table. Even the videos were in the fever of springtime, pop stars with little clothing jiggling to the sounds of overproduced music, running their hands across their own bronze skin or the bronze skin of others. Melissa shuffled closer on the chesterfield until her foot was touching his on the floor. Nathan stopped breathing. They watched another video. More skin, danc-ers with lips parted, backs arched, nipples erect. He swallowed.

When it happened it was a shock to them both. They were just suddenly kissing and, the shock was, unzipping and unbuttoning each other's clothes. There was no condom, or talk of one, just frenetic action, anxious fumbling. They were only having actual sex for twenty or thirty seconds before Nathan pulled back with a short moan, ejaculating onto the cushions of the couch. He col-lapsed beside her, pulling a blanket that was draped across the back of the sofa over their naked bodies. The television light bounced off the eggshell-coloured walls while the music continued on with its inexhaustible coital thump. Neither of them dared speak. And to his shame, a few minutes later, Nathan fell asleep.

When he woke, he had a hard time grappling with the fact that Melissa wasn't there. She was just *gone*. Upstairs somewhere. In her room maybe. Not wanting to think about what that might mean, he hurriedly got dressed and stepped up the stairs, walking through the house, quietly calling her name. And when he saw the headlights of her father's car fill the living room window, followed by the sound of its engine turning off in the driveway, he bolted out the back door.

They never talked about it again, though he was sure she'd told her friends, in the same way that he had borne all to Richard. Luckily, she appeared to be making an effort to treat him in the same way she always had. Seeing him as the entertainer that kept things light and easy while she remained the reluctant entertainee, who probably brooded heavily on all those light and easy things that were said.

Within a couple months, the air between them had almost reverted back to its normal feel and texture, and when the word was out that her parents would be away for this, the third weekend in July, it was clear, though unspoken, that Nathan and Richard would arrive at her door at some point. What would a party be without them?

Nathan removed the mickey from his pocket and took a swig, having to exaggeratedly lean forward just to gulp it down. Melissa, assuming it was for clownish effect, snickered.

"That good, is it?" she asked, her eyes casually scanning the faces of the people in the next room. Then Melissa froze. "Oh *shit!*" she whispered. "Is that Brad?"

"Uh. Yeah. It would seem so." Nathan also recognized the problem. Brad was a jock. A shoulder-guard-wearing, party-crashing, house-wrecking jock. And as the rule of thumb went: where there was one, there were many.

"Shit," she repeated and moved off in the direction of the back door, as if to bar it, raise the drawbridge, make it all okay with a single authoritative act.

While Nathan, on the other hand, knew it was hopeless. Things would soon get ugly, decline, spiral, and in anticipation of this, he was already working himself up into a state, was already ill at ease, anxious. He sipped his vodka, nodded his head to the music, still the same album, the CD player apparently set on repeat. "This bottle / of Steven's / awakens ancient feelings . . ."

Someone lit a cigarette, blew a stream of smoke under the lamp that was mounted in the centre of the ceiling, contraband in this non-smoking house. Others followed. No one cared.

He took another swig, making a concerted effort to try to enjoy himself, quickly, before the decay had become so prevalent it wouldn't be possible anymore. He looked around for Richard and, not finding him, started talking to someone else. While babbling, he heard his own voice, distant and amusing, trying to stay cool beneath his ordinary comic routine, heard himself trying to placate the anxiety rising in his lungs.

The vodka's non-flavour had less of a bite to it now, and he'd already reached the point where time had become choppy, lurching forward minutes at a time without the sensation of his having been present for all of them. He was clearly drunk, losing control in a situation that was losing control.

His conversation was interrupted by the sound of something heavy and glass toppling from a shelf and shattering, the music cutting out for a few seconds, CD skipping, laser lagging, searching, then catching again, rereading the binary code on the iridescent surface that gleamed, somewhere, hidden, deep in the machine. "Only in dreeeams . . ." Bass guitar slapping, dirty electric lead, drums building to a climax. "Only in dreeeeeeams . . ."

The girl he was talking to turned back and began chatting again while a fly landed on the rim of her glass, an inkspot floating in the transparency under her nose that she didn't quite notice. It was blue, glittering in the smoky light like a fallen sequin from a grad dress. The fly seemed to be fixing Nathan with its red eyes, seemed to know what was coming, rubbing its hands together with sinister focus.

Evidently his panic was beginning to get the best of him. Watching the girl's mouth move with slurry words, he tried to fight it back, wondering where the attribute of courage came from. Wasn't it possible that it was in his blood, coded in the helix of his genes somewhere? Surely he had *some* semblance of the mettle and bravery of his grandfather. He must. Even just a little tiny piece of it, gleaming, somewhere, deep in the machine.

Nathan caught the thick and skunky odour of hashish and looked over to see a tight circle of people in one of the corners passing around a homemade bong. At the same time a large vase in another corner was accidentally kicked over, tipping onto the carpet. He turned to look in the other direction and saw Richard, close to another one of the jocks who had surfaced, who was pointing out the flower in his hair, trying to mock him. But Richard was looking past the jock's finger, not really listening, focusing in the direction of the front door.

Then he saw Melissa, standing with her back against the wall with apparent abandon. There was nothing she could do either. And as he was admiring her devil-may-care expression, it wilted into something very different, something terrified, as if she were seeing the devil incarnate, and realized that he was something to care about after all. Her knees appeared to weaken, back sliding down the wall, hands covering her face, until she was squatting, out of sight.

A voice behind Nathan boomed above the sound of the electric guitars, "What in the *hell* is going on here!" The room spun around to face Melissa's parents, Mr. and Mrs. Johnson.

Mrs. Johnson was covering her mouth, trailing behind her husband, who was forcefully leading the way, shoving through the teens, his brow already glistening in a cold sweat, eyes wild. He was a large man, and his gestures even larger. He stopped in the midst of the frozen room, flabbergasted. "Who *are* all you . . . you . . . ?" He put a hand on top of his head as if to keep it from blowing off. "And how *dare* you . . . in . . . and . . . And are you," he pointed at the group in the corner with the bong, "are you doing *drugs* in my house?"

This would have been one of those opportune moments for the record player to scratch into silence, or like in the westerns, when the honky-tonk clank of the ivories faltered just before a gunfight, followed by the sound of a piano bench creaking over a wooden floor as the pianist ducked for cover. An appropriate quiet. Unfortunately this was a CD playing, enclosed in a glass cabinet. So the music went on, at the same volume, same album, same voice, having just started over again, back onto song one. The only sound in the hush of the room a blaring one.

"The choo-choo train left right on time / A ticket costs only your mind / The driver said, 'Hey man we go all the way' / And of course we were willing to paaaay . . ."

Someone nudged Nathan from behind, then someone else. He was, by default, the public relations guru among them. If he couldn't talk them out of this mess, no one could. He was nudged forward farther, by another hand, until the forest of backs and shoulders opened onto an obese and fuming middle-aged man.

Nathan was unnerved, panicky, trying desperately to conjure something from within, something strong and valiant, something that had to do with weeks of wartime ocean where U-boats lay in wait, or to do with jumping from a moving train, or battling unpredictable seas, something about his grandfather and the way he embraced adversity with a calm that made water look like a mirror. Unfortunately it felt like it slipped between his fingers.

Nathan cleared his throat. Everyone turned to him, listening, including, in his mind, the fly. "Right," he began, speaking above the stereo. "So, the thing is, no one's really to blame here, sir, because, well, frankly speaking, it was just a matter of . . . a miscommunication between the, uhm . . . the . . . well, what I think it really boils down to is the fact that there was a . . . uhm . . . Yeah, I'm dying here, aren't I? I am failing miserably at achieving any degree of eloquence, when I really just want to explain that this party, sir, Mr. Johnson, sir, was really, uhh . . . well it was . . ."

Cedric, teeth gritted, took three quick steps toward Nathan, crumpled the front of his priceless second-hand shirt into his fist, pulled him closer, and slapped him across the face. Lightly. No sound, no damage. But a clear message nonetheless. No one interjected, said a word, even moved.

Then something odd happened. Blinking hard, Mr. Johnson gave his head a shake and began looking around the room, hungrily taking in the details, as if trying to figure out exactly where he was. Once he was satisfied, he faced Nathan again, unclenching his shirt. "So. Guess the *big slap's* already taken place then." He stroked the crinkles in the fabric on Nathan's chest, trying to smooth them over.

The music was still blaring.

"And what was your name again, kid? Gnat or something like that. Nate? *Nathan*," he said, ostensibly answering himself. "Nathan." He nodded, looking around again, this time as if slightly embarrassed. "Well, Nathan. If only you knew how much that little slap I gave you, way back when, is gonna cost . . . in my life." He shook his head. "How much it's gonna change things for me." His brow was now creased, his posture dispirited. It was unsettling how instantly his rage had evaporated. Nathan wasn't sure if this meant more violence was about to be doled out. He took an uneasy step back.

People shifted, looked around at one another.

Melissa appeared beside Nathan. "You okay?" she asked him.

"Yeah, sure. Sure, fine."

She gave a sheepish glance at her father, "Dad . . ." she began, in a voice barely audible above the electric guitars.

"*Oh*, Melissa," Cedric said, "don't you worry. I'll get what I deserve. You just wait and see."

"What?" Melissa, squinting, looked around the room, not really knowing how to proceed. She was clearly in the wrong here, but her father was reacting to that wrong in the wrongest way he could.

"I mean," Cedric swallowed, "don't you . . . get it? I . . . I am not a great man." He pointed a quick finger at Melissa. "But you, I think you judge me like I should be, and . . ." He threw up his hands, at a loss. Then, to everyone's surprise, he stepped forward, toward his daughter, who stiffened as if getting ready to be thrown across the room. Cedric reached out and clasped on to Melissa's right arm, grinning, then awkwardly patted her in a plainly unpractised attempt to be affectionate. After that, he turned on his heels and walked out, stopping just before the hallway to right the vase that had tipped over onto the carpet there. It was a trendy melange of dried-and-dyed reeds and seedpods, which he stuffed back into the hole haphazardly before continuing on.

Now everyone looked to Melissa's mother, Julie, waiting for her to speak, to officially break up the party, usher everyone out the front doors, call the police: whatever she felt most appropriate. But she was too busy staring at her daughter, who was busy staring back. There seemed to be a kind of nonverbal exchange taking place, which didn't concern how much trouble she was in or even about that evening or the party at all. It was something else, something bigger. And Nathan would swear it was as if an offering were being made, an alliance, a pact.

Nathan shifted, cracked one of his knuckles.

And still no one had turned off the music.

I discovered them first with my hands
then explored them in slow light
lines of down floating along her skin
a dark mist, threaded fog
Gossamer body hair
finely patterned and
pointing in directions as limply
as wind-bent grass
It spilled from her navel
seeped from her jawline
swirled her forearms
I watched it all thirstily
never telling
stealing glances on café patios
in parasol shade
hoarding the details
the velvet shimmer
These markings on a creature
both consummate and elusive
wavering between aloof and skittish
like the tracks and traces of an animal
never seen, never taken
An untouchable pelage
touched

It was the first time Melissa had ever been to the seaside, let alone lived on one. Everything she looked at was a surprise, or bizarre, seemed to have sprouted directly from the pages of an implausible science fiction novel. She was most taken with the tidal pools, stepping out among the green anemones and their orifices of filament tentacles, the tiny sculpins invisible in their camouflage, shore crabs scuttling into recesses, limbs tucking tight, the hiss of seagrapes. She liked the tracks and traces in the wet sand that adjoined the pools, the life that had ventured out of them. And the purple, orange, and maroon starfish that clung to the rocks in expressive positions, their reaching arms, shrugging shoulders, hanging heads, splayed out on the barnacle-sprinkled surfaces like sailors having just crawled onto land from a shipwreck, limp and exhausted, reduced to ragged stickmen.

Emily had asked to sit on the rooftop outside, a request that somewhat confused the waitress seating her. It wasn't a nice day, a bit cool, mostly cloudy, and considering the time, the early afternoon lull between the lunch rush and dinner rush, she would most likely be the only person sitting there: a tall woman, robust and broad-shouldered, dressed in black, the solitary living shape amid two long rows of plastic chairs and weatherproof tables. To the waitress, it had seemed like such a bad idea that she'd asked twice if she really, *really* wanted to sit outside, pointing out the available tables everywhere else, in every corner of the dining room, where she would be able to blend quietly into the stylish decor, the post-postmodern lighting, the contemporary paintings on the walls as large and appealing to look into as windows. But Emily insisted. She had her reasons.

Pulling the plastic of her chair legs over the wooden planks, she ordered a drink, wanting a glass of wine but opting for an orange juice instead, thinking of her quartet's recital in a few hours. And oh, she'd said to the waitress before she'd slipped off to the bar, giving her a heads-up, she was waiting for someone.

She sipped her orange juice and played with her watch for a quarter of an hour. She'd been early, and Cedric was late. Though consciously late. It was the way he had been the last couple weeks, trying, in his own losing way, to play the game. She knew that he was probably somewhere close by, waiting in his car, parked and pretending to listen to the news or to a classical piece on the CBC (something he wouldn't have been caught dead doing only seven months ago), nodding his head in time to the movement, miming interest. All in an attempt to come across not quite as desperate as he really was.

His letter had appeared in her mailbox on Friday, late morning, as if brought by the postman, though wasn't stamped.

Emily,

Okay. You're right. I know we're not a perfect match. I know there's a lot of things I'm not. Not a violinist or composer, not a poet. In fact I'm really just a normal everyday guy. But I'm also a man that's developed this incredible need for you. And it's the first time in my life that I've felt it like this.

Since we spoke, I can't sleep, can't work, can't pull myself out of bed, only because of the thought (just the thought) of not having you, there, in some way. Everything suddenly looks so plain, feels so lost and empty.

I've never written a letter like this before either. (I don't think I've ever written a letter.) So please. I just want to talk. Please. At Remy's, 3:00, Sunday. Meet me there?

Please.

C

Ironically, it was one of the few things she liked about him, the fact that he wasn't a passionate man, wasn't a poet. She'd had her lion's share of fervid lovers, even married one, and they were never, in Emily's experience, quite what they were cracked up to be.

Emily Pereda had (according to her father) married too late and (according to her mother) divorced too early. Her marriage had lasted five years in total, but they were five years that had taken their toll, left her exhausted, etched unsightly lines around her mouth and the corners of her eyes.

They'd formally met at a wedding, though she'd heard of him before, even listened to him play once. Most of the musicians in the city knew of most of the other musicians in the city—just the way it was. She'd heard his name, Shane, listed off as someone that other people had played with, and she recalled that he was purported to be a solid musician, that he specialized in early music, and that he was rumoured to be good in bed. However, at the wedding in question, she hadn't found his playing to be all that much to write home about, and while sharing a tepid bottle of house wine after their set, she'd gotten into an argument with him about how smug he'd seemed concerning his performance. When they'd finally fallen quiet, it wasn't clear who'd won, so she'd offered to continue the discussion at his place, provided he had better wine, of course. Shane hesitated a long while, plainly baffled, before agreeing.

In the months that followed she found his tactics endearing, though never quite in the way he'd probably intended them to be. She felt like she was seeing him, as an impartial onlooker, considering most of his acts and gestures as being premeditated, what he perceived *she* would perceive as being winning and romantic. He would ask about the front yard of her childhood, go to her recitals to clap loudly from the back, and lift her heavy hair to kiss the nape of her neck. When walking past cedars or junipers, he would pluck a sprig from a branch, mulch it in his fingers, smell it, and hold them out to her as an offer to do the same. She rarely did, trying to smile in a manner that reflected she was seeing this all for what it really was; though he usually seemed to take it at face value, as an indication that she was genuinely impressed. She considered herself lucky that he'd never produced a red rose, as she wouldn't have been able to stop herself from laughing out loud.

She remembers the way he once knocked on her door with two snifters and a bottle of brandy, led her into the washroom, undressed her while filling the bathtub, helped her into it, and methodically washed her down, soaping every contour of her body, bit by bit, paying particular attention to her hands, pinching slippery suds into the weblike skin at the base of her fingers. The brandy was excellent. His method of shampooing was not. She remembers going over to his apartment, which was adorned with the bohemian intellectual standards, art prints advertising the museums they were bought in, ancient maps with galleons stencilled onto the seas and bobbing along curled and linear waves, and a self-assembled pinewood bookshelf that was teetering with volumes of Russian classics and selected works of philosophy that he'd probably never read or even paged through but had nevertheless arranged in alphabetical order, as if for quick reference; Dostoevsky, Kant, Nietzsche, Pushkin, Tolstoy. She would stand in his living room, snickering to herself, looking through his trinkets and CDs, a wineglass cradled to her chest, while he buzzed in the kitchen cooking a brightly coloured meal, cool jazz on the stereo, Chet Baker or Jimmy Giuffre, after having rushed around lighting candles as soon as she'd taken her shoes off at the door.

When Shane had proposed, she considered it for three minutes of thick silence, considered the long hours she had spent alone on Friday nights, how eager he was to please, then accepted with a shrug. "Sure."

Emily had never wanted children, ever, even when she was sixteen years old and full of pipe dreams and idyllic futures, when she could have fabricated idyllic offspring jumping through sprinklers on an idyllic lawn in front of an idyllic house. She hadn't. Instead she'd abhorred everything about kids for as long as she could remember. And it baffled her that, in this opinion, she was the exception and not the rule.

To start with, she hated parents, how mothers were, at first, only capable of talking in numbers: "I was in labour for eighteen hours," "he was seven pounds, three ounces," "she drinks 120 cc now," "he wakes up at three and then again at seven," "he knows four words so far," "grade one," "top two readers in the class," "95 per cent." And she hated how fathers were always on the sidelines, boasting in what was deemed to be a more objective manner, injecting words like "gifted," "advanced," and "precocious." Emily sometimes wanted to see a bar graph comparing "presumed future prodigies" to "actual prodigies that had surfaced from said presumptions." She was confident there was a considerable disparity between the two.

Beyond the parents, there were the creatures themselves; dirty, smelly, noisy, selfish, chaotic, thankless, and, most importantly in

Emily's view, dumb. They moved through stages that were all somehow equally disagreeable, from oozing diapers to drool and vomit, grunts and whines to ear-splitting tantrums, bruised knees and scratched elbows to mild concussions, barking orders to cold demands. And then, the clincher: at the moment that their blooming sexuality brings with it a swarm of new and disturbing worries to keep you up, again, all hours of the night, when they begin to display the rudiments of an adult mind where they might finally, finally have the ability to say something that could, potentially, waver on the line of interesting, of having the vague semblance of human dialogue, at that precise and potentially earth-shattering moment, they suddenly hate you. Only to blame you for their problems via your neglectful parenting and lack of nurturing understanding forthwith. And all of that for just hundreds of thousands of dollars and a few decades of your time. "Sure," she'd said to Shane, capping off her rant, which he was hearing for the first time in a motel room on their six-month anniversary. "Sounds fantastic. Best of luck finding a surrogate wife." She left to take a walk.

She imagined Shane behind her, grinning at the closed door, sure that she would eventually change her mind. She was, after all, a woman. It was natural for her to want children, a given almost. She'd come around. He probably would've bet on it.

And he would have lost.

This concept, of losing and winning, had always been present between them. Initially born from their unremitting arguments and polemics—from the need to prove or disprove, to build up a solid case in support of an opinion, or tear one down, it gradually transformed itself into something more, into an artful vying for ground, a constant attempt to gain the upper hand, seize territory. Their discourse had become something tactical, the private weighing out of victories and losses, every word measured for the cutting quality of its edge, syllables jutting from the sentences like bayonets. There were times when Emily would hear herself setting up for a costly forward advance, one that was sure to find them both sulking long afterwards (or retreating to bathrooms and bedsheets to charily lick their wounds), and it would occur to her that, at that moment, there was no real benefit to be made by causing damage, nor did she even want to. Yet she would. Fights about workspace, silence, selfishness, nickels and dimes, fridge magnets. Emily began to feel like a captive in the language that they'd developed between each other, tongue-tied in the dialect of combative exchange. How can we expect, she wondered—while he furiously washed the dishes, plates clanking above the major and minor scales that she was trying to warm up to—to fashion a lasting peace on a frontline when even armistices are written in the tongue of war? Soldiers and mercenaries are not trained to reconstruct, rebuild, start anew. They're not meant to. They've committed themselves to something else, know nothing else. Which meant, Emily began to suspect, that the greatest obstacle for engaged opponents who found themselves finally wishing for peace wasn't in figuring out how to lay their weapons down; it was in having taken up arms in the first place.

It was a month before their fifth anniversary when Shane mentioned the place in the country he wanted to show her, a place, he'd promised, that she was going to love. Everything about the idea had made her uneasy from the get-go, though she hadn't understood what his actual intentions were until she was there, standing in the cold and mildewed air of the brick-worked building, looking out from one of its windows. It was in the area where he'd grown up, on the outskirts of Beamsville, a small town on the Niagara Peninsula just across the lake from Toronto (whose bleary skyline could be seen from the shore on a clear day, writhing over a band of water mirage like gasoline vapour). The place belonged to friends of the family, a failed attempt at a guesthouse. Furniture unarranged and draped over with white sheets and mattress covers, to keep out the resourcefulness of moths and the patience of dust, armchairs and La-Z-Boys in the shape of Halloween ghouls, of children in ghost costumes with their eyeholes yet uncut, raising their arms in a still-framed "booOOooh," which was as soundless as wind under the doorsills.

The wood flooring crackled and moaned beneath her footsteps to the window, where she had stopped to look outside. In the yard it was early spring, fruit trees in bloom, grass the green of limes, shadows short and edged abruptly. She crossed her arms over her chest and tried to rub some warmth into her sides. Galaxies of particles churned in a slat of light at her shins.

"Well? What do you think? It's great, isn't it? I was thinking . . ." he shifted his weight onto a joint in the wood strips that complained with a whine, "I was thinking about the time off we both have, coming up in June, and . . . I was thinking that we could . . . that it would be good for us if we . . . you know, spent some . . . time."

Finally understanding what it was all about, and even appreciating it, she found she had little to say. Instead, she noticed the strand of a spiderweb hanging down from the top of the window frame. There was a tiny paint chip dangling from its tip, which was stirring, pivoting slightly, in miniscule degrees, as if of its own volition. A gleam of gesso clinging to the end of an invisible thread, like hope.

She sighed, leaning closer to the window as if tipping over with a towering weight, her forehead butting up softly against the glass, the sun shaving her cheekbones. She was thinking about the reality of his plan, thinking further afield than the reach of his good intentions, about what it would actually mean, the two of them being cooped up in a new and empty space for two weeks, where there were no familiar ambits to retreat across, no corners reconnaissanced for the hiding. Emily was no romantic. She knew that the kind of damage they'd inflicted by now was far beyond what could be held up to the most well-meaning lips and kissed better. Especially here, in the country of his youth, where they wouldn't even be on equal ground to try, where he would have an obvious latitudinal advantage, passing oak trees with his infant memories swinging under the branches, walking along vineyard rows where he'd harvested grapes as a teen, their stunted vines stretching out into dramatic renditions of the crucifix, muscles of bark flexed and contorted tighter than two thousand years of martyrdom. They'd kill each other.

She was as surprised as he was to hear herself say it. "I want . . ." she hadn't turned around, was still leaning against the window, "I want a divorce." She spoke into the glass, her breath spray-painting a misty halo in front of her mouth. "A quick and painless divorce," she added quietly.

She still hadn't turned around. There was a long pause while he looked for words that he was incapable of finding. The ghouls stood still.

"That's all," she murmured at the flowering trees of his salad days, the pink of the magnolias rusting at the fringes, their enormous petals unfurling until they dropped, white cups of silk gathering at the base of the trees like clothes at the foot of a nuptial bed. "It's all I want."

Contrary to the nature of their marriage, their divorce was, in fact, quick and painless. The only hang-up was a transitional twelve days when Emily didn't have an apartment; while waiting for one of the roommates to move out of a sober bungalow she'd found, she'd unwisely accepted an invitation from her parents to stay at their place.

She'd come from a large family, the middle child with five sisters and a brother. Both of her parents were school teachers, a profession, Emily held, that called to it only the most boring people. Her parents' one binding commonality was the way they approached raising their kids. Above all else, they wanted to foster their children's intellect, encourage them to be bold thinkers, to be analytical, critical, and, failing that, to at least become knowledgeable, cultivated, conversant. The manner in which they approached this was insisting that their children never be given chores or household duties: no cooking, cleaning, caring for younger siblings; so long as they were seen to be reading, studying, perfecting some sort of skill or art, they were exempt from everything they thought of as toilsome or menial. An approach that had Emily's parents, particularly her mother, working several times the amount of the average person, as well as rendering Emily utterly useless in the kitchen later on in her life, inept at controlling textile-incinerating irons, and the owner of underwear that was all three to six shades away from its original colour. Even now, at thirty-seven, she couldn't boil an egg without bungling it in some way, a fact she vehemently reproached her parents for whenever she saw them. Particularly her mother.

"I'm just worried about you," her mother had begun on her second night in the house, after brewing Emily an evening cup of tea in the kitchen. "Is that so wrong?"

"Some other time, will you, Mom?"

"Well, it's not going to get any easier, is it? At your age. To find a man. And this one was so clever. Certainly played well. Had a good job. Made it to the symphony." She broke off to look thoughtfully at the refrigerator. "And, sweetie, I'm afraid your big bones aren't getting any smaller."

Emily gave an acerbic look that her mother managed to evade.

"You *are* going to audition for a position in the symphony again this year, aren't you? You're bound to get it one of these times, hon."

Emily walked to the sink, poured her tea into it, clunked the cup into the steaming basin, and left the room.

Her mother's apprehensions about her attractiveness were ill founded. After her divorce, Emily was tired but hungry, and enjoyed a phase of casual flings and easygoing affairs that came about with little effort and were based almost entirely on sex. She met Cedric two years after her divorce, following what had been a disastrous experiment with a woman, a possessive and clingy violist who tipped easily into hysteria, a woman who'd had the habit of asking comprehensive questions about past lovers, then calling Emily hard and cold and brusque for her responses, criticisms that became self-fulfilling realities. When they split up, a door's trimming was damaged from the slamming, picture frames shattered. While one of her roommates helped her sweep up the mess, she told herself that this was the last of them, that what she needed now was some time alone, to plant a few shoots of calm in her life, however distractingly fruitful her soil happened to be.

When she was offered to play a gig for a retirement party at a golf course on the south shore of Lake Simcoe, she thought that getting out of the city and into the fresh air for an afternoon would do her good. The retiree was an insurance broker and classical aficionado whose company had splurged for an hour and a half of live Bruch and Dvořák at his reception. Emily's quartet played on a sunken stage while his associates, allies, and adversaries filed into the hall and mingled with cocktails in their hands, standing around, nursing tumblers and champagne flutes, schooners, and seidels. She'd glimpsed some of them giving a nudge, wink, and gesture toward the musicians, a cluster of the men stepping closer for a better look. One of them was watching her closely, eyeing the way her knees protruded from the black of her dress on either side of her cello, which was almost the size of a human body. When she finally met his eyes—a shallow, watery blue, framed in wrinkles he'd won from sunny fairways—he'd smiled and pushed his drink out into the air between them, as if to indicate how impressed he was with her precision, or was it her bowing technique, her controlled and understated expression? She looked back at her music stand, half-smirking at the absurdity.

During a short break midway through the performance she retreated outside with a glass of wine, a non-smoker's rendition of a cigarette break. Cedric had searched around until he'd found her there, on a terrace overlooking the wide green of the eighteenth hole. He accosted her with predictable compliments that progressed toward a predictable come-on. She sidestepped it by asking about him. He was, in fact, he'd instantly volunteered, recently divorced. (Likely the only thing they had in common, thought Emily, stepping out of her shoes to stretch the arches of her feet, toes splayed on the patio stones).

"So I guess you gotta practise a lot. Keep those hands in tip-top shape," Cedric said, watching the bare skin of her feet in the sun.

"If you do it well, you use your whole body actually," Emily offered as if to no one in particular.

"Your whole body, eh?" Cedric looked the whole of her body over. "That is really . . . interesting, you know . . ."

Listening to him speak she found him to be conservative, prudish, coarse, and provincial. And besides being fourteen years her senior, Emily thought he was irritatingly sure of himself, standing in front of her with his glass of sparkling wine, searing with confidence, a womanizer who'd been forced to philander for decades with the careful discretion of a married man but had, at long last, been unleashed from it. There was nothing stopping him now. He was overweight, unread, unwise, and on top of the world with it, limping into middle age with the notion that he was infallible. It was embarrassing really.

What was more, she understood that he'd been drawn to her image alone, that he was talking to the charcoal dress he assumed she always wore, to her refined lipstick and the practised way she could hold a wineglass. Emily knew how far off that mark she was, considering the previous hours that had brought her there; from her morning coffee in her scruffy sweater, with its murky stains and ratty holes along the hem, the squabble in the car concerning gas money, which diplomatically eased into who was dating whom. Which was in turn interrupted when one of the violinists realized they were lost, having turned onto a road of cracked pavement that gave way to gravel, dogs running out from driveways to chase their car, a quick blur of teeth and hackles, manic barking receding into the dust behind them, until they'd found the right road and pulled into the golf course anxious that they were late, their one-thousand-dollar station wagon—with fifty thousand dollars' worth of instruments crammed inside—the most rundown vehicle in the parking lot. And she knew what it would look like later, when they were finished playing, changing into jeans again, scoffing food from the posh mirrors of the caterer's trays in a back room, catching glimpses of her saliva-filmed fingers between the crumbs and picked-through remains of bocconcini and cocktail shrimp, of baba ghanouj and prosciutto.

Emily heard him speaking, and heard herself responding to it, but was stunned to hear how receptive she sounded, offering him all the right cues, maintaining her distance, but also the flow, the measured trickle toward intimacy. Then, without even meaning to, she let him know of a concert that she would be playing at the following week. He said he'd be there, watching it, and waiting to buy her a drink when it was over.

"You know," she'd responded, swirling her wine, holding it up to the afternoon clouds as if to check the vintage's legs. She gave it a long sniff, her nose deep in the glass, then sipped from it delicately, putting it back in the cup of her other hand with a finality akin to placing it on a table. "The truth is: I'm not all that sure you could handle me." She grinned mysteriously, looked away. As she surveyed an isolated curtain of rain in the distance, a watercolour smear in the sky drifting north, she could actually sense how smitten he was.

Emily intended on being more consistent with how she felt when she saw him next, more consequent. "You can't possibly be that naive," she'd said at one point. "I can't believe," her face in her hands, "that I'm actually sitting here with someone who could *think* something like that." Then, "You, my friend, are positively Neolithic. The year is 1999. Join us. Please." He had no idea how to respond, and seldom did. Instead he fished for compliments; there must have been *something* appealing about him. She gave him doubtful looks, sniggered randomly throughout the evening, as if to a string of amusing punchlines that rose from the occasion like gags from an improv, and when prompted to share these private jokes, she eluded the question, changed the subject, asked him to order another bottle. Which he did, perplexed, grasping at straws and ordering the second-to-last entry on the wine list, trying to impress, trying to get a handle on her, on the situation, on his complete powerlessness in it. Luckily the sex was great.

She insisted they not call "whatever it was they were doing" *dating*. They were doing what they were doing, she told him, and whatever it was, it didn't need a name. They met mostly on weekends, ate out, went to the first non-Hollywood films that Cedric had seen in his life, and even ushered in the new millennium together, in a bar on the rooftop of the Westin, getting drunk on a Mondavi and watching the fireworks while he checked his cell for messages every four minutes, worried about the imminent Y2K computer crash. She told him he should lighten up, that a little cataclysm would do the world good.

Emily continued to date other people, and if she slept with one of them, she made sure to tell him about it, often the next day, casually, adding that honesty was one of her few principles, and one she wasn't about to compromise in order to placate his soaring little ego. Then, in April, she made a sudden and capricious decision to cut off contact with him. She deleted his emails and answering machine messages for three weeks, after which he showed up at her doorstep uninvited, catching her with a bad book and bored to atrophy. She agreed to get some dinner with him, then went back to his place, where, in the morning, he'd said he was glad to have her back. She rolled out of bed and into her shoes, saying nothing.

It wasn't sitting well with her. There were days she felt horrible about the way things were going, even guilty. As well as days where she noticed him looking worse for wear, physically; he was dishevelled, stubbled cheeks, forehead blanched and lined with glistening pink folds. He smelled of addled sweat, amoeba-shaped blotches starching the armpits of his dress shirts. He sometimes said he would do anything she wanted him to. Anything, he would listlessly reinforce, staring so intently into her retinas that he seemed to be looking past her, emptily, emptied. She found him pathetic, saw him as a kind of addict, who was addicted—in the way, she believed, all addicts were—to his own destruction. And that was something she didn't want a role in, or implicated responsibility for. In fact the only thing she wanted was to ease him down gently, mercifully, to leave him behind, intact, just as he was before. Without so much as a trace that she'd been there.

Contrary to what everyone thought, Emily really was a compassionate woman, sensitive, perhaps even overly so. She'd never understood how others managed not to see her in that light. Sure she was outspoken, called a spade a spade, but that didn't make her any less sympathetic; it only made her humanity seem a bit askance, as if it were projecting itself at an angle that was, in comparison to everyone else, somewhat obtuse. Beneath that, however, she was one of the most sensitive people she'd ever met.

She remembers the night on Twyn Rivers Drive, in her first year of university, nineteen and driving her parents' car through a blind and moonless dark, two thumbs of light gliding over the road ahead of her, feeling their way along the mottles of the asphalt like brail. One of Emily's best friends lived on the city limits while her boyfriend at the time was in Pickering, just beyond it. A back road connected the two, passing through the city's largest natural area, the Rouge Valley, with its birch and hemlock stands, its migratory birds and swamps. And as Emily made the habit of never visiting one house without at least dropping by the other, she came to know the road quite well, had memorized its sequence of steep hills, blind corners, and single-lane bridges. She knew the straightaways where she could sink her foot low, knew the worst of the potholes, the places where you had to stray onto the other side of the road to miss them. There was very little traffic to worry about.

What she remembers best is the floating quiet just before the impact, the way her parents' Chevrolet seemed to be hovering in one place, thick and slow at eighty-three kilometres per hour. The deer had sprung out from nowhere, in a leap that arced to a stop directly in front of her car, the headlights brightening its coat until it was awash with it, glaring white, and sinking just out of her view. Before she could even touch the brakes, a hollow explosion shuddered the car, seemed to lift the wheels from the tarmac.

She pulled over and turned the vehicle off but left the lights on, only one headlight working now, its beam delineating tracers of insects whirling above the ditch. When she stepped outside she noticed that the hood was creased, a fender dented, the grill crushed with pieces missing from its centre, a silver smile with incisors knocked out. Then she heard the sound behind her, the deer on its side in the opposite ditch, running on the spot, kicking at the grass with all four of its legs, two of them broken. She could hear the terror in its breath, the wheezing panic. A hand over her mouth, Emily made her way toward the dying animal, her eyes slowly adjusting to what little light there was from the headlight still intact, pointing in the opposite direction and getting weaker the farther she walked. For reasons she can't understand, she was trying to step quietly, easing onto the sides of her feet. The air smelled of wet leaves. There was a hesitant toad croaking to her right.

Farther along on the pavement, she noticed a spray of black streaks flowering out from the point of impact, a thicker rope of the same colour trailing into the ditch, stringing together the cause with the effect. She saw movement in the grass and approached it until she could make out the deer's form, then the garbled kinks of its limbs, the way its ineffectual kicks were gradually slowing. She watched its eyes as they dimmed, massive and black, the bristles of its lashes fine-drawn and intricate but unblinking. Its mouth cracked open, some dark seeped out. Its tall ears became limp. With a last huff, it ran out of breath, the cold of the ground stiffening its joints, knotting its musculature, progressively stilling its movements. Until it stopped.

Emily's hand was still over her mouth.

She found herself thinking about the span of the deer's life, pictured it grazing on unseen slopes, twitching with attention, raising its head at anomalous sounds, always tentative, cautious, always wild, and living an entire life without having harmed anything but blades of grass. She contemplated whether something's life should be weighed against the damage that that life causes to the world around it. Which led her to an unsettling thought, to one of those notions she would allow herself to think of only once: there were individuals she knew—people, human beings—whom she would rather see in this animal's place, whom she would rather see die an untimely and unduly death in a ditch somewhere, like this, affecting things so little with their passing as to not even interrupt the amphibian-song in the surrounding grass. But it was a view that was quickly severed, plucked out, and quarantined, leaving her with nothing but a creaking toad and an ungulate that was beyond ever making a sound again.

She lowered her hand from her mouth, turned. Then she was running, to her car, lurching on her sneakers in the illumination from the distant headlight, into her seat, where she slammed the door and locked it shut. She fastened her seatbelt, turned the key in the ignition, took a long look at the dashboard of her parents' 1980 Impala, then slumped over the steering wheel and wept.

When Emily worked up the nerve to tell Cedric that it was finally and definitively over, she'd only found enough courage to do it over the phone. She told him that they'd never exactly been a perfect match, that it was probably time he moved on, found someone better. It was for the best, she promised; he would see that in time. She hurriedly hung up.

Two days later she found the letter in her mailbox, pleading, endorsed with a time and date, his summons to a parley. And one she had to show for. She owed the man that much.

When Cedric emerged from the stairwell he was in a rush that appeared authentic enough, checking the time on his cellphone, narrowly bumping into one of the closed parasols on the patio.

She wondered what had set him back, though wasn't about to ask. She intended this to be over quickly, to get to the point, and to cause as little a scene as possible.

"I'm so sorry I'm late," Cedric said, kissing his hello as if he were in Quebec, something she'd initiated once when he'd tried to sloppily kiss her goodbye on the mouth in public. "I had a noon hour of . . . complications." He settled into his seat, looked her over. "How are you?" he asked with sincerity.

Emily shrugged. "Okay. Fine." But now that he was there, she felt more uneasy than she had expected and looked around the patio as if for something that she'd misplaced, finding only a nick in the table's surface that begged picking at with her fingernail. She was trying to remember the order of what she wanted to say, the carefully worded sentences that she'd prepared. A policeman's siren started up nearby, gave out two long howls, then ceased.

"Look," she began, "I wanted to tell you that I'm really . . . sorry about the way things have . . ." But when she met his eyes, Emily cut herself short.

Cedric didn't look right. There was something odd in his smile, something strange in the way he was sitting there.

"You know what, Emily?" He swallowed. "There's no real reason to talk. I know what you're gonna say. I've heard it before, believe me. And I just . . . don't really want to waste this time with words. I think I just wanna—I don't know—take it in, I guess. Look at you. I haven't seen you in a long, long time, Em. Ages."

Emily tried to say something, but he stopped her, holding up his hand like a traffic cop, long-arming the words that were trying to get across without the appropriate signet. The gesture annoyed her, but she strained to let it go, to let him have it, what he was asking for, a minute of quiet. So she sat back and watched the curious grin on his face, watched him fixating on different aspects of her body, on her fingers, her knuckles, her throat, the tiny studs of her earrings, her cheekbones, her breasts held tight beneath her blouse, her too-broad shoulders, her blocky arms, the way her rib cage rose and fell with her breathing, lingering at her wrists, his eyes focusing as if he could see the eight delicate bones that floated beneath the skin there. Until, believing it to be enough, she stood from her chair and placed a hand on his shoulder as she passed. "Take care of yourself."

Cedric clung on to her hand, smelled it, ran a slow thumb over one of her nails, inspecting the half-moon of a lunula, then looked at another, as if to compare, and finally released his grip. She could feel him watching her until she'd stepped into the stairwell and was out of sight.

At her recital later that afternoon there wasn't much of a turn-out, a meagre audience of a few family members and the usual enthusiast couples, sitting in sporadic clumps, elderly and skeptical. There was, however, a husband and wife that kept catching Emily's eye, a Japanese couple who could have been anywhere between the ages of sixty-five and ninety. Neither of them were reading the program, both of them staring forward impartially, at the musicians, or in their direction anyway. The woman's eyes were deeply rimmed with crow's feet, decades of wind and sun folded into her skin, making her expression both wise and sad.

At one point, the woman noticed a piece of lint on her husband's sweater. She reached over and pinched it from the fabric, holding out her hand and rubbing her fingers together until she was sure it had dropped to the floor at her feet, her hand returning to her husband's shoulder to smooth over the spot where the lint had been, once, twice with the flat of her palm, which rolled off and folded neatly into her other hand that was resting on her lap. While she did this, her husband had continued to watch the stage without sentiment, half-staring at Emily as she tightened the horsehair of her bow and turned the page of her sheet music.

She would spend the night thinking of them both, picturing their faces, guessing at the decades spent between them, envisioning the one simple act over and over, unable to sleep.

Finally "hometown" had come to mean only weddings or
funerals, the usual faces mingling around either chairbacks
or tombstones. September this time, yellowing cottonwoods
frothing in the breeze, the hearse an oblong mirror

reflecting rows of satin flowers in plastic vases, dandelions
wilting from tin cans. It's a family plot, paid for in advance, blank
rectangles in the headstones, unengraved but already written
in stone. A Cessna drowned out the eulogy, and after the minister

had to compete with a woodpecker, plocking his way to a grub.
We stand amid wind damage, offerings of leaves untimely plucked
from their branches, grass clippings drifting the fringes of graves,
urns emptied of their Styrofoam-based bouquets, pulped like

confetti that's thrown to hail a new and momentous beginning.
Pedal-switch stepped on, the hydraulic lift lowered the coffin into
its green-carpeted enclave, basement floor in an elevator with no
doors to slide open, no pre-recorded voice to say you've arrived.

I try to sort out the complications of what I feel, coming back
to this place where everything seems to have shrunk, except
the trees and clouds and graveyards, which have swollen,
and wonder why it doesn't feel like I feel much at all;

watching the autumn gathering of robins hop between
the columns of burial plaques, stopping to tilt their heads,
cupping an ear to the ground as if listening for the
wriggling fingers of the past, but hearing only worms.

Melissa and her cross-country co-pilot counted backwards from their first day of classes to figure out that they had two days to spare on their road trip, which they planned on spending with worthy detours and extra sights. Annette offered once again to check out the town where Melissa was born, where it even sounded like she might have some family—on her dad's side anyway. But with the mention of her father, Melissa found herself feeling more drawn away from the place than to it and had bent over the map to find something else of interest nearby. (It was amazing to her how even the allusion to the existence of her father could change her mood for the worse, find her clenching her teeth and sighing, shaking her head in silence.) She soon found something of greater interest only an hour away, a provincial park with the attention-grabbing name of Writing-on-Stone, just along the American border.

They turned onto the network of secondary highways and township roads, Melissa fixated on the landscape again. Cows stepping amid their respective bevy of cowbirds (who skittered as attentive as underlings in wait at their beck and call), bovines chewing cud with a boredom that spoke of either pompous royalty or an exhaustive dimwittedness. The Mormon church spires spearing into the sky from every cluster of buildings big enough to name itself on the map, their pinnacles pointing up at the cirrus clouds, prairie plumes trailing a comb of white like ancient eyelashes dragging across a firmament iris, the dome of which was always stretching wider, more awake, attentive, scrutinizing the oil pumps in the abandoned distance below, those oblivious mule heads nodding sleepily at the ground, metronomes keeping time just to forget the hours they were leaving behind.

Hanif Khaled was lost. The hospital he was in, Montreal's Royal Victoria, was modelled after the one in Edinburgh, where the Scots had apparently been captivated with the idea of labyrinthine corridors, with a complex network of wards, wings, and divisions that was entirely mazelike. Hanif, in his third year of medical school at McGill, was doing his clerkship there, and that morning, with a short break between two of his lectures, he'd decided to nip a few floors up and get the results of a test he'd given to one of his patients the day before. He soon found himself in a wing he hadn't even known existed. To get to his second lecture from there, he opted for a clever shortcut, which only turned out to be a wasteful detour. Now he was pushing to be on time, walking fast, holding the strap of his backpack tight over his right shoulder, trying to keep it from bouncing noisily. He turned down a long hallway where two patients in baby-blue gowns were pushing their IV poles, shuffling gingerly, an exposed slice of freckled skin running down their backs. He could hear that there was a cluster of elevators farther along the hallway, their bells dinging on arrival, doors sliding open with a clattering grumble, where medical staff and visitors filed out of them, likely dispersing as they always did, with either hesitation or purpose and nothing in-between. He decided he would make his way there, thinking he might fair better on a different floor.

Once at the elevators, Hanif pressed both the up and down buttons, not quite sure which he was going to take. Absorbed in his own predicament, he was startled when a woman, also waiting for the elevator and standing behind him, tapped him on the shoulder. "Pardon me, doctor," she began, waiting for Hanif to turn around. "Would you mind if I asked you a question?"

Hanif was caught off guard. "Uhhh . . ." He glanced at a clock opposite the elevator doors—the same as every clock in the hospital, displaying the same time to every one of its hidden corners, plain white circles pinned against the intricate patterns of ornamental stone. This one was relaying to Hanif that he didn't have time to chat. "In fact-uhhh," he'd said, "I'm hactually not a docter. I'm a mediquel student. So . . ."

There was a disharmonious ding at his back, followed by the elevator doors heaving open. "I am . . . I am very sorrie," said Hanif, quickly stepping into the elevator, still facing the woman, "but I really avv to . . . I avv a . . ." He pointed to the floor, insinuating that he had urgent business to attend to in a lower ward.

The woman was staring at him pleadingly, clearly distressed. She had apparently had a very serious question to ask him. The doors slid closed between them. Instead of descending, the elevator began to climb.

Hanif sighed. He'd been given looks like this before, looks that, for him, managed to highlight the complications of how and why he'd chosen to study medicine in the first place. Looks that brought him back to an argument he'd had with his father, on the day he'd graduated from CEGEP at the top of the dean's list. Though Hanif had appreciated his father's confidence in him, he insisted he just didn't have what it took to be a doctor: detesting even the smallest levels of stress, functioning horribly in the mornings, and loving his easy schedule, a daily planner with enough empty slots to cram his demanding social life around. Nor, he'd added, did he have the drive, interest, or discipline to pursue it. Sorry, Yaba.

Hanif's father, Fineas, had disagreed. But he'd promised he would respect his son's decision, that he would support him in whatever he chose as an occupation, even if it happened to be the wrong one. Fineas himself was a doctor, and he and his wife, Nadia, had immigrated from Egypt, fled what had become a police state, just for the welfare and future prospects of their only son. But Fineas was also a man of his word, and through the years he never once said to Hanif that he'd settled to be less than what he had the potential to become. Though he believed that that was exactly what his son had done, and sat in the background, quietly, thinking it—watching Hanif's graduation as a physiotherapist three years later, watching his amateur downhill ski races throughout university, the slideshows of his California road trips, the unravelling of his car, toilet-papered again by his prankster friends—thinking it.

Hanif had coasted through a carefree decade as a physiotherapist, working at a chic sports-injury clinic in downtown Montreal. But nearing the end of that decade, he became aware of a nameless cerebral appetite. It was the kind of thing that felt like it had been quietly building for years and would no longer be sated by just another good book or weekend road trip. He was missing something, a challenge or test to pit himself against. Not knowing what else to do with it, he picked up a program for continuing education at McGill and browsed the course titles for night classes. Why not, he thought to himself, choosing the very first thing that stuck out for him, an introduction to Arabic: elementary reading, writing, and speaking. On the first evening there, he was asked the inevitable question, the teacher simply wanting to know why everyone had decided to take her course. The responses went around the room in a semicircle, creeping through the desk arrangement, and every answer to Hanif sounded more impressive than the next, the bar being raised incrementally until it was at the redhead boy beside him, who looked to be about twenty. "I just feel," the near-teenager said, "that, as of late, the Arabic world has become the scapegoat of choice in Western society, and I guess I'd just like to understand their culture a bit more, to maybe help curb that, uhm, tendency." The room nodded in thoughtful accord before shifting to Hanif, who looked to be more of an Arab than anyone in the room.

"And how about you?" asked the teacher, though ostensibly already knowing the answer—like others that were staring at him with discerning looks.

Hanif adjusted his sitting position, readjusted it. "I-ehh . . . don't know. Was just . . . interested."

In the fall of 2000, Hanif got a phone call from his mother, asking if he wouldn't mind coming along while Fineas had some tests done. She was afraid of the specialist jargon and terminology they would use while speaking to a fellow physician, and she hoped Hanif would be able to translate what was being said into palatable French. When Hanif asked what kind of specialist they were going to see, she said she imagined it had something to do with optometry. Fineas had been seeing double for a week now. Though he'd been complaining about peculiar smells around the house as well, like heated rubber tires in the kitchen. Hanif noted the dates, hung up the phone, and felt the blood drain from his face.

They found the tumours quickly enough but couldn't do much about them. They were small, and they were many. Hanif asked the different oncologists pointed questions, and hearing the ring of some kind of clinical training they would give him in-depth descriptions, justifications, and methodological reasons why it was impossible to operate, and that they would just have to see how he responded to chemotherapy, radiotherapy, and perhaps radio-surgery. In addition they would have to keep a close eye on the building pressure in his skull and be ready to take measures to curtail the effects, which were only sure to get worse. Whenever Fineas was informed of a change in his prognosis, he would let out a measured sigh. Nadia would ask him if he was all right. At which he would smile, say nothing.

The burgeoning cancer changed him in unexpected ways. He soon lost the patience he was known for, became easily annoyed, even spiteful, said things that a father never should. Like the evening he pulled Hanif closer and murmured into his face that Hanif, who'd been gifted enough to become a surgeon, was wasting his life massaging shoulders. Hanif pulled himself away, flung his father's hand off him, and called him a petty old man. They were words he didn't regret.

Five months later, Fineas was only speaking in Arabic. No one knew if this was a choice or a necessity, in the way that nobody knew how his experience of the world was changing as his neurons crammed ever tighter. Hanif understood enough of what was being said, either due to the course he'd taken or having picked some of the language up passively, overhearing his parents' arguments and endearments while living under their roof for twenty-three years. It was a foreign tongue that he had been around all his life; he was just never spoken to in Arabic, his parents probably imagining that he would integrate into Canadian society more easily that way, be better off *not* knowing it, richer.

As Fineas deteriorated, he was shifted around to different floors in different hospitals, corresponding to the complications that arose in his condition. After one of his moves, Nadia went home to get a few more of his things, personal effects that she brought into his room, set along the windowsills and bedside tables, things he never noticed were there. Hanif went to pick up his mother, arriving earlier than he'd said he would, only to find her with her forehead to the floor, standing up with the mechanicalness of ritual.

"Beh, que-ce que tu fais là?" He asked her what she was doing accusingly, because he knew.

She was unembarrassed. She not only admitted that she was praying but motioned for him to come and stand beside her, gesturing that he should join in. She could teach him, she'd offered, if he wanted, and added that his pronunciation in Arabic (at least in the few words she'd heard him say) was excellent. He would sound just like the calming Imams in the mosques of her youth. Come on, she encouraged, there was no reason to be ashamed.

Hanif's feet stayed very still on the tiled floor. "Mother," he said in Arabic, encouraged by the compliment, "I don't think you understand. I don't believe. I'm not a believer. What I believe, in fact, is that it won't do anything, for anyone."

"Hanif," she said, also in Arabic, the first time she'd ever addressed him in it. "I'm not asking you to believe. I'm asking you to pray. And it'll do something for me."

He looked out the window, ran a hand through his hair, then kicked off his shoes and stood beside her. She was right about his pronunciation, and in only minutes he'd learned the verses and positions. He'd always been such a clever boy.

That winter, Hanif, while certainly not feeling very clever—researching what might be going on in his father's skull, reading periodicals and journals, coyly looking for the laymen's abridgement—decided that studying for something medical would give him some welcome and needed stimulation. He prepared for his MCAT, curious to see what kind of marks he could get, wondering if he still had it in him. The score he received, however, wasn't much to write home about; much like his GPA, which he'd let slip near the end of his party-filled physiotherapy studies. Both numbers hovered just around the minimum requirements to be accepted into the Faculty of Medicine at McGill, the benchmark he was using to gauge his success. So, still unsure of whether he'd proven anything to himself, and with a little curiosity, and a little more abandon, he submitted an application, mentioning it to no one.

Fineas was moved into a palliative care ward. He was no longer speaking but would respond to both Arabic and French with a nod or shake of his head. Questions had to be brief and simplistic; he was easily confused. Are you tired? Are you uncomfortable? Are you in pain? He gave drunken nods to them all. On good days, he was still able to amble around a bit, but after he'd had several accidents when in the washroom alone they had him wearing incontinence pads and a catheter. He would sleep for days at a time, waking with a grogginess that no sunlight or fresh air ever managed to clear.

When Hanif was opening the letter from McGill he was inexplicably nervous. But reading that he'd been invited for the interviewing process, he became smug. Whereas his MCAT scores might have rightfully bruised his scholastic confidence, he knew that, socially, he was just as self-assured and articulate as he'd been in his early twenties, maybe even more so. On the scheduled day, he walked into the conference room like someone hosting a homey and intimate dinner party. In one interview, the panel, after laughing at an off-the-cuff joke he'd made, asked him what had sparked his interest in going into medical school, now, after having worked as a physiotherapist for ten years. Sitting with one leg crossed over the other, Hanif paused to a single, blinking image of his father, lying in his hospital bed only a few blocks away, his limbs and cheeks emaciating, a novel by Michel Tremblay placed within his reach, as if he might sit up and read from it at any moment. Hanif leaned forward and coughed, excusing himself tactfully, then gave the most winning response he could think of: that it was the natural progression for people in a curative field. He'd spent a decade treating physical injuries, and now it was time to expand beyond the same dislocations and knee operations he was always dealing with, time to learn about the broader scope of health and wellness, to take his already profound dedication to healing and bring it to another level. The chairman picked up a pen and thanked him for his answer, noting something on a sheet of paper. Hanif doubted they'd caught his hesitation.

The family had a meeting in the palliative ward to discuss Fineas's "end-of-life care." It was agreed that he would be more at ease and, perhaps, less bewildered at home, with nursing aides and physicians visiting regularly, as well as people on-call waiting to assist if need be. Once they'd set him up in his own living room, his condition altered. He slept less, was awake and in an animated state more, though it was anyone's guess how aware he actually was. He'd taken to pushing his head deep into his pillow, his bony spine arched, his eyes darting around in the air above him, never focusing or stalling, never fixing on any one object, a continuous jagged circle. The doctors had given him a month.

When Hanif received the second letter he didn't really know what to do with it, so he brought it over to his parents' place, sitting down in the living room with the envelope between his fingers. He talked with his mother about the slight changes in Fineas's condition from the previous afternoon. When she was finished they looked him over in silence for a while, watching as his eyes moved, Hanif thought, like an animal treading circles in a zoo, tamping a verbatim path of soil around and around its enclosure, never noticing the spectators' elbows hanging over the fence nearby. Hanif finally tapped the envelope and mumbled that he was on the waiting list at the Faculty of Medicine at McGill. Nadia turned to him rigidly, asking to see the letter, as if needing to verify its authenticity before getting excited. But once she'd skimmed it, she couldn't contain herself, and brought the piece of paper over to Fineas, holding it above him. "Hanif," she called down at him loudly in Arabic, "Hanif is going to be a doctor, Fineas! Isn't that wonderful news?" She held on to his shoulders and moved her head around, chasing his gaze. Finally, she looked back at Hanif, spoke sincerely. "You know. I think he heard. I think he knows." Fineas continued his manic search of the ceiling.

Then, on a Monday, three weeks later, Fineas appeared to be having an exceptionally good day. Just after lunch, Hanif stepped out, Nadia asking him to get some things at the grocery store, probably thinking of dessert or a refreshing afternoon snack: a cantaloupe, some grapefruit, a few oranges. While he was in the fruit aisle sorting the ripe from the green, and Nadia was wiping down the counters after finishing the lunch dishes, Fineas died. Hanif was the one that found him, placing the bag of groceries on the floor. He didn't call his mother in for a few minutes, wanting a moment alone with him. He sat on the edge of the bed and studied his father's face—the soft dents of his temples, the slackened muscles of his brow and cheeks—without really knowing why he was doing it. Then, for just a moment, Hanif Khaled let himself entertain a thought, a possibility. It was a fleeting indulgence really, whimsical, hopeful, and so he made a point of never sharing it with anyone, kept it tightly to himself. The following

Wednesday, Fineas was buried in the Islamic Cemetery in Saint-Laurent; on his right side, Hanif was intrigued to learn, facing Mecca.

Hanif was offered a placement, and, wavering until the last day he could decide, he finally accepted it. He took a leave from work and was plunged, almost instantly, into a surge of dense information that was steeped in opinions and politics. He struggled to keep on top of it and strained to ignore the contradictions that swirled in the undercurrents. The buzz-phrase of the day was "evidence-based medicine," where everything was either verifiable and could be plotted into an existing paradigm or discounted. Which, Hanif thought, was fair enough, until the next class would roll around and he would learn, for example, how clubbed fingers were a potential indicator of lung cancer. No, the professor would confess, there is no understandable connection between the disease and the symptom. But it had been seen enough, and was now accepted. The students duly noted it down. In the following class, the body would again be evinced as an apparatus that had been comprehensively mapped out, studied, and digitized. A human being was composed and comprised of a chemical soup that, as such, had restrictions, conventions, and rules that it must abide by. Therefore, one could ascertain what might be added or taken away to achieve the most advantageous effects. Mysteries, if there were any, were only a factor of time. They would be solved. And more likely sooner than later. At the end of these lectures, the students would stand as if for an ovation, shoving books into the hungry mouths of their backpacks, and file out the door to the next class.

He studied before bed, usually dozing off at his desk, head easing onto his arm "for just a second," sinking into a sleeve that smelled of the formaldehyde from his gross anatomy labs, the green-glass warmth of his lamp melting into his ear.

Meanwhile the first anniversary of Fineas's death loomed on the calendar, and only became more daunting the closer it crept, easing forward with its kindling of apprehensions and presentiments. When it finally arrived, it floated through the rooms where Nadia and Hanif were bracing for it, only to pass them by, dissipating into a completely normal day. It was an occurrence that would repeat itself, more or less, every year.

Hanif's second year of medical school was just as overwhelming as the previous. He had his first contact with patients, in a course where general practitioners were assigned groups of students to show around their clinics, where they were allowed to interview patients and perform some of the physical examinations.

When going into his third year, he'd had a physician tell him that working in hospitals was really just a nonstop game of catch-up, where all you were shooting for was to tie up the loose ends that had become frayed by the end of your shift, as to not leave anything unruly for the people behind you. When Hanif began his clerkship at the Royal Victoria Hospital, he was sure that that wouldn't be the case, as he would only be in charge of two or three patients on any given day. But even that proved to be thorny. He was always fighting the sensation that he didn't exactly know what he was supposed to be doing, straining to see the symptoms and diagrams that he'd memorized, the picture-perfect examples and case studies that had blistered from his textbooks. But he had no idea how these symptoms manifested themselves as permutations of other things and so could never be exactly sure what it was or what his next move should be. He took a cautious approach, ran tests that most would deem redundant, and took every opportunity he could to listen in on conversations between other physicians.

When his shifts were through, he was allowed to finish up his paperwork in some doctor's office that wasn't being used. He would slouch in its leather chair and stare dazed out into the hallway, where a series of plaques adorned the walls, commemorative inscriptions to chairmen, benefactors, and governors that bore seldom-used words such as "bestowal," "endowment," "bequest."

His head would often ease forward, lower, until it was resting on the desktop, which is how he would stay until a nurse walked by and poked her head into the room, asking if he was all right.

"Sorrie," he would say, rubbing his eyes, straightening his papers.

And now he was lost, and about to be late for his second lecture of the day, wandering around the labyrinth in the upper floors of the Royal Victoria Hospital without being able to find a substantial clue as to where he was. In the humming elevator, he was thinking of the woman who'd just wanted to ask him a question, thinking of the way he'd left her and how likely it was that he wouldn't have been able to give her an answer anyway. In fact, it struck Hanif that, lately, he wasn't really sure of anything. Not medical facts, not his studies, not the decisions in his life, not even why he was making them. It felt like his entire existence had become a losing game of catch-up.

The elevator doors slid open and he stepped out, looking up and down a new, unfamiliar corridor. A male nurse rounded a corner to his right, and Hanif, giving the man a quick glance, suddenly froze. It was striking how much this man resembled a younger version of his father. Hanif felt like he couldn't breathe. Cold seeped down the length of his vertebrae. The olive-skinned man, not knowing what to do with the loaded stare, addressed Hanif in passing. "Salaam," he said before disappearing around another corner. Hanif, watching the place where the man had left his sight, realized that he had said nothing in return.

He began breathing again, blinking hard. He shook his head and took in his surroundings as if for the first time. There were a few doors with uninspired Christmas decorations taped to their frames, which led to other places, other corridors. The floor below his feet was gleaming with polish, in contrast to the floorboards that had been nicked, scuffed, and marked by the polishing machine. The hallway was empty.

And Hanif Khaled was still lost.

Getting older
is convincing me that
a person's life is weighed out
by its shortcomings, its defeats
embarrassments
The things that made us
wince and cringe and cower
but somehow not shrivel
We kept on, less proud of course
less righteous, less right
but still plodding
walking the precarious cycle
from bendable bones to brittle ones
from fragile to frail
Meanwhile our ambitions and measures
compress with our spines
thin out with our scalps
Accomplishments scaling themselves down
to the size we always were
True, I've got a lovely daughter of twenty-eight
somewhere
but I've also drunk espresso with the pigeons
under the colonnades of Piazza San Marco
and stood to listen to an entire
song at Queen and Dundas
by a busking violinist with his
case hinged open
Which I threw a toonie into
before moving on
like I'd done with pennies as a kid
into bloated wishing wells

Bruno was curled up on the chesterfield beside her, the tip of his tail drooping over his nose. It was a deep sleep, his tabby eyes sealed tight, his purring having stopped long ago, even if Melissa's hand was still on his back. Melissa Johnson was focused on the book in her other hand, her thumb pressed into its crease, prying it open. When she'd finished the page she was reading, she grinned, removed her hand from the cat, and dog-eared the page's corner. Despite this movement, Bruno slept on. And would have continued to had Melissa not glanced into her empty teacup and calculated that there was enough time for another before work. Unfortunately for Bruno, the sofa was the antithesis of firm, the weakened springs creaking and sponging low when weighted, as well as springing widely back as she stood up, jostling him. The cat woke to give her a narrow-eyed glare as she disappeared into the kitchen, then tucked his face under his paw and let out a world-weary sigh. Outside in the boreal distance, a chainsaw puttered out. A crow complained in the quiet that was left behind. In the bay window in front of the sofa, a myriad of individual clouds—the kind that are only seen in autumn, small and shaped like blotchy snails with grey-bottomed bodies and white-furrowed shells—glided through the sky, all of them moving in the same direction, from one nameless place, to another.

After the kettle whistle rose to a squeal in the other room, deflating with the sound of its being taken off the burner, Melissa returned with a steaming mug, the tag of a teabag flapping lightly from its rim. She picked up her book again and sunk into the couch, where Bruno, deeply annoyed by yet another bounce of the cushions, stood to leave, though faltered with a stretch and a yawn, a trembling high-arched back, watching her settle in as if to judge how long she would be staying, his face a sleepy scowl.

Gradually, if reluctantly, he moved a little farther away and curled up again.

Just then, far below the clouds in the bay window, a sleek car drove into view and turned with certainty into her driveway. She looked up from her book, sure that this car, which she'd never seen before, would reverse out and drive away in the opposite direction, something that happened quite often on the road where she lived, an almost dead-end lane in the small town of Haliburton, Ontario. But whoever it was had turned off his car and was getting out, though with much less conviction than he'd had while pulling in. It was her father, Cedric, now slouching in her driveway, slamming the door while squinting through the front window, a hand held over his brow to function as a visor.

Melissa's lips hinged open.

The last time she'd seen him was four years ago. Which isn't to say that their communication had been severed by a dramatic episode, it was just that, as the years went by, there were fewer reasons to stay in touch. He did call her every year on her birthday, sounding pressed for time as usual, as if he were making the call between appointments, or snapping his fingers at a waiter to get the bill, maybe in traffic and changing lanes on his way to the golf course. Melissa ended these annual conversations with the feeling that he was just as happy as she was to hang up, each of them rolling their eyes as they pressed the red button on their respective receivers. Her last two birthdays he'd only gotten around to leaving a message on her answering machine, which suited her fine. She sure didn't call him for his birthdays. And he sure didn't call for Christmas, when Melissa and Julie were alone in the house together, the unilateral team of his opponents, as he likely saw them.

It was true that Melissa and her mother had become faithful allies leading up to the divorce. In fact, it was Melissa who'd instigated it. Cedric had always been far from the limelight of her grade-school plays and soccer matches, coming in late only to stand in the dim at the back with his standard set of excuses, which seemed to wear thin and weaken at the speed of Melissa's maturity. Until she was sixteen and her disappointment had turned into offhand acerbic remarks. Once, while Cedric was admonishing her about her physics grades, she'd asked him flat out, as if questioning the marks he'd had back in his own high-school English, what he thought the word "neglectful" meant. It snubbed him into a silence, encouraged her antagonism. Though it was a challenge she aimed at her mother instead of Cedric, pressing her with irksome questions when he wasn't around, gradually nudging her out into the wide agoraphobic open. Questions like: Are you happy in your marriage? How does it nurture you? Would you hope for me to find one just like it? Really? Why not?

But when she was seventeen and caught throwing a house party without permission, a line was drawn. On the evening in question, Cedric had slapped one of Melissa's friends (if you could call him that), and in so doing had (according to whispered conversations between Julie and Melissa) crossed a line himself. Either way, Cedric clamped down. It was high time she learned some respect, he'd said, giving her a grounding that was severe by any measure, even his. It was a punishment she readily, almost gladly, accepted. What it meant was more time at home with her mother, the two of them making the most of the evenings they had to spend together, cooking their favourite dishes, meals they knew Cedric would be late for (or more likely not show up for at all—calling at the last minute to tell Julie he would just have to microwave it when he got home, obliged into another cocktail with a very, very important client).

"You do know he's screwing other women, don't you?" Melissa inserted after one of these phone calls, the same night she convinced her mother to nurse the first gin and tonic of her life.

But Melissa's casual comment appeared to be going too far, costing Julie something that she couldn't quite afford. "Melissa. Please. I don't think that's any of your business."

"Mom, you say that like it's none of yours either."

Julie paused to look tiredly into her glass, then through it. "Maybe it isn't. You're young. These things are complicated."

"I think *you're* young. Nobody awards medals for living a miserable life, you know. At least martyrs can justify their suffering, have their belief to break even for them. While the rest of us are just too scared to take a daring stab at our own contentment. And sure, maybe you're not shooting for medals and monuments. But what about some peace? Just a bit. Haven't you earned at least that much by now?"

Whenever Julie failed to answer, Melissa felt a little more respect for her. It would take her another two years, with her daughter living at home throughout university, coaxing and prodding her toward it, before Julie would finally ask for a divorce.

When she did, Cedric was gobsmacked. He agreed almost laughingly, spitefully, as if he were daring her to try to survive out there in the big bad world-according-to-CNN without him. The settlement was a generous one for Julie, and within three months Cedric had moved the last of the things that had been deemed his out of the house. It was less an ordeal than either of them had expected. With an innocent old-fashionedness, they were stunned at how ready the system was for such an eventuality, a procedure already in place for them, with protocols to minimize the snags along the way and a modus operandi where, to combat the sensation of falling, you could merely cling to the handrails of the process itself. When the formalities were over, their relations remained amicable enough, even if Cedric went to great lengths to avoid hearing or seeing how, in the end, Julie could get along just fine in this scary world on her own. Better than fine really. In fact, Julie even came to enjoy her bi-monthly problem-solving quests, getting replacement light bulbs and oil changes; it was so much simpler, and less intimidating, than she'd imagined it being. While Cedric, unsettled after hearing from his mechanic about an easygoing run-in with Julie and a set of new brake pads, decided to find himself another garage, someone who was closer to his new place and who better understood the importance of keeping his mouth shut.

Meanwhile, Julie's relationship with Melissa took on a new shape, entered a confidence that often pushed the mother/daughter boundaries. It was no longer a taboo of loyalty to talk about Cedric's failings, which allowed for unspoken things about his youth and age to rise to the surface. Like the time they'd been at a dinner party and the wife of one of Cedric's clients, sitting next to him, calmly cleared her throat during the dessert, smiling politely, and stated that his hand seemed to be on her lap and would he please remove it. Julie had shot to her feet to clear away whatever dirty plates she could grab and remembers sniffling over the sink in the kitchen for no other reason than the fact that she wasn't able to slink out the back door and disappear from the debacle. She had to say goodbye to everyone, put on her shoes and coat, grin and bear it through the front door. Always having to face the music that she'd had no part in composing.

Melissa joined in with the same sentiments, recalling when she was fifteen and sitting bored at a barbecue in their backyard with some new guests, one of whom had pointed out how, lately, there were getting to be way too many panhandlers downtown, shoving their tinkling cardboard cups under everyone's noses, accosting passerbys with their hard-luck stories. And they were getting pushier too, he warned ominously. Which set her father off on his famous mugging tirade, telling the story of how he'd been robbed blind at a gas station once, in broad daylight. But then he took it a step further, mentioning how, if he'd owned a firearm, things would have been different. "I'm tellin' ya, if the same thing'd happened in the States, a regular guy like me, he would'a had a gun. And he would'a turned around, pulled it out, and pow, just like that . . ." he'd snapped his fingers, "just like that—the world's a better place. You know? I mean, these people, what do we . . . how can we just let them roam the streets like that? Shouldn't somebody be doing something about them? And I honestly don't care what. Just *do* something. You know?" He had searched the guests' faces for signs of accord, which they attempted to procure in as noncommittal way possible before quickly changing the subject. Hey, was that a *new* barbecue? And what *was* the marinade Julie was using for this chicken? Melissa remembered feeling suddenly nauseous, excusing herself to ease the door shut in her room where she could press play on her Cranberries CD and flop heavily onto her bedspread.

Julie and Melissa swapped these one-sided anecdotes until they'd run out of them, had grown weary of their simplistic villain-mongering, and began trending toward other topics, more productive ones, and, at times, things that they'd never thought of breaching before. Like what do you think or feel about such-and-such? What, if you could go back, would you do differently? Is there something you'd like to know, or do, or understand before you die? Is there anywhere in the world you've always wanted to go, and why? What (Melissa lifting her gin and tonic and motioning at the night sky, a salt spill of stars running along a smoggy pane, the quarter moon of her lime pinching the rim of her glass) do you believe?

She learned that her mother had always wanted to go to Ireland, to see the threads of hand-piled stones that macraméd the fields of rain-muddied grass there, and to listen, for one entire day, she'd said, to the most lovely accent in the English language. For Melissa, it was southern Spain, for the cubes of its Berber villages, the ornate ruins of its Moorish architecture, and to eavesdrop on the teenaged guitarists that she'd always imagined practising their flamenco in the parks. When Julie had heard this, she made a few phone calls, asked around, and managed to find Melissa a two-month au pair placement in the Andalusian city of Granada, if she wanted it, over her first summer break in university. Melissa couldn't wait, though kept offering to stay behind, even after she'd checked her bags in at the airport. But Julie had promised that she both wanted and needed the time alone. It would be good for her, she'd said, unpersuasively.

The months that Melissa spent in Spain taught her three things: she wasn't particularly gifted with four-year-olds, was even less talented (and potentially hopeless) at second language acquisition, and there was something about travelling that she absolutely adored. She thought that it had to do with the normalcy one found in other places. The way people got up, went to work and paid their bills, watched TV, walked their dogs and scolded their children, all in a different tongue, of course, but in roughly the same way we all do. However appealing the idea of ethnology was, it was really only the study of nuanced variation.

Melissa soon found her favourite place in the city, a barren hilltop above the Albayzín, crowned with an ancient wall and overlooking the Alhambra, far from the tourist squares below. It was a spot where she always felt somewhat daring, edgy, watching the young gypsy women with their flawless bellies bronzing in the late sun, their unwashed hair, so black it was indigo, glinting in its own oils, seedy men trailing behind them, scuffling along the dusty footpaths that snaked to the grottos and shanties of their homes farther off. None of them acknowledged her with anything outside of mild contempt, a dismissive enmity. She wasn't part of the landscape there, had no intimacy with it. She was only there to record it and move on, sitting on the bare clay with her Levi's blue jeans, a spiral-bound notebook pinned against the slope of her thighs, busily scribbling—a sketch, they thought, maybe a diary, travelogue. Whatever it was, they all seemed to judge, it was sure to be girlish and sentimental, have nothing to do with their reality.

When she returned to Toronto, still drunk with adventure, she transferred out of most of the courses she'd chosen the previous spring. She then registered into the recreation and tourism program, thinking that this was a sure way of getting her out of the city and travelling again. She wasn't a fan of the classes themselves, or of the sociable and cheery students that the curriculum drew, but she went through the motions anyway, wrote mediocre exams, uninspired papers, somehow sure that it would all pay off in the end. Meanwhile at home, Melissa shared her enthusiasm of "the new" and "dynamic" with her mother, giving her gifts of enrolment for her birthday, Christmas, Mother's Day, and, for no occasion at all, evening classes in Indian cooking, pottery, yoga, an introduction to painting. At winter's end, she bought Julie packets of exotic seeds for her springtime flower garden, and while she planted them in the cool yard, Melissa went through a list that she'd printed out with all the co-op positions and summer jobs that were open to her as a tourism student. Finally, the benefits. They narrowed them down to the four best-sounding jobs and Melissa applied to every one, receiving a single offer, a position helping to run a campground in British Columbia, on a beach in Tofino, Vancouver Island. She'd held out the minimum-wage contract for Julie to hold—with its stipulations of scrubbing bathroom stalls and quelling partiers that weren't abiding by the quiet curfew—as if it were a fragile and invaluable heirloom. Julie said she hoped she found what she was looking for.

One of her classmates, Annette, got the same job and proposed they use her hand-me-down car to drive them across the country, split the gas, keep each other awake. Annette wasn't Melissa's favourite of classmates, but she supposed the lure of the voyage would be enough to compensate for it. They left the day after their last exam and took the better part of a week to drive across the country.

The second day of the journey they'd driven too far, too late, having agreed to always find a place to camp before nightfall. Now they were on a desolate stretch in northern Ontario, the long dark becoming increasingly oppressive, both of them too inert and tired to search for a pull-off that would hide the car and allow them to set up their tent in the headlights without the worry of rural rednecks cruising by and discovering that they were alone, the scenario already played out in their heads: greasy dungarees and a baseball cap craning over the steering wheel to look for any boyfriends present, a gun rack and trophy feathers pinioned into his dash, the window rolling down with slow sadism. Gerls-needah-han-ith-anathenh? So they drove on, an eighth of a tank left, on the stereo Sarah McLachlan turned up to the cusp of distortion, the sorry sun-crusted speakers coughing dust, a familiar five-year-old cassette blathering on in order to ward off the squabble they both felt they could sink into. Finally, ahead, an oasis of streetlights with a roof of fluorescent tubing, harbouring a set of gas pumps. There was scaffolding along the walls of the store, the apparent tracing of a future wildlife mural; a moose, wolves, a trout on a fishing line flailing above water.

They stretched outside the car, electric buzz of fluorescence, nocturnal insects pattering the tin eaves above them, the lights so overswarmed with them they were foaming. It was Melissa's turn to stand at the nozzle, Annette's to pay and refill their Thermos mugs with the syrupy and jitter-inducing "gourmet coffee" that was found in push-button machines at every roadside gas station—Mochaccino, French Vanilla, English Toffee, bastardizations so far removed from their originals they'd become a creation unto themselves. She was also going to ask for the closest and safest paid campground, a cost, they'd agreed, they were willing to swallow.

Melissa pulled a sweater and the road atlas out of the car, slammed the door in the humming quiet, and ran her finger along the red line of the highway as if to measure how far they were from Thunder Bay. Just then a sizeable moth plopped onto the map next to her hand and became instantly still, probably sensing that there was something large and breathing hovering over it. The moth was pale green with a delicate maroon outline and a set of discerning eyes painted onto its wings. Two long lobes dropped from the mimicked face like tusks, the insect's body in the centre making up a kind of furry nose. It was the most striking moth Melissa had ever seen, and she found herself looking up at the lights, as if to find more of them there. Once, her friend Nathan (some might have referred to him as her old boyfriend), who was a great collector and retainer of factoids and useless trivia, had told her about the way moths had evolved to navigate by the strongest celestial light: the moon—if it wasn't new—or one of the brighter stars, Sirius, Arcturus, Alpha Centauri. Which is why, he'd said, when they pass by an artificial light, naturally assuming that it's going to stay in the same place in the sky, directly above them, for example, they have no choice but to circle it in order to keep it there, at that one fixed point in their vision. They're not, contrary to popular belief, attracted to light; they just can't seem to get past it, disoriented by their only means of orientation—like an arctic airplane heading continually west in a spiral around the magnetic pole. They're drawn into danger by a set of intuitions that they know only how to trust, into a blindness by the very way they see. And there was some aspect in that, considered Melissa, folding the map as the moth flew away to bounce off the lights again and Annette stepped out of the store, that was really, and quite wonderfully, human.

In the car she adjusted her Petzl headlamp on her forehead and picked up the spiral-bound notepad she kept near her feet, a pen slipped into the spine. As they pulled out onto the dark of the highway, Melissa started scribbling.

"The lady inside said there's a campground about forty minutes away. Cool?" asked Annette.

"Sure," Melissa said indifferently.

Annette flicked on her brights, checked the gauges. "So what are you writing?"

"Uhm . . . a journal," Melissa mumbled, though was obviously lying. Annette, slightly affronted, made a point to never ask about the notebook, or what it was for, again.

The next two days the road cut through mounded terraces of spruce and stagnant lakes, chiselled through brief walls of marbled granite, and straightened out through a stretch of aspens that dispersed into open fields and the red of granaries. Nunavut had just been christened its own territory only a month earlier, inspiring travellers to raise an inuksuk atop most of the prominent outcroppings, boulders, and benchmarks along the Trans-Canada Highway, a gesture, the two girls had agreed, that was somehow touching.

They crossed the Manitoba border into Saskatchewan, where Melissa, whether driving or as a passenger, fastidiously watched the landscape, finding the flatlands to be far from boring, a common complaint of people that traversed the country. It was true that there wasn't much to look at, but that, for her, only served to highlight what little there was to see. Whether it was the deviations in the geography: the buttes, eskers, draws, and coulees; or the manmade structures that seemed to stand out as a kind of proclamation, a defiance against the overwhelming expanse and isolation, even if they were in the very act of being defied: rusted and squeaking windmills above settlers' water wells and flattened homesteads, barbed wire draping along tilted fencelines, abandoned barns and farmhouses canting over in sagging parallelograms. The new generation machinery was painted in bold and resilient colours but was already dusting over with doubt. During her shifts as a passenger, Melissa never slept, not wanting to miss so much as a half-hour.

"This is like . . ." Annette broke one of their rare no-music-or-radio silences just after Medicine Hat, "it feels so Canadian, you know?"

"What does?" Melissa put her bare feet up onto the front of her seat, sipped from her half-litre coffee mug.

"I don't know . . . just . . . this," Annette gestured out in front of her, a hand sweeping the windshield. "You know, driving these huge distances with vintage tapes of Blue Rodeo and The Hip, grain silos and roadkill and irrigation sprinklers. All this stuff. Don't you think?"

But what Melissa thought was that she was about to come

across as a humbug again. Because to be honest, she'd always hated the question, had never seen the point of it really—all the literature and art collectives, the radio programs and television documentaries that explored the query of what it meant to be Canadian. In our scrambling need for an identity, thought Melissa, we'd opted for the worst way of acquiring one: namely by working backwards. We started with the naive idea that we could find a parameter for us all to fit inside, trace a silhouette with all the things we are and aren't, define a "we" by using the paltry measure of our few, few common denominators. Why should we care about the shape of the one paper-thin shell that might encapsulate us all? What kind of culture would be driven by such a manic search for its own confinement? If we spent half as much energy not in concentrating on what this fictitious capsule might look like, but instead on filling it, on cramming it with original art and thought and science and cuisine, on driving forward unimpeded by our own backward clichés and questions, those blurry lines would draw themselves. The truth was that Melissa didn't feel very Canadian, didn't feel moved when she saw her flag rippling in the wind. But she did feel that she liked the wind. And it's there, she knew, that the drawing should really begin. Right there. At the beginning.

"Well? Don't you think?" Annette repeated, a little impatient.

"Yeah. Yeah, I guess so." Melissa switched on the tape deck, turning it up a bit, rolled her window down farther, and went back to watching the fields as they moved past, fields strewn with hay bales now, like course-haired creatures, she fancied, hunched over and sleeping, oblivious to that exceptionally wide-open sky and the elephantine clouds that padded along the prairie with their shadows.

In the evening of day five, after they'd decided to take the shorter, though less scenic, southerly route through the Rockies, they passed through a city that Melissa had heard the name of innumerable times growing up. When she saw the first exit ramp slide away from their lane, she tried to look through the chain-linked fences that were choked with tumbleweeds and plastic bags, and over the concrete sound barriers into the town proper, as if straining to see something in particular.

"Are you looking for a restroom pull-off or something?" asked Annette. "Or you wanna get some orange juice for tomorrow morning again?"

"No," Melissa shrunk back into her seat, almost managing to look guilty. "It's kinda weird. This is where I was born. But then we moved to Toronto when I was two, so I have no memories of it."

"Really? Whoah. Well . . . I dunno—do you wanna stop or something?"

"Uhh. Not really."

"Whoah. So do you, like, still have family here and stuff?"

"No, not that I know of. My mom's parents moved to Burlington a few years after we did, and my dad's folks were killed in a car wreck when I was eleven, on some country road around here, I imagine. The story goes that my granddad was famous for falling asleep at the wheel. Something you can only be famous for for so long, I guess. So if I do have relatives here, they're distant ones. I remember my dad flying back every once in a while, just for weddings and funerals kind of thing, so, who knows, I might. But if I knocked on their door—I mean, what would I say to them?"

"Yeah, right," Annette acceded, doing an over-shoulder check and changing lanes. They'd driven past most of the exits to Lethbridge now and were cutting between the coulees, crossing a broad river valley where Melissa watched an extensive railroad bridge as it ran parallel to the highway, towering pylons as black as the coal it was initially built to transport. It struck her as one of those industrial eyesores that had since become quite funky, in that chic-urban steampunk kind of way. She was about to comment on it but didn't. They drove up the other side of the coulee where the highway opened onto a yawning skyline and a road-gridded carpet of prairie that unrolled all the way out to the Rockies. They found a cheap-enough campground just as the peaks started to rise and shoulder into the wide panorama that their eyes had become used to. It was near the site of a devastating landslide that had buried part of a town in 1903, the sprawling boulderfield so barren it could have happened yesterday. They clambered to the top of one of the larger rocks and ate submarine sandwiches for dinner, talking disjointedly about all the houses that had never been excavated in the wake of the disaster, the homes that were buried beneath them.

Two days later, after a ferry ride and a flat tire, which a brusque middle-aged woman had pulled over to help them change, counselling them on car maintenance and emergency preparedness as she did so, they pulled into Tofino. A few icebreaking activities transitioned smoothly into the orientation of their sleeping quarters, live-in policies, and the whereabouts of the cleaning supplies. Annette effortlessly fit in with the other staff, the rally of small talk and niceties, anecdotes of alcohol and university bashes. Melissa nevertheless felt herself budged out onto the wayside. She was beginning to come to terms with the fact that she was more socially awkward than she'd ever imagined herself being, more reserved, introverted. She reminded herself, however, that she hadn't come all this way for the party scene, for the marijuana nebulae and beach fires. She'd come here for the beach itself. Or for the ocean anyway.

It was the first time Melissa had ever been to the seaside, let alone lived on one. Everything she looked at was a surprise, or bizarre, seemed to have sprouted directly from the pages of an implausible science fiction novel. She was most taken with the tidal pools, stepping out among the green anemones and their orifices of filament tentacles, the tiny sculpins invisible in their camouflage, shore crabs scuttling into recesses, limbs tucking tight, the hiss of seagrapes. She liked the tracks and traces in the wet sand that adjoined the pools, the life that had ventured out of them. And the purple, orange, and maroon starfish that clung to the rocks in expressive positions, their reaching arms, shrugging shoulders, hanging heads, splayed out on the barnacle-sprinkled surfaces like sailors having just crawled onto land from a shipwreck, limp and exhausted, reduced to ragged stickmen.

Sometimes, falling asleep to the swelling rumble of the surf, she would think about the waves on McKenzie Beach, the campground's own, about the way they rolled in so consistently, insistently, unyielding, undying. She would lie in her tiny room that smelled of particleboard and new paint (which was already losing the battle against the mildew) and consider how long these waves had been rolling in for, in exactly the way they were then. And exactly as they are now. Right now. Rolling onto the sand, turning over in the sun, in the dark. Like they have for millennia. Like they will for millennia. Whatever way you stood beside it, the sea had a way of reshaping, of eroding, your humility.

Melissa would call home to tell Julie about most all of this, talking from a phone booth in the parking lot, leaning against the glass door to stare up at the lamp in the one streetlight of the parking lot, the bulb aswirl with a snow-flurry of moths. But enough about her, she would finally say, how about you, Mom, how are things over there? You enjoying your pottery classes again? What do you mean you talked to Dad? Yeah but, why bother? Seriously. A groan while hanging up the phone, the mood of her night suddenly soured.

On her days off she would walk into town, grey skies, drizzle brightening the colours of the yellow sea kayaks on the water, of the orange of the customers' survival suits aboard the whale-watching zodiacs. Girls on long skateboards steering clear of puddles; bicycles with surfboard racks, riders' arms drooping from the handlebars in a wet-dog slouch; organic coffee shops, soya sprouts in every sandwich; all while abrasive float planes bore down on the village overhead, with their pontoons like skis dangling from a blaring chairlift, the artists in their boutiques seemingly deaf to it, some of them white illustrators wearing crystal pendants, specializing in Haida art.

Looking back, it was more like the dog found Melissa than the other way around. She'd been reading on the beach one evening, with her back to the butt-end of a driftwood log, when it stepped out from behind her and sat down well within arm's reach, wagging its tail and watching her with a familiarity that suggested it had known Melissa all its life. While petting it, Melissa had looked around for the owner, assuming that, whoever they were, they were sure to be nearby. But after a long scratch that progressed to an ecstatic belly rub, no one had come forward or even seemed to be looking at her. She read on, a hand on the perky-eared mutt, a black mongrel that was lanky and long-haired, its fur salt-clotted, sand-speckled. An hour passed and still no owner. Then two, three. She finally walked the length of the beach, expecting the dog to spot its master for her, but failing to do so, she circled the entire campground with the dog in tow, hoping for the same. Nothing. The poor thing, she thought, looked to be pretty hungry too. She rummaged up a bag of chips and some milk-soaked bread and spilled it all out on the tarmac near her room. As night fell, wondering what she should do with it until the morning, where it was going to sleep, the dog suddenly stood up and sauntered off, back toward the beach, conversely, as if it had never met Melissa in its life. But the beach is where she found it the next evening, after it had spent most of the day with another prospective adopter. The pattern was set. Sometimes the people the dog had spent the day with would ask if Melissa was the owner, as it lay down next to her in the sand, as soon as she'd finished her shift. She would shrug her shoulders, say that no, it was a complete mystery who it belonged to, and both of them would look down at the dog, who would then jump to its feet and trot out to the waves to chase shorebirds. Melissa bought it some dog food in town and tried to guess its name, shouting common canine-sounding monikers out over the beach, watching for a reaction, and deduced that it was something that had a few syllables and ended with an "ah." A guess, she would learn, that was right on the mark.

It was a rare sunny day and she was taking her lunch break on the beach, a hand on the dog's belly while it squirmed on its back, mouth open, eyes closed, when a bearded man stopped at Melissa's feet and stood there, smiling. "Hi," Melissa said, squinting hard, thinking it a bit strange the way he'd approached.

"Hey," he replied, at which point the dog, recognizing his voice, spun around and sprung to its feet, giving him an excitable and long-awaited greeting. "See you found an interim owner again, eh pup?" While he patted her, he looked up at Melissa to speak. He had cold-green eyes and a thick leather string tied around his neck, the knot acting as the ornament, a pendulum keeping time over his clavicle. "She's probably 'lost' for about a week a month, on average. Though it's worse in the summer, when the people she adopts aren't locals and don't know she's mine. Takes a bit longer to find her. Hey, Lolita?" He thumped the drum of her rib cage. "Hmm? You unloyal little floozy." After this, having given a more than adequate conciliation dance, Lolita's ears cupped with attention at the waves where a group of plovers had landed on the shore. She was obliged to lope out and investigate, leaving Melissa and Jim (she would learn his name was) to talk idly about Lolita, the plight of the migratory birds that she ceaselessly accosted, and finally where each of them were from, what they were doing in Tofino for the summer. He was a surfer first and foremost, making ends meet by guiding sea kayak excursions through the tourist season. He lived off a logging road that was a bit of a drive from town, the main reason he was losing Lolita all the time, who would find a promising flock of birds while he was out surfing and then become a black dot in the fog-bank distance, eventually disappearing. Jim's home was apparently a shack he'd constructed himself, mostly out of salvaged lumber that he'd found in various places, including the beach he lived on, a rocky shoreline that had a good set of waves over the winter, with plenty of tidal pools and wildlife around. Actually, he'd said, if she ever wanted to come out and see it for herself, she was welcome to. Sensing her hesitation he added that she could bring a few friends, make a day trip out of it, see something new in the area.

Melissa thought it over, following Lolita as she traversed the beach in a wiry sprint, pivoting in an about-turn, and bounding back the same way she'd come. A child unexpectedly broke away from his parents to chase wildly after her. "Yeah. Sure, why not?"

It was the morning of Melissa's next day off, with three of the other campground workers, when they all piled into his corroded Datsun pickup. Jim collected another friend and some beer in town along the way, everyone settling into their places for the ride, in either the cab or the box, seat-belted in or balancing on the wheel wells. Melissa was in the back, where the wind whipped her hair so hard against her face that it stung and she had to duck down out of it, easing onto her back in the bed of the truck, hands behind her head, ankles crossed. Above the truck on the highway, a daytime moon was gliding between the trees, half full and following them, a crooked Cheshire-cat smile. They turned onto a gravel logging road where the leaves on the roadsides were frosted over with dust, the logging-truck tires kicking up clouds, coating the heavy leaves, smudging them like the skin of plums.

Lolita met them at the beach, the bustle of people hopping out of the back, scattering out along the rocks, throwing sticks that the dog couldn't have cared less about, Lolita curiously eyeing the pieces of wood as they bounded off the stones, then a quick bemused glance at the thrower. Melissa and Jim drank beer on a log overlooking the water, moss climbing the trees at their backs. She'd seen his simple shack that smelled of cedar, driftwood table chainsawed flat, a two-burner camp stove, foam bed, two jugs of water with plastic valves placed over a sink that he'd salvaged from a demolition site. He spoke with quiet satisfaction about his own resourcefulness and innovation. And before the end of the day, he'd leaned in and kissed her, inviting her to come back whenever she wanted. Like the next day she had off, he proposed, shrugging the potential in her direction. Melissa had smiled, given a nod. "Sure. I'd be into that."

It was how she spent every one of her days off for the rest of the summer. He would pick her up in the evening after work, and if it wasn't raining, they would wile their hours away in front of his fire pit; if it was, they would cook in his shack, the eaves trickling with long silver threads outside, while inside, the one window dripped with steam from his dented cooking pots. Among the pinecone artefacts and faded rocks on the windowsill was a small prism that he'd found, separating what it could of the feeble light that filtered through the rain clouds and the sweat of the glass, dealing out the dimmest hues onto the wood in front of it, the colours of a nighttime rainbow. They would prepare shellfish that they'd dug up themselves, Melissa setting his too-low table with plates and utensils that didn't have a single matching pair among them. During the meal, she would often ask him about surfing, never losing her fascination with how elusive he was about it. You just knew, he would say—you *knew*. When you started off surfing, it might take weeks before you actually stood up on your board. But once you did, after that first time, there was something you caught a glimpse of, there, during that brief moment when you were connected to—when you were actually a part of—an ocean swell rolling in. And it was something you couldn't see or learn or study anywhere else, it was just a sudden knowledge, a divinity; you *knew* that this was what living was all about. After listening to this, Melissa would look out the window, through the beaded curtain of droplets streaking the glass, and wonder what, for her, living was all about. Most of the time she thought she knew. Most of the time, she was pretty sure she had her own version of catching that glimpse.

They made love with an intensity and frequency that varied a great deal. Sometimes with a carnal fervour, rushed and impatient, pieces of clothing still left on, or the stitches strained to a slight ripping sound as they were being pulled off. Or they would take their time, often following a frigid evening swim, after which beads of seawater would seep from his beard for hours, globules sidling through the knots of its dense hair, shifting through the bristles like mercury. The only thing constant in their sex was a peculiarity of his, the way he would slide down afterwards, in the post-coital calm, and with his face near her breasts, run his fingers lightly around them, exploring their surface and touch as if it were a first-time experience, running his lips over them as if trying to find a word to describe their taste. Once, he fell asleep with her nipple in his mouth, and she cradled his head like a child, stroking the side of his beard. She thought then about how much things had changed since the first time she'd had sex, in her parents' basement at seventeen.

It had been with Nathan (who she still hung out with at times), with his nervous and hyperactive gestures. It was over within seconds, hurt, and ended with his falling asleep a few minutes later, facing her, his mouth open, teeth hanging, bad breath. She remembers how outrageously far it was from what she'd always been sure it was going to be. This act that had been such a taboo all her life, that had been seen as a rite of passage for so long, guarded by so many hurdles that she'd had to, not jump, but fumblingly knock down along the way, lifting the veil of guilt, of unshakeable societal views on purity and women; it was the one act and urge that was bolstered with enough trimmings and hype to give it centre stage (or at least an unacknowledged main role) in almost everything that people ever did; and there she was, lying on her parents' couch, having learned that, after all the buildup and anticipation, in reality, the act was just—utterly—lacking. An insight that felt overwhelming at the time, almost revolting. She'd eased off the couch, collected her clothes, and went up to her room where she slid open the drawer she kept her spiral-bound notebooks in, some empty, some full, and wrote the thing that she needed most to write.

How different it was now. How sustaining, enjoyable. It was understood between her and Jim that their relationship would be limited to a summer affair, and nothing more. Which, strangely, was what allowed her to be as involved as she was in it, as open, as present. Now when she eased away from the warmth under the sheets, it was only ever to put on her sandals and walk to the toilet outside, into a night that was wild and roiling and black, void of any artificial light. On the way she would think about the two bears she'd seen in the area before, foraging along the shore near the outhouse, eating seaweed and sending the scavenging ravens into flight; ravens with their moulted wings leaving spaces between their feathers like fronds of bracken, slats of grey sky sieving through before they landed in one of the arbutus trees nearby; those trees with their strange bark unfurling, illicitly peeling themselves back to naked ochre skins. And once she was there at the outhouse, she wouldn't close the door, having learned to appreciate even this, squatting over the toilet seat that Jim had carved, listening to the cedars tower, with their croaks and whispers, releasing volleys of collected raindrops every now and then, while below, the soaking wind would comb through the ferns and horsetail, their leaves dark and palaeozoic, where she imagined animals, crustaceans, and slugs, hidden and probing the busy shadows with their tentacles and whiskers. Walking back through these nights, slipping into a bed that was as warm as childhood.

At the end of that August in 1999, she packed her clothes and a jar of seashells that she'd collected over the summer into the back of Annette's car, gave Jim a tight hug and Lolita a pat (which the dog hardly noticed), and drove away. She hadn't exchanged an address or phone number with him, or even, it occurred to her on the ferry back to the mainland, learned what his last name was. Melissa, leaning on an upper-deck railing, watching the mossy islands slide past, knowing—with a kind of sudden knowledge— that if she were to do it all again, she wouldn't change a thing.

As Annette and Melissa threaded their way back through the mountains of British Columbia, they found themselves more at ease in each other's company, their silences more natural, less stiff. They'd taken the southern route again, where the foreranges were less extensive and the Rockies collapsed abruptly into the wide mat of the prairies, the evergreens dissolving into grass over only a few kilometres. When it happened, they'd changed the tape in the cassette player, turned the volume up, filling their immediate space, while the scenery emptied it.

They'd counted backwards from their first day of classes and figured out that they had two days to spare, which they planned on spending with worthy detours and extra sights. Annette offered once again to check out the town where Melissa was born, where it even sounded like she might have some family—on her dad's side anyway. But with the mention of her father, Melissa found herself feeling more drawn away from the place than to it and had bent over the map to find something else of interest nearby. (It was amazing to her how even the allusion to the *existence* of her father could change her mood for the worse, find her clenching her teeth and sighing, shaking her head in silence.) She soon found something of greater interest only an hour away, a provincial park with the attention-grabbing name of Writing-on-Stone, just along the American border.

They turned onto the network of secondary highways and township roads, Melissa fixated on the landscape again. Cows stepping amid their respective bevy of cowbirds (who skittered as attentive as underlings in wait at their beck and call), bovines chewing cud with a boredom that spoke of either pompous royalty or an exhaustive dimwittedness. The Mormon church spires spearing into the sky from every cluster of buildings big enough to name itself on the map, their pinnacles pointing up at the cirrus clouds, prairie plumes trailing a comb of white like ancient eyelashes dragging across a firmament iris, the dome of which was always stretching wider, more awake, attentive, scrutinizing the oil pumps in the abandoned distance below, those oblivious mule heads nodding sleepily at the ground, metronomes keeping time just to forget the hours they were leaving behind.

It was an impressive park, a small canyon of sandstone hoo-doos that created a maze of statues and figures, all carved out into an archetypal spaghetti western backdrop. The sandstone that made up the canyon was so soft you could etch into it with your fingernail, a conclusion that Melissa and Annette weren't the first to draw. The walls were patterned dense with carvings, icons, names, and graffiti, dating as far back as before horses had arrived to enter into the aboriginal petroglyphs, to the declaration of teenaged crushes that had been scraped into the rock only a week earlier. They explored the warren of chasms and runnels, Annette talking about the next semester of courses that they had coming up. Melissa listened, her stomach strangely knotted, feeling like school was still so far away. Too far even, out of her reach, out of her plans. At the same time, she felt like her ideals were changing, shifting, stretching, thinning, and she wasn't sure where she would find herself once they settled into place. As they made their way back to the campground, she also realized that her father was, again, invading her thoughts more than he should. She found herself thinking about the decisions he must have made, to end up where he was, who he was. At least she could be sure that, whatever her path ended up being, it would look nothing like his.

The next day they backtracked to fill up with gas in the town of Milk River. While Melissa paid, Annette stood at a phone booth, needing to call some people in Toronto to secure a room in someone's apartment for the coming year. Melissa waited for her while leaning against the car, looking around at the people filling up their tanks and squeegeeing their windshields, watching them too closely, inspiring self-consciousness. An older boat-sized car with a First Nations family inside, every seat occupied, pulled out of the parking lot and onto the road. Melissa, staring at them curiously, wondered if there was a reservation nearby, as well as wondering, for a moment at least, what life might be like on it. A young boy in the back knelt on the seat and waved at her through the rear window, and kept waving, his eyes dark, smile bright, shrinking as the vehicle receded down the road.

Melissa noticed the train that was standing still on a set of tracks across the highway and decided to cross the asphalt to take a better look. She walked up to the car that was most heavily graffitied, an enormous rusted barrel with the fadings of the words "Government of Canada" on its side, in two languages, streaked with corrosion, mechanical grease, and bird droppings. It made her think about how far this one car had travelled, how many times it had made its way across the country. Then she thought about that greater context, picturing the nation's trains whistling over desolate tracks, then of its planes, like stubby pieces of chalk pressed sideways and pulling across the length of blueboard skies, and the night roads that stitched the cities together through a patchwork of cricket rumours and bat-fluttering expanses; binding us, dividing us.

But these thoughts were soon interspersed by wonderings about school and debt, about travel and where she would find the money to do it, thoughts about her life, about her chances of becoming just another woman living a mostly painless fifty-two-week-a-year emptiness, interrupted, at best, twice, by all-inclusive resort packages. Thoughts that, maybe, the chances were pretty good.

It's interesting how countries, considered Melissa, have a way of having their way with us. Though, she countered, so does the world really, our biology, our nature, time, the cosmos. They all have their way with us. In the end, those inspirational posters and movies and New Age propaganda professing how one individual can make an enormous difference are wrong. In the end, there is room for our smallness, our insignificance. Infinite room.

And maybe, thought Melissa, sensing this, however vaguely— the immensity of where and how we fit into it all, what we're forced to dwarf ourselves in measurement against—it's almost natural that such an overwhelmingness manifests itself physically, inspires something tangible, like graffiti, something left behind for the wayfarer to read, see, witness. Even if it's simply to say, "I was here. *We* were here. Once." Isn't that why people scratch their initials and names into newly paved slabs of cement, brandishing sticks to etch out letters and dates, children squatting down to push their palms flat into the congealing mud, why travellers, merchants, and crusaders of antiquity inscribed other cultures' holy buildings and landmarks? They were all saying the same thing really. They were saying, quietly, soberly: "We weren't important. We weren't someone whom you would normally remember, someone who altered a heroic past or a courageous future. And why didn't we? Well, it turned out to be much, much bigger than us, so big that we couldn't. But we *could* change this wall, this train, this rock, this bathroom stall. Maybe even with something aesthetic or poetic, something thought-provoking, challenging, something that we drew or wrote in protest, disgust, dissent—or maybe, maybe it was just *something*. But something that was ours. Exactly ours. Put down in precisely the size and colour we intended it to be. It's not much, of course, but it was born solely from our choice to leave it behind. This, here, is our paltry stain that we've chosen over sterility, our tiny peripheral shout over silence."

Annette gave her quivering car horn a short bleat, and Melissa was soon sitting inside, pulling out and continuing their cross-country marathon. The next day, on the other side of Winnipeg, Melissa was behind the wheel and feeling suddenly settled, firm, her mind made up. She'd spent the entire morning thinking over the school year that she was going back to, affirming and reaffirming how certificates, diplomas, and degrees were just pieces of paper that had very little to do with knowledge, even less to do with intelligence, and absolutely nothing to do with wisdom. With the weightless satisfaction at having come to a decision, she spoke up, talking just above the radio. "Annette. I'm gonna drop out of university." She continued to look straight ahead, at the road, while Annette grappled with the gravity of what she was saying.

It took a while. "And do what?" she asked incredulously.

Melissa gave a shrug. "I'll figure it out." Nodding slowly, solid yellow line along the curve of the tarmac a creeping smile. "I'll figure it out."

It wasn't a decision that Julie held in high regard; in fact, she thought it was the worst idea she'd ever heard. But she also understood her daughter enough to know that no amount of dissuasion was going to work. After a month of Melissa's lounging in her room, mugs of tea, scribbling in her notebooks—with tiptoeing forays to the fridge whenever Julie was too far from the kitchen to intersect her, probably knowing what was coming—her mother finally implemented what she thought would be a reasonable renting scheme. No one likes a freeloader, she suggested. Melissa, stiffly agreeing, found a job at a café-bakery nearby, preparing salads, waiting tables, washing dishes, emptying a coffee cup with a tinkling of coins near the till labelled "Tips" at the end of every day. When it was slow in the afternoons, she read. And if the owner spotted her when she was, he would insist she clean the legs of the tables, the shelves, dust the light fixtures. He wasn't paying her minimum wage to just sit around you know.

Over the course of seven months she managed to save enough for a three-week backpacking trip through Mexico. She was proud that she'd stuffed everything she needed into a single daypack but saddened by the loss of her separate camera pack on the second-last day of the trip (unsure of whether she'd fallen victim to her own absentmindedness or to an exceedingly crafty thief). With no pictures or room for souvenirs, the postcards on her mother's fridge were the only evidence that the trip had ever taken place. Her Spanish certainly hadn't improved, having pointed at bright fruits in the market, the vendors grimacing: "Qwantto qwestta senniorre?" Sometimes, a papaya in hand, breakfast bought, Melissa had caught herself imagining the way her father would never have been able to survive in such a place. Not the way she could.

The following year, Julie, who'd never been the nagging type, started to drop careful suggestions about what Melissa could be doing, directions she might think of taking. It continued until Melissa, fearing the strain that was budding between them, started looking for apartments, and soon found a place at Markham and Dundas with two other roommates, the rent a steal, even if her room was windowless and claustrophobic, and the closest laundromat was a solid hike away. She'd also found a better waitressing job, in a newly renovated restaurant, upscale clientele, people with three credit cards in their wallets and the unspoken notion that the service industry owed them something for it. She dated one of the cooks there, and after him, a friend of one of the other waiters, always tending to shy away from relationships whenever things began to take on a serious tone. She visited her mother at least once a week, making dinner with her like they used to, nursing gin and tonics while standing on either side of the island in the kitchen. News of Cedric sometimes trickled into the conversation, things that Julie had picked up from friends who'd seen him around the city or from the occasional phone call that he gave her, a quick exchange to make sure everything was all right, his expectation that it should be palpable. "So, sweetie, everything's going okay, yeah? Oh, just hold on a second." Muffled voices slurring over the cupping of a mouthpiece. "Sorry, yeah . . . so, what was I saying?"

Then came the surprising meal when Julie confessed she didn't think Cedric was doing so well, that he'd sounded down on the phone, sunken. The grapevine had squeezed out the reason why, a simple enough story: he'd fallen for a woman who hadn't fallen back.

"But still," Julie had said, watching the ice as she swirled it in her glass, "there was something in his voice I've never heard before, something . . ." she took a sip, swallowed thoughtfully, "trodden."

"Well . . . good." Melissa, unmoved, leaned up against the island. "No? It's good for him. I mean, welcome to the club with the rest of us susceptible human beings. Glad he could join us at some point anyway."

Julie clicked her tongue. "Melissa," she said, making her way to the stove to check what was in the oven, "you and your tolerance that knows no bounds—until it comes to your own blood." She said this with a simple finality, not judging, not with the inflection of a lecture, just stating a bare and unpleasant fact. It was enough to get Melissa thinking a little more about it, though not quite enough thinking for her to change the way she spoke of him, to him.

Two years later, in 2002, Cedric invited Melissa out for lunch for her birthday and spent the first five minutes asking if she still had the travel bug, if she'd been anywhere lately, or had any plans to in the future. But the truth was that her interest in travel had since petered out, something that she felt, for no real reason she could put her finger on, a little self-conscious about, even ashamed of. Cedric almost appeared disappointed, telling her, shifting his utensils around on his serviette, how he'd been to Italy, how he'd decided that he just *had to* take a trip to Europe at some point in his life, and had gone alone, for a week, taking the trains around up north, the Alps on the horizon moving as slow as clouds. He'd taken lots of pictures if she wanted to see them, some time. Melissa, arms folded casually across her stomach, had a hard time believing him. It was astoundingly out of character; he'd always shunned everything that held even the slightest bit of risk, an inkling of adventure. She eyed him doubtfully, almost angrily. He wasn't supposed to change. It wasn't congruent with the way she saw him, some of the reasons she despised him. As they stood up from the table to leave, she felt it her duty as a waitress to point out that he wasn't leaving enough for a tip.

"Dad, it's the only real money they make. I think another couple bucks wouldn't put you out on the street, would it?"

Cedric rolled his eyes and dug into his pockets for some more change. "So it falls on me to pick up the slack of their stingy employers, huh?"

"Yes, St. Francis, it does. Actually—forget it." Melissa tossed a few dollars onto the table herself. "Can we go now?"

Melissa turned twenty-four, then twenty-five in the same apartment and job, the same disenchanting relationships, the same budget of just breaking even at the end of the month but with different books, art exhibits, and repertory films to give it all some flavour, as well as different places to sit with her notebooks on her lap, scribbling, always scribbling. It was probably enough, but it sure wasn't what she had in mind while crossing the country with Annette in her hand-me-down car when she was full of a fuel that she was sure would always be inexhaustible, the momentum that had seemed unstoppable, now rolling to a gravel-crumbling stall. She told herself that she needed a change, or at least to be open to one, should the opportunity present itself, never imagining that it would arise in the shape of shovels and a mud-caked wheelbarrow in her mother's backyard.

She'd gone there during the day, working the dinner shift, and had brought along a load of her dirty laundry. It was the spring of 2005, and her mother had decided to give the backyard a face-lift, getting the idea from a neighbour who had a long mound of creeping plants and splaying flowers. Melissa stumbled into an awkward conversation with one of the landscapers, a man named Troy, and the next afternoon, when Julie was out shopping, she invited him in for a coffee at the end of his work day. It came out that this was the last day he would be working there, repaying a favour to someone in the business, having brought the rocks down from a quarry up north. He worked in the field, did exactly the same thing really, but out of a small town in cottage country. He couldn't take the city, he'd said, too many people, too much noise and traffic and bustle. He had a nice place up there, tall stands of trees, a creek running along the border of his lot, hummingbirds at the feeders he put out every spring. She was welcome to come and visit sometime, make a day trip out of it, see something new, he proposed. Troy didn't quite understand the way she smiled at the offer and would have felt uncomfortable about it had she not quickly mentioned that she would be driving up north next week, which was a lie, but one she was willing to work around.

Melissa borrowed Julie's car the following Saturday and pulled into Troy's modest house in the picturesque town of Haliburton, where she stayed until Monday morning. On the day she returned it was raining, driving back through windshield-wiper squeaks, the sky not appearing nearly as dreary to her as it did washed and vernal and fresh. The trips to his house became a bi-monthly practice, then a weekly one. Until the snow had fallen, and the roads had become precarious, Melissa even sliding into a ditch on the way once, when he brought up, only for discussion he asserted, the possibility of her moving in. Melissa hardly had to think it over, the prospect of such a monumental reconstruction of her life so welcome that she couldn't pack her clothes and sublet her room fast enough. Thinking all the while of pippin-peppered snow crunching underfoot, of roads slinking away into the dark, leading nowhere; of winter branches dangling to the ground to point into curling drifts and tree wells, small stories left behind on their surfaces in the font of animal tracks—umlauts, tildes, circumflexes—punctuation that was both perplexingly foreign and universal.

Like most things in life, Melissa's move to Haliburton turned out to be even more than she'd thought it would be, and less. To start with, it wasn't a ravenous love that she felt for Troy; it was a slower, gentler kind, not as much falling as it was a careful kneeling, an easing onto a forest floor, where she would make small adjustments until she was perfectly comfortable. Then there were the things that had seemed so wildly eccentric at first that eventually became everyday: the radio stations with the call letters "Canoe FM," keeping pet food inside for fear of habituating bears, fake woodpeckers on power poles to stop the real ones from nesting inside, people driving short distances with ATVs, wild turkeys on the roads crossing languidly enough to delay motorists.

She worked at one of the cafés in town, then a deli, but began asking around for other possibilities. At a regional art exhibit, she met a woman who helped run one of the retirement homes in the area and had asked her a few questions about it. Melissa was soon enrolled at the local college, in the course that she needed to work at a home, and by the time she'd gotten her certificate was already employed at a retirement residence that was a short walk from where she and Troy lived.

It wasn't a glorious job. Most of it boiled down to a domestic tedium, assisting the residents to bathe, dress, eat, lie down, urinate, defecate, clipping and filing their fingernails, styling and hair spraying their sickly and thinning curls, and moving them from activity to program to scheduled event: crafts and board games, bingo and trivia, book readings and bread making. But there were some aspects of the work, like the intimacy that such human frailty lent itself to, that she enjoyed, valued. The sentimental stories and grossly inaccurate recollections that some of them shared with her, details that they conferred with so much buildup and bearing it was as if they were long-kept secrets.

Of course there were nights that—like everyone, she rationalized—she questioned her choices: moving there, her new line of work, her quiet life with Troy. Walking home in the winter dark, past living room windows that flickered with the blue flame of television, glazed faces that might have been watching fire if it weren't for the icy refractions, their expressions at once captivated and vacant, the intoxicating trance of nullity. Her legs involuntarily slowing to a stroll while the doubt-pokings of pine needles injected the skyline on either side of her, catching herself feeling lonely in her skin, isolated, insular. It was as if she were lacking something basic, some critical sustenance, an essential nutrient of some kind. And when she met Eamon Barham, what she found in him wasn't enough to quell this feeling entirely, but it was enough to appease it more than she'd ever thought she would.

He arrived at the home uneventfully, a nursing aide helping to set up his room, arranging things in a minimalist and uncluttered way, explaining some of the particulars in caring for him, as he was partially blind. He was seventy-four, a widower with no surviving siblings, no children, had had prostate cancer, kidney problems, and was somewhat underweight, moving around as if with the knowledge that, were he to fall, bones would break. During his third day at the home, Melissa had knocked on his door just to check on him, seeing as it was late morning and the staff had already grown accustomed to his sitting in front of a small portable stereo in his room at that time, listening attentively to the CBC. Whereas now, though they could hear that he was awake and moving around, his small stereo was quiet.

"Yes? Come in." Eamon's voice from the other side of the door was polite, if shy.

Melissa opened the door to find him sitting near the radio, tinkering with it. "Hello, Mr. Barham, how are you today?"

"All right. I guess," he said with an inflection that made the tone Melissa had used with him sound condescending, like she'd addressed someone who was half-deaf but who, in reality, could hear much better than her.

"You *guess?*" She adjusted her pitch. "What seems to be the problem?".

"Well, it's either this CD player's on the blink or my being blind as a bat has fouled things up again. My bet, unfortunately, is on the latter."

Melissa walked over and pressed play on the machine, saw the CD begin to spin, and an error message blink onto the display. When she opened it, she realized that he'd just put the CD in upside down, and turned it over for him. As she did so, he noticed how taken aback she was, that she'd frozen, held her breath.

"Don't worry. It's not nearly as frightening as you think."

"No, it's ... Uhm ... It's ... an audiobook. Of contemporary poetry, from New Zealand."

"Yes. It is. And perhaps you'd be so kind as to put it in correctly for me."

Melissa fumbled with the CD, inserting it into the player but didn't press play. "You know ..." her hand still on the machine, "there's a great site I know of, which is a yearly, kind of 'best of' anthology of New Zealand poems. It's really ... really quite good. I mean, if you'd like, I could always print a few of them up, or even the whole thing, and ..."

Eamon smiled. "You know, the doctors told me they could have operated in time to—*maybe*, they said—save enough of my vision to read." He spoke clearly but at an unhurried and deliberate pace. "Only they made the mistake of explaining the procedure to me beforehand. A simple local anaesthetic, they said, then they would probe, scrape, and cut away at my eyes and their inner workings. Can you *imagine* that? People huddled around your face, clamping your lids open and slitting along the glossy flesh of your eyeballs with a scalpel, throbbing spotlight, blood on their plastic gloves? Just hearing about it was enough, frankly, to have me settling on audiobooks and broadcasts for the few years I've got left."

"And people reading out loud."

"Yes. And people reading out loud. Perhaps, like these printed poems that you, Miss ... ?"

"Melissa."

"That you, Miss Melissa, might bring in and read to me at some point."

Melissa, giving a silent snicker, pressed play on the small stereo. "Well, I'll leave you to it."

"Thank you." Eamon spoke toward the door before she'd reached it. "And I look forward to listening."

But it was two days later, in reading the poetry that she'd promised him, that they both made the real discovery. He found her to be an excellent reader, never too dramatic, more inclined to understatement than to affected stress and pause, yet still managing to read with emotion. He was also pleasantly surprised by the selection she'd made from this "best of" collection. She had an eye. While Melissa found him to have a sharp critical ear, nodding contentedly at the cleanest images, seeming to catch the subtlest undercurrents. She learned that he'd been a literature professor at Trent University, and that it was only in his retirement, after he'd moved to live year-round at his cottage in the area, that he'd acquired his taste for the most recent poetry. The classics had their place, of course, he'd said, but it was what was happening in the twenty-first century that reassured him this was anything but a fading art. And he was determined to keep pace with it too, follow in the direction it was heading, until, he declared, he was too senile to care. In the meantime, it was one of those things that helped keep him sharp, he'd said, with an aimless wink.

So Melissa began spending her evenings and free time rereading the collections of yearly "best of" anthologies that she'd amassed over the years, earmarking the pages and poems she was convinced he would appreciate.

Before Eamon came along, she'd never had a conversation with anyone about poetry, and wasn't prepared for how similar two independently formed opinions could be. They loved the same poets, Ashbery, Hughes, Hirshfield, Collins; the same Canadians, early Atwood, late Purdy, Nowlan, Michaels, Birney; they staunchly agreed that poems should never be discussed in writing, and that when talked about, only the most regular language should be used—it was good, poor, brilliant, unclear—and that was all; though most of the time it amounted to even less, being boiled down to a single physical reaction after Melissa had finished reading, both of them pausing to consider the piece in silence, after which Eamon would finally give a nod, or a simper, a scowl, grin, which almost always mirrored Melissa's judgment exactly. Identical waves cancelling out sound, any need for discussion.

"So tell me," he asked her one day, a late morning in early spring while she was pushing him in a wheelchair outside, the snow thawing into mud, parting a path of dry concrete down the centre of the road. "Did your parents read poetry?"

"My mom, no; and my dad probably hasn't read a book in his sorry life."

"Mmm. I once read that being a father was waiting patiently, silently, for forgiveness."

Melissa, finding she had nothing to say to this, waited for him to speak again.

"And do you write any yourself, Miss Melissa?"

"Uh . . ." Melissa looked down at the top of his head, which was almost bald, a mole-blotted map of islands under the wispy clouds of his remnant hair. "Some."

He gave a single nod, turned his face up into the sunlight. "That's good."

But the truth was that she wrote more than some. She'd been writing poetry since she was fifteen, and had filled entire spiral-bound notebooks with it, the pages heavily edited in the same pen, words crossed out, sometimes whole lines, stanzas, arrows guiding others to their rightful places. And out of all of this poetry she'd produced, she was tempted to tell Eamon the thing she was most proud of concerning it, which had nothing to do with the poems she wrote, but with the ones that she destroyed.

It was the summer before she moved to Haliburton, still living in Toronto, pining for something in her life to overturn, when she picked up yet another book by an author she adored, Umberto Eco. In it, she came across a passage that struck her, something to the effect of: "Everyone writes poetry in their adolescence, but only true poets destroy it." The next time she was at her mother's house, she went into her old room, where she still kept a drawer that was full of her past notebooks. She spread them out on the desk and went through them, dividing the ones that were written when she was "too young"—when the verse was over-wrought and melancholic; only a teen would romanticize tragedy—and the ones that were written later, with the help of a little more perspective. And while flipping through the stapled pages and notebooks, she noticed that one of the compilations in a series of biographical poems that she'd written (this one in particular on the life of Primo Levi) was missing. And for some reason it annoyed her, searching more intently now, through every note-book and folder, leafing through the pages almost desperately, until she realized how absurd it was. What did it really matter if one of them had already been lost or thrown away? She only wanted to have it in her hands so she could place it in a neat pile with the others and burn it.

She went down into the Don Valley Brick Works with the stack of pages and a lighter, setting them down on a rock amid a tangle of small trees and long grass. She lit the wad of papers and straightened up, already satisfied, watching the line of char creep and boil, the corners curling like obscene gangrenous tongues, velvety and cresting to lick the roof of a mouth that wasn't there, and so continued to furl and lift, until they were floating, the ashes rising, whirling into the air, only to settle farther off, into the bushes and grass, the fireflies of their sparks still glowing. She stepped back, suddenly panicked, realizing the potential disaster. She ran over to one of the larger embers and stamped it into the reeds, looking over her shoulder as another feathery-grey parachute landed onto a shrub. She darted over there next, shoes crunching through thorny branches, then began moving out in a wide circle, patting and stomping, already humiliated, thinking in headlines, mortified that the cinders would spread, that the singeings of her scribbled lines might catch fire, the embers of her words growing into a swath of something wide and consuming and precarious, until she was laughing, madly laughing at the idea of it, knowing that this, her ridiculous scene, was sure to become a poem she would write out someday. Words smouldering to take on a life of their own.

She considered sharing this story with Eamon, was even sure that he'd appreciate it, but ultimately, she thought the better of it.

This last summer had been a dry one, and the leaves, desiccated and brittle on the branches, seemed eager to change colour and fall, the fingers of the willows tarnishing with amber, the bleeding canines of sumac drooping, the generous spilling of the aspens' golden coins onto the ground for children to pile and toss into the air like lottery winners.

They were outside again, in an afternoon that was cool and blowing, when Melissa asked him, sounding as if the question had been on her mind for hours but had been far too delicate to introduce. "Honestly, Eamon, sometimes—*most* of the time—I don't even know what it is. Do academics? Do you guys know?"

Eamon's mouth was open. He dug his nail into the corner of it, looking off to a slope of rose granite that descended out of the forest and plunged into the retirement home's lawn. "Poetry? No. We don't. Nor do I know anyone who would take a stab at its definition really."

"And doesn't that bother you sometimes? I mean, here's this thing that I can't picture ever living without, one of the oldest art forms in existence, and I don't even know, really, what it is. I mean, doesn't that . . . doesn't that bother you, somehow?"

Eamon blinked at the rock again. "No." He folded his hands in his lap, adjusted his weight on the bench that they were sitting on. "Though it is something I've thought about. And a fair bit at that. To start with, I think we all, poets or not, have the *feeling* of what poetry is. We know when something poignant, something song-worthy, passes through our lives, makes one of our days more of a story worth telling than just another empty orbit of the clock. We know what poetry is when we hear it, when we see it, touch it. That much is almost simple. But what poetry is to me, personally, is the larger complex that it produces, that we are embedded inside.

"If you think of your own life," he continued, "you might be able to string its narration together using the exotic beads of those few, most singular moments that you've experienced, the big turning points, the poems, until you could look at those glass colours all butted up together, side by side. But what you don't see looking at it—or even stop to consider—is that every human being that your path collides with *at* those poignant moments also has a string of beads, which is now intersecting with yours, and so is woven into it. And I think that this network of blindness to the poetry of other lives, this reluctance to penetrate such an expansive yet simple code—to admit the verse that is beneath everything, behind everyone, impelling its way through every existence, silently, cloaked and teeming—that we could exist without acknowledging this interplay around us, is, to me, exactly that: poetry. Poetry is being deaf to the extravagant choir that is behind you, below you, above you. But singing anyway. It is the collective and soundless cacophony of our solitary melodies, which is humming, even now, ringing in our ears with its almost perfect silence."

Melissa, looking into the shedding trees, thought this over, staring past the sloping granite and its splotches of lichen, past the branches, into the shadows between the twigs.

And it was something she kept thinking about, for weeks after-wards, even today, sitting peacefully on her couch before work, earmarking the pages she was going to read to Eamon later on this evening. And she probably would have continued to think about it, had her father not shown up out of the blue, without having seen her in more than four years.

Cedric was standing on her landing now, two feeble knocks and a glance over his shoulder, while waiting for her to open the door. Melissa was nervous, wondering what might have sparked such a visit, panning through the worst-case scenarios, a shaky hand on the latch, only opening the door enough to squeeze her body into the gap. "Wow. Dad. Hi. What—uh . . . what are you doing here?"

Cedric almost seemed as confused as she was. "Melissa. Hey. How are ya, kiddo? You've uh . . . you've grown up a bit. But look good, healthy." An ungainly pause, trying hard to be a pleasant one. "Yeah. So. Would you . . ." he looked past her, into the house. "Could I . . . come in?"

"Uhm, yeah, sure, yeah, here." She flung the door open and stepped back until she was standing in front of the bay window, waiting to find out what was happening, her arms crossed, one of her hips cocked to the side. "So . . . What's up?" Melissa catalogued the changes in his body since last she'd seen him, his belly protruding a little more, a bit of added flesh sagging beneath his chin, hair growing thinner.

"Oh nothing." He sighed, looking around the room. "I just thought I'd drop by and . . ." He cleared his throat, turned back to her. "Actually, you know, I might as well cut the crap. The truth is that, well, something . . . crazy's happening inside my head, and . . . and I'm here . . . because . . . Well, I don't really know what I'm doing here, to be honest."

"Right. Uhm. Dad, you're not making any sense. Just so you know." He looked so out of place, standing here among her private things, in the living room of her intimate world.

"I know."

"Okay. So." Melissa lifted a hand to scrunch at her hair. "Uh, do you want some tea or something?"

Cedric inhaled, seemed to hold his breath. "No, thanks."

"Coffee?"

"Look . . . See this weekend, I drove out here to meet a new client, who invited me to . . . play some golf at a new course that . . . isn't all that far from here. And, well, I was on my way home, and passed by a sign with your town on it—or the town your mother told me you were living in anyway."

"Okay. So you thought you'd just . . . drop by? I mean, it's nice to see you and all, but, I haven't *really* heard from you in a while, Dad. It's kind of . . . odd, just stopping in like this. No?"

"Well, see that's the thing. I . . . didn't stop in. I just . . . kept driving. I mean, I chickened out, is what I'm saying. Because it would've been too awkward and, you know, like you say, it's been a long time. But, see, the point is that I *wished* it, you know? I *wished* I'd had the balls to turn around, and pull into your driveway, and maybe, maybe even say that I always, I don't know, that I was . . . that I know that I've been . . . a bit of a . . ."

"Dad." Melissa was taken aback at how quiet her voice was. "You don't . . . have to . . ."

"I know. But I didn't . . . I mean, do . . . a lot of things . . . that I . . . wish I had, and . . . and . . ."

"Yeah. Well." Melissa swallowed, shifting her weight onto her other hip, recrossing her arms. "So, anyway, you were saying, you turned around and you . . . ? How did you know . . . where I live? Did you stop and ask someone or something?"

Cedric waved a hand to give a simple answer but found, confusingly, that he didn't have one. "I . . ." he searched the carpet near his feet, then the coffee table. "That's a good point. I . . . you know I don't know. I just . . . I . . . just came. I just . . . drove here."

As Cedric looked back up at her, the room was wavering, the paint becoming unfocused, the pictures on the walls shaking in a soundless blur. Then his daughter, standing in front of him, flickered into transparency a few times, reappearing as solid and concrete as she was before, watching him, waiting for him to answer. Then her image flickered again, much in the way that the old eight millimetre projectors did, he thought, just before reaching the end of a reel or slipping through an amateur splice job, a few frames from a blank section flittering in, flashing out; or like words, words that you know you've seen in a text before, being repeated somewhere else, lighting up, fading away. Until her form fluttered a last time and vanished from in front of him, instantly reappearing on the couch, sitting there now, suddenly comfortable, reading an earmarked page, a cup of tea in her other hand, like she'd never gotten up to answer the door in the first place.

"Melissa." Cedric heard that his voice had become hollow, fragmented, remote. He could barely hear it himself, while she, judging by her lack of reaction, couldn't hear it at all. He spoke louder, almost a shout, "Melissa!" Nothing.

The cat, a young tabby, who had been staring groggily into the centre of the room, approximately where Cedric was standing, swished its tail, an ear cupping to the side. Its tired stare rose a bit, nearing Cedric's face, distantly listening to something, for something.

Cedric, baffled and squinting, turned around to look at his car in the driveway. It wasn't there. Then he lifted his hand in front of his face, looked down at his feet, his legs, and things started to become clear to him, started to fall into place. Of course, he thought, of course. It had been almost obvious, the whole time. He'd just never let himself consider it.

He turned again to his daughter on the couch. "You know what's crazy?" he asked in a normal volume, not trying to get her attention anymore, speaking at her, not with her. "I've been trying to convince all these people—these people who I open my eyes to and flash away from a minute later—trying to convince them that something was happening to me, something strange and profound and mysterious. I've been trying to get them to believe that this experience was real, that it was important, and . . . While there was really only one person that had to *get* it, you know? That had to believe what this was all about." And finally—finally—Cedric did. He understood. And with that understanding, he grinned softly.

He noticed from the cover of her book that she was reading poetry, and it made him think of something else he wanted to say. "Melissa." The cat's glare lifted to another part of the room, still searching distractedly, sleepily. "You probably don't remember this, but you weren't there when I picked up the last of my things from the house, and your mother wasn't either. And with no one around, do you know what I did? I went into your room, where you kept all those poems you were always writing, and I looked through some of them, even read a few. I picked one, for no real reason that I can remember, and took it with me. Stole it. I kept it in the top drawer of my desk. It was a long poem, or a series of them anyway, stapled together, numbered with roman numerals. They were recounting a man's life, a famous chemist or botanist I think, something like that. And I can't help but think that, maybe, when you find out . . . you might write something like it . . . about me. My life. You know. Maybe."

The cat, giving up on the sounds, put its chin onto the sofa and closed its eyes, intent on finding sleep again as soon as it could. It licked its tiny lips, swallowed, sighed.

Melissa turned the page.

In the living room's bay window, a myriad of individual clouds—the kind that are only seen in autumn—glided through the sky, all of them moving in the same direction. From one nameless place, to another.

(**xii**)

How gently the tires rolled off the shoulder,
swathing through the grass to the trees;
where some of the smaller ones splintered
and the thickest were bark-gashed, bleeding resin.

The quiet that followed was a devoted one, assuring,
the only sound the vivid foliage, dropping
with a gentle plink onto the roof, tapping
the pulverized safety glass, its intricate geometry
opaque and glimmering as crystalline snow, leaves
sliding down it with the fffff of toboggans.
Like torn triangles of construction paper,
they piled onto the wipers,
a glueless collage.

Meanwhile the powder from the airbags cascaded a slat of sun,
dust pale as talcum, or as the flour I was once allowed to touch
on frosted rolling pins, doughy countertops where
cookie-cut entrails lay limp and forgotten.

Resting my head against the driving wheel
I found the pillow to be hard and rubber-coated,
far from the afternoon bed of an elementary sick day;
an observation I tried to get out of my head, tried to replace
with something a little more inspired or noteworthy, momentous.

But I never did.

The phone was red. And what William hated most about it, besides the fact that it was inconveniently mounted on a wall in a tight corner (and at a strange angle), was that when it rang it was so gratingly loud that you could actually see the cherry receiver quavering as you picked it up. He shook his head in the relieving silence, put it to his ear. "Yes?" Then he leaned over the tiny and strangely angled desk to write on a pad of paper there, pen out of his jacket pocket, clicked and already jotting down the information, a glance at his watch, time and date scrawled onto the top left-hand corner. "Mm-hmm, all right. And how long ago did the call come in? Mm-hmm. Okay. So you're more or less ten minutes away then, is that about right, John? All right. We'll be ready for you. Thanks." William hung up, fiddling with the twists of the phone cord afterwards, flattening them against the wall, and stepped back out of the corner, giving the receiver a final disapproving look.

William walked into the reception area and listed off the information to one of the nurses in passing, who put down what she was doing and walked away in a relative hurry. He continued down the hall to a small office where Hanif Khaled, who'd just arrived for his shift, was looking over some patients' charts. Technically, William was free to go, having handed off his responsibilities to Hanif the moment the intern had arrived, but he also knew that, with a call like this, coming from the red phone as it had, he wouldn't be leaving any time soon. Not that that was a problem; it was the nature of the beast of rural medicine really, and something you had to get used to if you wanted to practise it.

"Hanif," William spoke in a low and direct tone. "It *sounds* . . ." he checked his watch, "like we've got a code coming in in about eight minutes. Janet's prepping the room now. So uh . . ." he adjusted the watch on his wrist, "I'll be staying behind to help out of course."

Hanif, who, in the few days that he'd been there had already made the impression of being a confident and competent intern, paled a bit with the news, though quickly postured and gave a solid nod, already on his toes and striding out of the room. "Thank you. I would . . . appreciate thahd very much, Doctor Kirbee."

He rounded the corner and in a glimmer of subtle body language, William, who was following right behind him, understood—without needing to verify or point it out—that so far in Hanif's brief career, he hadn't yet handled a code, and maybe hadn't even assisted in one. This would be his first. William hoped things went well for him.

William Kirby had been a doctor in Haliburton for twenty-four years. He'd schooled in London, Ontario, grown up in Oshawa, and spent every summer of his childhood on Spruce Lake, one of the hundreds of bodies of water around Haliburton, jumping from his parents' dock, with the family's golden retriever stretching out in the dripping air behind him. When he'd made the move from the city, it was in 1983, the same week a Boeing 767 sunk out of the sky due to a metric conversion error with its fuel levels, having to land on a small Manitoba runway as a jawdroppingly oversized glider. William remembers talking about the incident with the neighbour on either side of him, and getting the feeling that there was going to be more to this rural living than what he'd drawn from holiday recollections and reveries. To begin with, he realized that people there could be divided into two groups, his neighbours representative of one each: vacationers and locals. The former thought of themselves, unequivocally, as the latter; and the latter detested, unequivocally, the former.

This being the middle of October, it was the time of year when, with the last of the leaves, the last of the vacationers left; and so was also a time when William, as a local, was supposed to rejoice at their departure, supposed to be glad for the rustling quietude they left behind; squirrels free to skitter along the baring branches frenetic and nervy, the sound of fishing boats eerily absent, while hunters patrolled the back roads with their guns and camouflage, beer-bellied soldiers ranked and filed for winter bragging rights. But, truth be told, he found himself more leaden than lightened, found the shoulder season one that made his shoulders hunch, turned him inward, left him more introspective and reticent. He noticed the smell of leaves that burned through the autumn drizzle, the mist of raindrops seeming less to put out the fires and more to feed the smoke. Noticed the pine needles that collected along the windward shores, floating and undulating on the surfaces of the lakes, pressed into a tight carpet of geometric patterns, sodden-matchstick mosaics. He became aware of the autumn flowers speckling the ditches in their carefully subdued hues, drawing little attention to themselves, as if deliberately, as if working quietly and tirelessly at some mysterious aim, something that hovered just above their mere survival, stamens prodding spellbindingly into the cool air: witch hazel, goldenrod, ladies' tress, aster.

William Kirby knew that, to many people, such observations might be considered flights of fancy, which were discordant with his profession and personality. But he didn't see it that way. Einstein had often quoted that a sense of the mystic—that a wonderment at what is all around us, yet impenetrable—was the germ of all true science and art. William agreed. He loved medicine (and all the sciences really) because of the driving force behind them, the disciplined and systematic search to understand what we don't when it would be better for humanity if we did. And William didn't see this teasing out of the natural world's mysteries as an attempt to control them, but as a means of being closer to them, and even, in some way, to honour them, revere them.

With opinions like these, it was incredible to think that he'd been called a skeptic more than a few times in his life and, once, even a cynic. Though he remembered the circumstances. The problem was, thought William, that people naturally linked any kind of infatuation with the mystical with things of a much less credible nature. Like the ridiculous pseudosciences (astrology, numerology, phrenology) or the endless splay of New Age egocentricities. Now these things, on the other hand, William was happy to dismiss with a snide remark or roll of the eyes. Sure the mystical was alluring, a kind of intoxicant, but if he found that others, or even himself, were crossing the line, feeling a little light-headed with it, it was best, in William's opinion, to stamp a solid foot on the ground and keep it there. One must—*must*—always fall firmly on the side of reason, on quantifiable, evidence-based principles that could stand up to peer review and rigorous scrutiny.

Which is maybe why William liked to keep a thumb on the pulse of how quickly things were changing, scrolling through the biggest online science magazines in the evenings, why he was a devout follower of *Boing Boing*. Because every passing week saw incidents surfacing that laws hadn't yet been designed for, or had even considered; let alone corresponding ethical codes and conduct. The speed at which society was being asked to adapt was an exponential one. A fact that most people probably found daunting, but which seemed to fuel William, absorb him. All the more because the upshots and spinoffs of the progressive global village, the urban displacements, eclectic cosmopolitana, and the newly invented alternative lifestyles could even be seen in rural Ontario life.

There was Lynn, with her tattoos and piercings, living just up the road with another woman her age, both of them young enough to be his daughters. The couple had bought a small farm on the outskirts of town and had slotted themselves into the same chores and rounds that the family before them had maintained, every day, for more than fifty years. They kept chickens, horses, a few milk cows, a large enough garden to keep them cooking over the summer and fill their freezer for the winter. He'd met Lynn like he met most people, as a patient, which, as with most people, led to cordial hellos in passing, but then, as a pleasant surprise, to a few eggs or surplus produce from her vegetable patch, handed over the fence when he sauntered by on his daily walks. Once, William saw her feeding a few of those eggs, presumably rotten ones, to her horses, holding them out in front of their noses, one at a time, until the horse had wrapped its velvety mouth around it, lifted its head, rolled the egg down the length of its tongue, and quietly crushed it at the back of its throat. Until he saw this, he had no idea that a horse would eat an egg. Another time, around New Year's, she gave him a chicken she'd butchered herself. A young woman from the city, butchering a chicken. William imagined the physical act, how she would do it, how discomfiting it probably was, knowing he couldn't do it himself.

Then there was Jack, living along the Drag River Walkway, who welded sculptures together out of salvaged metal. Or Walter, the hunting outfitter who'd moved there from Kansas City, spoke with what sounded like an exaggerated American accent and had a certificate in animal-assisted therapy, his clientele split between gruff hunters and timid children, rifle casings jingling in his pockets while he coaxed a youthful hand to pet a therapy llama.

Even the most no-nonsense people in the area could have hidden eccentricities to them, say things that surprised you. Like two years ago, when William had had a double load of firewood brought in and piled under his deck in the backyard. It was the third year that he'd gotten his wood from the same guy, Steven Greig, who spent the season cutting, drying, and delivering it himself; though William knew that he also worked on a selective logging crew, doing some tree pruning and other grunt work for a horticulturalist in town, some snow plowing for a contractor in the winter. He was a serious fellow, quiet, hard-working, who always wore a stern expression. He lived with a local woman with similar traits, and they had three children, whom they'd christened with interesting names that William had a hard time remembering, like Nodin and Sade. As he was finishing with the wood—immaculate rows, stacked into stable walls, already divided into thick rolls and halved logs that could be easily cut into kindling—William decided he would give him a little extra this year, waiting for him to run his sleeve across his brow before handing him a beer.

"Thanks," Steven had said, twisting the bottle open but not taking a sip until he'd caught his breath. They stepped into William's spacious backyard.

"You do good work, Steve. Thanks a lot."

Steven nodded firmly.

"So," William, straining for a bit of light conversation, "your last name's Greig. Is that British? German? What is that?"

"Hell if I know." Steven shrugged, almost cutting himself short with a swill of beer.

"So did you grow up up north then? Sudbury or something?"

"No . . ." he said hesitantly, a deep mumble. "No-no. Grew up all over the place. Mostly in Tronno, I guess. Kind of an orphan. Kind of a street kid. Gettin' inta all kinds a trouble."

William studied his face, suddenly intent on his expression, trying to read into the details between the words. "Who knew? Living on the street, eh?" He took a swig of beer himself, shook his head. "Wow."

Steven took another steep sip. "Yup," he said with finality. They chatted about the yard for a few minutes before Steven handed his empty bottle back to William. "Thanks for the beer. Gotta get goin'. Send ya the bill."

"Hey, thanks a lot again. It looks great under there. No kiddin'."

"N'probems. Anytime. Bye." He walked to his truck, visibly self-conscious, and jostled into the cab, slamming the door hard.

William watched the truck as he pulled away, wondering about him, never having thought of Steven as one of those people who might be coming out on the better end of a tough life. He wondered what kind of trouble he'd gotten into, knowing, at the same time however, that he'd never find out. Then, as the truck turned onto the road, William saw that one of Steven's kids had written into the thin layer of dirt that coated the vehicle's paintjob, a child's fingertip dragging clean the words *DaDs Truk*. William smiled. He was beginning to develop a weakness for graffiti. With a fling of his arms, he drained the last of both of the bottles onto the grass and went back inside.

William followed Hanif into the crash room, where Janet had turned on the machines and instruments and was busy checking the monitor. Hanif asked her where the crash cart was, and after she'd pointed to it, he began going through the items, seeming overly calm, moving fluidly, lifting the glass vials to read the labels. "The atropine is . . . ? Oh wait, eer it is. Sorrie."

William, leaving Hanif to sort through it himself, walked through to the staging area and opened the bay doors, a burst of autumn air sighing into the building. He stepped outside, checking his watch. In the crisp distance, the approaching siren could already be heard. William scratched at his palm, sauntered out onto the ramp where he saw a car driving by on the township road in front of the hospital, loose leaves chasing close behind it, caught in the eddy of its slipstream like just-married cans tied to the bumper of a honeymoon car. He caught a single flash of the approaching ambulance strobe out of the corner of his eye while looking just beyond the township road, at the marsh on the other side of it, remembering what had happened to him early last wcck.

William had been on the way out the door for his daily stroll when his wife asked him to find her a few cattails for a dried-grass arrangement she wanted to put into a tall vase by the fire. So William grabbed the pruners on his way out of the yard and climbed along the old road, now a trail, making his way past the bare spot that looked over the town, the steeples of the churches the tallest points, towering high, almighty, though unused and unthought-of. The trail continued to where it branched off to circle the marsh, which he descended toward, thinking about the logistics of cutting cattails and bringing them back intact. As usual, he was alone on the trail, which he was happy for, appreciative of the space and quiet.

He found them easy enough, jutting out of the marsh's edge, though most of them had already gone to seed, their brown velvet splitting along a seam that seemed to bleed out with a type of downy cotton. He decided he would pick them anyway, let his wife be the judge of whether she could use them or not, but as soon as he walked into the reeds he found himself stepping onto a ground that was veiled and unnaturally soft, which had him rethinking the idea. He stopped, looked around. A few remnants of fall colours were standing out against the browns and greys of early winter, a yellow leaf caught in the sepia culms, a brush-dab of maroon, a fist of rust. There were also birds, he realized, twittering and chirring in the rushes in front of him, hidden. On a whim, he clapped, just once, never for a moment imagining that it would have the effect that it did.

The entire marsh seemed to erupt, and the sky darkened with hundreds, maybe thousands, of small black birds. They formed a bleary cloud that spread and thinned itself one moment, then condensed and folded in on itself the next; but it was always whorled and synchronous, always acting as one. Like history. Like a nation. There was a point when the flock passed low over his head, and he was sure he felt the wind of their countless wings, and flinched beneath its tremolo, ducking low into the sedges. Then the flock collected and spiralled above the marsh that was farthest away from him and, rather abruptly, sunk into the reeds again, leaving the autumn air empty but for their sounds, now remote and muted.

When he stepped out of the rushes several minutes later, without having procured a single cattail, he looked both ways along the trail, as if about to cross the street, and was somehow disappointed to see that no one else was there, that he was still alone. And as he stood on the edge of the marsh again, he was struck with a strange sensation, a thought. It occurred to him that there might be someone else out there who'd experienced exactly what he just had, who had stood in some rushes mesmerized and half-frightened by a swirling flock of blackbirds. And for some reason—he couldn't even begin to say why—it was important that that person existed. He continued on, thinking of who they might be, imagining a younger woman, an older man, crouched in another marsh, another time. When he got home, he apologized to his wife for not bringing her back any cattails. He said nothing about the blackbirds.

And now he found himself looking for them here, in this other marsh, scanning for a brief flapping or flutter above the wetland as the ambulance sped closer, but didn't manage to spot anything. He began to step backwards, back into the crash room, the sirens switched off as the vehicle turned into the hospital's driveway, the engine wheezing with a final acceleration before it reached the staging area, where everyone was more than ready for it.

The rear doors flung open, stretcher wheeled out. The paramedic that had been treating the patient in the back moved along with him, giving chest compressions as he sidestepped into the crash room. There, a collection of hands gripped on to the large man and slid him onto a proper bed, hoisting on the count of three.

As this was happening, the paramedic that had been driving held the patient's chart out in front of him and brought everyone up to speed. "Okay: fifty-eight-year-old male; single motor-vehicle accident off Highway 118; found unresponsive behind the wheel; no trauma noted per se, except for minor laceration to right arm; gentleman extracted from vehicle without difficulty; no pulse on arrival, chest compressions were begun; hooked up to AED and found patient to have ventricular fibrillation; shocked once, got a brief pulse, which fell into pulseless v-fib again; shocked a second time, got some electrical activity, but no pulse. We've been bagging and masking with chest compressions for thirteen minutes now."

"Thanks, John," William, his back already turned to the paramedics, prepared to intubate while Janet hooked Cedric up to the cardiac monitor.

"Doctor Kirby," Hanif said, busy watching the screen, waiting to see what would come up on it, "Can you intubate please? Oh yes. I see. Good."

William had worked the laryngoscope into Cedric's mouth, found the slot between the vocal chords, and fed the plastic tubing inside, fixing it onto his cheeks with stretchy material and tape. The lower part of Cedric's face was now obscured.

The paramedic continued with chest compressions, numbering them off under his breath, ". . . five-and-six-and-seven-and-eight-and-nine-and-*thirty*. Breathe."

The other paramedic, who had just taken position at Cedric's head and connected the bag and mask to the tube, gave two squeezes of air.

Everyone paused to look at the monitor. But there wasn't much to see. No sound, no movement, no squiggling lines.

"Asystole. Okay," Hanif said. "Okay. I think we should try for a shockable rhythm. Let's cut his clothes off and get a Foley in please." A forty-five-second flurry of hands, medical scissors, yanking fists of fabric, and Cedric was naked with a catheter in his bladder, his bloodless urine a good sign.

"Okay. Continue compressions please. Janette, let's get an IV in heach arm." Hanif sidled around to one of the arms and Janet handed him a needle for insertion. "Thank you." He bent low, his face close to Cedric's skin, fingers massaging into the flesh, looking for a vein. He found it, pierced the epidermis, taped.

The doctor liked what he was seeing with Hanif. In William's book, it was the little things that counted, the cordial transitions, the methodical, though still human, interactions that had to take place quickly and efficiently. He hadn't gotten to know the resident on any kind of personal level, hadn't invited him for a drink or quick lunch, Hanif having only been there since the beginning of the month.

He'd apparently chosen to do a four-week elective in Ontario for a few reasons: specializing in family medicine, he'd been looking for a place where the problems he would have to deal with were sure to run the gamut, but he also wanted to be around, and interact in, colloquial English, a combination that was hard to come by in his native province of Quebec. Ontario, of course, dove at the chance to help him out. Quebecers, thought William, they've always gotten the red-carpet treatment. Then, checking himself, he wondered if that was really the case or just the way we liked to conjure it.

At least Quebec is where William *assumed* Hanif's roots were, even if, judging from his looks and name, along with the throaty pronunciation he'd given to an Arabic word that came up in conversation the week before, he might have been from North Africa or the Middle East. William supposed he was Muslim, though couldn't really say why. It probably had to do with how thoroughly polite he was, as if he were trying to take up as little social space as possible, knowing how cramped the scaremongering world felt with even the presence of his religion.

Hanif took a vial of epinephrine from the crash cart and drew a little more than a milligram into a syringe, hastily injecting it into one of the IVs.

William switched with the paramedic who was giving the compressions, as he was heaving audibly from the exercise, getting tired. "Thanks," the man said breathlessly.

Both the doctor and the intern stopped at the end of the cycle, pausing to glare up at the monitor, hoping the drug would have an effect. But there was nothing.

Hanif, jumping the gun on the three-minute mark before he could inject more medication, followed the epinephrine up with forty units of vasopressin, into the other arm. Another cycle. Another pause, all eyes on the monitor. Waiting for a sound, a beep, a leaping spike. No activity.

Hanif cleared his throat. He took his stethoscope from his neck and listened on the side of Cedric's chest. "Okay. We avv bilateral breath sound with the bagging." He lifted one of Cedric's eyelids to check for pupil constriction with a penlight, ran his cold finger along the bottom of Cedric's eye. There was no reaction to either. "Okay."

At the two-minute-and-fifty-second mark, he injected one milligram of atropine and drew blood to be sent to the lab, William's whispering the only sound in the room: "three-and-four-and-five-and-six-and-seven-and-eight-and-nine-and-*twenty*-and-one-and-two-and . . ."

Seven cycles of CPR. The quiet was becoming an uncomfortable one. Both the paramedics, with little to do, stood, shifted, watched, wordless.

Janet picked up the chart to write out the steps that they'd taken so far, the type and quantity of what they'd administered, eyeing the blank monitor every few minutes. She wasn't noting the information hurriedly.

Hanif injected more epinephrine, more atropine. Janet noted it down. She stopped looking at the screen.

William began to exchange glances with Hanif more frequently, until he eventually broke the silence, huffing, tired, "And what's our time?"

Hanif checked his watch, knowing that they had far exceeded the fifteen minutes that, even if they had been chasing a vague rhythm, and had done everything perfectly, would be enough to cause brain death. "Let's just do two more cycles. Then we'll . . . then we'll see." He injected the last milligram of atropine, having reached the maximum dosage, and stepped away from Cedric, toward the monitor, reading through the empty digits, watching the bottom of the graphs, his eyes busy, the screen calm.

In the room, on the bases of the instruments and bed, the wheels teetered stationary, idle. The clinical apparatuses shed indistinct shadows onto the mottled flooring. Empty hooks on the IV stands curled, their ellipses glimmering, rigid. On the soap dispenser above the sink, a lobe of foam sagged from its tip, gradually clotting in the dry air. The cloth of the bed gripped tightly on to its folds and wrinkles.

When the two cycles of CPR were finished, Hanif put his hands in his pockets, looked at the toes of his shoes.

William, having stopped, took a step away from the bed. "So," he said, waiting long enough for his own breathing to return to normal before speaking, "I guess we should call it."

"Right," Hanif agreed, then leaned over Cedric to do one last test for pupil restriction. Without seeing an inkling of a reaction, he straightened up, comparing his watch with the clock on the wall. Janet, pen poised above the corresponding box on the chart, scribbled the numbers down as he said them. "4:43 PM."

"Okay."

"Okay."

A crackle on the radio from the ambulance just outside sent one of the paramedics to check on it, the other paramedic trailing awkwardly behind him. "We should probably be getting back. So . . ."

William waved. "Go ahead. Thanks again, John."

Janet was turning Cedric's driver's licence over in her hand, writing things down. "I'll uh . . . I'll call his information into the station so they can notify the family."

"Thanks, Janette," Hanif mumbled after her.

The two men, alone in the room, stood around the body for a moment or two, William making his way to the monitor and turning it off. He found himself watching Hanif as he did so, considering the possibility that this might be the very first death Hanif had ever witnessed, the first body (besides the inert cadavers that he'd had to dissect in his gross anatomy labs) that he'd ever seen. And there was something about the way he was looking at the man's face, as if studying it—looking over the soft dents of Cedric's temples, the slackened muscles of his brow and cheeks—which made William aware that, for some unseen reason, this was more than just a poignant experience for the resident.

William offered what he could. "As I'm sure you know, sometimes, with massive heart attacks, there's really nothing medical science can do. We did our best."

"I know, yes. But still, it gets you . . ." Hanif broke off with a heavy sigh. "I mean, I'm wondering . . . right now . . . Do you . . . ? What do you think happens when our body dies?"

William stiffened, became noticeably nervous, worried that the conversation was about to spiral in the direction of fluffy clouds and paradise, of Allah and seventy virgins; or was it seventy-two? William wasn't sure. He felt suddenly ignorant, realizing that his knowledge of Islam didn't go far beyond the discriminatory media and its regurgitated stereotypes. If he was about to have a sensitive religious dialogue, he was entirely unarmed for it. He half-cringed to clarify, "You don't . . . mean, as in: Is there a heaven, do you?"

Hanif flashed him a dreary glance. "No. Of course not."

They both snickered, releasing some of the tension.

"What I meant was," Hanif continued, "medically, *scientifically*, what do you think happens inside the cerebral cortex, to consciousness, while the brain is in the hact of shutting down? What do you make of these things like tunnels of light and your life blinking before your eyes?"

William was focusing on the part of Hanif's tone that almost sounded hopeful, as if it were important that this peaceable summation occurred. He also realized that this wasn't a question he'd given a great deal of thought to. Though he did know that when you witnessed someone die, or even saw a body just after it had passed, there was a definite finality in their posture and presence, something that was unquestionable, complete. It was as if, in their deepest physiology, they had flicked a switch, an unequivocal, polarized switch. And William doubted very much that there was any kind of lingering between the *On* and *Off* position of that switch.

But he also felt, and perhaps more importantly, that Hanif's question, with its strange pang of hope mixed into it, was a dangerous one, one that fell on the other side of that line that William liked to draw, between hard science and everything else.

"So you're asking what I think happens to consciousness . . . as the brain shuts down?" William repeated, plainly stalling.

"Yes. That is what I'm asking. What do you think?"

Finally, reluctantly, William squared his shoulders to Hanif and answered him in a calm, deadpan voice, "Nothing." He honestly hoped he wasn't offending the man. That was just the way it was. He was sure of it. "Nothing happens."

A pause. "Right," said Hanif, turning to look at Cedric again, though in a way that insinuated how, while that was close, it was somehow not quite—not exactly—what he, himself, believed.

Epilogue

The autumn that Cedric passed away brought with it unexpected gifts. One of them was the funeral itself. Melissa had sat in her appointed seat, among the featured mourners, looking calmly at the rouged and powdered face of her late father, his hands folded in a serene way that, Melissa considered, was quite unlike him. She teared, consoling her mother beside her, and wasn't at all prepared for what she saw when she turned around at the end of the service and looked through the faces of the other people in attendance. It struck her that she knew almost none of them. Ex-business partners, ex-lovers, ex-friends. It was disconcerting to think how some of them might know her father's story much better than she did. It was disconcerting that she had never thought of her father's life as a story.

Then came the day that Julie handed her a brown envelope. Julie had been asked to go through his personal effects, and had found it, in the top drawer of his desk. It was a series of poems that Melissa had written and stapled together when she was younger, about the life of Primo Levi, the paper now supple and yellowed.

"Wait . . . He stole this from me."

"Yes." Julie grinned. "I think he did."

This time around, Melissa didn't destroy the poems. She kept them in the same envelope, and left them sitting on her own desk, where they lay perfectly still.

That winter Eamon also passed away. It happened abruptly, and due to complications after he'd caught pneumonia. Melissa was the only one at his burial. She had written him a warm elegy, one that she had imagined herself reading during the service but couldn't quite bring herself to do it. Instead, she folded the paper into a tight rectangle and dropped it into the winter ground to be buried along with him. She lay fresh flowers at his grave. They froze.

At her home, cuticles of snow grew along the windows. The winter air was seldom windy, and mostly grey. Nights were long, the harbour of her bed inviting. She took a bit of time off work, spent much of it in silence, the refrigerator humming to itself in the kitchen nearby.

The envelope of poems that Cedric had stolen from her still lay on her desk. Sometimes she caught herself watching its brown lines and divots.

Until, one afternoon, she took out a spiral notebook, sat down, and set out to write an elegy for him, Cedric. Her father.

(i)

Reaching up to the frosted copper handle
and opening the door to air
so warm it stings the cheeks

Supper steaming at the window
with the sweet breath of fried onions
Mittens drying on the furnace duct
beside a lunchbox lined with breadcrumbs . . .

Acknowledgments

This book, like every book ever written, is fictional. That said, everything in it is either based on real people, real stories, or real history. If there are any discrepancies of facts within (or my interpretation of them), the blame lies entirely with me, the teller of these stories, and not with the people who inspired, lived, or shared them.

In the chronological order of the chapters, I'd like to recognize and express my gratitude to the following people:

For the school-teacher chapter: Greg Ellis and the Galt Museum Archives in Lethbridge, the librarians at the Lethbridge Public Library; Angie Warkup; and Linda Nugent, who gave critical feedback and invaluable anecdotes for the proceeding four chapters as well.

For the Ukrainian chapter: Father Mark Bayrock, Jack Peak, Joe Lavorato, and Tekla Berkedale.

For the First Nations chapter: William Singer III for his patient storytelling, Kelly Tail Feathers for his studious fact-checking, Robbie Plaited-hair, Jeff Doherty, and inspiration from the brilliant writer that is Sherman Alexie.

For the hippie chapter: Lucy Carlson, and the library staff at Lethbridge College.

For the Greece and textile-mill chapter: an anonymous (and shockingly corrupt) landlady of my past, Stefan Fournier, Kenn Hale for useful legal information, and George Arnokouros for language and cultural accuracies.

For the inner-city youth chapter: immeasurable thanks to Deb Mallet for her life story, and to Anthony Suppa and Larisa Williams.

For the South African chapter: Michael Mercier for his legal advice, Rick Holden, Gail Leuzinger, Irving Hexham, Lee White, Brianna Sharpe, and an enormous thanks to Nicki Mosley.

For the Ottawa youth chapter: Jeff Lindberg, Brian Silcoff at the Ottawa Archives, Glenn Garwood, Ralph Getson with his inexhaustible Maritime fishing information, and the Archives of the Canadian War Museum.

For the musician chapter: Ellie Nimeroski and Mechtild Schnell.

For the physiotherapist in Montreal chapter: Andrew Kahlil for his story, Nadine Baladi, Joe Baladi for perspective on life under Nasser, and Sarah Thomas.

For the Melissa chapter: Brenda Fortier, the sea-kayaking guru John Dowd and his unfaithful dog, Lolita, Karen McMullen for all her teenaged details, Mike McKenzie, Mathieu Valade, and J.P. McCarthy for Canadian surfer information, and Silva Johansson, who helped with coastal wildlife questions.

And for the final doctor chapter: the people at the archives of the Haliburton *Echo* and the Minden *Times*, and again, Andrew Kahlil, for always pointing me in the right medical direction.

I would also like to express colossal thanks to Sandy McMullen, with her eager insights, recommendations, and fact-checking on all of the Toronto chapters; to my parents for sending me some direly needed grocery money on the very last leg of the journey; to Joyce Gilmour, who was a devout proofreader and friend throughout; to Lynn Coady, for her brilliant editorial eye; and finally to Ruth Linka, for taking a chance on me and this book.

Mark Lavorato is a musician, photographer, and professional nomad. His freelance work has been published in over twenty-five magazines including *Ascent, Orange Room Review,* and *Poetry Canada.* Mark is also the author of a collection of poetry called *Wayworn Wooden Floors* (2012), and his first novel, *Veracity* (2007) is available on his website at marklavorato.com. Mark currently resides in Montreal, but his wandering habits may soon take him elsewhere.